Quest of the Sapphire

OTHER BOOKS BY A. E. SMITH

Journey of the Pearl
A Gift for Gracelyn

Quest of the Sapphire

A. E. Smith

RESOURCE *Publications* · Eugene, Oregon

QUEST OF THE SAPPHIRE

Resource Publications
An Imprint of Wipf and Stock Publishers
199 W. 8th Ave., Suite 3
Eugene, OR 97401

www.wipfandstock.com

PAPERBACK ISBN: 978-1-5326-9628-2
HARDCOVER ISBN: 978-1-5326-9629-9
EBOOK ISBN: 978-1-5326-9630-5

Manufactured in the U.S.A.   10/23/19

For Ken and Kenna Marie.

Preface

————⚬⚬⚬————

Two thousand years ago, people saw Jesus, heard his words, were healed by him, and were taught by him. I have always wondered how they lived before and after they met the Son of God. Since it is unlikely that I will ever know the stories of their lives, I invite these people into my imagination and onto the pages of my books. I hope they come to life for you as they have for me.

In this historical drama, *Quest of the Sapphire,* Book Two, I continue the story of Centurion Adan Clovius Longinus who turned to the crowd of hecklers at Jesus's crucifixion and announced, *"This must have been the Son of God!"* In this story, Adan's seventeen-year-old twin sons, Marco and Aquila, discover that God truly works in mysterious, and sometimes, confusing ways, for the good of mankind.

For the purpose of this story, the Pompeii earthquake of 62 A.D. and the eruption of Vesuvius in 79 A.D. occurred thirty years sooner. From the first minor eruption of Vesuvius until the first of six deadly pyroclastic surges (super-heated mud and volcanic debris) there was time to escape to safety, and many did. The dates of the eruptions have been questioned due to prevailing wind patterns, and the lack of summer fruit preserved in Pompeii. In 2018, Italian archeologists uncovered an inscription in Pompeii dated October 17, which eliminates the August 24–25 timeframe. The suggested dates of October 24–25 will be used in this novel. It is estimated that ten thousand people died as a direct result of the eruptions. Human remains are still being found in the affected cities and surrounding roads.

The Torch of Helene is now referred to as St. Elmo's Fire, a phenomenon in which a luminous electrical discharge appears on a ship or aircraft during a storm.

The Festival of Vulcanalia was celebrated around August 23 but moved to October, also for the purpose of this story.

The Prophecy Box is based on an artifact in the National Archaeological Museum of Athens and will be featured in *Secret of the Ruby,* Book Three.

Words in italics are either direct quotes from the Bible, words of emphasis, or words in a language other than English.

I extend my gratitude to my editor, Sandra Woolsey, for her dedicated skill, patience, and enduring friendship. If you find an error, which you probably will, it's not her fault. I have an irresistible tendency to change things every time I look at my pages.

Chapter 1

Road to Jerusalem, a Farewell Letter, and Arrow the Horse

———— ⬡ ————

Marcus Clovius Longinus, known as Marco by his family, wanted to be a hero even though he had no specific plan, no idea of what it would cost him, or how many people it would hurt. He thought about telling his twin brother of his search for adventure, but Aquila would undoubtedly demand to go with him. Also, if Marco found success, would it be due to his efforts, or his brother's? Would others assume it was Aquila who had solved all the difficulties? Would Aquila take command as he often did? Marco could not take that risk. If he was to prove himself, he had to go alone.

Marco, a Roman teenager living in the 1ˢᵗ century A.D., was the youngest son of Adan and Dulcibella Longinus. His father, Centurion Adan Clovius Longinus, was famous. He was the centurion who came back from the dead after five thousand soldiers witnessed his and fifteen *legionaries'* executions. King Herod was forced by Roman law to execute them when Simon Peter escaped from their custody, even though he suspected Felix Valentius orchestrated the "escape" to instigate the execution of sixteen of his enemies. Adan Longinus testified that an angel escorted Peter from their custody, but that made no difference. The sentences of death were carried out. There was a reasonable explanation as to how Adan survived his execution, but for most of the soldiers who saw him months later, very much alive, their superstitions were confirmed. Centurion Longinus, having the dark-ringed amber eyes of a wolf, must be a *lupus versipellis*, a werewolf. The twins had the same wolf-like eyes as their father, which led some to the same superstitious conclusion about them.

Aquila, the older son by nineteen minutes, concentrated on explanations of natural wonders, inventions, and solutions to observable problems. Marco concentrated on the unjust customs of the times, daydreamed of rescuing hapless victims, and battling enemies he conjured in his imagination. The twins' drastically different personalities were an ironic contradiction to their identical appearance. Aquila set his mind on becoming a successful inventor. Marco set his heart on saving the world.

Marco lit a candle with an ember from the fireplace in the main room of their cottage. It was once the guest house for his grandparents' villa but was converted to his parents' home when they wed. The house was perched on a cliff overlooking the Mediterranean Sea near Caesarea on the coast of Samaria. It was the only place he had ever lived. He dreaded how his parents would react when they discovered his absence. They would worry and, most likely, be angry with him.

Marco read the letter he had written for his parents one last time.

"Father, Mother, I had to leave. Now that I am seventeen and of age, I must follow my heart and discover God's plan for me. I have been thinking of this venture a long time and waiting for the right opportunity. Please do not worry about me. You have always taught me to trust in God and go where the Spirit leads me, so that's what I'm doing. Father, please do not follow me. Tell my sister, Longina, and Aquila, especially, that I will miss them. Tell Grandmother Iovita and Grandfather Marcus that I will miss them, too. Tell Uncle Niko, Aunt Marina, Adriana and Titus that I will miss them as well. Please tell Aquila I am sorry I couldn't take him with me. It would be too cruel for both of us to leave you. I will return when I have accomplished my mission—whatever that may be. Pray for me. Your son, Marco."

He blew out the candle and started for the front door. A noise from Aquila's bedroom stopped him. "Aquila," he hissed, "are you awake?" He padded softly back to his brother's doorway. He stood and waited but there was only silence. He turned and walked back to the front door. Just for a moment, Marco hesitated. He wanted to tell his brother what he was doing but his pride held him back. He had to do this alone or it would be meaningless. Aquila was always helping him out of one mess or another. For once, he was going to prove to the family—and himself—that he could accomplish something significant on his own.

Marco walked down the path to his grandparents' villa and entered through the kitchen door. He made his way in the darkness to the main hall and put the letter on the table next to his mother's favorite chair, and he started for the front door. He had thought about slipping the letter under his parents' bedroom door, but Aquila often woke them in the morning if they overslept. Marco didn't want him to find the letter. He might hide it or even destroy it out of spite for being left behind.

Guilt twisted in Marco's heart. Today was his and Aquila's seventeenth birthday. Celebrations were planned, but he had to act now due to uncontrollable circumstances. The opportunity to travel with an armed guard and the merchant who hired them was too good to pass up. He paused, retraced his steps, and reached for the letter. The sudden desire to tear it into shreds almost overwhelmed him, but he stayed his hand. He had to trust in his own determination and courage. He blew out the candle and waited until his eyes adjusted to the soft darkness of the moonlit night.

Marco slung his knapsack over his shoulder and slipped out into the night. Outside of the barn, he lowered the knapsack and checked the contents one last time. He had extra clothes, the obsidian razor his father gave him, a small copper disc for a mirror, and a blanket. Romans prided themselves on being clean-shaven with short-cropped hair so he wanted to keep up his best appearance. He counted the bronze, copper, and silver coins in his coin pouch. He only had a few, but he planned to find work along the way. Satisfied he had everything necessary, he crept into the barn and saddled one of the pack horses. His own horse snorted disapproval. Marco went to his horse's stall and rubbed a hand along the jet-black Friesian's neck.

"I'm sorry Wingshadow. You can't go with me. I'll be back. I promise. Father will take good care of you. I'll miss you, but you'll be safer here than with me."

Wingshadow stomped a hoof, backed away from Marco, and flattened her ears back against her head. The horse let out a high-pitched squeal as if she were trying to raise an alarm.

Marco waved his hand defensively. "No, Wingshadow! You'll wake everyone up. I know you don't understand why I'm leaving you, but it's too dangerous. Someone will try to steal you for sure. No one will look twice at the pack horse—or me."

Wingshadow moved forward until her chest pressed against the railing of her stall. She extended her head as if inviting Marco to rub her forehead. Marco placed his hands on the sides of the horse's head and looked into her eyes.

"Maybe you do understand," whispered Marco. "It is because I love you that I don't take you with me. Blackfire would never forgive me if something bad happened to you, since you're his daughter and all. Blackfire may be an old horse, but he still has heart. He would grieve if I took you away from him."

In the stall next to Wingshadow, Blackfire shifted to face Marco. He nickered low in his chest and tossed his head.

"See? Your father agrees with me. You need to stay here." Marco sighed. He knew he was projecting his own feelings about the grief he was about to cause his father and the whole family. "There's another reason you must stay here. They will know that I'll come back if you're still here." This time it was Wingshadow that nickered a deep-throated rumble of acceptance.

Marco rubbed the horse's neck and patted her shoulder. "I'll be back." He left Wingshadow's stall and led the old pack horse through the doors and closed them softly. Wingshadow turned toward the door with her ears stiff and facing forward, alert for the sound of Marco's voice. When there was only silence, the horse turned away and went back to sleep.

The moon was full and lit his way as Marco left the Cornelius estate behind. He wasn't even sure that his travel plans would work. He tried to think of an alternate plan as he rode down the switchbacks of the cliff road, but nothing came to mind. He would need to follow the shore of the Mediterranean Sea until he reached the Ocean View Inn. His hope was to join a cloth merchant he had met at the inn. Marco knew that traveling alone would be suicidal. Overhearing the travel plans of the merchant presented the opportunity he couldn't pass up. The merchant was on his way back to Jerusalem, which Marco thought was as good a place as any. His father and Aquila would most certainly try to find him, but they wouldn't know what direction he had taken. Marco hoped they would think he had gone somewhere other than Jerusalem since the city was in a constant state of agitation between the occupying Romans and the resident Jewish population.

The first few hours of daylight would be the most critical for Marco's success. As a centurion at the garrison in Caesarea, Adan Longinus would be able to order his men to search for his son in all directions. However, Marco hoped that his many hours of lead time would enable him to avoid the soldiers and his father. He winced at the thought of how humiliating it would be if he were found quickly and dragged back home. He wished he could think of some type of disguise, but decided that if God was on his side, he would succeed in making it all the way to Jerusalem. After all, hadn't he prayed fervently for a chance to prove himself to his father and grandfathers, to be as courageous as them, and to face all challenges? Surely, since God presented this opportunity, leaving was what he should do, but the anxiety in the pit of his stomach made him wonder, at least for a moment, if he were being childishly foolish.

Marco pulled on the reins and his horse stopped without argument. The horse looked back at his master and waited patiently. Marcus took a deep breath. "It's too late to change my mind. I'm committed to seeing this through. I would feel like a coward if I gave up now."

The soft breeze ruffled his hair as the scent of the sea stirred his senses. The sound of the dancing waves soothed his doubt and he pressed on. With the light of the moon, he could see the city of Caesarea ahead. Marco gazed in the direction of Jerusalem, seeing more in his mind's eye than the reality of the landscape of craggy limestone and sandstone bluffs and hills.

"Father nearly died there, twice," Marco announced to his horse. The pack animal turned his ears back to listen to his rider's voice. "Since Jerusalem was the place my father became a hero, it will be the place for me to do the same. I'm sure of it." The horse looked back at Marco and shifted his weight, content to go nowhere. The young man tapped the horse's flank with his heels and took the road that went through Apollonia and on to Joppa, which would set him on his way to Jerusalem. "I suppose if you're going to carry me into adventures, I should give you a name. I can't tell my stories starting with, 'One night, under a full moon, I set out for Jerusalem riding a—brown horse.' No, that will not do. How about something that sounds strong like Warrior?"

The horse lowered his head and sneezed.

"Maybe not," muttered Marco. He gave it some more thought and then announced, "I know. I will be the Archer and you will be my Arrow. Yes, I like that. I now christen you, Arrow, my loyal, four-legged companion."

Arrow stumbled on something in the road and blinked back at his master.

Marco sighed. "Some arrows might be a bit dull, I guess, but you'll do. Now all I need to do is catch up with the cloth merchant in Apollonia. Let's hope he did not change his plans."

Chapter 2

Discovery and Dismay in Caesarea

Dulcibella opened her eyes to the sound of birds singing outside the window of the bedroom she shared with her husband, Adan. She smiled to think of the plans she had for the day. She and her daughter, Longina, who had married the assistant architect to King Herod in Caesarea, would meet at the Ocean View Inn to visit with Nikolaus's wife, Marina, and their daughter, Adriana. Adan and Nikolaus had plans to take the twins and Titus, Nikolaus's son, to the town of Dora to inspect a horse that Titus had his heart set on. Dulcibella thought it should be a fun day for everyone, especially for Aquila and Marco since it was their seventeenth birthday. There would be a special celebration that night for the entire family.

Dulcibella sat up and jostled Adan by the shoulder. "Are you awake? The boys will be eager to get going. Niko and Titus will be here soon if I know those two."

Adan rolled to his back and slowly opened his eyes. He sat up and ran his fingers through his thick, black hair. "I'm awake—now. They're probably riding up the cliff road as we speak. Titus has been looking forward to this day all month. I hope he is pleased with the horse."

"He said this colt is a dapple gray and looks a lot like Venustas," said Dulcibella. "Do you miss Venustas since my father gave Blackfire to you? She always perks up her ears when she hears your voice. I think she misses you."

"Yes, we are old friends, the two of us, but your lighter weight is much easier on her aged back. Blackfire, despite his age, could carry both of us without effort." Adan threw the blankets off. He pulled on a fresh tunic and laced his sandals. "It's a good thing that Blackfire sired the two foals we gave to the twins. We could not have afforded to buy them. But Aquila and Marco have not taken them for granted. They take good care of them, especially Marco."

"With your supervision, of course," smiled Dulcibella. "No one knows horses better than you, Adan. But I am glad to see the boys accept their responsibility. I'm sure Andreas and his sons would do all the work and never complain if you allowed it."

Adan grunted. "And end up with a couple of pampered, useless sons? Aquila wouldn't mind getting help with Nighthawk, but Marco would never let someone else touch Wingshadow. I've stood outside the stable and listened to him talk to that horse. I swear it seems like a two-way conversation. I wonder where he got the idea that horses and dogs speak Latin."

Dulcibella smiled at him tenderly. "You don't know *anyone* else who talks to animals as if they understand every word?"

He reached for her as she squealed with feigned alarm. "Are you implying that I really am a wolf creature and can speak 'Animal'? Such ridiculous notions!" He laughed as he easily overcame her "struggle" to escape. She was laughing too hard to even pretend resistance and snuggled into his embrace.

"As much as I love the wolf in you, we better get our boys up and ready to go. You know how their Uncle Niko hates to be kept waiting."

Adan indulged in stealing a long kiss before Dulcibella reluctantly slipped out of his arms. "I'll see if Cook has breakfast started. Mother and Father should be up by now."

"Marcus and Iovita are probably on the roof terrace watching the sunrise. Since *Primus Pilus* Centurion Cornelius retired, that seems to be their usual morning and evening routine."

Dulcibella smiled at Adan's use of her father's official title. She left the bedroom and padded down the hall to Marco's and Aquila's rooms. Aquila was still asleep but needed little urging to get up. Dulcibella looked in Marco's room, but he wasn't there. Mildly surprised, she searched the rest of the cottage only to find that he was not there either. She walked down the path to the main house and entered through the kitchen door. Her father was just entering the kitchen. Iovita was coming down the stairs.

"Where are the twins?" Marcus asked. "I thought they would be dressed by now."

"I just woke Aquila, but Marco wasn't in the house."

Her father frowned. "I haven't seen him either."

"He must be in the stables," suggested Dulcibella. "You know how particular he is with that horse." She hurried through the great room and walked to the stables. Marco wasn't there, but his coal-black Friesian horse was in his stall. She sighed with relief until she spotted the empty stall. The brown pack horse was gone and so was Marco's saddle. Fear made her mouth go dry. She rushed back to the house and was about to call for her father when she saw the sheet of papyrus propped against the vase on the side table.

Dulcibella snatched up the letter and hurriedly read it. She clapped a hand over her mouth in shock. When she turned to run back to the kitchen, her father was watching her with concern.

"What is it, Bella? Where is my grandson?" Marcus demanded.

She tried to hold back the tears of panic. "He's gone! I've got to get Adan." She thrust the letter into his hand and hurried out to the cottage. It didn't take much explaining after Adan, Aquila, and Dulcibella joined Marcus and Iovita. Dulcibella read the letter aloud. Iovita collapsed in a chair and dropped her head to her hands.

"What could he possibly be thinking?" demanded Adan. He frowned in frustration and took the letter from Dulcibella. He scanned it again and slapped it down on the table. "Why would he think this was such a great plan if he had to sneak off in the middle of the night?"

Dulcibella whispered into his ear, "Come with me, please. We need to talk in private." She led him out of the kitchen door to their favorite high-backed bench under the ancient oak tree on the terrace. She gazed down on the ocean waves lapping at the beach at the foot of the cliff. Adan glared off into space.

"I don't even know what direction he's taken," exclaimed Adan. "I'll send *legionaries* to every road out of here. When we find Marco, I will make him understand that immature, irresponsible behavior will not be tolerated in this family."

"Adan, think for a moment," said Dulcibella gently. "Was it immature, irresponsible behavior that made you enlist in the army against your father's wishes? Or was it the need to establish your independence and make your own decisions?"

"I joined the army, Dulcie! I didn't run off without a means of support. That decision got me a respectable, lifetime career with benefits for the whole family, I might add."

"As fearful as I am for our son, I do not believe he did this on a whim. Think about it, Adan. Marco has heard about your deeds, if not from you, from Niko and Serapio. He knows that you joined the army against your parents' wishes and went on to do great things. He has heard the stories about his Grandfather Marcus and his Grandfather Aquila. Both brave men who rose to great challenges and succeeded. Our sons may be identical twins, but they have very different personalities. Aquila thinks of inventions and explanations for how the natural world works. He enjoys inventing machines to make a task easier. He is content to watch and learn and experiment. But Marco—he dreams of adventure. He doesn't care about saving people from work. He cares about saving people from injustice. Please try and get inside his mind and heart before you assume the worst. I do not believe he has done this lightly or without concern for our feelings. If he did not care, he would not have left a letter. And there's something else."

"What is it?" Adan snapped impatiently.

"He didn't take Wingshadow. He took that old pack horse. I believe he didn't want to take the chance of something bad happening to his pride and joy. I know he believes that he can take care of himself. His youth makes him think he is invulnerable. But he does realize that others would not think twice about ambushing a solitary young man to steal such a stunning horse. Also, he will draw little attention on that old brown horse. He has thought this plan through a little better than you realize."

Adan leaned his elbows on his knees and massaged his temples. He looked up with a chagrined expression. "I just hope we can catch up with him before he gets himself in trouble."

"I might be able to help with that," said Nikolaus as he and Titus walked across the terrace. "Iovita showed me the letter. Titus and I were surprised that you and the twins weren't waiting for us down at the beach. I knew something was wrong."

"We're in shock, Niko," said Adan. "I can't believe Marco would be so—so selfish."

"Well, at least I have a good idea where he went," said Nikolaus. "One of my patrons, who sells linen and purple dye, always stays at my inn when he does business in Caesarea. He was explaining his plans to me when Titus and Marco came out to help with the horses. This businessman, named Florinus, always travels with a group of hired guards. I noticed that Marco was deep in conversation with Florinus. I thought it was odd at the time but forgot to ask him later what they discussed. I suspect that Marco may have met up with Florinus in Apollonia to travel with his armed guards. If so, Marco is on his way to Jerusalem. That's where Florinus lives."

"Then, that's where I'll go," declared Adan.

"As will I," added Nikolaus. "The two of us should be able to talk some sense into that dreamer's head of his."

"Adan, how many soldiers can you take with you?" asked Dulcibella.

"As many as I need. Centurion Tacitus was very grateful that Marcus sponsored him to take his place in Caesarea. Out of gratitude, he told me he would grant me whatever I need, anytime. Tacitus desperately wanted out of Jerusalem after Tribune Salvitto retired. There is constant political turmoil there. If there's going to be a rebellion against Rome, it will start in Jerusalem. Fighting could erupt at any time. Marco has no idea what's ahead of him."

"We made a promise to each other that once we married, we would never be parted again," said Dulcibella. Her eyes softened with sadness. "I suppose that was a rash promise."

"No, it is a promise that we will keep," declared Adan. "We may be physically parted for a short while, but I still have your heart right here," he pressed his hand on the center of his chest, "and you still have my heart—"

Dulcibella pressed her hand over the center of her chest, "right here." She smiled at the memory of their oath to "trade hearts" the first day of their betrothal nineteen years ago.

The back-kitchen door slammed shut. Marcus and Aquila soon joined them. "Iovita is getting Cook to throw together a quick breakfast," said Marcus. "Andreas is preparing the horses. I'm sure you want to be after my grandson as soon as possible."

"Father, I think I should go with you," said Aquila.

"Absolutely, not!" retorted Adan.

"Adan, hear him out," said Marcus. "He has a good reason for going."

"I was only thinking that it would save a great deal of time and false leads," said Aquila. "There will be no possibility of misidentification when you ask people if they've seen Marco, with his twin brother standing right next to you."

Dulcibella nodded but said nothing. Adan sighed and glanced at her. Their eyes met and understanding passed between them. "Unfortunately, you're right, Aquila. Even though our eye color makes us distinctive, there would be no chance of a mistake with you there. Besides, I imagine that Marco might resist me and your uncle, but with the three of us, he might be persuaded to come home. Come on. Let's eat, pack and be on our way. I'll send Andreas with a letter to Tacitus so that our escort soldiers will be waiting at the crossroads."

"I think I should go with you as well," announced Titus.

"I appreciate your dedication to your cousin, Titus," said Nikolaus, "but I will need you at the inn to help your mother with the daily chores. It will be a great blessing knowing that your mother is not alone. Besides, we'll only be gone a week at the most. We'll find Marco in Jerusalem and come straight back here. Then I'll take you to Dora for that horse you want. I promise."

"I understand, Father," said Titus. "I will do as you ask but I have a suggestion. I think Grandfather Pitio should come stay with us while you're gone. Uncle Gnaeus won't mind sharing his company for a few days. It will be good for Mother to spend time with him as well."

Nikolaus grasped his son's shoulder. "You are wise beyond your years, Titus. I know I can depend on you. And I'm sorry about the trip to Dora. I'll make it up to you when I get back."

"No need for Marco to mess everything up for the whole family," said Marcus. "I can take Titus to Dora today. Andreas and his sons can go with us. It will be a nice break for them from their usual work and I wouldn't mind getting out of the house for the day."

"Thank you, Sir," said Titus, visibly brightening at the proposal. "I welcome the offer and your company. Is it all right with you, Father?"

"Of course," said Nikolaus. "Chances are we will be back in a few days with Marco in tow, but if not, you'll have your new horse. No doubt, Marco will have had seven adventures between now and sunset and be ready to come home." The others smiled, hoping that his prediction would come true, but Dulcibella knew in her heart that it would not.

Chapter 3

Jerusalem, Blackmail, and Centurion Thracius

Marco reined Arrow to a stop outside the Apollonia Inn. It would be tricky to contact the merchant without Uncle Gnaeus, Aunt Marina, or his great uncle, Pitio, seeing him. The sun was eagerly reaching for the horizon as he dropped from the saddle and led Arrow to a clump of trees. Perhaps they would get a few hours rest before Florinus left Apollonia. The thrill of "escaping" in the night had been replaced with fatigue and hunger. Marco sat on the grass next to where his horse contentedly grazed and kept an eye on the front gate of the inn. A few people came and went, but Florinus did not make an appearance.

Marco was getting worried. Perhaps the merchant had changed his mind and was still in Caesarea or had left a day earlier than he had previously planned and was already in Joppa. When the sun was well above the horizon, he put a stick in the ground and drew a line in the sand along the shadow. He would wait one more hour. If the merchant did not appear, he would go on to Joppa and take his chances with the dangers of travel.

The gate opened and several heavily armed men emerged leading their horses. They glanced up and down the road before giving way to Florinus who followed with his horse. Several more men followed, leading their horses and the pack horses. Marco breathed a sigh of relief and stood up to hail the merchant.

"Sir, over here!" shouted Marco. "Remember me? You said I could travel with you."

Florinus waved back and beckoned to the young man. "Yes, I remember. You're the son of Centurion Longinus. Yes?"

"I am," Marco confirmed with pride. The title of centurion carried its own brand of respect and he never missed a chance to use it.

"Come along then," said Florinus. "I have a day's business in Joppa, but we'll be on our way to Jerusalem after that. I hope you're not in too big of a hurry." There was an odd tone to the man's voice. He watched Marco closely while he waited for a response.

"Oh, no, not in too much of a hurry," he lied.

Florinus noted the attempt to sound casual. "Do your parents know that you have taken leave of them, Marcus?"

"Of course, why wouldn't they? And you can call me Marco. My grandfather, *Primus Pilus* Centurion Cornelius uses Marcus for his *praenomen*. I was named after him. He's retired now, but still greatly respected in all of Judea."

"Ah, so the great Centurion Cornelius is your grandfather. Interesting. Since your father is a centurion, why didn't he send you with escort soldiers? And why are you riding on a broken-down, old horse. Surely, the son of a centurion would ride a high-bred steed."

Marco struggled to think of a rational lie to explain the discrepancies. "Father said he didn't have any men to spare and Wingshadow is recovering from a snakebite. She'll be fine in a week or so." He looked at the merchant helplessly.

The man chuckled and shook a finger at Marco. "You have no skill at lying, young man. Let me guess—you have run away from home. Am I correct?"

Marco hung his head, but only for a moment. "I have not run away, since that would imply that I'm not going back. I have come of age and I think it is time that I do something besides study my lessons and do chores. Honestly, I have felt for some time that I have a mission. I am depending on my faith and obeying God's call. That's how I see it."

Florinus laughed. "Which god would that be? Personally, I find the gods to be ignorant and self-serving. Or do you mean the Hebrew God, Yahweh? You don't need to bother with an answer. I really don't care. But I welcome your company, Marco. We shall have much to discuss as we go on our way."

The travelers stopped in Joppa and spent the day going from shop to shop so Florinus could sell the last of his cloth. Marco tried to stay as unobtrusive as possible so as not to attract attention. The unusual color of his eyes caused some observers to mutter among themselves while they kept a suspicious watch on him.

When Marco and Aquila were together among strangers, whispers of superstitious fears often reached their ears. However, the presence of their father or his soldiers belayed any action beyond vague murmuring and guarded glances. There was never a serious problem among the residents of Caesarea. There was hardly a well-established household that had not asked Centurion Longinus for advice about a sick horse or dog.

Adan's healing touch and calming voice were well known among the soldiers as well. Adan's knowledge and skill with disease and surgeries cast him more as a healer than a soldier, at least until someone was foolish enough to challenge him. Being fluent in Greek, Egyptian, and Hebrew enabled him to connect with the many non-Roman soldiers who had enlisted to gain Roman citizenship. He had passed his knowledge of these languages and healing techniques on to his children, making sure they had teachers to complement his efforts.

Unfortunately, many people outside of Caesarea were suspicious of Adan and his sons. The pale-amber color and dark outer ring of their eyes looked so wolf-like; people were often visibly uncomfortable around them. Even a *primus pilus* centurion leading a charge against a band of rebels once ordered, "Put Longinus in the front line. Let's see what they can do against a wolf demon." A few cohort centurions laughed. The others didn't think it was a joke.

Adan had hoped that his sons would not be ostracized as he was when growing up in Rome. His oldest child, Longina, had bluish-green eyes, giving them the same turquoise look of Dulcibella's eyes. Adan and his sons inherited the rare eye color from his mother's Parthian father. Adan's mother, Marsetina, had copper-colored eyes, but her father's eyes were more yellow and lighter in hue.

Florinus's mood lightened when he sold the last of the purple dye. Even with an armed guard, he was anxious carrying such a highly prized commodity. They left for Jerusalem the next day. The increased cart and horse traffic as they approached the western gate into the city slowed them down. The air smelled of acrid dust kicked up by the hooves of horses and donkeys and the wooden wheels of carts and wagons. The dry breeze did little to freshen the air, pungent with animal dung as well as human waste thrown into the streets from upstairs windows. The hired guards kept their employer and Marco surrounded to prevent any unwanted contact with the congestion of street vendors, beggars, and shoppers. They made their way to the home of Florinus, a large two-story structure built of Judean limestone.

Florinus invited Marco in with a flourishing wave of his hand. "Come in, Marco, and let us conclude our business. Please, sit. My slaves will bring us refreshment."

"I appreciate that, but what do you mean—conclude our business? Have I missed something?"

Florinus's eyebrows shot up in surprise. "I am referring to the payment for my guards' services. Did you think you would benefit from their presence without compensating me?"

Marco was startled, "You didn't say anything about payment when we first talked. You had plenty of opportunity to tell me that I would owe you money. How much payment are you talking about?"

"Oh, I think fifty *denarii* should suffice," said Florinus as he glanced over Marco's shoulder. Marco looked around to find two of the guards standing in the doorway. "Of course, if you prefer, I can send word to your father that you owe me this sum. I'm sure he would be eager to pay your debt and escort you home." He smiled, but his expression remained watchful.

Marco glared at the man. "Fifty *denarii* is an outrageous sum for two days of travel. Your threat to summon my father means nothing. Do you know of Serapio's *Suppelex*? Regulus Novius Serapio is a close friend of the family. I'm sure he will loan me a reasonable fee for your guards' service, but it definitely won't be such a ridiculous amount."

"I have heard of this Serapio," said Florinus, "but I have a better idea. Perhaps you can rest easy in the Antonia's pit while we wait for your father to arrive. Unless you have the money on you. I would offer to take your horse for payment, but that old nag isn't worth the grass it eats." Florinus nodded at the men now standing behind Marco's chair. Before he could make a move, the men grabbed Marco by the arms and lashed his wrists together behind his back.

"Have you lost your mind?" demanded Marco as the men started to take him from the room. "My father will have your head for this! You can't falsely charge me with anything, much less have me thrown in the pit."

Florinus studied Marco for a moment. "You're probably right."

Marcus sighed with relief. "Then untie me at once!"

"Oh, you misunderstand. You're probably right about not throwing you in the pit. The *legionaries* will probably chain you to the wall in Holding, being that you're a Roman citizen. I think they reserve the pit for prisoners of war and runaway slaves." Florinus gestured in Marco's direction. "Take him and explain how he has stolen from me. Here's the writ of complaint." He handed one of the men a small scroll.

"You already had this set up," accused Marco. "You deliberately didn't express any demand for payment in the hope I wouldn't have the money."

The merchant laughed. "Do you have the money? Because if you do, I can take back my writ and I won't send for your father to come and fetch you."

Marco's mouth dropped open. "You're blackmailing me! You're not asking for payment; you're demanding a ransom."

"Do—you—have—the—money?" Florinus asked with a malevolent smirk. At Marco's silence, he gestured at his guards to proceed. The men hauled Marco out into the street and headed for the Antonia. He shouted furiously at them, but his threats fell on deaf ears. The townspeople stared at the unusual sight of a young Roman under arrest.

"My father is Centurion Adan Clovius Longinus," announced Marco to anyone who looked his way. "This arrest is unlawful! My grandfather is *Primus Pilus* Centurion Marcus Claudius Cornelius. I demand that you release me immediately!"

One of the mercenaries stopped and spun Marco around to face him. "Not another word out of your mouth, thief, or I'll shut your mouth for you. I saw your horse. Do you really think we believe a centurion's son would even allow his dead corpse to be slung over a long-toothed nag like that? We've seen slaves riding better horses than yours."

The man jerked Marco around and they continued to the gates of the Antonio. As they trooped through the streets, he began to understand the danger he was in. If only he could get word to Serapio. The family had visited Jerusalem every year and always stayed with Serapio and his wife, Fabiana. After Nebetka, their son, was married, Marco and Aquila were often invited to stay for months while Serapio taught them the same wood crafting skills he had taught Adan when he was a teenager. Marco knew that Serapio and Fabiana would drop everything to come to his rescue if they knew he was in trouble.

The *legionaries* presented Marco to the soldier in charge of processing prisoners. Hearing the name Longinus had little effect since it was a common name. He was hauled into Holding and chained by the wrists to the wall. He sat on the floor and took in his surroundings. The detention room was built with the usual limestone walls, hard-packed dirt floor and a wood beam ceiling, a standard design. The long wooden table and the two benches on either side, which ran down the center of the room, could seat a dozen men or more. There were no latticed windows in the room, but torches burned in the wall brackets.

Marco glanced around at the other prisoners and thought that he would not like to be in the dark with them, even though they were chained as he was. He watched the soldiers to see who seemed to be in charge. It didn't take long to see who stood apart from the *legionaries* gambling in a corner of the room and those gossiping among themselves.

"You there," called out Marco. "You must be in charge. I need to speak with you."

The *legionary's* irritation was unmistakable. "How dare you speak to me without addressing me as 'Sir!'"

"All right then, Sir, I need to get a message to a friend of my family. His name is Regulus Novius Serapio. He's a furniture mak . . . "

"I know who he is, thief," the soldier interrupted. "How will you pay someone to take a message for you?"

"My father, Centurion Adan Clovius Longinus, will pay someone handsomely since Serapio is as much a member of my family as my twin brother," boasted Marco.

The soldier sneered at him angrily. "If you disrespect the title of centurion with your lies again, you'll be sorry. Centurion Longinus means something to us here at the Antonia and there's no way he is related to a thief."

"I'm no thief. The merchant never gave me a chance to pay him. He has practically kidnapped me by falsely charging me." Marco eyed the man resentfully. "And don't call me thief! I have a name, which is probably more than you have."

An elderly prisoner next to Marco shot him a concerned look. He quickly whispered, "If you want to live, do *not* apologize!"

"What? Why should I . . . "

Marco didn't get a chance to finish the sentence. The *legionary* snatched him up from the floor by the front of his tunic. He growled in Marco's face, "Are you saying that my mother was a harlot, boy?" The soldier shook him and pinned him to the wall.

"Sir, I'm sorry, but you have to . . . "

The prisoner who had whispered the warning rolled his eyes and groaned. "First thing out of his mouth, 'I'm sorry!' No one ever listens to me."

The *legionary* clenched a beefy hand around Marco's throat. "You're sorry! You're *sorry*? Do you think that makes everything all better?" Marco tried to reach for the man's hand but the chains prevented him. He couldn't breath and his vision began to blur. Out of instinct, Marco kneed the man in the groin hard enough to make him let go. The soldier doubled over in pain. Marco gasped for air, sunk to the floor, and braced himself for retaliation. The *legionary* stumbled back to the bench and sat down heavily.

The soldier's voice was thick with malice. "I don't think you're nearly sorry enough, boy!" He came to his feet and pulled a dagger from his belt. He knelt next to Marco and grasped him by the hair. He placed the edge of his dagger against Marco's cheekbone. "I think you need a scar to complement your evil eyes."

The bar on the outside of the door scraped in its casing and the door swung open.

"Centurion present!" shouted one of the other soldiers. The *legionaries* stood up at attention. Marco's attacker spun around and slipped his dagger back in the sheath on his belt.

"Porcius, what do you think you're doing?" shouted the centurion. "I saw you through the window." He pointed at the small barred opening in the door. "Have you forgotten what happens to the soldier in charge when a prisoner is mistreated?"

"I was just going to scare him, Sir," said Porcius. "He was disrespectful. He's a thief and a liar. You can see that he is unharmed."

The centurion stepped closer and eyed the red marks on Marco's neck. The man faced Porcius. Without warning, he grabbed the soldier by the throat and squeezed until Porcius stumbled back and fell to the bench. "Scare him like *that*?" The centurion released the soldier.

The soldier coughed and rubbed his throat. "Centurion," the man swallowed hard, "Centurion Thracius, I meant no harm. He disrespected the name of the centurion that died and came back to life. I was only defending the man's honor."

Thracius's eyes flashed with anger. "Yes, we all remember how well you honored the man when you bragged on your eagerness to execute him, Porcius." He glared at Marco. "How did this boy disrespect Centurion Longinus?"

"He claims to be his son."

Thracius focused on the prisoner. "Look at me." Marco looked into the man's eyes, not knowing what to expect. Thracius knelt on a knee. "Are you the son of Adas Longinus?"

Marco frowned. "Yes, but he changed his *praenomen* to Adan before I was born."

"Why did he choose that *praenomen*?"

"Adan was the name of the son of my father's closest friend, Regulus Serapio. The boy had died, so Serapio offered the *praenomen* to my father after he survived his execution." Marco swallowed hard and waited for the centurion's response.

Thracius stood up and sat down on the bench. Satisfaction brightened his features. "Your facts are correct and so is the color of your eyes. There's a slight difference, but not much. You must have inherited the dark-green around the irises from your mother."

Marco felt a flush of hope. "Do you know my parents?"

"I do. Both of them. Why were you arrested? Surely the son of Longinus is not so bored with life that he steals for the thrill of being chained to a wall."

"I am not a thief. The merchant I traveled with did not tell me that he expected to be paid fifty *denarii* until we were at his home here in Jerusalem. We were on the road only two days and I would have paid him a reasonable fee, but he didn't give me a chance. He ordered my arrest before I could do anything. He still has my horse, too. Arrow is just a pack horse, but I'm fond of the old nag."

Thracius stood up and laughed. "Yes, you are definitely the son of Adan Longinus. I never saw a man who cares about animals like he does. What is your *praenomen*?"

"Marcus, Sir—I am named after my grandfather *Primus Pilus* Centurion Marcus Claudius Cornelius," he responded as he raised his chin with pride. "But everyone calls me Marco.

"Well, Marco, I'm afraid you're stuck here in Jerusalem until we can get you before a judge. However, I can keep you in my custody if you promise to not run away. Can you do that?"

"Yes, Sir. Thank you, Sir. But can I get a message to Serapio? He's the one . . . "

"I know who Serapio is, Marco. Everyone in Jerusalem knows Serapio. Instead of a message, how 'bout I escort you to him? I'd like to see the ol' one-eyed *gladiator* anyway. It's been months since I've stopped by for a chat."

Thracius took the shackle key from the coin pouch attached to his belt and unlocked Marco's chains. The centurion put a hand down and helped him to his feet. Porcius watched their departure with resentful eyes. The *legionary* was persistently ridiculed for his tendency to grovel when face-to-face with his commanders, but uncooperative and churlish behind their backs. The other cohort centurions wondered why Thracius didn't dishonorably discharge Porcius, who was referred to as the pig man for reasons other than his name. But even the lowest rung on a ladder is useful, and Thracius knew exactly how to use Porcius.

Chapter 4

Commander Lysias, Calais, and Silver Coins

———— ⟨≈≈≈⟩ ————

Centurion Thracius and Marco left Holding. They stopped by the office of Commander Claudius Lysias, the man who had been assigned to take Tribune Salvitto's place when he retired. Thracius requested that the son of Centurion Longinus be allowed to remain in his custody until he could be presented to a judge. Lysias granted the request on the grounds that Marco would return that evening to tell him the full story of his father's legendary "return" to life. Marco eagerly agreed. Thracius and Marco went to the huge limestone building that held the stables and the slave quarters.

"I hope Arrow is not being mistreated," said Marco. "He's a gentle ol' nag."

"We'll find out soon. We're going to pay a visit to Florinus, first, and then we'll go to Serapio's shop." Thracius stopped at the arena gate and whistled. A slave trotted out from the stable at the centurion's summons. "Tell Calais to saddle my horse and a spare horse."

The slave hurried back into the building. Thracius and Marco talked while they waited. Thracius saw the slave in charge of his horse's care approaching with the two horses and opened the gate. Marco stepped into the arena and held his hand out for the reins. The slave looked up as he passed the reins to Marco. Quite unexpectedly, Marco looked him in the eye.

"Sir!" cried the slave, "do you know Centurion Longinus?"

"Silence, slave!" demanded Thracius. "How dare you speak without permission."

"Centurion, wait," pleaded Marco. "I want to hear why he is asking about my father."

Rashly oblivious to the threatening glare of the centurion, the slave pressed ahead. "Centurion Longinus is your father? Is he here? In Jerusalem?"

Marco shook his head. "No, it's just me. How do you know my father?"

"I was brought here as a young boy when my mother was forced to sell me. Centurion Longinus took me under his protection and taught me how to tend to the horses. I would have done anything for him, even unto death." He glanced in Thracius's direction. "He always called me by my name."

"Your name is Calais? Did I hear it correctly?" asked Marco, remembering Thracius's command to the first slave.

"Yes. I am the only one left from your father's Saturday class."

"I want to talk with you some more. I'll find you when I get back. My name is Marcus Clovius Longinus, but everyone calls me Marco."

Calais's eyes widened with surprise. To be told another's name was to be acknowledged as an equal. The last doubt that he was talking with the son of Longinus vanished. No other free man, except Centurion Longinus, had ever introduced himself to Calais since he became a slave. He handed the reins over and dropped to his hands and knees next to Thracius's horse, knowing that protocol required him to "back up" the elder man first. The centurion placed a foot squarely in the center of the slave's back and straddled the saddle.

Thracius urged his horse into a trot, "Marco, I'll be at the gate. I need to speak with the guards." Marco nodded and took the reins of his horse as the centurion left the arena.

When Calais started to get on his hands and knees, Marco stopped him. "No need, Calais. My father taught us that we didn't deserve to own a horse if we couldn't get in the saddle by our own strength. Marco grasped the left-front saddle horn and swung his leg. He pulled himself into the saddle.

"That is what Centurion Longinus always did," said Calais with pride. "I never once saw him use a slave to back him up. Does he still have Venustas, that beautiful dapple-gray Arabian?"

Marco smiled. "Yes, we still have Venustas, but now my mother rides her and father rides Blackfire, a Friesian from *Hispaniola*. My horse's name is Wingshadow; she was sired by Blackfire, but I left her in Caesarea."

"I remember seeing a black Friesian stallion ridden by the man that came with Centurion Longinus when he first came back from the dead."

"Yes, that was Blackfire," Marco said proudly. "My Grandfather Marcus was riding him. That's who I am named after. I better go. I'll find you later, Calais, and then we can talk more." Marco urged his horse into a trot to catch up with Thracius.

Calais watched from the arena as Marco and Thracius left the fortress grounds. Surely, it was a sign from the gods at last, thought Calais. The son of one of the few men he had ever trusted had come into his life. Perhaps there was hope, after all, he thought as he walked back into the building.

"Why is he here alone?" whispered Calais to himself. "Has he run away?"

"Who are you talking to, Crazy Calais?" asked a slave who had been watching from the shadows.

Another slave added, "One look into the wolf eyes of that boy and you're muttering to yourself. Of course, you mutter to yourself anyway since no one else will talk to you."

"Leave me alone," demanded Calais. "The centurion has come for me, as I have told you."

The two slaves snickered. One of them scoffed, "Where is he? Will he sweep you out of here in a gold-covered chariot?" He made a swishing motion with his hand and bowed.

"More likely, the Wolf will eat you alive," said the other slave.

They exchanged exaggerated expressions of fright and threw trembling hands in the air. They doubled over in raucous laughter. One of them made chomping noises with his teeth. Calais picked up a shovel that was left outside a stall and raised it like a club. The slaves' eyes widened in alarm. They decided it was a good time to make a hasty departure.

Calais watched them run off before he set the shovel down. He smiled to think that his dusty old dream of hope might actually come true. "Go ahead and laugh for now. We'll see who is laughing when I walk out of here a free man."

Thracius and Marco threaded their way among pedestrians and donkey-drawn carts until they found the home of Florinus. The centurion ignored the bell attached to the courtyard wall and threw the gate open. He strode up the walkway to the inner front portal and pounded on the door. A flushed servant opened the door and stepped back when she saw the uniform of a centurion.

"Take us to your master immediately," demanded Thracius without introduction. Marco blinked apologetically at the startled servant but remained silent. The servant led them to an inner room Florinus used as an office and timidly announced there were visitors.

Florinus looked up from his papyrus and set his pen on the table. He stared at Thracius and asked, "Why do you barge into my home like a tax collector? Who are you and what do you want?"

"My name is Centurion Thracius. This young man, the son of Centurion Adan Longinus, is in my custody. You have accused him of theft. I counter the charge with an accusation of usury. This young man traveled two days with your guards. The standard fee for such services is four *denarii* per day, not twenty-five. If you do not accept the payment of eight *denarii*, I will arrest you and both of you can go before the judge together."

Florinus studied the centurion before he spoke. "Perhaps I made a hasty decision. Do you have the payment with you?"

"I do," said Thracius.

"Well, then, I accept," said Florinus as he stood and extended his open palm.

"First, give me a writ of no charges and hand over his horse," countered the centurion.

The merchant threw him a peeved look and called out to his servant. She appeared immediately. "Get that brown horse and bring it around to the courtyard." The girl disappeared. The merchant scribbled out a writ on a half-page of papyrus, and again extended his open palm.

Thracius snatched the writ from his hand and read it. "When we have the horse, you will get your money." He turned and strode out of the room. Marco followed at his heels.

"Thank you, Centurion. I will pay you back," said Marco as they exited the front door.

"Don't bother. I owe your father much more than eight *denarii*. However, I am surprised the merchant gave in so easily. Perhaps there is another reason he does not want to come before a judge. But no matter. Is this your horse?"

Marco clicked his tongue in annoyance at seeing the girl bring the saddled horse so quickly, meaning Arrow had never been unsaddled. He checked the horse over for injuries while Thracius handed the money to the servant. Marco led Arrow to a public water tank instead of climbing in the saddle. The poor horse drank long enough to tell both men that he had not been given water after the trip from Joppa.

Marco angrily snapped, "I'd like to make Florinus go without water. How could anyone be so cruel? I should file my own charges against him."

"Leave well enough alone, Marco," said Thracius with a tone of impatience. "Come on, let's file this writ back at the Antonia and then go see Serapio. Once we've filed the writ, you'll be free to go wherever you want."

They rode back to the fortress and Thracius presented Marco and the writ to Commander Lysias. He stamped both the arrest writ and the cancelation with his signature ring.

"I would still like you to dine with me this evening, Marco," said the commander. "I want to hear all about your father. You can stay in the guest quarters tonight."

"Thank you, Sir. That is very gracious of you. May I leave my horse in the stables tonight? He doesn't eat much and will be no trouble."

Commander Lysias grinned at Marco's concern. "The stable slaves will see to your horse. Now, gentlemen, you will have to excuse me. I have inspections for the rest of the afternoon. I look forward to hearing about the centurion that came back from the ashes of death."

"Sir, my father wasn't . . . "

"Yes, Commander Lysias," interrupted Thracius. "We will return on time." He gave Marco a subtle shake of his head in warning when the commander looked away. Lysias dismissed Thracius, and he and Marco left.

As they walked across the grounds Thracius cautioned Marco. "You can tell him the whole story tonight, but I would be careful about correcting him on any facts that he favors. And make very sure you are not late. That would not go well for you."

"I shouldn't talk to slaves, apologize to soldiers, correct falsehoods, or be late for dinner. Any other rules I should know about?"

Thracius laughed but it was not the sound of amusement. "I'm sure there are. I'm still learning them, myself."

Chapter 5

A Riot, an Unlawful Command,
and a Purple Sapphire

⸻◦⦿⦿◦⸻

M arco and Thracius left the office, climbed back in the saddle, and rode out into the street. It wasn't far to Serapio's from the Antonia but people running and shouting in the streets diverted their attention.

"I wonder what's going on," called Marco.

The centurion grumbled angrily. "Sounds like another riot. I better look into it."

"I'll go with you."

The loudest shouting came from a crowd in front of the temple and Thracius knew what that meant. The riot would have religious implications and emotions would run high. As they approached, several squads rushed past them led by Commander Lysias.

"Look! The commander, himself, is in the thick of this one," cried Thracius. "He must have been inspecting a construction detail nearby."

Being on horseback, Marco and Thracius could easily see the rioting men. At the center of the fray was a single man being beaten by an angry mob. When the mob saw the commander and his *legionaries*, they stopped beating the helpless victim, but continued to shout at him. The commander ordered the man to be secured with chains and demanded to know what he had done. Angry voices fused incoherently. Unable to determine the man's crime, the commander ordered that the prisoner be taken to the Antonia. Thracius rode into the melee of rioters and helped get the prisoner back to the Antonia. When they reached the stairs of the barracks, which was the safest place to conduct an improvised interrogation, the crowd became even more agitated. Soldiers were forced to beat them back, and people were getting injured. Thracius shouted to the commander that they should carry the prisoner inside. Marco thought the man looked familiar, but his face was too bloody to recognize. He urged Arrow closer to get a better look. When the shouting grew louder, Arrow let out an agitated squeal and laid his ears back. Even the emotion-charged mob knew what that meant. They did not want to get trampled and backed out of the way.

Then the bloodied prisoner spoke with the commander and they stopped mid-way up the stairs. The beaten man motioned with his hand and spoke aloud. A great silence fell over the crowd when they heard him speak in Hebrew. "*I am indeed a Jew, born in Tarsus of Cilicia, but brought up in this city at the feet of Gamaliel.*"

Marco recognized his voice even before he could see his face. It was Paul. He had come with others to visit at his home when Marco was quite young. His grandfather and parents spoke highly of Paul and often went to visit him while he lived with Philip in Caesarea. His cousin, Titus, studied with Paul and Philip. Marco and Aquila had been invited to join Titus, but after a few lessons, they lost interest, unlike their cousin who continued his studies for years.

Staying close to Thracius, Marco listened to what Paul had to say. He spoke of the times he persecuted the Jews who believed in Yeshua. He described how he consented to the death of Stephen who was killed in the street for professing that Yeshua was the Messiah. Marco remembered his father telling him about this event. He said that Stephen even forgave his killers before he died. Then Paul described a vision he had while in a trance. Yeshua had said to him, "*Depart, for I will send you far from here to the Gentiles.*"

The tumult erupted once again and the soldiers had to take Paul into the barracks. Thracius decided they had seen enough and motioned for Marco to follow him. The centurion reined his horse away from the crowd. Marco caught up with him.

"Centurion, please, we need to follow them inside," pleaded Marco. "I know this man and I need to speak with him."

"It's too dangerous to be around these people when they get like this. Commander Lysias has the riot under control," argued Thracius.

"No, I need to see Paul. Please Centurion, let me speak with him. Also, he is a Roman citizen. If a soldier does him harm, it will bring penalty on the commander."

"All right. Let's go." Thracius shouted for several of the soldiers holding the crowd back to stay with their horses. "Stay right behind me, Marco."

Marco and Thracius entered the barracks in time to hear Commander Lysias order soldiers to interrogate Paul under scourging. Thracius stepped to Paul's side as the men were binding Paul with leather straps.

Paul asked Thracius, "*Is it lawful for you to scourge a man who is a Roman, and uncondemned?*"

"No, it is not. I will inform the commander," said Thracius. He ordered the soldiers to stop and gave Marco a grateful glance. He approached Commander Lysias who stood at the other side of the room. "*Take care what you do, for this man is a Roman.*"

The commander was surprised that Paul had not told him this immediately. Commander Lysias, being a Greek citizen, admitted he had to pay a great deal of money for his high level of Roman citizenship which had more benefits than the limited citizenship given to enlisted soldiers.

When Paul confirmed that he was a Roman citizen by birth, the commander and the other soldiers withdrew. Commander Lysias could already be faulted for violating Roman law by putting Paul in chains. He was angry that Paul had only hinted at being a Roman citizen when he first took him into custody. Lysias left the prisoner under Centurion Thracius's custody, which removed his responsibility for Paul's safety. They brought Paul a chair and water to wash his bruised and bleeding face. One of the soldiers handed him a linen towel.

Marco drew closer. "Do you remember me, Sir? I am Marcus, son of Centurion Adan Clovius Longinus. You taught the Way of Yeshua to my cousin Titus when you lived with Philip in Caesarea."

Paul patted his face dry and smiled. "Of course, I remember you and your family. Don't they call you Marco? Your grandfather and father came to me often in those days." Marco nodded eagerly, pleased that he remembered after so many years. Paul looked at him questioningly. "But what are you doing here? This is a dangerous city for a young man to be traveling alone."

"I am not entirely alone," answered Marco, "Centurion Thracius is a friend."

Paul eyed him suspiciously. "Do not tell me you have run away, young man! I would be disappointed if you have. We are to honor our father and mother, not cause them pain with disobedience."

Marco returned his gaze with defiance. "I am not dishonoring my parents. I am living up to their high standards. My father and grandfathers are great men, and I want to be like them. I know God has a mission for me. He just hasn't told me what it is yet."

"I agree that your father and Centurion Cornelius are great men. I do not know about your grandfather Longinus, but I'm sure you are right. Why do you think your father is a great man?" Paul asked.

"Everyone knows why," countered Marco. "Even though King Herod offered him a reprieve from death three times, my father refused to denounce Yeshua or allow a slave to take his place. Three times he offered life to my father and he refused, saying it would be a life of dishonor if he accepted. But God caused my father to survive his execution. Everyone knows the story. Centurion Longinus is a legend. He is the Wolf Commander."

Paul nodded. "I can see that you are very proud of him. You should be, but there is so much more to his honor than that. Adan Longinus revealed courage in ways that most men would not even think of doing. In the face of terrible danger, he fulfilled God's plan."

Marco frowned. "What do you mean? Are you talking about how he followed his orders to crucify Yeshua? He had to follow orders. Centurion Valentius made sure he got the assignment. He was hoping the people of Jerusalem would riot to save Yeshua, and my father and his men would be killed."

"Valentius gave the orders but he was not in charge; God was—and is. Your father did carry out the crucifixion, but Yeshua forgave him and his men. Don't you know that?"

Marco couldn't look Paul in the eye. Adan had told his children about the event.

Paul spoke gently, "Marco, look at me. You have nothing to be ashamed of on your father's account. When I first met your father, I didn't know that he was the centurion who executed Yeshua. Even Silas didn't know. Luke had asked Adan to tell us about his experiences with Theophilus Salvitto because he was writing several accounts about Yeshua for Theophilus. Your father came back to us the next week and told us about Yeshua's crucifixion. It was deeply painful for him to tell us what happened. He said, 'I have been forgiven by God, Yeshua, his mother, and his closest followers, but I ask for your forgiveness as well.' It was then that I told him how I had persecuted the men and women of the Way with all my strength and how Yeshua spoke to me on the road to Damascus. I suggested that we forgive each other, once and for all. I met your parents years after Yeshua was crucified, yet your father still grieved for the agony he inflicted as if the crucifixion had just happened."

Marco took in a deep breath. "Will he ever stop grieving?"

"No, I don't think so. God forgets our sins when he forgives us, but we cannot."

"Then God must have been punishing him for something, knowing how it would cause him pain for the rest of his life."

"No, Marco, it was not punishment, it was a necessary task. One that had to be done. Let me explain. There is a very special reason why God chose Adan to be in charge. Because he is fluent in Hebrew, he heard everything Yeshua and the thief managed to say. No other centurion at the Antonia spoke Hebrew."

"Why was that important?"

"Luke was shocked when he heard what the thief, Demas, said and how he believed in Yeshua and asked Yeshua to remember him when he came into his kingdom. Then Yeshua told Demas, '*Today, you will be with me in Paradise.*' No one had ever told us this detail. John was there, but too far away to hear. The women were too shattered with grief to hear, even if they had been close enough. Your father was the only living person who had heard and understood what Yeshua and Demas said to each other. I know of no other account that describes how the thief believed while he was on the cross. Even though Demas had lived a life of sin and admitted that he was crucified for good reason, Yeshua promised him eternal life in paradise because he believed. This is a message the world needs to hear. The Holy Spirit made sure Adan remembered every word. I believe the story of the dying thief will be retold throughout history. It is proof that even at the moment of death, eternal life can be granted."

"Adan had an important role in the fulfillment of God's plan to make sure that all mankind would know that salvation is possible even until death. As long as there is life, the offer of salvation is always there. Just as important, when Yeshua died, your father turned to the crowd and announced, '*This must have been the Son of God.*' His statement of faith will be repeated throughout history."

"I didn't know about this. Father never told me. He has told me precious little about himself. Mother never mentions any of it. Uncle Niko and Serapio have told me a few stories, but I'd rather hear them from my father."

"Yes, I know of Serapio and Fabiana," said Paul. "Everyone in Jerusalem has heard of Serapio. But there's more to the story, Marco. Your parents did one of the most amazing things any person can do."

Marco's eyes widened with surprise. "Really? What was that?"

"It is a very, very difficult thing to do and comes with a great temptation *not* to do it. The only thing greater would be to sacrifice one's own life so that another would live." Paul waited for the young man to process his words. Marco looked at him encouragingly. Even Thracius listened intently. "I see I have piqued your curiosity."

Marco nodded eagerly.

"Then I shall tell you," said Paul. "Do you know about the blue pearl?"

"I know a pearl is the most valuable treasure on earth. Only kings and emperors possess pearls."

"Usually, yes," agreed Paul. "But your parents owned the most spectacular blue pearl that has ever existed. It was given to your father when he rescued an old tax collector named Zacchaeus who had acquired the pearl at great cost. Robbers were attacking Zacchaeus, and your father chased them away. He then carried the mortally wounded man on his horse to the man's home where he died in peace. Zacchaeus gave the pearl to Adan before he died."

Paul shook a finger at Marco for emphasis. "Do not let anyone tell you that your father stole the pearl after Zacchaeus died. Adan tried to give the pearl to Mary, the mother of Yeshua. If he had stolen it, he would not have given it away. But the story gets even better. During a gathering, a man *named Agabus, stood up and prophesied by the Spirit that there would be a great famine throughout all the world, which came to pass in the days of Claudius Caesar.* I told your parents that we were collecting donations to deliver to the people of greatest need. Your mother and father gave me the blue pearl to save countless people from starvation. That was an extraordinary act of generosity. I once owned that same pearl, but I sold it when I was young. Your parents gave it to me without a moment's hesitation. That is what makes them great heroes. They have more heart than all the people in all of Judea combined, including me."

"This is unbelievable," said Marco, shaking his head. "They could have bought all of Caesarea with that pearl and lived like royalty. Longina, Aquila, and I would have been rich beyond anyone in all of Judea."

Paul smiled and sighed. "Don't you understand, Marco? They have acquired the greatest treasure anyone can have, and that is treasure in heaven which can never be taken from them or destroyed. A cup of wine or vinegar will dissolve the most valuable pearl in a few hours, but treasure in heaven lasts forever. So, tell me, are you ready to do such heroic acts of sacrifice, far from cheering crowds or grateful admirers? Other than

God, only Luke, Silas, and I knew about your parents astounding act of love. And now, you and Thracius know."

Marco looked away. "I had no idea my parents were so—unselfish."

"Ah, we should pray for your tendency toward wild exaggeration," quipped Paul.

Thracius chuckled at the pink flush that spread across Marco's face. He bit his lower lip and sat in silence for a moment. "I think I should go home and apologize. I know they will forgive me. I truly thought I was doing God's will, but I left secretly. I was afraid they would stop me."

"And why would they do that if it was God's will for you to go?"

Again, Marco blushed. He didn't have an answer.

"God does have a plan for you, Marco, but even I do not work without direction, a means of support, and the aid of a friend or two. I think it would be wise for you to return home," said Paul. Thracius nodded agreement.

"What will happen to you, Paul?" asked Marco. "Will you be safe?"

"No worries," he said with a shrug of his shoulders. "What happens is God's will. I speak when I can. I write when I can. I go where God directs me. And he does direct me. I do not traverse the world in random leaps and bounds. I follow God's instructions."

"But how will I know what God's instructions are?" asked Marco. "I do not have visions or go into trances. I do not have dreams of inspired commands. They would be easy to follow."

"God's directions are rarely easy to follow and are often beyond our understanding. Emotions can also be misleading and fleeting," Paul chuckled, "especially if one is young and impulsive. Beware of Satan's tricks, Marco. Satan's children are lies, temptation, and bitterness. You are blessed with a loving family that honors God and Yeshua above all else. Do not take them for granted. They will not live in this world forever."

Marco wanted to discuss his parents further, but the commander returned and informed Paul that he would be kept overnight in Holding.

"I have so many more questions, Paul," said Marco.

"And we will talk again, young man. Of that, I am certain."

They said their farewells and Marco left with Thracius.

"It is too late now to go to Serapio's if you are to meet with the tribune for dinner," said Thracius. "You really don't want to be late. Commander Lysias is not tolerant of tardiness."

"I guess I can get over to Serapio's first thing in the morning," suggested Marco. "But I hate to return home now, with nothing to show for my efforts. I feel like a failure."

"I know you think you have wasted your efforts, but have you really?" Thracius glanced at the young man to gauge his reaction. "Did you not learn amazing things about your parents? If you had not met up with Paul, would you ever have learned about the pearl and how your father told Paul and Luke about the thief?"

"Well, that is something valuable, I know, but knowing it does not make *me* a great hero," Marco frowned at himself. He knew how childish that sounded.

"You will never do anything great if your motive is self-serving. I think you have behaved rashly and should return home," said Thracius. "To be without a plan is to wander into the night with wild animals and robbers behind every tree just waiting for you to trip over your own feet."

Marco frowned at the criticism but made no reply. They headed back to the Antonia, passing a few street vendors still selling their wares despite the lowering sun. One man caught Marco's eye. He looked a lot like Gnaeus Ovidus, his Uncle Niko's brother-in-law. The man saw Marco staring and mistook it for interest in his merchandise. He started to hold up a few of his best items but took a second look at the horse Marco was riding. He pulled one of the necklaces from his right hand and held up the others.

"Young man," the vendor called out, "would you be interested in a beautiful trinket for your sweetheart, or for your mother. Women do love pretty things and I have quite an exquisite assortment."

Marco was tempted to ignore the man and pass by, but the necklace the man chose not to display intrigued him. "What about that one? The one you don't want to show me."

The merchant blinked in disappointment. "This one is quite expensive, young Sir. It is one of a kind. A purple sapphire from the Far East. That is where one must go to find sapphires and rubies. We have no such gems in Judea or in Greece, my native land. They are difficult to work with due to their great hardness. One must use a *diamanti*, a diamond, to tool the etching. Diamond can carve anything and never wears away, but it is not much good for anything else."

The merchant was proud of his merchandise even if a sale was unlikely. "This necklace is strung on a quality leather cord. It is the only sapphire I have of this color. Would you like to inspect it?" Normally, the street vendor would not trust handing his merchandise to someone on a horse who could easily run off without paying, but the presence of the centurion assured him that the young man would not risk arrest.

Marco took the necklace and turned the crystal slowly to look at it more closely.

"It is a fine stone of the rarest color," said the merchant. "Most sapphires are gray and not suitable for jewelry. The blue ones are favored for rings since they are more common. Yellow and pink sapphires can be desirable. However, the purple sapphire is the rarest of all the sapphires. See the hexagonal shape and how the crystal faces shine with a soft luster. Purple is the color of royalty. The color of kings. Have you ever heard of anyone who owns a purple sapphire?"

Marco smiled, thinking of the stories Nikolaus had told him. "As a matter of fact, I have. My aunt has a purple sapphire, or so I've heard. I've never met her. She lives in Herculaneum in Italy." Marco frowned as he inspected the crystal. "All six of the crystal faces are scratched."

"On no, those are not mere scratches, but words. There is quite a story attached to this necklace. There once was a man who had been blind since birth. Even as a grown man, he had to live with his parents. Then a great healer named Yeshua of Nazareth took pity on him. He made a poultice of mud, put it on the blind man's eyes, and told him, '*Go, wash in the pool of Siloam.' So he went and washed, and came back seeing.* It caused a great uproar because the healer had done this miracle on the Hebrew Sabbath. Being Greek, I do not understand the reason for the dilemma, but the healed man was denounced and thrown out of the temple because he swore that Yeshua had to be from God and not a sinner. Many years passed and then the healed man died of old age. His family did not have money for a proper burial so they asked if I would buy his necklace. As you know, it is a grievous dishonor to leave a dead body to be scavenged by wild animals. Out of the kindness of my heart, I offered a fair price for this necklace. The man was buried according to Jewish custom." He beamed at Marco and Thracius, expecting their praise for his altruism.

Marco smiled with approval, but Thracius grunted in disbelief, suspecting the merchant paid the family far less than what the necklace was worth.

"What do the words mean?" asked Marco. "The words etched on the sapphire?"

"That I cannot tell you, young Sir. Sapphires come from the Far East, so I suspect the words are of the ancient language of Tamil spoken in the land of India. As a Roman, you might know the country as *Hindustan*. The mystery of the language lends mystery to the message. Yes? As I told you, it takes great effort to carve a sapphire. Whatever is written on the stone must be extremely valuable. One can easily imagine that the crystal speaks of something even more valuable than the sapphire itself. The message might send you on a quest for fame, as well as fortune. Perhaps it describes the way to a great treasure in faraway lands."

"Tamil, you say?" asked Marco. "It looks similar to Hebrew, but I don't read Hebrew."

"I am only guessing, young Sir, but since sapphires come from India, wouldn't it be logical for the message to be written in Tamil?"

Thracius grunted with scorn. "You would say anything to make a sale."

"I am dismayed at your lack of insight, Centurion," said the merchant unabashed by his skepticism. "Remember, this necklace belonged to a man born blind who received his sight by an astonishing miracle. His family told me that after he was healed, he never took the necklace off, even while he slept."

Marco smiled enthusiastically, but Thracius glared at the merchant. "If it speaks of such a great treasure, why didn't the man collect it himself?"

The merchant shrugged. "Who can say that he did not? What is treasured by one may be cast away by another. Or perhaps the man never had the message translated."

"How did the blind man come by the necklace?" asked Marco.

"*Once* blind, young Sir, but healed. How he acquired the necklace is a mystery."

Marco considered his words. "You say that the message could send me on a quest for a great treasure." Marco whispered under his breath, "Can a person be a treasure? Aunt Dionysia is a treasure to Uncle Niko." As he studied the crystal, the street vendor studied him.

"I can see that you are captivated by this necklace, young Sir," said the vendor. "The stone has magical properties. It can protect you from all evil. It protected the once-blind man. He died peacefully of old age. Isn't that what we all desire?"

"Rubbish," grumbled Thracius. "It is a hunk of mineral; nothing more. Come on, Marco. Give it back and let's go."

Marco set his jaw defiantly. "I do not believe in magic, but the stone is intriguing. How much do you want for it?"

The street vendor smiled. "Forty *denarii*. That's all. It is worth much more, but for you since you're such a polite young man, I'll give you a special discount. How about thirty?"

"I can give you one *denarius*. That's all I have."

The street vendor's eager smile vanished. "You insult me with such mockery, young man! The stone is worth much more than I'm asking."

"That's all I have," exclaimed Marco "Thirty *denarii* would buy a man. You ask too much."

"Enough!" growled Thracius. "Here." He opened his money pouch. "Throw in that bloodstone amulet you've got hanging on your neck and I'll pay you two *aureuii*."

The merchant's eyes gleamed with pleasure. "I'll take gold over silver any day."

"Bloodstone?" Marco frowned. He had never heard of such a thing.

Thracius shrugged. "Green is my favorite color. What can I say?"

Marco looked confused. "Green! Why is it called bloodstone?"

The merchant handed the amulet to Marco. "See the red splashes in the green. Looks like blood spatter."

Thracius laughed at the look on Marco's face. He gestured at Arrow. "*Ohe,* do I look at this run-down horse of yours like that? I like this shade of green. You like this old nag. We're even." Thracius handed two gold coins to the merchant.

"Now let's go. Commander Lysias will have me flogged if I get you back late."

The man smiled at the coins. "Well done, Centurion. The boy will have many adventures with this necklace. Remember, young Sir, follow the purple sapphire. It will lead you to your destiny. May your quest be great and memorable."

Thracius waved the vendor off. "It's just a rock. Be gone with you!"

Marco put the leather cord around his neck. "Thank you, again, Centurion. I owe you much money now, but I will find a way to repay it if you can be patient with me."

"No, you don't owe me anything. As I said, I owe your father much more than that."

Thracius pressed his heels into his horse's flank. Marco followed suit and they trotted down the main road leading to the Antonia.

"Centurion, several times now you have mentioned a debt to my father. Why?"

"Adan Longinus gave me something that I needed. It was an answer to a question."

"What was the question?" implored Marco, curious at how words could be so valuable.

"A man named Lucius Equitius Octavean saw someone just before he was executed while he stood next to your father, the last of the sixteen to die. It was someone no one else could see. But I know it happened. I was Octavean's executioner. They called him The Lion, but not just because his initials were LEO. He was fearless in battle and had the stature of a king. He could have been a centurion, but it didn't work out that way. It haunted me until your father explained who Octavean saw. That was also the first time I met Serapio. I was there at his *Suppelex* when Octavean's mother tried to kill your mother and nearly killed your father."

"*What!*" exclaimed Marco. "I have never heard about this! How many more secrets have my parents kept from me?"

"Perhaps if you had shown proper maturity, they would have told you all of these things. Maybe even if you were at home this very moment, they would sit you down and say, 'Now that you have come of age, we have some things to tell you.' But you took off. Too bad for you."

"I guess I deserve that, but I will be asking some questions when I get home."

"The answers you seek may be lost," said Thracius with a sullen tone. "Parents don't live forever. Do not make the mistake I did when I thought I had all the time in the world. My father could have shed light on a few family issues, but he died unexpectedly."

They finished the trip back to the Antonia in silence. Marco grasped the purple sapphire and thought of Dionysia and the merchant's words. "Follow the purple sapphire. It will lead you to your destiny." Marco knew what he was supposed to do. A slow smile brightened his face. He would not be going home just yet, after all.

Chapter 6

Joppa, a Broken Wheel, and Serapio

A dan, Nikolaus, Aquila, and two escort soldiers traveled to Simon the tanner's house in Joppa where they always stayed when they traveled to and from Jerusalem. Simon looked forward to their visits, but this time, the mood was somber. He sympathized with Adan and his family since his own sons had left as soon as they came of age and rarely visited. It was hard to let go of one's children, no matter how mature or capable they may be. However, Simon thought it was particularly selfish and ill-conceived for seventeen-year-old Marcus to leave without warning.

Simon hauled in a good quantity of fish for their supper. His wife grilled the fish and served it with garum, a favorite Roman fish sauce, boiled asparagus and carrots. The host and hostess were hoping that dinner would distract them from their depression, at least while they ate.

Adan pulled another hunk of bread from the wheat loaf and dipped it in herb-flavored olive oil. "I just can't understand why Marco would take off without so much as a hint. It feels more like he was kidnapped. Why would he run away?"

"Because he's only thinking of himself," said Aquila. "He claims that God has some big plan for him yet he has no idea what it could be. What a joke! I know what's really going on."

Adan and Nikolaus exchanged a look, but Aquila avoided their eye.

"Do you want to explain it to us?" asked Nikolaus.

"Isn't it obvious?" demanded Aquila. "He wants your attention, Father, and it worked. Don't you see? I do everything you ask of me. I do all the chores you assign to me even though I have twice as many as Marco. I have never even argued with you about it. You call to me and I drop everything to come running. What does Marco do? He leaves a job half done so I finish it. If he messes things up, I take care of it. And what do I get for being the responsible one? More work! But what happens when Marco does the most irresponsible thing? We go running after him."

Adan frowned to hear the anger in his son's voice. "If you're so angry with your brother, why did you insist on coming with me to look for him?"

Aquila shrugged his shoulders. "I thought you could use my help."

"And have time with your father—without Marco to interfere?" asked Nikolaus gently.

"Aquila, is that true?" asked Adan.

"I don't know. Maybe," said Aquila, not looking either one of them in the eye.

"I haven't spent much time with either one of you lately," admitted Adan.

"Not *any* time," muttered Aquila under his breath.

"What?" asked Adan. "If you have something to say, let's hear it."

"All right. Sometimes we just want to listen to you, to hear about your experiences. From you, not hearsay from others. Why have you told us so little about yourself? We have questions that you won't answer, so you know what Marco does? He fills in the gaps with his own imagination. Sometimes Marco sits under the oak tree staring out at the sea for hours. I ask what he's doing and he says, 'Thinking.' I say, 'Thinking about what?' and he says, 'About the adventures I will have, just like Father and Uncle Niko.' Marco wants to skip the lessons and go straight to being some kind of warrior without all the hard work in between. He wants to be a great hero so everyone will admire him. He imagines the soldiers cheering for you in Herod's Theater and forgets that you were about to be executed. He visualizes the soldiers swarming to rescue you in Herod's Palace, crashing their shields down on the stone, making sparks fly, and shouting 'Hail, King Herod!' He forgets that Herod had ordered your execution for a second time and could have beheaded you right there in front of Mother. Marco dreams of admiring cheers and forgets about the pain that came first. But I do the work, not the daydreaming. I get things done. I don't sit around fantasizing."

"I see what you do for the family, Aquila," said Adan. "Don't I tell you how much I appreciate your efforts?"

Aquila didn't answer. Instead, he thanked Simon and his wife for the meal and asked to be excused. Adan waved a hand in frustration. Aquila got up and left the room. Adan looked at Nikolaus questioningly, but he shrugged his shoulders at a loss of what to do.

Adan ran his fingers through his hair. "I'm beginning to think I don't know either one of my sons very well. Aquila is right about one thing. I don't talk about myself much. I tried that one time and Marco threw it in my face. He even used it against me."

Nikolaus frowned. "What are you talking about?"

Adan waved a dismissive hand. "Nothing. It was nothing." He looked away and sighed. "How am I supposed to know what to do? How have I missed all this conflict between them? Dulcie seems to have this situation figured out, but I don't have her wisdom when it comes to figuring people out. It seems my sons are just as angry with me as they are with each other."

"Adan, you didn't grow up with siblings. The dynamics between children and parents is complicated. Children want the approval of their parents, but at the same time, they resent parental authority. Children compete for their parents' attention but are disappointed when the attention produces criticism. Parents have to teach their children responsibility without discouraging their natural abilities. Being a good parent is the hardest job anyone will ever have."

"Then how does a man learn to be a good father?"

"Trial and error, brother. Trial and error."

"Great. My sons will despise me for the mistakes I make."

"Neither of them despises you, Adan," said Nikolaus. "I think they want you to be proud of them. They don't realize you're already proud of them."

"I think that's the point, Niko. Why don't they? I'm sure I have told them many times."

"Have you?" asked Nikolaus in a subdued tone. "Have you told them in your actions, not just your words?"

Adan glared at his brother with annoyance.

"I mean," explained Nikolaus, "have you given them equal responsibility? Do you assign them a task and then get out of the way so they will learn from their mistakes? Or do you step in and take over because you want the job done your way? You must let them stumble and fall sometimes, Adan. You need to encourage them to keep trying without taking over. No, the job will not be perfectly done, but they will learn and profit from the learning. You have to trust them even when they falter."

"I've tried, but Marco doesn't follow through and Aquila resents my suggestions," Adan declared. "What else am I supposed to do? Coddle them?"

"Adan," Nikolaus said in a softened tone, "you once relinquished all control to me when I was still a slave in your custody. You practically invited me to escape when you said you would not hunt me down. You told me you would take responsibility for my escape. What did I do?"

"You ran off in the middle of the night."

"That's right, but then I came back—on my own. You told me that I had made a decision of a man, not a child, and certainly not a slave. I had just turned seventeen, like Aquila and Marco. You gave me permission to fail so that I could succeed. Have you done that with your own sons?"

Adan didn't answer.

Nikolaus continued, "I have seen the disappointment on Marco's face when you asked Aquila or Titus to do a difficult task and left nothing for him to do. He wants to earn your respect. I believe he feels like this is the only way to do it. This is the only way he can succeed at something without your interference. As for Aquila—he wants your companionship, not your lectures. Your sons are not your *legionaries* needing to be ordered around. They want you to share yourself with them, not your criticism and rules."

"I have to instruct them, don't I? Why was Longina so easy to deal with? She was like a sponge, soaking up everything Dulcie and I taught her. Look at her now, happily married, tending to her husband and her children. Why can't the twins be that easy?"

"You cannot compare one child to another. Longina is her own person as are each of the twins. Look at Titus and Adriana. My children are completely different. Titus wants to study and teach the Way of Yeshua, nothing else. Adriana wants to manage the inn. Who do you think I usually depend on the most? It certainly isn't Titus, but is he doing what God intended for him to do? Yes! Our children may need to answer a calling that we, as their parents, don't always understand, or find convenient. However, they can surprise you. I'm depending on Titus while I'm chasing after my nephew. He accepted the task without argument. But there's more to his cooperation, too. It is also a way for him to spend time with his grandfather, who he dearly loves."

Adan looked away. "I would have gladly debated any issue with Marco instead of running after him and being worried sick." He gestured impatiently. "Enough of all this talk. I just hope we find him in Jerusalem. I know he must have gone there, and I think he'll go to Serapio's first. He'll want a good meal and a bed to sleep in free of charge, if nothing else."

"See there?" said Nikolaus with a wink. "You *do* believe that Marco has a practical side."

Adan snorted. "Ah, so there's hope for my parenting skills, after all?"

"Well, I don't know if I'd go that far." Nikolaus gave him a grin.

"Thanks for the encouragement, Niko. My confidence is growing in leaps and bounds."

Nikolaus laughed. "I aim to please, brother."

Adan, Aquila, Nikolaus, and the escort soldiers eventually bedded down for the night on Simon's rooftop and left with the rising sun the next morning. Their trip from Joppa to Jerusalem seemed to take much too long, especially since Adan didn't know if they were going in the right direction. Marco could have gone anywhere, including boarding a ship in Joppa or heading north toward Dora.

Along the road, as they neared Emmaus, they came upon a family whose wagon had a broken wheel. They were desperate for help. It would delay them to stop, but Adan knew what a dangerous situation it was for the family. They removed the wheel. Nikolaus and the soldiers stayed with the family while Adan and Aquila took the wheel to Emmaus. There Adan found a woodworker's shop and repaired the wheel himself using the skills Serapio taught him years ago. Adan paid the shop owner for the use of his tools, which pleased the man. He had not expected compensation. Aquila offered a suggestion that would strengthen the rim of the wheel, possibly preventing future breaks. Adan was surprised that he had never thought of the idea but was impressed that Aquila had. Together they fixed the wheel, then took it back and reattached it. The owner of the wagon offered to pay Adan. When he refused payment, the man threw back the wagon tarp revealing loaves of bread and jars of honeycomb. He insisted that Adan and his group each take a loaf of bread. He gave Adan a jar of honey which they passed around to each other as they rode, dipping pieces of bread into the honey. They entered Jerusalem just before sunset, when the city gates would be closed for the night.

Once inside Jerusalem's walls, the same feeling of anxiety settled over Adan that he always felt until he reminded himself that Serapio, Fabiana, and Nebetka were there, and Felix Valentius was not. Even though Valentius had been executed for high treason, Adan would never forget the vindictive persecution Valentius waged against him for two years. The pain of those memories was fading as the years passed but being in Jerusalem always brought them back into sharp focus.

The escort soldiers moved into protective positions around their commander and his family as they made their way down the congested streets. The acrid air burned the throat and eyes of those unaccustomed to the dirt streets of the city. Adan appreciated the stone-paved streets of Rome and wished the emperor would use some of the tax money to pave, at least, the main streets in Jerusalem. With every passing wagon, cart, or mounted patrol, the travelers, street beggars and shop venders were subjected to choking clouds of dust.

Merchants and street beggars called out as they passed by. The occasional mounted and foot patrols that they encountered acknowledged Adan and paused at attention until he moved on. Some of the decurions and *legionaries* stared at Adan with wide eyes, recognizing him as the centurion who came back from the dead. When his back was to them, they quickly huddled in whispered conversation, speculating on why the Wolf Commander had come to Jerusalem. Not all the soldiers recognized him, but all of them had heard of him.

Adan felt a lifting relief as he reined Blackfire to a halt in front of Serapio's *Suppelex*. He dropped from the saddle and strode in through the open door of the shop. Serapio was twisting a reed around a section of a chair seat when he looked toward the darkened doorway. He had changed little over the years except his full head of hair and beard were steaked with iron gray. There was one very notable difference. Even though everyone in Jerusalem still referred to him as "the one-eyed *gladiator*" the blind, milky-blue eye was now deep brown as it had been before Theo Salvitto's niece, Drusia, took a short sword to Serapio's face. It had taken years for Serapio to come to terms with his guilt as a killer for the entertainment of the masses. With Adan's encouragement, God's healing touch through Simon Peter, and Serapio's faith, his full eyesight was restored.

When Adan appeared in the doorway, Serapio exclaimed with a hearty laugh, "Well, there stands my most favorite centurion in the entire world! What an unexpected treat! What brings you to my humble shop?"

Adan frowned to see genuine surprise on Serapio's face. "He's not here, is he?"

Now it was Serapio's turn to frown. "I would say it is very good to see you, Adan, but you don't look happy to see me. And who were you expecting to find here?" He saw Nikolaus and Aquila. "Where is—the other one?" It was hard enough telling the twins apart when they were together but nearly impossible when they were apart.

Adan lowered his head. His broad shoulders seem to sag as he swallowed hard. "I felt sure Marco would be here, Serapio. I am sorry to not return your warm welcome as I should have. But he has taken off and we aren't sure where he has gone. I thought he would be here with you and Fabiana. Perhaps he went to the Antonia, except I don't know why he would do that." Adan looked around. "Where is Fabiana?"

"Ana is helping with a sick grandchild over at Nebetka's tonight. The illness is not serious, but she gets nervous when children are sick, more so than most, as you can imagine. She will be back in the morning, but she will be sorry to have missed even one hour with you."

Adan stepped out the door to order the escort soldiers to go on to the Antonia and to meet back with him in the morning. He gave the *principales legionary* an introduction written on a small scroll to give them access to the enlisted men's guest quarters and cafeteria.

Serapio pulled some chairs from the back of the shop and asked for details about Marco. "We will find him, Adan," he said with assurance. "He still might be here. Think about it; would he come to the very place you figured he would go to first? If he's here, he will come to see me, but he may be laying low for now. He's not an idiot, you know. I mean, he is his father's son and you've always been a cunning wolf."

Adan blustered at the comment. "This cunning wolf feels outsmarted by a child, at this point." He realized the slip as Aquila started to correct him. "*Ohe*, that's right. He's not a child anymore. We could have looked for him today if we had not been delayed outside of Emmaus. As it was, they nearly caught our horses' tails in the city gates when they shut them for the night. It probably doesn't matter. If he doesn't want us to find him, we won't. I just hope he's not in trouble. The world is full of evil and Marco is blind to it. He is much too trusting."

"Marco can be naïve about somethings, but not everything," pointed out Nikolaus. "Have some faith, brother. You have taught him well. I don't believe he will leap into truly dangerous situations as blindly as you fear."

Adan gave his brother an angry scowl. "Are you sure about that?"

Nikolaus frowned and gave him a puzzled look but said nothing.

Serapio lit a few oil lamps with an ember from the fireplace. It was getting dark. The golden glow of the moon was just beginning to appear at the eastern horizon.

Serapio caught Nikolaus and Aquila's eye and motioned for them to join him upstairs. "Let me talk with him alone," said Serapio. "You two can use Nebetka's old room. I'll bring you some supper and then you can get some sleep. Adan and I will tend to the horses. I've got a spare mat for the roof, which is where I'm sure he will end up. I'll see you two in the morning. I'm sorry your reason for being here is unpleasant, but I am glad to see both of you."

Serapio went down the stairs and motioned for Adan to join him. "Let's go tend to your horses." Blackfire raised his head in greeting at the sight of Adan in the doorway.

After the horses were cared for, Serapio took food and drink up to Nikolaus and Aquila, and then he and Adan shared a loaf of bread and dried mutton.

"I still can't believe Marco would do this," groaned Adan. "I've been in shock ever since Dulcie put that letter in my hand. She is a strong woman, but naturally, she fears for our children, not because they take heedless risks, but because the rest of the world is a dangerous place, especially for one as inexperienced as Marco."

"Don't sell him short, Adan," countered Serapio.

"I'm trying not to, but up until a few days ago, I thought he could never disappoint me." Adan hung his head. "Well—other than that one time."

Serapio frowned. "What happened?"

Adan put his thoughts in order. "I set all three kids down to have a talk, one of those serious kinds where you feel sick and your mouth goes dry. I told them about Yeshua's execution and my part in it. I wanted them to know what forgiveness did for me. I thought they understood when I admitted my greatest guilt to them. Longina cried and hugged me. She thanked me for trusting her with my darkest moment. Aquila and Marco expressed their sorrow that I had to take part in the crucifixion—or so I thought at the time." Adan got up and walked to the open doorway. He looked out into the night and felt the chilled breeze that wafted along the street. Serapio waited in silence.

Adan came back and sat down. "It had been nearly a year since I told them about the crucifixion. Then a month ago, we were going for supplies when we came upon a man who was terrified and wounded. Marco immediately offered to help him. He was going to take the man on his horse and run for it. I stopped him and began questioning the man. Marco was furious. He said the man must be a runaway slave and we had to help him before it was too late. I said he was an impulsive fool to endanger himself like that."

"Adan, he's young. He reacted without thinking. But to call him a fool, especially in front of his brother—that must have deeply humiliated him."

Adan wasn't listening. "Look, all I'm saying is that we didn't know the facts about this man. Marco jumped in without even considering that he may be dangerous. Then soldiers came and took the man into custody. They said he was a runaway slave who, according to witnesses, had murdered his master. Also, when another slave confronted him, the murderer had killed him as well. That made no difference to Marco. He was furious with me. I explained that murder was never justified, even for a cruel master. He said the witnesses could have been lying and the murdered slave might have actually been the killer. I said that was possible. That's why we have trials to determine the truth. I said if the man is found guilty, he should be executed. Marco said he could be found guilty and still be innocent. I said that was highly unlikely. That's when Marco said—" Adan paused and rubbed his hand across his mouth. He looked away and bowed his head.

"Just say it, Adan."

Adan raised his head. "Marco said, 'You're right. We all know that an innocent man has *never* been crucified.' I was speechless. I entrusted Marco with my darkest grief and he used it against me. Not only that, but for a moment he looked at me with pure loathing. It wasn't my imagination. Aquila was staring at him with the same shock that must have been on my face. I couldn't speak for the rest of the way into town. For days, we avoided each other. I kept thinking he would apologize, but he hasn't brought it up. Dulcie says I need to be patient, and that when the time is right, we will both know what to say. I haven't told Niko." Adan sighed heavily. "I guess, I don't want him to be disappointed with Marco."

Serapio shifted in his chair and cleared his throat. "With just Marco? Or both of you?"

Adan gave his friend a tired look. "Sometimes I'd rather deal with two hundred raw recruits than my two sons. Being someone's father is the hardest job I've ever had."

"We bring our children into adulthood the best way we know how," said Serapio, "but we make mistakes, and they suffer for our mistakes. They in turn, make their own mistakes. And the cycle goes around and round. He lashed out because you called him a fool when he thought he was doing the right thing by coming to a victim's rescue. He is trying to prove to you *and himself*, that he is perfectly capable of putting the needs of someone else before his own in a beneficial way. He wants you to be proud of him, Adan, not ashamed of him."

"I know I messed up, Serapio," Adan said glumly. "But I don't know what to do about it. When Mary, Yeshua's mother, forgave me and required me to forgive myself, she also warned me that I may be tempted to take the guilt back. She said that others may condemn me. I never thought that my own son would be one of those 'others.' I have tried to forget those terrible words, and that look on his face. Yet, that one moment burns a new scar in my heart every day."

"Yes, we know what even one ill-advised statement can do to a person," said Serapio.

Adan nodded dejectedly. "I hear you. To think that Felix Valentius hated me because of what my grandfather, Livius Longinus, said to him decades before still astounds me. I guess, it shouldn't. Resentment often festers. The tiny mustard seed grows into a huge tree."

"The seed of resentment will die if it is not given nourishment. And here's the trick—only *you* can withhold that nourishment. If you hold on to what Marco said in anger, you will be no better than Valentius."

Adan nodded, but said nothing. He had convinced himself that Marco had acted only out of selfishness, but now, he needed to evaluate his own contributing factors. He would not make excuses for Marco's behavior, but neither should he make excuses for his own actions. Adan decided that when he found his wayward son, he would apologize for his harsh condemnation.

Chapter 7

Jerusalem, Jealousy, and a Scheme

⬤⬤

Centurion Thracius managed to return Marco to the Antonia on time, but Commander Lysias sent word that a situation had arisen which required his attention and he would have to reschedule. Thracius took Marco to the guest quarters and warned him not to leave the fortress until the writ canceling the charge of theft could be properly recorded. The centurion assured him that he would take him to Serapio's the next day. Rather than summon a slave, Marco took Arrow to the stables himself. He wanted to talk to Calais. He led his horse up and down the rows of stalls until he found the young man.

Calais looked up from brushing down a horse when he heard his name. He was surprised to see Marco since only fellow slaves called each other by name.

"How can I serve you, Sir?" Calais asked.

"I need to put my horse in a stall for the night. Are there any vacant ones?"

"Of course! Anything for the son of Centurion Longinus." He stepped out of the stall and took Arrow's reins. "There's one at the end of the row. I'll take good care of him and make sure he has plenty of hay and water."

"I'll come with you," said Marco. "I really would like to talk with you about my father. When did you meet him? How old were you then?"

Calais paused for a moment. "Very young. I met him after I heard about the Saturday classes. Everyone talked about how he always handed out food at the end of each lesson. Naturally, I wanted to be on his team. At first, it was just to get something good to eat, but later, it was more than that—much more. It was said that he wouldn't take the youngest boys, so I told him I was eleven. I was barely eight, but tall for my age, so he didn't question it. I am twenty-six years old now, the same age your father was when I met him."

"And I just turned seventeen. What an odd coincidence."

"A coincidence? For what?" asked Calais.

"My Uncle Niko was seventeen and my father was twenty-six when they met. Then they became brothers the same year. I'm seventeen and you're twenty-six. Maybe we'll become brothers, too." Marco was startled at the undisguised anger on the slave's face, but it was gone in an instant.

Calais looked away. "Forgive me, Sir. I have offended you somehow."

Marco was confused. "What? I don't understand. Did I say something wrong?"

"Of course not, Sir! I am Commander Lysias's property much like his horse. It is not a crime to mock someone's horse."

"I wasn't mocking you, Calais," said Marco. "Even though I admit it is unlikely we could ever be brothers. I'm sorry you took it that way."

Calais stopped at the stall and opened the gate. He led Arrow inside and removed his bridle and saddle. Arrow went straight to the hay piled in a corner. Calais opened a spigot over the water trough in the stall. The spigot was connected by a lead pipe from a water tank that was elevated above the level of the troughs in each stall. There was a tank for each row of stalls. The stable slaves rotated their other duties with filling the tanks each day from the wells. While Arrow ate, Calais brushed the horse down.

Marco watched him work. "Tell me about Niko. Was he always close to my father?"

Calais stopped and stared at Marco. "There was no one here named Niko and I don't remember the centurion having a brother. Niko doesn't sound like a Roman name."

"I mean Nikolaus Kokinos, the slave who was in charge of my father's stable team."

Calais blinked in astonishment. "Are you saying that the Nikolaus who is now your father's brother—legally—is the same Nikolaus who was a slave here at the Antonia? The Greek slave?" He turned away to concentrate on his task. "Forgive me, again, Sir! I had no idea you were talking about Nikolaus."

"Don't worry about it," Marco said nonchalantly. "Of course, I never knew Nikolaus when he was a slave. For me, he's always been Uncle Niko."

Calais paused in his work and looked Marco in the eye. "Nikolaus the lowly stable slave is now the brother of the great Centurion Longinus." Bitterness made his throat tighten. "How did he become a brother to the centurion?"

"My grandfather, Aquila Longinus, adopted him soon after my parents were married." Marco frowned at the stiff, angry movements of the slave as he brushed Arrow.

"I see," said Calais after a long pause. "So, Uncle Niko lives off the wealth of your family, doing nothing but whatever pleases him?"

"No, he works hard," Marco answered defensively. "He owns an inn in Caesarea, and is co-owner of the flour mill, and the owner of two wine shops. He was given a huge reward for turning in evidence that the slave of Centurion Valentius was really the famous murderer, Alexander Nisos."

"You mean Demitre. I remember him. He lorded his favored position over everyone in the slave quarters. Too bad he died of a broken neck. He should have been crucified."

Marco was surprised at the vehemence in the slave's voice. "Well, as I was saying, Niko bought the Ocean View Inn in Caesarea with the reward money. He married my

Aunt Marina soon after he and my parents got back from Rome and Herculaneum. They invited Niko to go with them to find his sister, Dionysia, who is a slave in Herculaneum. He wanted to buy her freedom, but she refused to leave her children. Her master is her children's father. I've never even met her."

Calais's eyes gleamed with envy. "Nikolaus is a rich man now. How wonderful for him."

"He sure is," Marco said, missing Calais's caustic tone. "Father has invested in Niko's businesses and is turning a good profit. My Grandfather Marcus, who I'm named after, also invested so Uncle Niko was able to buy the wine shops. He and my father are true brothers in every sense of the word except for biology, of course. When my father survived his execution in Herod's theater, Serapio came here and talked Salvitto into selling Nikolaus to him. Serapio took him straight to my father and they registered his canceled slavery contract the next day. I wish I could have been there to see that."

"I wish I could have been there as well." Calais said, barely able to subdue a sarcastic tone. "Without Nikolaus," he muttered to himself.

"What? I didn't hear you."

"Unimportant, Sir. Just telling your horse to stop stepping on my foot. I remember when Nikolaus was sold as if it were yesterday. I was assigned to scrub the *latrinae* channels at the time, even though I had done nothing wrong, so I didn't see him leave. It was the worst time for me here at the Antonia. That's when Centurion Longinus went away. Nikolaus went away, and Onesimus went away. He was sold like Nikolaus. *Latrinae* duty is reserved for the most humiliating punishment. Sometimes *legionaries* are even given the job if they have really messed up. A *principales* assigned me to it until Tribune Salvitto found out. I had been at it all day before he saw me. Tribune Salvitto made that *principales* stand outside his office holding a rock in each hand for the rest of the day. I'll never forget that. Tribune Salvitto said, 'Nobody punishes my slaves without my permission.' And he gave me a loaf of wheat bread. It was the most delicious bread I'd ever tasted, or so it seemed at the time."

Marco looked at Calais with sympathy. "I wish you weren't a slave. If I had enough money, I would buy you and set you free." He looked away, until the silence grew uncomfortable. "Tell me about Serapio. Why is he called the one-eyed *gladiator*? He has two perfectly good eyes."

"He didn't always," replied Calais. "You can still see the scar. That was from a sword across the face that blinded his eye. It used to look kind of milky with a bluish discoloration like a blue cloud in a white sky. They say that a follower of The Way healed him and gave his full sight back to him. But the nickname stuck. I wish a follower of The Way would heal me. You can't see the worst scars, but I feel them every day."

Calais glanced over at Marco. "They say that Mosaic Law allows a Hebrew to safeguard a slave in his household if he can make it inside his gate. The Jew's home becomes a sanctuary. I find that interesting. Their commandments include 'You shall not steal,' but they can keep someone else's property. That is the way of the world. Confusion and contradiction."

"Calais, what would you be willing to do for your freedom?"

The slave arched an eyebrow. "Is that a trick question?"

Marco snorted and gave him a lopsided grin. "I guess it was. Why don't you run away?"

"Commander Lysias would not hesitate to hire the slave hunters. They are very good at their work. Look at me. You're not the only one with unusual eyes. Slave hunters are professionals and they have a communication system with detailed descriptions of runaways. How long would it take them to spot a green-eyed Greek? Lysias wouldn't kill me since I make a lot of money for him, but he would brand my forehead with the letters FUG for *fugitivus*. As you know, once a slave is branded a fugitive, or scarred from a scourging, he or she can never be free. He would punish me every day for the rest of my life. That would be my best situation. Do you know what the worst would be?"

Marco shook his head dejectedly, not wanting to hear the answer.

"Lysias would have me crucified—for practice. He would be paid a bonus to compensate for his loss of property. That's the way they teach the new soldiers how to cause the most pain for the longest time before the male or female slave dies from dehydration and exhaustion. I don't wish to be a practice boy for new recruits."

"But what if they would never even look for you? Would you go?"

"Why are you asking me these questions?" Calais stopped brushing the horse and eyed Marco with suspicion. "If I knew that no one would hunt me down, of course I would leave. Wouldn't anybody?" He turned back to his task.

Marco pursed his lips in thought. "Centurion Thracius bought an amulet for me, a purple sapphire like the sapphire my Aunt Dionysia has. The merchant said to follow the purple sapphire. Not just 'follow the sapphire,' he said, 'follow the *purple* sapphire.' I think that was a message from God." He pulled on the cord to reveal the stone. "If you could leave, would you go with me? I could use your help. I want to save my aunt from slavery, too. After we bring her to Caesarea, you would be free to go wherever you want."

Calais paused before he started to clean out Arrow's hooves with a hoof pick. A cascade of emotions coursed through his mind in an instant. "I would do anything to go with you. The only one who would notice is Commander Lysias because he rents me out to most of the cohort centurions. He would miss that income, as if he didn't make enough money already. Only your father and Tribune Salvitto cared about me. The tribune cared because I was his property. But your father cared because I was his favorite. He was kind to me. I was safe with him. He kept the other soldiers from abusing me." Calais concentrated on his task without looking up. "I loved him like a father." He whispered to himself, "I still dream about him."

Before Marco could ask him what he had said, Calais continued, "He gave me extra food, even wheat bread. That's against the rules, you know. He didn't care. Of course, no one challenged the Wolf commander. The *legionaries* wouldn't admit it, but they were afraid of him. Most of them thought he was a werewolf. Because he was so young, a few believed he must have been given the title of centurion as a special favor. Those who thought he was a werewolf said he was ancient because werewolves are immortal. When he died on the stage, they were confused. Then he came back to life and they were convinced. No more confusion. Some of the men were terrified, saying he came back for revenge. Four squads were put to death because Valentius had them drugged and then paid someone to smuggle the prisoner, a Galilean, out of Holding. We all thought Valentius had killed the Galilean, but then *he* showed up again, just like your father. Some said it was the Hebrew God, *Yahweh,* who brought them back to life. I don't believe in *Yahweh.* He doesn't even have a statue you can pray to. I don't believe in anything I can't see."

Marco exclaimed, "But you can see him, well, you can see his creation. It's all around us."

Calais finished cleaning the last hoof. He tied the leather thongs attached to the hoof pick to his belt. Marco saw the name 'Lysias' sown onto the wide, thick belt worn by all slaves. Calais looked Marco in the eye. "Your father only took Nikolaus with him when he went to Caesarea because Tribune Salvitto assigned Nikolaus to serve him. Centurion Longinus wanted to take me. I know he did, but I was Tribune Salvitto's personal property so he must have told him no." He reached for the gate latch. Marco backed up to let him out. He walked to the next stall. "Please forgive me. I have to tend to many more horses."

Marco followed him and stood outside the gate, leaning his elbows on the top. "Don't apologize. I know you have work to do. But Tribune Salvitto didn't assign Uncle Niko to my father. He requested Niko and paid for his services."

Calais turned away to hide his anger. "I don't think so. Centurion Longinus would never have left me here if he had known what some of the soldiers would do. They took advantage of his absence." Calais straightened up from cleaning out the next horse's hooves. "When I thought your father was dead, and then Nikolaus was sold, and Onesimus was sold, I wanted to die. Everyone I had ever cared about was gone. I was alone, but that wasn't the worst part. When Centurion Longinus went away, I lost my protector. Your father kept his team of stable slaves behind his shield. None of us were beaten or abused or used for pleasure. When your father went to Caesarea, we lost his protection. One of the *legionaries* told me that it was my own fault. He said, 'If you were an ugly slave, no one would have you.' The only reason I am still alive is that Tribune Salvitto transferred me to the kitchen when he sold Onesimus. But there were still times I couldn't avoid a drunk soldier and I paid the price, one way or another. So, you ask me if I would go with you if no one would hunt me down? In a heartbeat!"

"A heartbeat?" said Marco. "That's it! A heartbeat. It worked for my father. They thought he was dead so he got away and no one came looking for him. What if they think you're dead?"

Calais gaped at him. "I thought you were going to buy my slave contract like your father did for Nikolaus. How can you make them think I am dead? They burn dead slaves out in the crematory. That is, after the pit is full of enough bodies to warrant the use of the wood."

"Exactly. The bodies are piled in the pit until there's enough. They would dump you out there. No. Even better, I would volunteer to take your body, since you knew my father, and then I would come back and get you when it's night. We would slip out of here and find a way to Herculaneum. I would tell everyone that you are a family servant. Far from here, no one would suspect. If anyone sees the brand on your arm, I'll explain how you were once a slave, but my father freed you. That's what the Longinus family does. We free every slave we can."

"How could I possibly look dead enough to fool anyone? I would be sold to the mines and you'd be arrested for helping me escape. What would your father say about that?"

Anger flashed in Marco's amber eyes. "He would say that I was an impulsive fool, but I don't care. I'm going to prove him wrong, because I'm going to rescue you *and* my aunt. I can be just as brave as he is." He pressed his hand over the sapphire under his tunic.

Marco sighed and chewed his bottom lip in thought. "But my mother would cry if she knew what I was doing. She worries when something bad happens to anyone in our family, and then Father is gentle and kind with her. He's always kind to her and my sister, Longina, and to Grandmother Iovita and Aunt Marina. He's strict with me. Not so much with my brother, but he's really hard on me. Apparently, he sees the best in everyone but me."

"Centurion Longinus is a good man. You're lucky to have a father like him. How can you complain?" He didn't even try to disguise the annoyance in his voice.

Marco shrugged sheepishly. "I have my reasons."

Calais bent down to clean the last hoof. "I remember what a family is supposed to be like. My parents loved me, but then my father was killed in an accident. A tower in Siloam collapsed and killed eighteen people. My father was one of them. We had immigrated there from Greece to avoid barbarian marauders, only to lose Father to an accident. My mother tried to find work, but in the end, she had to let me go. She said I'd starve to death if I stayed with her. I would rather have starved. There are some things worse than death. You think I could really escape this place? How could I possibly fake being dead? They won't take your word for it. They'll stick a knife in my heart to see if I move. I've seen them do that before."

"It will be tricky. We'd be taking a big risk."

Calais straightened up from his work and glared at Marco. "You mean *I'll* be taking a big risk, the biggest. If I'm not crucified, Lysias might sell me to a copper mine. Do you know how they get the ore out of a mine?"

"No, I never thought about it. Is it difficult?"

Calais looked away to hide his exasperation. "You stand on top of a huge wheel. The outer rim of the wheel is made of shovel-edged compartments. You have to keep your balance while stepping on the shovel edges to make the wheel turn. You must stand far enough back from the top so your weight makes the wheel turn, but you have to step forward, just right, to keep from falling off. The wheel turns, which scrapes the ore from the wall of the mine. Other slaves move the wheel forward at its base. Then more slaves shovel up the loosened ore at the bottom of the wheel and dump it in carts pulled by, you guessed it, more slaves. A once healthy man lasts about eight months before he dies. His corpse is left to rot where he falls. The other slaves step over the corpses, barely noticing. It's dark, after all. The air is suffocating with ore dust and smoke from the torches so you can barely smell the putrefying flesh. That works out nicely, don't you think? You work for sixteen hours every single day. You might get a few water breaks, if the guards don't spill it first. Any slave who slacks off or passes out loses a water break. They work to eat, but they're given just enough to avoid starvation. Once a year, the slaves are sent down to clear away human remains so they can move the wheel and carts through the mine tunnels. As I said, there are some things worse than death. In the copper mines, death is the *best* thing. So, forgive me if I'm not excited about your plan."

Marco lowered his head. "I'm sorry. I didn't know. How do you know all this?"

"My older brother was a guard in a mine for five months. It's a horrible job even for the guards, but it was all he could find. He managed to earn enough to pay off my father's debts so our mother wouldn't have to sell herself on the street. He would have kept at it for the family's sake, but he was fired when they caught him giving extra food to the slaves. This all happened only because my father and I were walking by the Siloam tower at the worst possible moment on that terrible day. The tower began to crumble, we stopped and looked up. Blocks of stone began to fall and my father literally threw me out of the way. A stone block crushed him. A woman grabbed me and covered my face with her shawl. She took me to my mother. I never got to thank her for saving me from seeing my father's crushed body. You're angry with your father. I can see that. But you still have a father, and I bet he would have done the same thing for you that my father did for me. You think he has mistreated you? What did he do? Shout at you? Make you do extra chores? Such brutality! I wonder why you waited so long to escape such an abusive father."

Marco was shocked to hear a slave reprimand him, but shame reduced him to silence. Once again, the thought that he should return home echoed in his mind but he pushed it away. He raised his head and found Calais watching him. The slave turned away and resumed his work.

"You're right, Calais. I have taken my father and my privilege for granted. I have a good life, and have never been afraid for my security, or even wanted for anything. That only makes me want to prove myself even more. I know I am supposed to save my Aunt Dionysia. Uncle Niko and my father have gone to Herculaneum twice, but came back without her. It makes my uncle sad for the longest time. I just thought that I could help you, as well as my aunt. There are poisonous plants that make a man appear to be dead. When my father nearly died in Herod's theater, they had poisoned him with belladonna. We can't use that because he would have died later at Serapio's house if God had not healed him through Simon Peter."

"Simon Peter? He was the prisoner that escaped from your father's custody. Then your father did help him?"

"No! It was an angel of God that took Peter out. My father saw it happen. Lucius Octavean wanted to kill Peter to get Valentius executed. What is done to the prisoner is done to the lead commander. But Father saved Peter. That's why God saved Father when he died in Herod's theater. And he really did die, but when Valentius hit him on the chest out of anger, Father's heart started beating again. It was later that Peter healed Father from the poison."

"I think that is the man who healed the one-eyed *gladiator*. He's still around here. It drives the Sanhedrin crazy, but they don't dare confront men like him. Not usually, at least. Sometimes the men of the Way leave but they always come back. I think they're all idiots. I'd run so fast; they wouldn't even see me. I'd just be a flash of light, and they would think I was a god."

"There's only one God, Calais," declared Marcos. "If you believe in him, he will help you."

"Yes, and we can see how much God has helped me and my family so far." Calais finished with that horse and moved to the next stall.

"Well, I'm with you now," Marco said brightly. "I know we will succeed. When we get back with Dionysia, I'm sure Father will offer you a job in Caesarea or maybe Uncle Niko will hire you to manage one of his wine shops. I will pray and ask God to help us, and he will. We just have to have faith."

"God is your slave, then? He does whatever you demand?" growled Calais as he began brushing the horse down.

Marco's grin faded. "No. It's not like that. If it is the right thing to do, God will help us."

"And if it's the wrong thing? I could die a slow, agonizing death. I think, I don't like this plan. I've got it better here now. The soldiers like to make sport with the youngest boys. Other than the occasional fist in the face, they mostly leave me alone." He glanced over at Marco. "I know you mean well, but I don't know you. What if you changed your mind and decided you don't need me? What if someone recognizes me before we can get away and alerts Commander Lysias?"

"We'll get out of Jerusalem immediately and go where no one knows you. I'm not going to change my mind, either. You can trust me, Calais."

"I trusted your father and he left me. I trusted Tribune Salvitto and he sold me to Commander Lysias." He stopped and leveled his eyes at Marco. "I trusted Nikolaus and he betrayed me. *I* was your father's favorite, not that back-stabbing, simpering . . . never mind. You wouldn't understand."

The accusations of betrayal hung in the air like a poisonous stench. Marco clenched his teeth in frustration. "My father had no choice. He couldn't take his whole stable team. He was supposed to be dead, after all. I'm sure he would have found a way to free you, too, if it were possible. I don't know what happened between you and Uncle—between you and Nikolaus, but he's a good man. He would do anything now to help you to freedom. I know he would."

"From what you have told me, they didn't give me a second thought," Calais said. "Your father could have sent that *gladiator* to buy me, too, especially since Tribune Salvitto owned me personally. Salvitto bought me and Onesimus together for his own use but decided to train us here at the Antonia. Then he sold Onesimus to some rich man named Philemon and sold me to Commander Lysias. I take care of his horse first, and he takes a fee from the other cohort centurions for me to tend their horses. I had to work hard to get this position; I used what I learned from your father's Saturday classes."

Calais looked Marco in the eye. "I did everything I could to win your father's praise. Yet, now you tell me, he *selected* Nikolaus to be his assistant in Caesarea and *paid* for his services. All this time, I have been content thinking that Salvitto assigned Nikolaus to the job because he wasn't the tribune's personal slave, like me, but just a piece of Antonia property. Still, Nikolaus thought he was better than the rest of us. Always telling us how rich his family had been and that his father was famous. Poor little boy Nikolaus lost his whole family, except for that sister he always went on and on about. They were all lies, I'm sure."

"Uncle Niko is not a liar!" Marco angrily retorted, "Everything he said was true. My Grandfather Aquila had heard of Nicandros, Niko's father, and his architectural masterpieces." He stepped back from the low gate. "But you're probably right. It won't work and we'll get caught, and then your death will be my fault. Forget I ever said anything about getting you out of here. I was just trying to help!"

Marco turned away and strode up the row of stalls. He could feel Calais watching him. He crossed the arena and headed for the guest quarters. He wondered how anyone could be content to remain a slave when he was offered the chance for freedom. Perhaps this was why his father had chosen Nikolaus, who had never been content to be a slave.

Calais leaned against the low gate and bowed his head. "That went well. I have proven myself to be more stupid than you," he told the horse. It turned its head toward him and snorted. "Now I will always wonder, what if? Maybe I should apologize. He most definitely is the son of Centurion Longinus. He looks just like him. Even if we fail, I'll be rid of this life, if you can call it a life." The horse flicked its tail and went back to eating.

The slave finished with that horse and moved to the next stall. The animal laid its ears back and raised its head threateningly. This horse was aggressive and didn't like anyone coming into the stall. Calais cautiously reached for a halter hanging from the gate. "Come on, you evil old dragon, let me do my job. It's not like I've ever done anything to hurt you." The horse turned its ears toward the slave and loudly exhaled as if it were bored.

Calais set the halter down and slowly reached for the horse. It huffed and snorted but allowed the young man to rub its muzzle and forehead as he began to talk softly. "Let us get close and win your trust. Then they stick in the knife. But that little trick can go both ways." Calais untied his hoof pick from his belt and leaned down to grasp the horse's left front ankle. He stopped and straightened up. But what if it worked? "I will be free to do whatever I want," he reasoned aloud. "Marco will take my loyalty for granted, thinking I will feel indebted to him. He will trust me as I trusted his father. I can play the loyal servant until I no longer need him. Then I will make Centurion Longinus wish he had never left me behind. I wonder if he will grieve for his son as long as I have grieved for him." A malicious smile crossed his face but not for long. The smile faded into a look of misery. "And then my hope will be lost forever." He sat down at the feet of the horse and dropped his head in his hands.

Calais raised his head and got to his feet. He had never worked in a copper mine, but his life at the Antonia was a treadwheel all the same, one short step from falling into oblivion. He would apologize to Marco the next day and swear on his life to help him rescue Nikolaus's sister. As soon as he and Marco were far from Jerusalem, he would leave the boy and disappear. He would finally have his life back.

Chapter 8

Larkspur, Friends Reunite, and an Ominous Oath

Marco rose early, grabbed a quick breakfast at the officers' cafeteria, and saddled Arrow himself, hoping to avoid Calais for now. He left the Antonia before Thracius could find him and possibly interfere with his plans. He knew that the writ clearing him of the charge of theft had been filed with Commander Lysias. Thracius was just making an excuse to keep an eye on him. For all Marco knew, Thracius had sent word to Caesarea and his father was on his way to Jerusalem to take him home. Even though it was not quite the second hour, street vendors were out in droves and shop owners had their doors wide open. Just in case Calais changed his mind, Marco wanted to be prepared. A few merchants called out their inventory as he passed by. Most glanced at his horse and ignored him. The smell of smoke from morning cook fires hung in the air. The street dust had settled during the night, but now cartwheels and horse hooves were churning the fine particles of silt. Marco kept an eye out for someone selling flowering plants. The vendors usually grew the plants on their roof tops where they would not be stolen or trampled. He went from street to street until he was about to give up. Several vendors were selling flowers, but not the kind he needed. He turned down the last street and spotted a sign with blossoms painted on it hanging over the door of a shop. The owner had a variety of plants potted in small ceramic vases. Marco slipped down from the saddle when he spotted what he was looking for.

"Those violet flowers are quite lovely," he said to the woman when she glanced at him. "Are those larkspurs? My sweetheart loves those."

The woman smiled, not wanting to offend him, but she could see that he probably couldn't afford her prices. "Yes, they are quite lovely this time of year."

"I need to find one in a small vase so she can easily carry it from window to window."

The woman pursed her lips at the deception. She knew he wanted something small because that was all he could afford. "How about this one? It's the smallest one I have. The flowers are quite fresh. I planted this one only a few weeks ago."

Marco fingered the petals. The seeds of larkspur were poisonous and so were the leaves if they were young. The poison could cause the appearance of death but was not as deadly as belladonna. "This one will do nicely. How much do you want for it?" They haggled over the price until the woman finally made her last offer and Marco accepted. He climbed back in the saddle and she handed the ceramic pot to him. He needed a few more items and set off to find the appropriate shop.

* * *

Many streets over, on the other side of town, Adan, Nikolaus, Aquila, Fabiana, and Serapio were eating breakfast while they discussed how best to locate Marco.

"I'm sure he would have made contact at the Antonia," said Adan. He might have stayed at the guest quarters for at least one night."

"You think that because that's where you would go, Father," said Aquila. "I would find an inn that would let me work off the price of a night's stay. He could be anywhere, if he's here in Jerusalem, at all."

"That makes sense," agreed Serapio. "Aquila and I can investigate the inns while you and Nikolaus go to the Antonia. We can meet back here at the sixth hour and then decide what to do. I feel sure he's here somewhere. Fabiana, if he shows up while we're out, lock him in a room if you have to."

"Are you saying that my fascinating conversation won't do the trick?"

Serapio chuckled. He appreciated her attempt to lighten the downcast mood of the others.

Aquila and Serapio headed for the section of town with inns and shops. Adan and Nikolaus rode to the open gates of the Antonia. As they neared the gates, the two men shared the same touch of unease. The best memories they had of the fortress was when they were exiting the gates, not entering them. The entry guards came to attention at the sight of Adan's apparel, but their jaws dropped in shock when they recognized the man. Nikolaus smiled at their open astonishment. He had not considered that Adan would still be recognized among the soldiers.

"Sir! Are you Centurion Adas Clovius Longinus?" called out the *principales* on duty. "The man who came back from the dead?"

"My *praenomen* is Adan. Tell your commander that I wish to speak with him if it is convenient?"

The soldier took off at a run for the office that was once Tribune Salvitto's. Adan and Nikolaus continued across the quad and reined in their horses at the arena fence. Several of the stable slaves came forward to ask for instructions. One boy stole a look at Adan and turned on his heel to run back into the building. Thinking of the four years he was a slave made Nikolaus nauseous, but he couldn't keep from staring at the limestone building where he used to work.

A young man emerged from the shadows of the open building. It was Calais. He stopped and studied the men before he moved closer. "Centurion Longinus. It has been a long time. It is good to see you again, Sir." He focused on Adan without acknowledging Nikolaus.

Adan tilted his head slightly in concentration, trying to place why he looked familiar. "Calais? Is that you?"

"It is, Centurion. I am the last one here from your Saturday class."

"It is good to see you," said Adan as he glanced at Nikolaus. "I'm sure you remember your teammate, Nikolaus."

Calais didn't even glance at him. "I recognize the horse. One of those golden horses. His name is Inventio if I recall correctly. He shines like real gold in the sunlight. I see you no longer have the dapple-gray Arabian, Centurion. Venustas was a beautiful creature, and this horse is equally majestic. I don't remember you having this stallion, but I do remember seeing him. When you came back from the dead, the man with you was riding this horse. What is the horse's name, if I may ask?"

"You have an incredible memory for horses, Calais. His name is Blackfire. The man who was riding him that day is my father-in-law. He gave the stallion to me when he retired from the army. We still have Venustas. I gave her back to my wife. Venustas thanks me every time my petite wife climbs into the saddle."

Calais grinned. "Yes, Sir, I understand. The muscle of a man outweighs the gentle contours of a woman."

Nikolaus cleared his throat at the inappropriate comment, especially coming from a slave. But Adan shot him a cautionary glance. "Perhaps you can help us, Calais. We are looking for my son. Have you seen him here?"

"Yes, Sir. He was here yesterday when I tended to his horse. The horse is gone now and I have not seen him this morning. Perhaps he has left or simply gone on an errand."

Adan and Nikolaus exchanged glances of relief. At least, they were on the right path.

"Did he introduce himself," asked Nikolaus, "or did you recognize a family resemblance?"

"He introduced himself!" snapped Calais, looking Nikolaus in the eye for the first time. "But I'm not stupid. Any idiot could see who he is. You're asking how I could possibly know his name since men of status never introduce themselves to common slaves?"

"I only wondered if he was using an alias," said Nikolaus patiently.

Adan decided to ignore the unpleasant exchange. "Calais, did you speak with him? Did he tell you anything about his plans?"

"No Sir," responded Calais. His bad humor was instantly gone. "He didn't share any plans with me. In fact, he said he had no idea where he would go next. Mostly, he talked of other things."

"Like what?"

"That he misses his mother. That you have a volatile temper, which is mostly directed at him. Forgive me, Centurion, but you asked and that's what he said." He watched for Adan's reaction. When he saw that it was safe to proceed, he added, "He said that he was just as brave as you and would prove it. But he didn't say how he planned to do that." Looking past the two men, Calais saw Commander Lysias approaching. "May I take your horses for you, Sir? I will make sure they have water and hay."

"That won't be necessary, Calais. But thank you for the offer," said Adan.

Calais smiled. "I remember that, too."

"What is that?"

"You are the only soldier who thanked me for doing my job. I would have done anything for you, Centurion, if you had given me the chance."

Adan blinked at the candor and started to reply, but Commander Claudius Lysias interrupted him with an enthusiastic greeting. Adan and Nikolaus greeted the man with equal eagerness. When Adan glanced around, Calais had turned his back and was walking away. It was inappropriate for a slave to leave the presence of his superiors without permission. Adan glanced at Nikolaus and saw him frowning at the retreating figure.

He caught Adan's eye and arched an eyebrow in disapproval. "That was odd."

Commander Lysias extended a hand to Adan. "Centurion Longinus, this is quite an honor. It's not every day that an immortal presents himself here at the Antonia."

Adan shook his hand but ignored the comment. "Commander Lysias, allow me to introduce my brother, Nikolaus." Lysias shook Nikolaus's offered hand but returned his attention to Adan.

"I suppose you're here to take your son home," Lysias said. "Young men can be rebellious at times. He is safe, however, and I can have him rounded up if you wish."

"I assure you, Commander, I do not want my son rounded up but I appreciate the offer. He is not rebellious, but I'm afraid he feels the need to prove himself. We only want to assure him that he has nothing to prove."

The commander pursed his lips and nodded. "I see. In that case, you can speak with him tonight if you don't find him before then. We were to have dinner together last night, but I had to reschedule. Please, join us this evening if it is convenient. We've got a situation here with a prisoner, a Pharisee from Tarsus of Cilicia. As usual, religious debates among these people turned violent and I'm trying to keep the city under control."

Adan and Nikolaus exchanged glances. "Would this prisoner be named Paul?" asked Adan.

"That is his name. Do you know of him?"

"Commander, would you allow me to speak with him?" said Adan. "He is a good friend. I have known him for many years."

"Of course, Centurion. I would take you to him, but obviously you know the way. I'll have my slave take your horses to a stall."

"That will not be necessary," said Adan. "They can stay here. We may need to leave in a hurry. It is good to meet you, Commander. We will see you this evening."

Adan and Nikolaus headed for Holding. The guards at the entrance to the Prisoner Holding building came to attention. Adan signaled for them to open the door. He and Nikolaus strode down the hall, glancing through the barred openings in the doors to the interrogation rooms. They stopped in front of the room where Paul sat on a bench. Adan opened the door.

Paul was sitting with his hands on his knees and his eyes closed. He was meditating, content to wait for events to take their course. He raised his head when the door opened but was surprised to see good friends. They warmly greeted each other.

"Paul, it grieves me to see you in custody," said Adan. "I wish I could release you."

"If Titus were here with you," said Nikolaus, "we wouldn't be able to pry him out of the room."

"It is most gratifying to see the two of you," said Paul. "I suppose you are here to find Marco. He is a fine young man, Adan. Don't be too hard on him. He has heart; he just needs to learn that one must also have experience." They discussed Paul's situation and how they might be able to help. The discussion turned back to Marco. Paul told them what they had discussed. As they talked, there was a knock on the door. Adan opened it himself to find a young Hebrew boy standing in the doorway.

"Please, Centurion, I must speak urgently with my uncle," he said. Adan ushered him inside and closed the door. Introductions were exchanged.

"Uncle, I have heard of a plot to take your life. Some forty men have taken an oath to assassinate you. I was passing down a corridor in the Hall of Hewn Stones and stopped outside the door when I heard them mention your name. A man said, '*We have bound ourselves under a great oath that we will eat nothing until we have killed Paul. Now you, therefore, together with the council, suggest to the commander that he be brought down to you tomorrow, as though you were going to make further inquiries concerning him; but we are ready to kill him before he comes near.*' I am sure those were his exact words."

"You have done well," said Paul.

Adan opened the door and spoke to the *legionary*. "Bring Centurion Thracius here."

As they waited, Paul's nephew told them the names of some of the men he saw as they left the room. When Thracius arrived, he was quite pleased to see Adan and Nikolaus. Whenever they came to visit Serapio and Fabiana, they made a point to visit with Thracius as well. Paul asked his nephew to repeat the oath he overheard. Thracius left to inform the commander of the plan to assassinate Paul.

Adan and Thracius knew that Lysias could not take the chance of Paul being killed. Since Paul was not sentenced to death, Lysias would be forced to execute the centurion in charge if Paul was killed. Whatever happened to a prisoner, not under the sentence of death, would be done to the highest commanding officer in charge

Thracius returned with Commander Lysias who took Paul's nephew aside and listened to him intently. He cautioned the young man, "*Tell no one that you have revealed these things to me.*" He then had the boy escorted from the Antonia.

Commander Lysias knew that forty men lying in wait between the Antonia and the Hall of Hewn Stones, where the Sanhedrin met every day, would result in injury and possibly death among his own soldiers as well. "Centurion Thracius, you and another centurion will *prepare two hundred legionaries, seventy horsemen, and two hundred spearmen to go to Caesarea at the third hour of the night.* Provide horses for Paul and *bring him safely to Felix the governor.* This group of forty conspirators may grow to twice as many before the day is over. Perhaps they will break their vow at the sight of four hundred and seventy armed soldiers. I'll write a letter to Governor Felix informing him of the situation and that I told Paul's accusers to make their charges before him in Caesarea. That should avert this bloodbath."

Adan looked at Nikolaus with a silent question. He nodded agreement. "Sir, if we may," said Adan, "My brother and I would like to accompany your men, with your permission. We have two escort soldiers traveling with us as well."

"What about your son, Centurion?"

"I'm sure that both of my sons will be joining us tonight."

"As you wish, Centurion. Frankly, I think your presence will give the men confidence. One doesn't go into battle every day with a man who has come back from the dead."

"I was dead for only a few moments. But I know of someone who was dead for three days and returned to life. I can tell you about him if you're interested."

"I'm always eager to hear a good story, Centurion." Lysias ordered the *legionary* outside the door to bring more chairs. Paul and Adan exchanged smiles. Their combined experiences were sure to keep Lysias's attention.

Chapter 9

Blueberries, Pomona, and
a Story from the Past

—————⟡⟡⟡—————

M arco needed to find blueberries. He would smear the juice of the berries on Calais's lips and fingernails and rub flour on the young man's face. The combined sickly pale skin and bluish lips and nails would produce the look of death. The oil from crushed leaves and stems of the larkspur would paralyze voluntary movement, but not the heart or lungs if given in the right amount. To be sure of the dosage, he stopped at a *pharmacopolium* to ask the chief pharmacist for advice. Marco claimed he had to transport an aggressive, full-grown mastiff. The pharmacist asked the weight of the dog and the length of time the animal would need to be subdued and made a few calculations. He was quite informative until Marco refused to buy any potions or herbs that he suggested. He told Marco to stop wasting his time and escorted him to the door. When he saw the young man take the reins of an old pack horse, he made a sour face and turned away.

Marco didn't care. He had the information he needed. He had learned how to gauge the dosage and possible side effects. The poison would make Calais vomit, but that would add to the look of disease. No one would handle the body or linger at the scene any longer than necessary. That's when he would volunteer to transport the "dead" slave to the crematory to honor Calais's previous service to Marco's father. His explanation for involving himself should suffice. Soldiers would be assigned to assist him, no doubt, but they would not want to get close enough to detect any signs of life. Marco was certain he had thought of everything.

Marco had the larkspur and flour, but the blueberries were more challenging. After passing carts offering pomegranates and figs, Marco found a woman sitting in front of her small house selling peaches, apricots, and a selection of berries, including blueberries. She was in her mid-forties, with soft brown eyes and chestnut-colored hair, which was unusual for Judeans. Marco dismounted and forgot to feign disinterest in her wares by immediately asking what she wanted for the blueberries. The woman sensed an easy sale. She looked more intently at Marco and frowned. She had seen someone else with eyes like his.

"It is unusual to see a young Roman like yourself shopping for food. Has your wife sent you on this task?" She watched his expression closely.

"No, I'm not married," Marco replied. "I don't live here. Just visiting."

"That surprises me," said the woman. "Such a strapping, handsome young man like you. Who are you? The son of the Antonia commander, or one of his brave centurions?"

Marco smiled at the compliment and took it at face value. The presence of Arrow should have made him suspicious of her flattery.

"I am the son of a centurion," he said proudly. "You might have heard of him. They call him the Wolf Commander. My name is Marcus Clovius Longinus, and he is Adan Clovius Longinus. Everyone calls me Marco since my grandfather, *Primus Pilus* Centurion Marcus Cornelius, has the same *praenomen*."

The woman smiled at Marco's childish attempt to impress her. "Ah, the Wolf Commander. Yes, I saw him once. He's the one who came back from the dead." She patted the bench she sat on. "Please, sit with me. My name is Pomona. You can tell me about your famous father and maybe I can tell you a story. Business is slow for now. Come and sit with me and I'll let you have the berries for free."

Marco smiled at his good fortune. He had spent nearly all his remaining money on the larkspur so the offer was surely a good omen in his quest to free Calais. He told her about how his father protected Simon Peter and how Valentius had plotted to get the sixteen soldiers killed, but was himself executed for treason. The woman listened intently.

"Now it's you turn," Marco said. "Tell me a story and then I'll be on my way."

"As you wish." She waved her hand in a gesture of graciousness. "There once was a woman, named Eliana who worked for me. She cooked and kept the place clean. She wasn't much good for anything else, but she did have some fascinating stories to tell and I do love a good story. Once there was an uprising in Samaria, and Rome sent the army to stop it. There was a dashing, young cohort centurion who was very brave in battle and a fine, honorable man. He was ordered to subdue a large village. He had a full cohort of 600 well-trained men so he was confident. They successfully put down the rebellion, or so they thought, but were ambushed before they could enjoy their victory. Hundreds of men from his cohort died and the centurion was gravely wounded." Pomona averted her eyes. She found his penetrating gaze disturbing.

She licked her lips and continued. "His second-in-command knew of a woman among the prisoners who was an accomplished healer. That woman was Eliana. The Roman officer told her that if she saved the life of his commander, she would not be sold as a slave, but if he died, she would die. Eliana agreed to treat the centurion. At first, she tended him night and day only to save herself. But he was weakened and vulnerable. She took pity on him and as he healed, they fell in love. He could not marry her, for he was already married, but he loved her. They had a child, a girl who stole his heart away just as her mother had done. The centurion swore to Eliana that he would take care of her and their daughter for the rest of their lives. He went back to his wife, but he sent money every month to Eliana in the capital city of Samaria. His wife died and he was transferred to Jerusalem. He found Eliana and moved her to Jerusalem. Since she was a Samaritan, he wed her secretly so as not to bring judgment upon her. That centurion was the very man you told me committed treason against Rome, Felix Pomponius Valentius."

Pomona watched for Marco's reaction. She was not disappointed. He seemed shocked to learn that Felix Valentius was more than just a traitor.

Pomona continued. "Eliana never spoke a word against him. He was kind to her when he could have turned his back on her. Sadly, their daughter died at a young age, but Eliana lived out a long life. In his later years, opium took control of him. Eliana blamed herself for his addiction because even after he was healed, she was not strong enough to withhold the opium he craved. Eliana died a few years before the centurion was executed in Rome for the charge of treason you have so proudly retold to me. Eliana told me she was his best kept secret. Even his slave, Demitre, didn't know about her. He told her once, 'Never let Demitre know about us. He might use our love against us. It is in his nature and he won't be able to stop himself.' Isn't that an odd thing to say about one's own slave?"

Marco frowned and nodded. "Yes, but we know now that Demitre was not his real name. He was the famous murderer, Alexander Nisos."

The woman shrugged. "What people think they know about someone is sometimes incomplete. Take you, for example, do you think Valentius was as good a man as Eliana thought? And if he was, could other people have lied about him. Do you think that is possible?"

Marco was losing interest. He needed to talk with Calais, and see Serapio and Fabiana, but this woman was droning on and on about a man Marco knew was evil to the core. "I doubt it. Valentius was a greedy liar, who cheated his way up the ladder to high treason. The emperor had him executed, didn't he? That's all we need to remember about him." Marco stood up to leave. Perhaps if he had seen the look on Pomona's face, he might have realized that there was more to her story, but he missed the flash of hatred in her eyes. "Thank you for the blueberries. I will put them to good use." He climbed in the saddle, nodded at her, and turned Arrow down the lane in the direction of Commerce Road and Sheep Gate Street, the address of Serapio's shop.

The woman watched as he rode away. She spoke aloud to his retreating figure. "You left before I could tell you the best part. I am the child of a centurion as well, because the daughter of Felix and Eliana did not die. Her name is Pomona—my name. And you, Marcus Clovius Longinus, will regret that you ever saw my face."

Pomona rose from the bench and walked into her shop. She slammed the door with rage. The arrogant smirk on Marco's face swam before her. In the shelter of her home, she allowed the demons of wrath to erupt. She grabbed the first object at hand and threw it against the wall. The ceramic vase shattered into pieces.

Marco nudged Arrow into a trot and smiled to himself at the anticipation of seeing Serapio and Fabiana. Most likely, they would lecture him for disappearing from home, but in the end, they would hug him with affection. However, he needed to stop at the Antonia first and find Calais.

When he passed through the fortress gates and headed for the arena, he saw Black-fire and Inventio in the arena, tethered to the fence railing. He looked around in panic, but when he didn't see Adan or Nikolaus, he hurried into the arena and led Arrow into the barn area. At the end of a row, he found Calais cleaning out a stall.

"Calais, I need to talk with you, but I have to hurry," exclaimed Marco. "My father and uncle are here. Did you see them?"

Calais dumped soiled hay into a hand cart and set the shovel down. "I talked with them. Your father asked if I knew what you were planning to do and I said that you had not shared that information with me. He seemed very calm to me, considering his son is missing. Not worried or anything." Calais watched for Marco's reaction. He was rewarded with a flash of disappointment in Marco's eyes.

"Are you still afraid to leave this place behind forever? I have everything you need to fake your death. There will be no slave hunters looking for you, professional or otherwise." Marco took the potted flower out of his knapsack. "Do you have a bowl? You'll need to crush the leaves and stems." Marco seemed to have forgotten Calais had rejected his plan.

Calais opened a knapsack that he was allowed to keep. He pulled out a small bowl used to get water from the horse troughs. "Here, that's all I have. I apologize for losing faith in your plan. I've decided to go with you."

Marco smiled in relief as he took a smooth rock from his knapsack. He plucked the leaves and a few stems from the larkspur and put them in the bowl. Using the rock, he crushed the vegetation until a small amount of liquid pooled in the bowl. He took a glass vial with a cork stopper from his knapsack and poured the poison into the vial. Marco handed the vial to Calais.

"What if I get too much poison? Could I really die?"

Marco shook his head emphatically. "No! I asked the chief chemist, who specializes in plant and seed medications. I'm sure the dosage is right. Do not take the poison until I tell you. We must time things perfectly. Drink only half of it to start with. If you don't feel any effects in half an hour, take the rest of it. But remember; do *not* start with the full amount. Give your body a chance to react to the first dose or it could be fatal. Do you understand?" Calais nodded.

Marco explained the purpose of the flour and blueberries. "You'll be able to hear, but you'll be paralyzed. You'll be conscious, at least sometimes. Remember, timing is everything. I have to go see Serapio now but I'll come back in a few hours. Be ready. You won't be able to take anything with you, obviously, and I'll find you a horse. You'll only be in the crematory for a short time. You'll see, Calais, you can trust me. I'll be back soon. When you see me, you'll know it is the right time. We'll need to act quickly before my father interferes."

"Wait. There is one thing I need you to do." Calais reached into his knapsack. "Here, could you hold this for me. My father carved it for me on my sixth birthday. It is all I have left."

"What is it?" Marco put out his hand. Calais set a small wooden owl in his palm.

"It is the owl of wisdom, Athena's pet. I've managed to keep it for twenty years and I don't want to leave it behind."

"Athena, the goddess of wisdom." Marco took the round-eyed creature, its wings folded tightly against the body. "It's beautiful and so detailed. Your father was very talented."

Calais smiled. "Yes, and kind and patient. Your father reminds me of him."

Marco bit his lip in shame and avoided Calais's gaze. "I'm sorry you lost your father. I don't know what I'd do if my father was gone." He put the owl in his knapsack. "I'll take very good care of—does it have a name?"

"She does. I named her Sofi. The Greek word for wise, as in wise woman."

"I promise to protect Sofi until I can give her back," declared Marco.

They discussed a few more details and Calais hid the supplies in the stall he was cleaning. Marco led Arrow out of the stables and into the arena. After a quick look around, he climbed in the saddle, hurried out of the Antonia, and headed for Serapio's. He was only a few houses away when Aquila came around the side of the shop leading Nighthawk. Marco reined Arrow to a stop and watched from behind a courtyard wall. Serapio and Fabiana came out of the house to speak with Aquila. Serapio laced his fingers into a stirrup and helped Aquila into the saddle. Aquila smiled to himself; Serapio must not know his father's rule about climbing in the saddle without assistance. Aquila headed down the street in the direction of the Antonia.

Marco waited until Aquila was well past and urged Arrow into the throng of pedestrians, vendors and street beggars. He slid from the saddle and approached Serapio's door.

"Did you forget something, Aquila?" called out Serapio.

Marco blinked at the big man until a broad grin brightened his face. "No, Sir! I never forget anything."

Serapio threw his hands out and strode toward the doorway. "Marco, you sneaky little imp! You have the whole family scared to death! How long have you been in Jerusalem? Have you been to the Antonia? You better have just now stepped foot in this town because if you didn't come here first, I shall chew you out until sundown." With that, Serapio gave him his most enthusiastic bear hug until Fabiana rescued him with a gentle hug of her own.

Marco laughed at the expressions on their faces. "It is good to see the two of you. I just saw Aquila leave here. I saw Blackfire and Inventio at the Antonia."

Fabiana ushered them over to chairs while she found goblets for wine. Serapio looked Marco over. "At least, you don't look the worse for wear. Please tell us you have come to your senses and are going back home."

Marco made a face. "I was going to, but then I think I was given a message from God. Well, maybe two messages. If I tell you my plan you both have to promise to keep it secret."

"I will make no such promise," declared Serapio. "Your father needs to know what is going on inside that head of yours."

Marco sighed loudly in frustration. "Fine. I'll tell you anyway. I believe that I am supposed to go to Herculaneum to rescue Uncle Niko's sister, Dionysia."

Serapio and Fabiana gaped at him in stunned silence.

"You don't have to look so shocked," declared Marco resentfully. "I can do this!"

"You're going to steal a man's slave?" asked Serapio. "God tells us not to steal. Don't you think that's a problem?"

"I don't plan on stealing her, just rescuing her. Look at this." Marco pulled the leather cord from around his neck. "The vendor told me to 'follow the purple sapphire' like this one." He placed the hexagonal crystal in Fabiana's outstretched hand. "Dionysia has a purple sapphire. I think this was God's way of telling me that I am to bring her back to Caesarea." Fabiana handed the sapphire to Serapio who gave it back to Marco with barely a glance.

"But before I can save Dionysia, I need to help a slave at the Antonia to die. Well, not literally die, just look dead so he can go with me without being hunted down. Will you help me?"

Serapio stared at him in dismay. "Have you lost your mind, Marco?"

Marco glared at him. "I thought you would help considering you were once a slave."

Serapio rubbed his forehead. "Did this man talk you into this?"

"No. Actually, he told me to forget about it."

"Ah, so he's a smart slave. How do you think you'll accomplish this deception without his cooperation? What would stop him from accusing you of trying to steal him to save his own skin if your attempt fails? You do remember the penalty for stealing someone's property, don't you? It might not be just a fine and a stern lecture. Roman citizens can be executed for theft, depending on the value of the stolen property or the harshness of the judge. You won't be crucified, but you could get beheaded. You'll be just as dead, just quicker."

Marco frowned. "I'm willing to take that chance since Calais is. He changed his mind. I already gave him everything he needs to fake his death. It worked for my father. Why wouldn't it work for Calais? Once I get him out of the city, he will be safe."

"It's not that simple," said Fabiana. "He would still have to work to have money for food and lodging. Work is not easy to find and people will not take strangers in as apprentices. You might get him away from his master, only to have him starve to death in the street."

"But he won't be alone," countered Marco. "He'll be with me. He was a member of my father's stable team. In fact, he's the last one left at the Antonia. He said that he would have done anything for father if he had been given the chance. Father didn't give me a chance either. Calais and I have much in common. We both want to prove our worth."

"Marco, your father loves you more than he loves his own life," said Serapio. "He would literally die in your place if it came to that. You have nothing to prove to him. He already loves you just the way you are. I also think you're projecting your sentiment on to Calais. I seriously doubt he cares about pleasing your father more than staying alive."

Marco's voice was edged with resentment. "If Father loves me so much why does he treat me like a failure? He even called me a fool in front of Aquila. And I trust Calais. Father did. That's why he put Calais on his team."

Serapio's expression soured. "Do you think Adan really sees you as a fool or was it fear for your safety? He told me about the runaway slave who murdered his master and another slave. He admits that his words were harsh. But all of us have said things we wish we could take back, like that ugly thing you said to him about Yeshua's death? It was cruel and unmerited. You used your father's grief against him after he trusted you with his greatest shame."

Marco hung his head. "I know. It just came out before I could stop myself."

"Like when your father called you a fool. It just came out? How is that any different from what you did? You find fault with Adan, but you make an excuse for yourself."

Marco jumped to his feet and walked to the open door. He stood watching the people passing by for a few moments. "I don't know what to do about it."

"Yes, you do," said Serapio. "Talk to him. If neither one of you talks this out, it will remain between you like a chasm. Is that what you want?"

"Of course not," muttered Marco as he faced Serapio.

"Prove it," said Serapio. The two glared at each other, until Marco's shoulders sagged and he sat down again. Fabiana touched his arm.

"You need to think this through," she said gently. "God really may want you to go to Dionysia, but not like this. Not without your family's help."

"Ana is right, Marco. You need to put away your pride and be honest with yourself. Nothing we ever do is for only one reason. I think you have other motives for running off like this, more than just doing something brave. You might not even realize it." Serapio touched the scar on his face. "Did you know that I used to be half blind?"

"I didn't until I asked Calais why they call you the one-eyed *gladiator*."

"For years, every time Yeshua came to Jerusalem, I had the opportunity to get my full sight back. I know he would have healed me because I saw him heal others countless times. Still, I told myself, and your father, that I kept my blindness as a reminder to never glorify myself at the cost of someone's life. Theo Salvitto's brother committed suicide on my sword in the arena and I celebrated over his dead body. It was Theo's niece, Drusia, who slashed me with her father's sword. Then Theo retired from the army and moved back to Rome."

Serapio ran his finger down the scar. "With Theo gone, I wasn't so keen on being half blind, anymore. Truth is, I resented Drusia for blinding me. I resented Theo for not taking his brother out of the arena, and I resented his brother most of all. I refused to take Drusia's life, which I had the right to do. I wanted Theo to *never* forget that I spared Drusia's life. He couldn't look at me without feeling guilty. That was exactly what I wanted him to feel. I used his guilt to free Nikolaus, so it was for a good cause. However, I used it against him in subtle ways that benefitted my business. Salvitto talked up my furniture to every aristocrat he knew. That is one reason I have been so successful. When he left, there was no benefit to my blindness."

Serapio sighed and shook his head. "I finally admitted the truth to myself and God. Then I confessed it to Peter. He said he had asked Yeshua why he hadn't healed me. Yeshua said that my true blindness was in my heart. He said that my heart would have to heal first before my eye could be healed. When he told me that, I let go of the bitterness. We prayed together. Peter laid his hand over my eye. I felt nothing, but when he removed his hand, I could see."

Marco hung his head in thought. Fabiana said, "Could it be that you have run from your father, not to prove yourself, but to hurt him for hurting you? What you both said was wrong. But scaring your family half to death is also wrong."

"Maybe I did want to hurt him." Marco looked at them questioningly, "But first, will you help me free Calais? He said father was the only one who ever showed him kindness, but then he left Calais at the Antonia and didn't give him another thought. We need to help Calais."

"Do you have any kind of plan?" asked Serapio, hoping that he didn't.

"I do!" Marco grinned at them. "I've already given Calais everything he needs to play dead. He's just waiting for me to tell him it's time."

Serapio groaned. "Wonderful. Now we'll all get arrested."

Chapter 10

Deception, Poison, and a Hostage

Calais fingered the vial of poison and wished that he had some way to test its effects. He thought about the oldest pack horses, but none of them were under his care. If a horse died under suspicious circumstances, the slave in charge would be seriously punished, if not executed. However, the main reason Calais decided against a "test" was that it would use up the amount of poison Marco had given him. He had said to start with half of the poison, but under no circumstances drink the whole amount at once. Unfortunately, there was no anecdote for the poison. Calais had to ingest a precise amount for success. He thought about the confident way Marco declared that nothing could go wrong because God was on their side. Marco's faith did not reassure Calais. After all, Marco was not risking his life against the word of some medicine chemist hoping to make a sale.

The slave dropped the vial down the front of his tunic and felt for the slight bulge just above his belt. He finished with the last of the centurions' horses and walked out along the row of stalls until he reached the opening to the arena. He was surprised to see another magnificent, coal-black horse like the one Centurion Longinus rode. He stopped dead in his tracks. Marco was standing next to the stately black horse, looking around as if he were trying to locate someone. Calais glanced around the arena but didn't see Arrow. Marco must have had another slave put the horse in a stall. Calais started toward the centurion's son, curious why he had returned so quickly from visiting with Serapio.

Calais hesitated, fearful of what he was about to do. He approached his co-conspirator and spoke in a low voice. "Is it time?"

The centurion's son turned around and eyed him guardedly. "Are you talking to me?"

Calais paled with fear. "You told me to wait for you. Have you changed your mind?" His mouth went dry at the indifference in the young man's eyes.

"Changed my mind about what?" He looked Calais up and down with a frown. He knew the slave must think he was Marco. He had seen that confused look a thousand times.

Calais felt as if someone had punched him in the stomach. "You talked me into escaping from this place. You begged me to trust you."

"I've never begged for anything in my life." Aquila studied Calais with narrowed eyes. "I don't even know who you are."

Aquila knew what the consequences would be for his brother if he were caught abetting a runaway slave, but impersonating Marco would avert the potential fiasco. Aquila would do what he always did—clean up his brother's mistakes.

Calais felt the color drain from his face. "Why are you betraying me?" He reached inside the neck of his tunic and pulled out the vial. "You gave me this!" He thrust the vial toward Aquila who coldly glanced at it.

Aquila smirked. "No, I didn't." He gave Calais one last look of disdain and turned away. He headed for the building across from the arena. He didn't know what function it served but there were two soldiers guarding the door. He could feel the slave's eyes on him. As he walked, the impact of the panic on the slave's face made him hesitate and he nearly stopped. Maybe he should not let the young man think that Marco had betrayed him. Then he remembered the pain in his mother's eyes when she first discovered Marco's letter. Her anxiety tore at his heart. Leaving in the dead of night had been the worst thing Marco had ever done, and Aquila wanted him to pay the consequences. He quickened his pace and approached the guards. He made a show of speaking with the guards and then deliberately pointed in the direction of the arena. Calais was still standing near the fence, watching him. The slave turned on his heel and fled into the stables.

Aquila felt a surge of regret but pushed the feeling aside. "I am Aquila Clovius Longinus. Have you seen my father, Centurion Adan Clovius Longinus? That's his horse over there, at the arena." The guards looked where he pointed and nodded. They confirmed that Adan was with a prisoner from Tarsus. One of them escorted him to the interrogation room.

* * *

A few streets over, at Serapio's *Suppelex*, Marco finished explaining his plan for faking Calais's death. Serapio and Fabiana made a few suggestions since they could not talk him out of it. However, they both thought that the slave would probably not take the poison anyway. The situation would take care of itself, especially since Adan, Nikolaus, and Aquila were at the Antonia. Adan would set Marco straight and they would be on their way home by tomorrow.

Marco said his farewell and assured them that they would be meeting Calais soon. He headed for the Antonia and rode Arrow in through the open gates. When he saw his family's horses at the arena fence, he rode Arrow quickly into the building and searched the rows of stalls for Calais. He asked other slaves if they had seen him, but they only shook their heads. Marco glanced down the last row and was about to leave until he looked more closely. The gate of the last stall was open. He dropped from the saddle and led Arrow to the stall.

Calais was lying on his side in the straw. His face was deathly pale. His eyes were slightly opened in narrow slits. The empty vial was near his outstretched hand. There was vomit in the hay and on his lips.

"No!" cried Marco as he dropped to his knees. He shook Calais by the shoulder, but there was no response. "Why didn't you wait?" He snatched up the vial. It was empty. "Why did you take all of it?" Marco leaped to his feet and ran down the row of stalls out to the arena. His father, Uncle Niko, and Aquila were just leaving the incarceration building with Commander Lysias.

Marco ran to them, not caring that their search for him had abruptly ended. "Come quick! Hurry! It's Calais. I think he's killed himself!" Without waiting to see if they followed, Marco ran back across the quad for the arena.

Relief at finding Marco was overshadowed by his fearful pronouncement. Adan and Nikolaus only hesitated long enough to exchange worried glances and then ran to follow Marco. Aquila didn't move. Commander Lysias nearly bumped into him in his haste to follow Adan and Nikolaus. Marco hurriedly explained to his family how he met Calais when they caught up with him. They reached the end of the last row of stalls and found the slave as Marco had left him.

Adan went down on a knee and pressed his finger to the young man's neck. "He's dead."

"What killed him?" grumbled Commander Lysias.

Adan gently checked Calais for injuries. There were no wounds. He saw the open vial in the hay but didn't touch it. "Judging by the pallor of his skin and this vial, I'd say he took poison. This is such a shame. Calais was always a good and loyal aide." Adan stood up and glanced around. "Where is Aquila?"

Nikolaus looked around. "He came out of Holding with us."

Aquila stepped into view and slowly walked through the stall gate. He looked in and saw Calais on the ground. "Is he dead?"

"I'm afraid so," said Adan.

"I can't believe he would do this to me," growled Lysias. "I was good to him, the ungrateful lout. I let him eat every day and gave him a new tunic once a year. I let him get as much water as he wanted while he worked. I let him have a loaf of wheat bread whenever a new centurion signed up for his services. And now I'll have to deal with his carcass."

Adan turned to Lysias. "Didn't you let him pay the monthly fee for a benevolent service? They provide for cremation and an urn."

Lysias sneered. "And waste a whole *dupondius* once a month? I don't care what happens to his ashes. I'll have to waste manpower to get him hauled off to the crematory, as it is. I'll not waste one copper coin on an urn or a storage niche. Funeral insurance shouldn't even be offered to slaves. It's a waste of space to fill up burial niches with slaves' urns. Since he took his own life, the government better reimburse me for the cremation cost. That's what we pay taxes for, isn't it?" It was clear that the story of Yeshua that Adan and Paul told Lysias meant nothing to him.

"Don't bother wasting your precious manpower," Adan snapped. "I will take care of his cremation myself."

"As you wish, Centurion," said Lysias, "but do it quickly. We leave tonight to escort Paul to Caesarea. I won't wait for you." He left the stall and strode away. His heavy tread echoed his irritation at losing his slave.

Adan turned to the others. "Niko, why don't you and Aquila go get . . . Aquila?"

Aquila was staring at Calais in horror. He looked up and met Marco's eyes. Something unspoken passed between the two of them. Marco's eyes widened with shock.

"*You* did this—didn't you? You pretended to be me," Marco cried.

"Aquila, what is he talking about?" demanded Adan.

"I was going to help Calais gain his freedom," exclaimed Marco. "We were going to fake his death like what happened to you, Father, in Herod's theater. I gave Calais the poison of larkspur, but he was supposed to only start with half of it. I gave him flour to make his face pale and blueberries to make his lips blue so they would think he was dead. I was going to volunteer to take the body to the crematory and then take him to Serapio's when it was safe. Serapio and Fabiana were going to help. Calais wasn't supposed to really die." Marco looked at Aquila. "But he saw you, and thought it was me? What did you say to him? Tell me!"

"I'm sorry," groaned Aquila. "I thought I was saving you from getting in trouble. I thought you were going to help him escape, you know, the usual way, by running. I knew if the soldiers or the slave hunters caught him, you could be executed. He belonged to the commander of the Antonia, no less!"

Marco turned and ran out of the stall. He grabbed Arrow's reins and jumped into the saddle.

"Marco. *Marco!* Get back here!" shouted Adan.

"Let him go," said Nikolaus. "Nothing you say will help, not now."

Adan spun around to face Aquila. "If harm comes to your brother because of this, I will hold you responsible." Adan looked at Nikolaus, silently asking him if he would take care of Calais. Nikolaus nodded. Adan hurried down the row of stalls to the arena. Grabbing the reins of Blackfire, he vaulted into the saddle. He didn't see Arrow anywhere, but the soldiers on gate duty told him that a young man had galloped out of the fortress on an old brown horse.

Adan turned Blackfire down the street toward Serapio's house, but Marco was headed in the opposite direction. He wandered up and down streets, trying to come to terms with Calais's death. How could his plan have gone so wrong? How could Aquila have been so cruel as to make the young man think that he was betraying him? He swore that he would never forgive his brother for deceiving Calais. Aquila had to have realized that Calais thought the escape plan would be reported to Lysias. Calais would either been flogged within an inch of death or sold to the mines. Terrified of both alternatives, Calais chose death by his own hand.

After wandering aimlessly, Marco found himself on the street where he had bought the blueberries. The woman was not in sight, but he recognized the front of the house and the bench she had sat on. Marcos found himself sliding out of the saddle and knocking on the front door.

The door opened. "What do you want?" the same woman demanded. "I'm fresh out of berries and stories. Go away." She started to close the door.

"Please, I need to tell you why I wanted the berries," said Marco.

Pomona saw his misery. She had seen the same haunted look in her father's eyes. She hesitated, but backed away and let him in. She waved a hand toward a chair. Marco sat down and leaned his forehead on his hand. She pulled a stool over and sat down.

"I just killed someone," said Marco.

The woman gasped and threw her hand to her chest. "And you bring this trouble to my home? Do you know what they'll do to me if they find you here?"

"No. It's not like that. I didn't literally kill him. He killed himself, but it was my fault." Marco explained the plan. As he talked, a plan of her own took shape. She listened as she got up to pour him a goblet of wine. He didn't see her add a pinch of a powdery substance. Marco took the wine without question and emptied the goblet. He was thirsty. He talked on. She asked questions, many questions, even repeated a few of the same questions. When a lethargic feeling came over him, he frowned up at her as she stood up. "Why am I so tired? I must be more exhausted than I thought."

"Come and lie down. Rest. You'll feel better soon." She helped him to a straw mattress in the corner of the room. "You should know; I lied to you earlier today. The daughter of Eliana and Felix Valentius is not dead. Her name is Pomona and she's standing right in front of you."

Marco swallowed hard and tried to rise on his elbows, but the room swam around him. "Wh—what did you give me? Is it poison?"

"No, I didn't poison you. But you are my hostage until your father comes for you. You better hope that he does." She went outside and found a boy who lived in the house next door. "Carry a message for me and I will pay you. Find a Roman named Centurion Longinus. He might be at the Antonia, but if not, someone there will know where he is. Tell him, and I want you to say this exactly, 'I have your son. Come alone and you can have him back.' Repeat it back to me." The boy dutifully repeated the message. "Good. If you bring the man here quickly, I'll pay you even more."

The boy took off at a run. Pomona went back into her house. Marco was asleep with one foot on the floor and an arm dropped across his chest. She lifted his foot and pushed his leg back on the bed. She poured herself a goblet of wine and waited.

It was well over an hour before a knock sounded at her door. She opened it to find the neighbor boy standing with his hand out and Adan behind him. She paid the boy a few copper *dupondii* and invited Adan inside.

Adan took one look at Marco. "What have you done to him?"

"Put him to sleep, Centurion," she answered. "He'll wake up in about an hour."

"Why is he here?"

"He wanted blueberries. I gave them to him because he listened to my story."

"What do you want? A reward? I suppose he told you how he ran away?" Adan checked Marco's eyes and laid a hand over his heart. The beat was steady.

"Yes, I do want a reward, but not in gold or silver. I want you to listen like he did."

"Who are you?" Adan demanded.

"My name is Pomona. My father was Felix Valentius." She watched as conflicting emotions crossed his face. She had heard the rumors and wondered if he really could be a werewolf. She suppressed a shiver and continued, "I lied to your son. I told him Eliana and Felix were married after his wife, Julia, died. My mother and father never married, but he did love her and she loved him. If he had married her, there would have been an official document and he feared for her safety. Father had many enemies."

"I didn't know Valentius had any other children besides Aurelius. You want me to listen? You have all my attention," said Adan. He sat in the chair Pomona offered him.

She stared at the floor for a moment before she began to speak. "You have heard of the Samaritan rebellion? Centurion Tacitus was given the lead command. You might also know that my father outranked Tacitus. He was an underling compared to my father. There were only two cohort centurions higher in rank than Father in the whole legion. He was on his way to becoming a *primus pilus* centurion, but the emperor wanted to grant a favor to Tacitus for a past debt so my father and his cohort of six hundred men were put under Tacitus's command. Injury was, literally, added to insult. The wounds Father sustained in that final battle nearly killed him. That's when my mother, Eliana, agreed to care for him. At first, she only did what had to be done to survive. But Father grew to trust her gentle touch and soothing voice. He fell in love with her. As time went on and Father healed, she fell in love with him. Then it came time for his court martial for disobeying orders, or so they claimed. In the end, he was only reduced in pay and rank, from the 3rd cohort, down to the 10th. However, one judge voted for his execution by *fustuarium*, death by stoning. That judge was your grandfather, Livius Clovius Longinus. He told my father that being reduced in pay and rank was an insult to the dead soldiers. He said that even *fustuarium* was too lenient. Longinus said he would have charged him with treason so the surviving soldiers could have crucified him.

"I know my grandfather made harsh comments to Valentius."

"Yes, he said other cruel things, but I don't remember what they were."

Adan looked at her sharply. "That surprises me. Even I remember the exact words Aurelius repeated to me. 'You're a pathetic excuse for a centurion and a disgusting excuse for a man.' Your father said the exact same words to me once."

"Father told me that the judges voted against Longinus's recommendation. He was angry for being overruled so he berated my father to his face. Father laughed it off, saying it was only the ranting of a bitter old man who was put in his place."

Adan frowned. "How can that be? Aurelius told me that his father was obsessed with my grandfather's condemnation. He said Valentius, 'ate and drank those words and wore them like a second skin.' Those were his exact words."

"How could Aurelius have told you this? He drowned when the *Scarlet Jade* sank in a storm, before you came here from Caesarea. That's what Father told me."

Adan frowned at the unintentional mistake. As far as he knew, Aurelius had not shared his true identity with anyone else after taking the name of a drowning victim as his own. Pomona didn't seem to notice that Adan didn't answer her question as she continued with her story.

"Father was devastated when Aurelius died. I never met him, of course, but his death took Father over the edge. He was already suffering from his opium addiction before Aurelius drowned. His addiction made him irrational and paranoid. My mother said it was her fault because she couldn't bear to see him in pain. She never denied him the opium even after he had healed. Father was a good man before Aurelius's death took his heart and the opium took his mind."

Pomona saw that Adan was intently listening and she continued. "Father knew life would be very difficult for me so he made provisions. When we moved here, he bought an educated, Greek slave woman, named Calypso, to be my teacher and to help Mother. She taught me to read both Greek and Latin. Before she was a slave, she came here with her husband and they were happy. They had a family until her husband was killed in an accident. Her adult children scattered after that. She eventually had to accept slavery or starve. I loved listening to Calypso's stories of her homeland, Greece, and Persia, where she lived for a few years as a child. Her father worked for a small group of astrologers there."

"Do you mean the *Magi*?" asked Adan. "That must have been fascinating for a child. The *Magi* are truly a mystical sect. Calypso's stories must have been entertaining."

"They were. I miss Calypso as much as I miss Mother. Sometimes, she taught a lesson by telling me a story. One time she told me about the ancient Greek historian, Herodotus, who wrote *The Histories* five hundred years ago. Herodotus reported that fox-sized, furry ants in Persia would dig up gold nuggets the size of walnuts when they dug their underground tunnels. Herodotus said that the people would wait until the sun was high and hot in the sky for the ants to go underground. Then they would collect the gold. Calypso asked me if I believed Herodotus's report. I said, 'Does everyone else believe it?' Calypso said, 'Yes, they do.'"

"I've heard this story, too," said Adan. "My mother swore it was true."

Pomona smiled. "I told Calypso that since everyone believed Herodotus, it must be true. She laughed and said, 'Never let the beliefs of others be the only reason you believe. Search for the truth and form your own conclusions.' Father heard her story too, and he asked me if I had ever seen fox-sized, furry ants. When I said I had not, he said, 'Could the creatures have actually been groundhogs or moles?' He said, 'Perhaps Herodotus, not understanding the Persian language, mistranslated what others told him. And that it was not gold nuggets, but gold dust.' I said that maybe the whole report is false. But Father said that in every report, there is usually a nugget of truth. He said nugget and smiled when I laughed at that. I'll never forget our philosophical discussions. I greatly miss those times. Father didn't talk about these things with Mother, but he did with me, until the opium stole him away." She smiled but there was sorrow in her eyes.

Adan frowned to think that the man he had hated could have been such a good father to his illegitimate daughter. He would have doubted the story if he had heard it from anyone else.

"Where is Calypso now?" asked Adan.

"When Mother was dying, she decreed Calypso's freedom and I upheld her final wishes, but I miss Calypso as much as I miss her." Pomona shrugged with resigned acceptance. "Calypso left and never looked back. I loved her, but her love for home was stronger than her love for me." She folded her hands in her lap and continued. "After Father's wife died, he said that we were his only family, just me and my mother. He said Aurelius treated him like a stranger he had accidently bumped into in a crowd, polite but guarded. Father always hoped for a reconciliation, even after Aurelius changed his *nomen* to Julius, but it never happened. So, Father moved us to every city he was stationed in. We had to be very careful, especially because of Demitre. Father said that Demitre must never know about us. He was afraid of him. I asked him why he didn't sell Demitre. He said Demitre had once protected him and Julia, nearly at the cost of his own life. I asked Father, 'Then why would he harm you now?' Father said, 'He can't help it. It's in his nature.' We never spoke of Demitre again, but after that I was afraid of him, too."

"You don't know the whole story, Pomona," said Adan.

"Then tell me, Centurion. What is the whole story?"

Adan hesitated. As far as he knew, Aurelius had trusted only him with his secret. However, Pomona was Aurelius's last living relative.

"Demitre was the murderer, Alexander Nisos, but he was also Julia's half-brother. Demitre was your father's brother-in-law. But more importantly, Aurelius didn't drown in the storm. We were both young men when I met your brother, so it was many years ago. He assumed the identity of a passenger who had drowned. He wanted a clean slate—a new life."

Pomona silently considered the revelation. "You could tell me anything and I would have no way of knowing if it were true."

"There is proof, if it hasn't been destroyed. Aurelius told me he sent a letter to Tribune Salvitto with another letter inside addressed to Demitre. My friend Serapio confirmed this when Salvitto told him about it. It was to be delivered to Demitre if he outlived Valentius. Aurelius had confessed assuming the dead man's identity and asked that Demitre send for him so they could be reunited. They were uncle and nephew, after all. Family. According to Serapio, Tribune Salvitto couldn't remember the name of the centurion who sent the letter. Aurelius had legally changed his name, so it wouldn't have been familiar to Salvitto."

"My brother is still alive. I wonder if he is married and has children. Perhaps I have nieces and nephews. I would have a family again if Aurelius accepted me."

"I wish I knew the name he assumed. You might be able to find him, if he's still alive."

Pomona gave him a sad smile. "What is a name, but a string of letters? If we are meant to find each other, it will happen. Accepting me as family is another matter."

"You might be surprised, Pomona. Aurelius went to your father's trial in Rome. The evidence was daunting, but he refused to forsake him. He bribed the jailor so he could speak with Valentius one last time. Aurelius told me that the greatest shock of his life was to see the joy on his father's face when he saw him. He said there was no anger, no accusations, or even bitterness, only happiness to see that his son was alive. Aurelius said that one moment changed everything he had ever felt about his father. Valentius was executed, but Aurelius knows his father loved him."

"Again, what does that mean for me?" Pomona asked.

"You are a blood relative. Only love seals a stronger bond than blood. If Aurelius held to his father, despite all that had happened, would he turn away from you so quickly?"

"Perhaps. Perhaps not. However, I take comfort in knowing I have family out there."

A voice sounded from the bed. "Pomona, I am so sorry I said those things about your father." Marco sat up and leaned his head on his hands. "*Ohe*, I have such a headache."

"How long have you been awake?" demanded Adan.

"Long enough to know that I have made a huge mess of everything," Marco grumbled. "And worst of all, Calais is dead because of me. We need to go, Father, and tend to his remains."

"Serapio will take care of Calais," assured Adan. "I gave him money to pay for a private cremation. Serapio will make the arrangements tomorrow and it will be done. Serapio and Fabiana will keep the body at their home overnight. His remains will be safe under their watch."

"I want to be with him when the torch is lit," declared Marco.

"No, we leave tonight. We will travel with Paul to Caesarea. I have already given my word to Paul that the four of us will travel with him along with our escort soldiers."

"Fine," Marco said bitterly, "but I will not ride next to Aquila."

Pomona looked at Adan questioningly, but Adan did not explain. "We must be going, Pomona. Do not give up on Aurelius. You never know what twists and turns life will take, especially when you least expect it." Adan thanked her for sending for him and handed her a silver *denarius*. "For the blueberries you gave him."

"They would only have cost two *dupondii*."

"I know."

She smiled and took the coin.

Chapter 11

A Missing Belt, a Search,
and the Crematory

———⊶⊱⊰⊷———

Adan and Marco mounted their horses and headed in the direction of Serapio's house. Marco spoke first. "Why didn't you ever tell me all those things. The things you told that woman?"

"You weren't ready to hear them, Marco. And that woman's name is Pomona. You should have thanked her for sending for me. She could have done you harm if she wanted to."

"She kind of did," said Marco, rubbing his forehead. "My head is killing me."

"You deserve it," muttered Adan.

"Thanks, Father, your sympathy is appreciated."

"You're welcome. Now, you want to tell me why you took off in the middle of the night? Your mother is beside herself with worry."

Marco hung his head. "I'm sorry, Father. I will apologize to her and make things right when I get home. I just wanted to show you that . . . " His voice trailed off.

"Show me that you could do something great on your own? Is that it?" Adan glared at his son. "Leaving without permission, without a plan, without resources, that was your idea of something great?"

Marco clenched his teeth. How could he ever get his father to understand that there seemed to be no other way? "How could I do anything else? You won't let me do anything! You always gave more responsibility to Aquila and Longina, than to me. Honestly, Father, you turn to Andreas more than me. What important task have you ever trusted me to do?"

"I trusted you to understand why I had to crucify God's Son."

The answer stung Marco like the strike of a scorpion. His face burned with shame as he looked away from the pain in his father's eyes.

Adan saw his son's humiliation and softened his tone. "And yes, you are right. Not all convicted men are guilty. I was wrong to criticize you so harshly, especially in front of your brother. For that, I am sorry. Even though your actions were unwise, you did it out of the kindness of your heart. The problem is, Marco, what if he had been armed and you were alone. He could have injured or killed you to steal your horse. He would have run Wingshadow to death."

The thought of his own peril barely registered, but the suggestion that Wingshadow could have been killed turned Marco's stomach. He knew any horse could be literally run to death. They rode on in silence until a donkey cart abruptly turned onto the road in front of Adan. Blackfire reared in protest.

"How could you miss seeing this horse!" Adan shouted at the man who was trying to rein the donkey over to the side of the street. Marco anxiously frowned at his father. Such an ill-mannered show of anger was rare for Adan even with negligent *legionaries*. Marco realized that the stress of his departure had taken a greater toll on his father than he had anticipated.

"Father, I am sorry for using Yeshua's death against you," said Marco. He watched his father's face, trying to decipher his reaction. "It was mean and ugly. I really do understand why Yeshua had to die and why God wanted you to carry out the execution. Paul explained to me that Luke wrote down what you heard Yeshua and the thief say to each other. It was really important, and you understood because you speak Hebrew. Father, please forgive me for what I said. I know you'll never forget my ugly words, but I deeply regret saying them."

Relief smoothed the tension in Adan's face. "I believe you, Marco. We both needed to apologize to each other and we have. Let's try to put it behind us." He reined Blackfire to a stop in front of Serapio's house. Fabiana met them at the door as they dismounted. Marco tied Arrow's reins to a hitching post. Adan did not secure Blackfire's reins, knowing he would not move from where the reins touched the ground. Marco gave Fabiana a hug and went into the house. Adan stood outside where he could talk with her out of earshot of Marco.

"Is Serapio back yet with Calais's body?" Adan asked.

"No, not yet. I am so sorry this has happened, Adan. We are broken hearted about the loss of this young man's life, but we are equally sad for Aquila and Marco. It will be a long time before this rift between them heals."

"I'm afraid that forgiving themselves may be harder than forgiving each other," said Adan.

"Don't count on that," said Fabiana. "For most, it is usually easier to blame someone else. Both Aquila and Marco thought they were doing the right thing. This was a brutal lesson. I hope they learned something positive from it."

Adan started to reply but saw Serapio coming down the street on his cart. Serapio reined his donkey to a stop and climbed down.

"His body is in there." He pointed to the tarp covering the cart. "I was trying to find out if Calais set aside provisions with the funerary service, *Society of Diana and Antinous*. They guarantee cremation, an urn, and a *columbaria* niche for the urn, but there was no record of provision for Calais. I used some of the money you gave me to buy an urn and a niche in the *columbaria* here, but his body will have to stay in the stable tonight. The cremation is scheduled for tomorrow morning."

"Thank you for this, Serapio. It seems you're destined to clean up the Longinus family's messes. Are Niko and Aquila still at the Antonia?"

Serapio nodded as he led the donkey to the little barn built onto the back of his house. "Aquila is avoiding Marco. He's volunteered to keep Paul company. Niko is with them."

"Hopefully, they will talk some sense into Aquila's head," said Adan.

"What? And ruin a perfectly good record of mule-headedness for the Longinus clan? You should be ashamed of even suggesting such sacrilege." Serapio pulled the outer stable doors open.

Adan sighed. "You know us so well."

They led the donkey into the little barn and unhitched the cart. Serapio slid the wood beam through the braces on the double doors to protect his horse and donkey from thieves.

"Shall we invite Marco to say farewell to Calais?" asked Serapio as he removed the donkey's harness and bridle.

"Yes, he will want to do that," agreed Adan as he opened the interior barn door to the house. "I'll go get him."

Adan returned with Marco and Fabiana. Marco walked to the cart and reached for the tarp. He hesitated, but then pulled the corner of the cloth away, revealing the body of Calais. Marco's eyes clouded, but he said nothing. His expression was a mask of regret. He extended a fist and opened it to reveal the little wooden owl. "I promised to keep her safe until I could give her back to you." He started to set the owl in one of Calais's hands. "No. You wouldn't want her to burn." He closed his hand on the little figurine.

Adan stepped over to stand next to him. He rested a hand gently on Marco's shoulder. "Calais is in God's hands now, Marco. Neither you, nor your brother, could have predicted what would happen. Your intentions were good, but life is complex and often confusing. Sometimes it is best to wait for others to ask for help."

Fabiana spoke softly as she touched his arm. "Marco, no matter what you may think, the final decision was Calais's and his alone. He died by his own hand. You and Aquila were involved, but ultimately, despair and loneliness overcame his will to live. You can blame yourself for the rest of your life, which will change nothing, or you can learn from this and be wiser."

Marco looked into Calais's still face. "I am sorry. I never meant for this to happen." He moved the tarp back over the body and turned away. Without another word or a glance at the others, Marco went back into the house. The others followed him. From inside the house, Serapio shut the connecting stable door and slid the bolt. It was an old habit from when there was only an open stable outside the back door. The small barn with its locked outer doors added to their security but Serapio still locked the door between the barn and the house.

"I am sorry, too," said Adan. "I should have realized how devoted he was to me and bought his slavery contract, as I did Niko's. I can only imagine the despair he must have felt when all three of his only friends left at the same time. Salvitto had just sold Onesimus the day before Niko left." Adan took a deep breath. "We need to leave. We must get back to the Antonia. We will be leaving at the third hour of the night."

Marco nodded without a word. They said their farewells to Serapio and Fabiana. Adan lingered long enough to give Fabiana one more hug before they leaped onto their horses and trotted down the street toward the fortress.

They arrived at the Antonia to find preparations under way to escort Paul out of the city. Commander Lysias was taking no chances. He knew the original number of forty oath-takers could have doubled, if not tripled by now. He had been in Jerusalem long enough to know how deadly serious the Hebrews were about their religious beliefs. Lysias also suspected the Sanhedrin would demand, if Paul were injured or killed, that the same be done to him personally, along with the two centurions in charge of the escort. The Sanhedrin despised Paul, and saw him as a traitor, but they also hated Lysias. The Jewish leaders would not hesitate to use Roman law to their advantage.

Centurion Thracius had an idea that might help and he shared it with Commander Lysias. "I'll make sure," said Thracius, "that *Legionary* Porcius overhears me telling my *principales* to take Paul over to the Hall of Hewn Stones tomorrow afternoon with a couple of squads. Porcius will waste no time selling the information to someone with the Sanhedrin. He knows there's a large detail being dispatched tonight to transport a prisoner, but I'll make sure he thinks it is someone other than Paul. The oath-takers will relax, thinking they will only have to contend with a few soldiers tomorrow afternoon."

"I like it," said Commander Lysias. "Do it." Thracius nodded and left to find his *principales*.

Having just arrived at the Antonia, Adan and Marco walked their horses through the arena and found stalls for Blackfire and Arrow. Adan put a hand on Marco's shoulder. "Son, I know you're angry with Aquila, but he had no intention of doing Calais harm."

Marco eyed his father coldly. "Are you sure? Either he is very foolish to think that Calais would simply dismiss my apparent betrayal as a slight inconvenience, or he didn't want me to succeed without his involvement. He wants all the praise and glory and can't stand to think that I might outshine him just this once. You have told us how your parents freed many slaves. You freed Uncle Niko. I want to be like that, Father! I want to be like you. Why can't you understand that?" Marco brushed past him to walk away.

Adan watched his son as he left the stables and strode across the quad toward the prisoner detention building. Marco spoke briefly to the guards and walked inside.

Adan leaned his arm on the gate of the stall. Blackfire tossed his head and snorted. His thick, wavy mane flared back and forth with each head toss. Adan rubbed the horse's forehead and behind his ears. Blackfire lowered his head contentedly. "I should go after him, but what will I say," Adan muttered to the horse. The trip to Caesarea was going to be a very long journey, for many reasons.

Adan found Marco with Paul, but Aquila was not with them. Thinking he needed to let Marco have time to talk with Paul, he went looking for Aquila. He found him in the guest quarters.

Aquila looked up when his father stepped thorough the doorway. "Did you find Marco?"

"I did. He was with a woman who sold him some blueberries earlier today. She was kind enough to send for me and keep Marco there."

"In her kindness, did she demand a reward?" retorted Aquila.

Adan looked at his son sharply. "Why do you assume the worst? She wanted nothing from me, but to listen to her story. As it turns out, her name is Pomona and she is the daughter of Felix Valentius and his mistress, Eliana. She's had it rough, being half Samaritan and half Roman; both are intensely hated by the Jews. She revealed a side of Valentius I never suspected."

"I'm sorry. I guess I'm just in a bad mood. Why can't I ever say the right thing?"

"Aquila, I understand why you're angry with yourself. But you had no idea that Calais would kill himself. You did, in fact, judge the situation correctly. Marco was going to help him escape, but you didn't know about the poison."

Aquila grimaced with guilt. "That's not entirely true. He held up a vial and said, 'You gave this to me!' I should have realized something in that vial was important to Marco's plan. If I'd asked a few questions," he paused and frowned, "Calais might still be alive."

"Well, you can what-if this or that, but it won't change anything. You and your brother are going to have to settle this when we get home. For now, we need to concentrate on helping Paul get to Caesarea safely."

The door opened and Nikolaus walked in. Adan spoke with him quietly. Aquila tried to rest, but his thoughts went from the empty stare of Calais's pallid face to the shocked disappointment on Marco's face. Aquila lay wide awake despite his exhaustion.

Finally, it was time to leave. Adan and Commander Lysias, along with a hundred *legionaries* mixed in with a hundred spearmen took the lead. The seventy horsemen came next with Paul, Nikolaus, and Aquila in the center of them. Last came the remaining one hundred *legionaries* with the remaining one hundred spearmen. Centurion Thracius and Marco rode among the spearman. Only the moon would light their way since torches would not be used. They left Jerusalem by the closest city gate and followed the outer road surrounding the city wall until they could head northwest for Antipatris.

Aquila stayed with Paul all night, while Marco stayed close to Centurion Thracius. Nikolaus maneuvered back and forth between Adan and Thracius, conveying updates on their status. They were greatly relieved when they left Jerusalem behind without incident.

If archers had attacked from the top of the city walls, it would have been difficult to defend themselves. From then on, Aquila stayed with his father in the lead.

Nikolaus glanced at Adan. "Forty Zealots are going to starve to death since they swore to not eat until Paul was dead. Religious fanatics are the most willing to commit brutal acts of violence, even against themselves if they can't hurt their victims."

"Yes, to declare such an oath is a serious matter. It's a good thing they did not make a blood covenant," said Adan.

"What is a blood covenant?" asked Aquila.

"It is enacted when two people want to pledge an unbreakable vow. A perfect animal, without blemish, is cut completely in two. Certain animals are used because their life's blood and innocence cancel out sin. The two halves are laid out with a narrow path between them where the blood flows. The two people making the covenant walk together through the blood. Then they say, "May this be done to me if I break this covenant."

"Do they really do that?" Aquila asked with revulsion. "It sounds awful."

"Perhaps to you, but to the Hebrews, it means that the covenant is so binding that it will result in the death of anyone who breaks it. Blood is life. When God sent Yeshua to be sacrificed, in essence he was swearing the ultimate blood covenant with all humanity. Through his Son, God shed his own blood and said, 'I have shed My blood for you. I will be your God and you will be My people.' God promises to remain bonded to every believer forever."

"Have you ever told Marco about a blood covenant?" asked Aquila.

"No. Why do you ask?"

"Because if you had, I would make him enter into one with me."

Adan looked at his son sternly. "You would have to *ask*, Aquila, not demand such a thing. The covenant must be agreed to willingly by both oath-takers. What would be your purpose?"

"To swear that we will never keep anything secret from each other again."

Adan heard the pain in his son's voice. "Aquila, it must seem like you and Marco will never get past the death of Calais, but you will. Give it time. You two are brothers. You need each other now and you always will."

"Did Marco need me when he left the house in the middle of the night?"

"Yes," answered Adan. "He just didn't know it."

Father and son rode on in silence.

* * *

Serapio and Fabiana awoke to a mourning dove sitting on the lattice of a window, softly cooing. It turned its head to and fro as it sang. The bird took flight when Fabiana sat up.

Serapio let out a long, low breath. "That was an omen. I'm sure Calais would agree with me, if he could." He got out of bed and put on a tunic. He buckled his belt and shuffled out of the room to go downstairs. He stirred the remaining embers of the cook fire and added kindling to get the flames going. He unlocked the door to the barn and looked in the cart.

Serapio burst back into the room. Fabiana was coming down the stairs. "Calais—*he's gone!* The body is gone! The double doors had to be unbarred from the inside! He left this." He held up a wide belt. "It reeks of horse urine. There's the name 'Lysias' stitched on it with the title 'Commander' underneath. This is Calais's belt." He tossed the belt into the fire.

Fabiana gawked at him in shock. "Wha—what are you saying? Calais is *alive*?"

"And we have no way of warning Adan any time soon," exclaimed Serapio. "Calais tried to kill himself because he thought Marco betrayed him. I'm afraid he will want to even the score. He couldn't have gotten far, not in his condition. I'll take the horse and look for him."

"Apio, be careful," cried Fabiana. "He might see you first and do something rash. And if you find him, what will you do? You know what they'll do to him."

"I will explain to him about Aquila. That will cool his anger at Marco. Then I'll offer to get him out of Jerusalem. But I must find him before he leaves the city and goes after Marco."

Serapio quickly saddled his horse and went out into the streets. He tried to think where he would go if he were sick and afraid. He asked discreet questions among the street vendors and beggars. If any of them had seen someone matching Calais's description, they usually claimed ignorance. After several false leads, Serapio found a shop keeper who remembered Calais.

"Early this morning there was a young man like you described, half dead with sickness. I gave him bread in hopes he would leave. He did leave but first he said the oddest thing. He said, 'Will they give him stone for his bread in Tartarus? I hope it breaks his teeth.' I yelled at him, 'Be gone, leper!' I didn't dare touch him. Then I slammed my door shut."

"How long ago was this?"

"He was here a little before the first hour, but now that the city gates are open, he could be anywhere."

"Why did you think he had leprosy?"

The merchant pursed his lips. "I didn't, really, but I don't take chances. He was sick from something."

"Was he wearing shabby clothes, old sandals—no belt?"

"Maybe." The merchant shrugged. "I remember his eyes. Empty looking, the color of olives when they're still green. His face looked washed out, like there was no blood in his veins. Why are you looking for him?"

"He's the son of a friend of mine. He's been a little out of his mind, if you know what I mean," said Serapio, hoping that he sounded convincing. "What direction did he go?"

"Who knows? All I know is that he was gone when I reopened my door."

Serapio groaned in frustration. He looked up and down the street and tried to think. Where would someone go who was sick and confused? He rode from shop to shop, asking questions, but no one offered any promising leads until he spoke to a woman selling pottery.

"I saw the young man you describe. He was missing his belt, like you said. He was staggering as he walked and collapsed." She pointed to the public water fountain. "Right there in the street. A patrol came along. They yelled at him to get out of the street. They thought he was drunk. One of the soldiers poked at him with his sword when he didn't move. Then he stabbed the body like they do to see if the blood flows out."

Serapio frowned. He knew what that meant. "He didn't bleed."

The woman shook her head. "I was close. I could see. Dead bodies don't bleed. The soldiers left and came back with a cart. They took the body away only a short time ago."

Serapio bowed his head, feeling both relief for Marco, but sorrow for Calais. Serapio headed for the crematory outside the city. When he entered the walled complex, the smell of burnt flesh, decomposition, and oily smoke assailed his senses. This was a place abhorred by the Hebrews but insisted upon by the Romans who always incinerated their dead. There were several small buildings designed for private cremations, as well as large pits for burning the bodies of dead slaves, criminals, unwanted babies, and prisoners of war. Serapio rode slowly among the pits and buildings looking for any sign of Calais. He found a body lying face down among other corpses in the fourth pit and dropped from the saddle to peer at it more closely. This body drew his attention because he not only had the same appearance as Calais, he was also still clothed, except the belt was missing.

The cremators saw no reason to waste clothing that could be resold; therefore, it was unusual to find a clothed body in the pits. Serapio saw a man come out of one of the buildings. He went into a shed and came out with a torch which he lit at the ember pot. The man slowly made his way to the pit where Serapio stood.

"This body here," Serapio pointed to the clothed corpse, "how long has he been here?"

"Do you not see my slave belt?" He gestured at the name sown onto the thick, wide belt. "I am the property of this man. He tells me what to do. I don't ask questions. Besides, this is the pit for dead slaves. No one asks questions about them."

"Why is this one still clothed?"

The slave approached the pit and looked in. "How should I know?" He lifted the torch to toss it into the pit. Serapio grasped his wrist and snatched the torch from him.

"You will answer me first," insisted Serapio. "Why is only his belt missing?"

"I don't know; but if I were dying, I'd yank this cursed thing off and bury it in sheep dung." He looked down at the still body of the young slave. "But most likely, whoever dumped him here took the belt to prove to the owner that he's dead."

"And his clothes?" persisted Serapio.

"If he died of leprosy," the man shrugged, "they burn the clothes with the body."

"I see no signs of leprosy."

The man leaned forward for another glance. "You can't see his face or the front of his body. You know how lepers can't feel pain. The rats eat on them when they're asleep. If he slept on his back, the rats would go for the . . . "

"I know how it is with leprosy," snapped Serapio.

"Well, then I don't know," the man muttered. "If soldiers brought him in, they usually take the clothes for themselves." He shrugged his shoulders with indifference. "What does it matter?"

While they talked, the body never moved. One arm was twisted at an unnatural angle and the body was sprawled as if it had been tossed—or had fallen. It had to be Calais. His first day of freedom was also his last day of life.

Serapio handed the torch back to the slave. The man tossed it into the center of the pit. The oiled wood easily caught fire. The slave hurried away and disappeared into the main building. Serapio peered down on the young man as the flames grew higher. The fire slowly spread out from the center where the torch had fallen. Serapio had seen enough.

If the corpse was not Calais and he fully recovered, Marco could be in danger as well as Aquila. Calais knew where they lived and where Adan worked. He could hire himself out to any traveling merchant who needed someone to tend his horses and merchandise. There would be no public notices announcing a reward for a young, runaway Greek slave with dark hair and gray-green eyes. Serapio was in a dilemma. According to the law, he should report to Commander Lysias that Calais might be alive no matter how slim the chance. Lysias would inform a registered slave hunter, instigating a pursuit. Serapio loathed slavery in any form but he especially hated the professional slave hunters who were brutally efficient. However, Serapio also understood that Calais might seek revenge on Marco or Aquila. No matter what he did, there could be tragic results.

Serapio thought about finding the cremator to ask about the young man the soldiers brought in, but it would probably be an exercise in futility. There were so many bodies. Serapio doubted that the cremator ever asked where they came from as long as a family member or the government paid the cremation fee. Serapio sighed in anguish. He would go home and discuss the situation with Fabiana. The pain in his heart eased, knowing he could rely on her wisdom to help him decide what to do.

Chapter 12

Road to Caesarea, Harsh Words, and a Warning

Once the escort reached Antipatris, Centurion Thracius sent the other centurion, the two hundred *legionaries* and the two hundred spearmen back to Jerusalem. Protected by the seventy horsemen, they continued to Caesarea. Adan decided his sons needed to confront their mutual hostility before they reached home. He ordered Aquila to join Marco.

"Aquila, don't leave his side until the two of you have settled your differences," Adan demanded. "I won't have you and your brother upsetting your mother any more than she already is. Do you understand?"

Aquila set his jaw and cast sullen eyes over his shoulder. "He is the one who upset Mother. Why should I go talk to him? He should come crawling to me."

"And you should be crawling to Calais to apologize. But wait—you can't—he's dead."

Aquila bowed his head. "I would apologize to Calais if I could, but Marco started all this mess. Why should I be the first to give in?"

"Go talk to him. Now!"

Aquila turned Nighthawk back to join the rear of the escort where Centurion Thracius and Marco now rode. When Aquila came alongside, Thracius urged his horse into a trot and caught up with Adan in the lead to leave Aquila alone with Marco.

"What do you want?" grumbled Marco.

Aquila begrudgingly glanced at his brother but centered his attention on Arrow. "At least you weren't a complete idiot. Someone would have stolen Wingshadow."

Marco refused to look at him. "You mean kidnapped her. You steal saddles and bridles. You kidnap horses."

Aquila rolled his eyes. "Please. They're animals, not people."

Marco frowned with annoyance. "I said, what do you want?"

"Me? I don't want anything. Father has ordered us to settle our differences before we get home so Mother won't be upset. The great and noble centurion has spoken."

Marco threw him a surly look. They rode in silence until Marco's anger got the better of him. "Why did you pretend to be me? And don't give me that 'I was just keeping you safe, brother.' You had to have known how terrified Calais would feel. I'm sure he assumed you would report him. Did you really think he would shrug it off and go pick mud out of horses' hooves while he waited to be beaten?"

"Did you really think the whole family would cheer with blissful glee when we discovered you had slunk away in the middle of the night?" cried Aquila. "Marco, I thought you were going to run away with that slave. When you got caught, and you would have been caught, you could have been seriously punished. How was I supposed to know what was in that vial?"

"You knew about the vial?" Marco snapped. "Why didn't you ask Calais what it was for? Or better yet, why didn't you tell him, '*Ohe*, you got the wrong brother! Let me go find him.'"

"Right. As if I knew exactly where you were. Besides, you would have done it anyway." Aquila clenched his teeth in frustration. "I'm sorry. Alright? I really didn't mean for that slave to kill himself."

"That slave had a name," growled Marco. "His name was Calais. He worshipped the ground Father walked on. He would have done anything for him." Marco swallowed hard. His voice softened. "He would have done anything for me."

Aquila looked at him sharply. "What do you think I do? Who always takes up your slack? Why didn't you take me with you? If I couldn't talk you out of it, I would have gone with you. Don't you understand? If we had gone together, Mother and Father wouldn't have been so worried. We have always looked out for each other. Why didn't you trust me?"

"It's not about trust!" cried Marco. "I didn't leave you out. I left you in peace. I needed to prove to Father that I'm not a—never mind."

"Not a fool?" said Aquila. "That's what you were going to say, wasn't it? But then you did the most foolish thing you've ever done. You just took off with no idea what you were doing and upset everybody. Your little escapade has only proven that you *are* a fool, Marco, and now we have to drag you home with nothing to show for your bravado."

Marco blanched at the impact of his callous words. He knew Aquila was right. He would return home a disgrace, a failure, with nothing to redeem himself. His voice went flat. All signs of emotion left his face. "You won't be dragging me anywhere." He dug his heels into Arrow's flanks and left his brother staring after him.

The escort traveled all day and reached the garrison of Caesarea before nightfall. Centurion Thracius presented Commander Lysias's letter and Paul to Governor Felix. The governor commanded that Paul should be held in Herod's Praetorium until his accusers arrived from Jerusalem. In the bustle, Adan lost track of his sons, but it didn't take long to find Aquila in the stables. He was brushing Nighthawk after giving him hay and water.

"Where is your brother?" Adan asked as he brought Blackfire into the same stall.

Aquila shrugged a shoulder. "How should I know? I'm not his master."

"Aquila! Don't take that tone with me. Did you two get your differences settled?"

"I don't know. He took off in a huff. I haven't seen him since." Aquila continued to brush Nighthawk without looking at his father. "I don't know what you think we're supposed to say to each other. He's angry with me about that sla . . . about Calais, and I'm angry with him for tearing the family up just so he can go on some ridiculous adventure. Why don't you let him go? Let him get in trouble. It'll teach him a lesson. Besides, you've got me, Father. You can depend on me." When Aquila heard no response, he glanced around; his father was gone.

Adan strode through the garrison asking if anyone had seen Marco. No one had. He found Nikolaus, and together they continued the search. One of the horsemen who had ridden with them from Jerusalem approached.

"Sir, I heard that you are looking for your son," said the cavalryman. "I did not think anything of it at the time, but I saw the one riding the old brown horse, break ranks and head toward a grove of trees before we reached the garrison. I thought, you know, maybe he just needed a nature call, Sir."

Adan asked for the details of the exact location. The grove of trees stood next to a road that split off to the west leading to the shore of the Mediterranean Sea, and to the north leading to Dora, a port city north of Caesarea. Cargo ships went out every day from both ports. It was common knowledge that many ship captains hired crews off the docks, no questions asked. Fear made Adan's mouth go dry. He knew Marco was not on his way home.

"Come on, we have to find Thracius," said Adan. "He spent the most time with Marco and he might know something, even if he doesn't realize it. I don't think Marco is here at the garrison."

They hurried to find Thracius. He was just leaving the arena outside the stables. Adan told him what he suspected about Marco's whereabouts. "Did he say anything to you that might hint at what he plans to do?" asked Adan.

Thracius frowned and shook his head slowly. "No, he didn't share any plans with me."

"Did he say anything or do anything that might suggest his frame of mind?" asked Nikolaus, but Thracius again shook his head. "Did he ask if you knew anyone who could be a guide or where he could acquire passage on a ship? He would have to work off the cost of passage since he has no money."

"No. Believe me, if I knew anything, I would tell you. He was in trouble with a merchant who charged him with theft, but other than that we talked about you, Adan, and Felix Valentius."

"Theft? What are you talking about?" demanded Adan.

Thracius told him about Florinus and his attempt to exploit Marco. "I was impressed with the way he handled himself with Florinus. He kept his head when he was arrested and thrown into Holding. But I have to be honest; I was surprised when he let a street vender manipulate him into buying a worthless amulet. I wouldn't have thought him to be superstitious."

"Not Marco. I taught my children to deal with facts not imaginary reasoning," countered Adan. "Marco may be a dreamer, but he's never been superstitious."

Nikolaus gave Adan a sympathetic look. "He's not finding fault, Adan. He doesn't know Marco like you do. Let the man talk."

Thracius looked at Adan sheepishly. "I meant no criticism. This street vendor caught Marco's eye, and I suspect the man knew he had him hooked. Marco was, in fact, quite taken with this one amulet. It was a single stone on a leather cord. The man wanted thirty *denarii* for it and Marco only had one, but he was quite taken with the crystal. The merchant claimed it had a secret message written on it that would lead to a great treasure. Those street peddlers say that about any bit of rock or figurine. He saw that Marco was taking it all in so he piled it on, even claimed the stone would protect him from evil. Of course, they always spout a babble of lies just to make a sale. I bought the thing for him just so we could get back to the Antonia in time for supper."

"An amulet?" asked Nikolaus with a confused frown. "I've never known Marco to be interested in trinkets. Also, the Marco I know would never 'take charity' from someone."

"That's true, which makes his attraction to this amulet even more curious," said Adan. "He told me about the travel fee you paid to the merchant, Thracius. I will work the debt out of Marco later, but for now I will pay you what he owes."

Thracius flipped a hand. "Adan, I appreciate the offer, but you don't owe me a thing. Let's leave it at that. As for Marco, he really liked that amulet. He was fascinated with it."

"Was there something special about it," asked Adan.

"Not really. I've seen much prettier crystals, ones you can see through. This one was opaque. A sapphire. I admit, the color was unusual. It was purple."

"Purple! A purple sapphire? You're sure?" Nikolaus asked.

Adan frowned at the sudden intensity in Nikolaus's voice. "Does that mean something to you, Niko?"

"Yes, my sister has a purple sapphire that my father gave to our mother on their wedding day. It is carved into the knot of Hercules. I told Marco about it once. Thracius, did he say anything to you about Dionysia, owning a purple sapphire?"

"As a matter of fact, he did," said Thracius. "Yes, Dionysia was the name he mentioned. He said that she lives in Herculaneum with her master and his wife. He said he has never met her, but he whispered something about her being a treasure to you, Nikolaus."

"But he didn't say anything about going there?" asked Nikolaus.

"No, but I saw the look on his face when the merchant said, 'Follow the purple sapphire. It will lead you to your destiny.' His whole face lit up. I thought he was being foolish to believe such rubbish, but maybe that was not what he was thinking at all. The look in those eyes of his could have been, well, maybe—inspiration."

"That's it," declared Adan. "That's his mission. He's going to find Dionysia. That's why he wanted to free Calais. He wanted a traveling companion he could trust."

Nikolaus sighed. "Yes, just like I am to you. He wants to repeat our history, Adan. Your history. Whether he realizes it or not."

"Adan, Niko, you'll have to excuse me," said Thracius. "I need to report to Commander Tacitus. I'll find you before you leave if I have any relevant news."

Adan and Niko thanked the centurion for his help. They watched in silence as he walked toward Commander Tacitus's office.

"Niko, what you said about Marco repeating our history. It might look that way, but I freed you legally. Then you made your own decision to stay with me. Contrary to that, Marco expected Calais to stay with him. He will not be content to find Dionysia, shake hands, and be on his way. He plans to take her away so you two can be reunited. He knows you tried to secure her freedom, but she wouldn't leave her children. They're grown now and both married. Aren't they living in Rome?"

"Yes, as of the last few years according to Dionysia's letters," said Nikolaus.

"I think Marco is determined to do this, no matter how dangerous or illegal it is. I know he's thinking that if he can return home with Dionysia, he will be welcomed as the conquering hero and everything will be forgiven."

"I think you're right, but there's nothing we can do about it until tomorrow," said Nikolaus. "We can't find him in the dark if he doesn't want to be found. We can head out in the morning and maybe catch up with him by the end of the day. He's going to have to sleep sometime, and trees grow faster than that pack horse can walk. We'll find him, Adan."

Adan was deep in thought. "Niko, I'm not sure that is what we should do. We can bring him home, but he'll just leave again, first chance he gets. He is of age now. He's too determined for this to be just a whim. Perhaps I should leave him alone. Maybe Aquila is right. He just wanted my attention and he got it. Maybe he just needs some time on his own. He'll come home when he gets hungry and desperate. And I'll be watching to welcome him home."

Nikolaus was about to respond when a mounted courier from Jerusalem approached. He reined his horse to a stop and asked, "Sir, are you Centurion Longinus?" The courier looked Adan in the eye and handed him a scroll without waiting for an answer. "This message is from Regulus Serapio in Jerusalem. He said it is most urgent."

"Thank you," said Adan as he broke the seal on the scroll. He quickly scanned the message. Nikolaus frowned to see concern crease his brother's brow.

Adan handed the scroll to Nikolaus who read it aloud, "Adan, I have reason to believe that Calais may be alive. When I went to take his body for cremation, I discovered that he was gone. I tracked him to a shop owner who gave him bread. Then a street vendor told me someone who matched Calais's description collapsed and died in the street. It may have been his body in a crematory pit, but I am not certain it was him. Take care! If the body in the pit was not his, he may be a danger to Marco. Calais said to the shop owner, 'Will they give him stone for his bread in Tartarus? I hope it breaks his teeth.' I am nearly certain that the dead body I saw was Calais, but in an overabundance of caution, I give you warning. Go with God and be safe."

Nikolaus rolled the scroll up and grimaced. "This really complicates things. We must assume that Calais is alive and will seek revenge. We also have to assume that he knows Marco's plan to go to Herculaneum."

"Yes, this changes everything," said Adan. He thought for moment, tight-lipped and tense. His tension eased when he reached a decision. "I can't take the chance that Calais is dead. I know where Marco is going. I'll follow him. If he gets himself into more trouble than he can handle, I'll be right behind him. But I'm not going to force him to come home, not this time. I will track him, but I won't interfere."

"I'll go with you, Adan," declared Nikolaus. "Titus and Pitio will help Marina run the inn. Adriana and her husband have decided to live at the inn permanently. Marina will understand."

"But you'll be gone from Marina for at least four months, maybe five. I can get a leave of absence from Commander Tacitus," said Adan, "and I can take a few soldiers with me. Are you sure you want to do this?"

"I can't believe you're even asking that question. You're my brother and he's my nephew. I'm going with you." Nikolaus pointed over Adan's shoulder. "Look! There's Aquila. You better tell him what's in that scroll. Calais might find him before he finds Marco."

"Father, did you find him?" Aquila asked as he joined them.

"No. He's gone, but you better read this," said Adan as he handed the scroll to his son. "It's from Serapio."

Aquila read the message and then re-read it. He looked from his father to his uncle. "This is great news! Now we know Calais is alive so no harm done, right?"

"Wrong, Aquila!" exclaimed Adan. "We don't know that he is alive, but if he is, he might go after Marco for revenge. You may have intended to protect your brother from arrest, but instead, you may have put him in danger. Sounds like Calais wants revenge."

Nikolaus frowned at Adan. "That was not Aquila's intention."

Adan motioned toward several benches that lined the arena fence. It gave him time to gather his thoughts as the three of them walked to a bench and sat down.

Adan softened his tone. "Aquila, the worst thing you can do to a person is destroy his dreams. It doesn't matter if they are irrational or even delusional, because they offer hope. From what I can gather, Calais survived his life as a slave because he dreamed of my coming for him some day. For eighteen years he clung to that belief. Then Marco showed up and gave him hope. His dream seemed possible once again, especially when

I showed up next. All the times we went to visit Serapio and Fabiana, I never once considered going to the Antonia to find Calais. It never occurred to me. But I doubt he knew of my visits to Jerusalem, so he kept the dream alive in his heart. When you pretended to be Marco, you crushed his dream. Now both you and your brother may be in danger if he is alive."

Aquila curled his lip in disgust. "He didn't really try to kill himself. He was just pretending and heard every word we said."

"I wish that were the case," said Adan, "then he would know that Marco didn't betray him. His eyes were slightly open and that only happens when someone is dead or close to it."

"There's something I should have told you," said Nikolaus as he looked at Adan. "When you were arrested for Peter's escape, Calais told me he couldn't live without your protection. He said you were the only one at the Antonia who had shown him kindness. The best thing that happened to him was when you invited him to be in your Saturday class. I explained to him how fortunate he was to stand behind your shield. That shield went away when we were in Caesarea those four months. I heard that Calais was a favorite plaything among the *legionaries* while we were gone. He was so happy when we got back. He thought everything would go back to the way it was. The day you were supposed to be executed; Calais tried to kill himself."

Adan looked away in sorrow. "The life of a child in slavery is worse than—everything."

Nikolaus understood all too well. "One of the other slaves found Calais the afternoon of the executions. He had tried to hang himself with the reins of a bridle. The slave lifted him up and called for help. They untied the leather and took him to Tribune Salvitto. Salvitto was kind to him and even summoned a *medicus*. Afterward, Salvitto reassigned him to the officers' cafeteria to take Onesimus's place. I don't know what happened after that since Serapio came for me the next day. I didn't tell you about Calais because I thought you might think I was ungrateful. You know, give someone a loaf of bread and he asks for the flour mill as well. I told myself that Calais would be all right, and that Cook would protect him like he did Onesimus."

"I have no one to blame but myself," said Adan. "I should have realized what was in his heart. His actions spoke of his loyalty, and I abandoned him, twice now."

Aquila came to his feet. "It doesn't matter if Calais is alive or dead. There's no need to be worried about Marco. He was mad, so he tossed me aside like I was some useless pair of old sandals and just took off, *again*, but he was headed in the direction of Caesarea. He's probably at home by now." Aquila turned on his heel and stalked away.

"Aquila might be right," muttered Adan. "Maybe we're overreacting. That road leads to a crossroads to either Dora or Caesarea. Maybe he just wanted to be alone to think. He could have gotten home while we were sitting here debating the situation."

Nikolaus clapped a hand on his brother's shoulder. "Let's go find out. If he's not there, then we know where he's going." The two men headed for the stables.

Chapter 13

A Decision, an Apparition, and Redirection

———— ⟨※⟩ ————

The thought of going home as a failure was more than Marco could stomach. The rage that boiled inside him was equal to his determination to prove Aquila wrong. Finding passage on a ship to Herculaneum would be a challenge, but one he could manage. He would hire out in Dora as an oarsman on a troop transport ship or a cargo ship. The pay was less than what a *legionary* made, but it would do. If he could not find work in Dora, there was always Sycaminum or Ptolomais farther north. As Arrow plodded along, Marco thought of the various plans he had devised to rescue Dionysia. Buying her slave contract was probably out of the question since Uncle Niko had offered to do that more than once. Marco didn't have any money, anyway.

Marco knew that both of Dionysia's children were married. Uncle Niko had shared the good news from his sister's letters. He feared that Dionysia might still be held back if she wished to live near them since they both lived in Rome. His greatest fear, however, was that Decimus may have sold her. She was thirty-seven years old now, and he may have grown tired of her. The last time Marco asked Uncle Niko about his sister, he said that she was doing well according to her most recent letter, received three months ago. Many things could have changed since the letter was written. He wouldn't have any answers until he reached Herculaneum.

"Well, Arrow, I guess I'm going to travel this path on faith," Marco proclaimed. The horse glanced back over a shoulder to catch a glimpse of his master. Marco also glanced over his own shoulder a few times, but there were no riders approaching from behind. He tried to feel relief that his father and uncle had not caught up with him, but he found himself brooding at their absence.

A new thought came to Marco and he pulled up on the reins. The horse came to a stop and looked back at him. "Perhaps just going to Jerusalem," he announced to Arrow, "and finding the purple sapphire was what I was supposed to do for now. I had

89

to encounter that street vendor in Jerusalem to discover my mission. Now, I need to go home and prepare for it. Make some money. Devise a plan. Leave with Father and Mother's blessing this time. Yes, that's it. Now I know what to do."

Marco tapped a heel against Arrow's flank and the horse grudgingly moved. Marco was approaching the intersection with a road to Dora and the other road leading home. Horse and rider drew near to the split. Marco only hesitated a moment before he turned Arrow toward the road to Caesarea. When he got home, he would explain what he wanted to do for Dionysia and see if anyone in the family would help him. If they didn't, he would leave again when he was fully prepared.

Marco was feeling good about his decision. He was studying the familiar landscape as Arrow plodded along. Suddenly he was startled to see the figure of a young man standing in the road. No one had been there a moment before. Marco reined Arrow to a stop and looked more closely. The man was just standing there, not moving, veiled by the shadow of a terebinth tree near the side of the road.

"*Ohe,* are you lost!" Marco shouted.

There was no response. Marco peered more closely. The young man had dark hair, was taller than average, and was wearing a ragged tunic and sandals. Marco noticed that his belt was missing, which was odd. He would have nothing to attach a coin pouch to or hold an item dropped inside his tunic. When the man neither moved nor spoke, Marco frowned and glanced around nervously. It was common practice for robbers to ambush travelers, but it would be a brazen act to attack so close to the garrison. A gust of wind swept past the still figure. Dust puffed up from the road and swirled into the field of wild grass and thistles on the other side. Yet the man's clothes did not flutter with the wind. A chill went up Marco's spine, even though the man presented no threat. He simply stood there as if he were waiting for something to happen.

Marco waved an arm. "Do you need help?" The figure's rigid stance was unnatural. Losing patience, Marco urged Arrow in the direction of the solitary man. The horse laid his ears back flat against his skull and balked. He turned aside despite Marco's efforts. When Arrow let out a high-pitched squeal, Marco knew there was danger. He looked over his shoulder but no one was there. Arrow spun away, but Marco reined him back to face the solitary young man.

The figure had vanished.

Marco looked around frantically. "What! Where did he go? There's nowhere to go." The ground was flat around the road with little vegetation and no large boulders to hide behind. He pressed his heels into Arrow's flanks and trotted up to the spot where the figure had stood. He reined his horse around in a full circle. He thought about footprints. He couldn't see any, but Arrow's hooves may have wiped them out. There was a cluster of trees not too far from the road, but could the man have run to them so quickly? Marco reined Arrow toward the trees. The horse again balked and laid his ears back. A feeling of dread snaked up Marco's spine. He had tried to ignore his own senses, but the truth was undeniable. The figure in the road had looked like Calais.

Marco spun Arrow around to retrace his steps to the intersection. The thought of seeing the mysterious figure again made him cringe. He took the road to Dora and pressed his heels into Arrow's flanks. The horse, unusually motivated, leaped into a canter, and fled from the road to Caesarea.

After a few minutes, Marco slowed Arrow to a walk. He fished around in his knapsack and found the little wooden owl. "Sofi, was that Calais? If you answer me, I'll know I have lost my mind." He started to put the figurine back in his knapsack, but put the little owl in his coin pouch instead. "You'll be safer there, Sofi." He looked over his shoulder to make sure he was alone. "Perhaps this is where I'm supposed to go, anyway," he told the horse. "That couldn't have been Calais. He's dead. But whoever he was, he sure scared you, didn't he?" He patted the horse's neck. "Well, I guess we're going to Dora after all. It must be God's will."

* * *

Adan and Nikolaus would have disagreed that any of Marco's schemes were God's will. Adan found Aquila and joined Nikolaus in the garrison's barn. They saddled Blackfire, Nighthawk and Inventio in record time, and bid Centurion Thracius farewell. The three men took the road that led to the shoreline of the Mediterranean and turned north until they reached the cliff road to the Cornelius estate. Andreas saw them clear the curve at the top of the path and hurried to meet them.

"I'm so sorry, Adan," said Andreas when he saw that there was no one else. "I felt sure you would come home with Marco."

"Well, that answers my question. He's not here. We almost brought him home," said Adan with a surly glance at Aquila. "We got him as far as the garrison, but he took off again."

"He may still show up before sunset," suggested Nikolaus. "We can go to Dora first thing in the morning and ask around. Maybe he just wants us to come after him."

"Why should we?" asked Aquila with a frown.

"Because he is your brother," said Dulcibella. No one had noticed her slip around from the terrace where she had been watching the road. "Marco would do the same for you."

Andreas took the reins of Blackfire and Nighthawk and led them to the stables. Nikolaus had not dismounted. "Dulcibella, we will find him," said Nikolaus. "I'll be back in the morning, but for now I need to go home and talk things over with Marina." He reined Inventio around and headed for the cliff road.

"Niko, thank you for coming with us," Adan called out.

Nikolaus waved a hand in the air. "You would have done the same for me."

Adan managed a brief smile, but then caught Aquila's eye. He tilted his head toward the house. "Go on in the house, Aquila. Tell your grandparents what happened." Adan turned to Dulcibella and gathered her in his arms.

"Are you going after him again?"

Adan frowned in thought. "I won't treat him like a hostage. He is of age now. I would have offered an escort to accompany him to Herculaneum, if he had come home." He took a deep breath. "But there's another problem, a potentially dangerous complication. Let's go sit on the bench. I need to tell you everything that has happened." He took Dulcibella's hand and led her to the bench under the ancient oak tree. He gazed over the sea. It mirrored his restive mood.

Adan told Dulcibella about the amulet and how he had reacted to the words of the merchant when he said, 'Follow the purple sapphire.' He put his thoughts in order and continued. "Niko has told Marco many times how he wished Dionysia could live here. We think he's going to Herculaneum to free Dionysia. There is something else. I'm afraid Aquila may have pushed his brother to take off again when we were almost home." Adan told her about Calais's death and how Aquila had pretended to be Marco.

"This breaks my heart," said Dulcibella sadly. "No doubt, Calais thought Aquila was telling the guards that he was planning an escape. It's easy to understand why he killed himself."

Adan stiffened. Dulcibella shot him a glance. "What is it?"

"That's the complication. Calais might not be dead. When Serapio went to take the body, it was gone. Serapio had barred the doors from the inside, of course. Only Calais could have removed the bar." Adan told her about Serapio's warning. "If that dead body in the pit was not Calais, the twins could be in danger."

Dulcibella stared at Adan in shock. "You have to find Marco! Take Aquila with you. If Calais sees Marco and Aquila together, he'll understand what happened. He'll be angry with Aquila, but it might pacify him enough to leave our sons alone."

"If Calais is alive, it lets Aquila off the hook sort of, but it leaves Marco in a bad way. If Calais is dead, Aquila is guilty of contributing to his suicide. None of this would be happening if I had freed Calais all those years ago."

Dulcibella took Adan's hand in hers and ran her fingers over the scars of the cross in his palm. "Does condemning yourself change the situation?"

He glanced down at the scars and sighed. "No, of course not. What is done cannot be undone. I will follow Marco, but not to dissuade him. If I find him, I'll offer my help. If he refuses it, then so be it. I have to let him go."

"I believe everything happens for a reason even if we do not understand it. Following Marco will allow Aquila to have time with you and Niko, without interference. You really do spend most of your energy on Marco."

"I have to. He's constantly messing up one thing or another."

Dulcibella's voice softened. "Did you ever consider that he might do it on purpose?"

Adan frowned. "On purpose? Why would he do that? He gets in trouble for it."

"He also gets your attention for it. Lots of attention. Lots of your time. Getting into a little trouble is always better than being ignored," said Dulcibella gently.

"I don't ignore my sons," exclaimed Adan. When Dulcibella said nothing, he glanced at her. "Do I?'

"Sometimes."

Adan sighed. "Why are children so difficult? Can't I just yank them by the scruff of the neck into adulthood?"

Dulcibella laughed softly. "You could try that. Might make them taller."

Adan grinned and patted her hand. "What would I do without you, Dulcie?"

"I don't know." She smiled. "Let's not find out."

Adan laughed and got up. "We will leave in the morning. I need to talk to Marcus and Iovita. They may think of something that will help."

"Send Aquila out here to me, please," said Dulcibella. "We're going to have a chat."

Adan went into the house. Aquila trudged across the terrace and sank onto the bench next to his mother. "I suppose you're going to chew me out," he stated with a disheartened tone.

"Would it help?"

Aquila shrugged and refused to look his mother in the eye.

"I didn't think so," said Dulcibella. "Aquila, I know you think Marco neglected you by leaving you behind. But you must understand that what he did is not about his relationship with you. It's about his relationship with himself. You feel good about yourself when you solve a mechanical or science problem. Marco feels good about himself when he solves a social problem. If he had taken you with him, then that good feeling would be cut in half."

"So, he's being selfish," declared Aquila.

"In a way, yes, and so are you."

Aquila glared at Dulcibella. "How am I being selfish?"

"You want all of your good feeling, and you want half of Marco's good feeling as well. Do you include him on your projects, or your experiments?"

Aquila shrugged. "No. He'd probably just get in the way."

"Perhaps Marco thought that *you* would get in his way."

"Well, there's nothing I can do now. He's gone and I made things so much worse anyway. Why should I even try?"

"Because you love your brother. That's why you keep trying."

"He's not going to let me do anything now," retorted Aquila. "He blames me for Calais's suicide." He lowered his head. "There's something else, Mother. I said something to him. It was harsh. Marco would have come home with us if I had not taunted him. I am sorry. Even when he comes home, this won't be over. I know he will not forgive me for deceiving Calais."

"You cannot predict what Marco will feel or do. You can only ask his forgiveness just as you ask God for forgiveness. What Marco does is up to him. You will have done everything you can." Dulcibella placed a gentle hand on his shoulder.

Aquila looked his mother in the eye. "I know God forgives me. But if we don't come home with Marco—if he never comes home—will *you* forgive me?"

Dulcibella stood up and leaned on the balustrade. She gazed out over the sea and whispered, "I hope so. For my own sake."

Chapter 14

Justus, Elizabeth, and a
Broken Vase in Dora

———— ⌘ ————

Marco knew the port city of Dora was a four-mile walk from his home on the cliff. He figured it would be sunset by the time the others reached the villa and discovered he wasn't there. He was sure they would not travel to Dora until the next day. That would give him time to find a place to stay until he could hire out on a ship bound for Herculaneum. In the meantime, he would need to stay vigilant in case his father came looking for him.

Once he reached the city, Marco offered to work in exchange for a night's lodging, but the shopkeepers were closing for the night and didn't need his services. It was getting late and danger always lurked in the darkness. On the road, there was no way to see if thieves waited in ambush, wild animals prowled, or delapidated bridges and roads loomed ahead. Thieves also huddled in the shadows within every city, waiting to attack. Shouting or banging on doors rarely resulted in assistance or refuge. Few were willing to put themselves in peril for a stranger.

When the shopkeepers refused his offer, Marco resorted to homeowners but was waved off or ignored. He spied a Galilean, judging by his attire, who was in his late sixties and about to lock his gate for the night.

"Sir, I am trying to find a place for the night or possibly longer. I can work for my lodging and supper. Please, is there some work I can do for you?" Marco anxiously waited for an answer.

The man looked him up and down. He studied Marco's face long enough to make the young man blink with embarrassment.

"What is your name?" asked the man.

"Marcus Clovius Longinus, Sir. My father is—not with me." Marco nervously coughed, aware that a centurion's name would not please a Galilean. "If you have no work to offer me, I will find work in the city tomorrow and come back to pay you. I'll leave my horse and saddle with you to guarantee my return."

"Well, Marcus Clovius Longinus, can you clean out the stall and haul in fresh hay tonight? If so, and you do a satisfactory job, you may stay. My wife will set another plate at the table. All our children are grown and gone. She will enjoy having company."

"Thank you very much, Sir. What should I call you?"

"My name is Joseph Barsabas Justus, but I prefer to be called by my surname Justus."

"Everyone calls me Marco. I am very grateful to you, Justus." He slid out of the saddle and led Arrow through the gate, which Justus locked behind him.

"If I may ask, Marco, did you leave your good horse at home?"

Marco caught his amused tone and smiled. "Yes, I did. I have a black Friesian named Wingshadow. I would never risk her welfare on a trip like this. How did you know?"

"Just a hunch," said Justus with a smile. "I see this horse is well cared for, however. That speaks highly of you. Animals are God's creation and not to be mistreated. Even when we used to sacrifice animals to cover our sins, we were to do it as painlessly as possible."

"You speak of that in the past tense, Sir. Do you no longer sin?" Now Marco had an amused tone and Justus smiled.

"Unfortunately, we still sin, but we no longer need to sacrifice animals to atone for it. The final blood sacrifice has been shed. There can be no greater sacrifice than God's own blood."

"You speak of Yeshua, God's Son," said Marco. Absent-mindedly, he laid his hand over his heart where the purple sapphire rested.

Justus blinked at him in surprise. "I do. Are you a believer?"

"I am. My grandfather, who I am named after, is Marcus Claudius Cornelius. He and our family were baptized by Simon Peter."

"You are welcome here, Marco. Come. Let me introduce you to my wife, Elizabeth."

Marco wondered what Justus would do if he knew that his father was Yeshua's executioner, but he wasn't curious enough to find out. He did not want to jeopardize having a safe place for the night.

"I have to ask, Sir, if you don't mind telling me. Why did you accept my offer? Everyone else turned me away."

Justus looked Marco in the eye with a steady gaze. "I have heard of another who has eyes like yours. When you said you are believer, I knew. Centurion Longinus is your father. Yes?" Justus held the stable door open and stepped aside. "After you."

Marco stopped and stared. "Since you know who my father is, you must know that he was in charge of crucifying Yeshua. Why do you still offer me hospitality?"

"Because Yeshua had to be sacrificed. Someone had to do it. I also know what else your father did. He defended Peter when he was in custody at the Antonia and refused to deny Yeshua before King Herod. One should never consider half the story. Wouldn't you agree?"

"Yes, Sir. Thank you, Sir." Marco sighed with relief.

Justus gestured for Marco to take Arrow to the last stall. "Tend to your horse first. Clean out the old hay and replace it with fresh, then come into the house. Quickly now. Supper will be ready soon."

Marco took care of Arrow and cleared away the old straw in the stalls as fast as he could. Dispersing the fresh straw was the easier part of the job. When he finished and knocked on the door, a woman in her early sixties opened it. She was small and thin, but her large brown eyes spoke of quiet authority. She smiled and stepped back for him to enter. It was a modest home made of mudbrick reinforced with straw. The wooden furniture was plain, but well-made and sturdy. The interior walls were plastered and whitewashed, giving the house a clean look. The dirt floor was well swept and the cook fire was in the corner of the house to keep the smoke from escaping into the room.

"You must be Marco, the centurion's son," said the woman. "Please come in and join us. My name is Elizabeth." She gestured for him to enter.

Marco gratefully took a place at the table. Elizabeth filled a bowl with mutton and vegetable stew and set it in front of him, along with bread. She set a bowl of olive oil at the center of the table for dipping the bread, and set a cup filled with wine in front of him. Then she served her husband and set her own food out last.

Marco wanted to gulp the stew down since he was hungry but managed to maintain good table manners, to his mother's credit. In between mouthfuls of stew, he asked, "How do you know my father?"

"John, the son of Zebedee, told me about him," said Justus. "All of Yeshua's disciples know about your father. He said *'Truly, this was the Son of God!'* at Yeshua's crucifixion and it will never be forgotten. Neither will the conversion of your grandfather, Cornelius. We accepted that Yeshua was sacrificed for all people because of the belief of your family."

Marco stopped with the spoon midway to his mouth. He glanced at Elizabeth then back at Justus. "Does that mean my father and grandfather are famous?"

Justus smiled. "Famous? I suppose you could say that. The story of Longinus and Cornelius are told among all the believers. You are welcome to stay here as long as you are in Dora. Even though we will, most certainly, need to buy extra food at the marketplace." He looked at his wife with laugher in his eyes. "Please, continue your dinner. You were enjoying it most appreciatively."

Marco blushed, but spoke quickly to cover his embarrassment. "I know Yeshua had to die, but my father told us that he knew Yeshua was innocent when he executed him. He knew it, yet he did it anyway. How can you be so kind to me, knowing I am his son?"

"Do you think your father did this thing all by himself? Do you think that Centurion Longinus was the only man who killed the Son of God? Marco, every person in existence and yet to be born, killed Yeshua. Your father was chosen by God to carry out the sacrifice, but he did not take Yeshua's life. The final blood sacrifice was *given* by

Yeshua, not taken from him. Do you not know of all the other things your father did? He was God's instrument for many good works. I suspect that he still is."

Marco thought about this for a moment before he went back to the stew. "This mutton is very good, Elizabeth. I hope there's enough for all three of us."

Elizabeth laughed and winked at her husband. "It is a good thing we have raised five children, all with healthy appetites."

Marco smiled. Their amused banter eased his tension from the day's events. "Did you know Yeshua, personally? Did you ever talk to him?"

"I did. I knew him and all his disciples. I volunteered to replace Judas Iscariot after he betrayed our Lord. Two of us were nominated. We drew lots and the lots named Matthias. I was happy for Matthias. I knew that God had other tasks for me. When God shuts a door, another one will open. It is best to go through the door he opens rather than trying to force your way through one he has shut."

"How do you know if God has shut a door or if life is simply being complicated and confusing?" asked Marco.

"Is there a difference?" Justus countered.

"What do you mean?"

"All people are God's creation, subject to his will," explained Justus. "Therefore, God's bidding is always fulfilled, one way or the other. But if you set out on a mission that runs counter to God's plan, the way becomes murky and directionless. You will fail, but God never does. Evil is always vanquished, but sometimes it seems to take a long time for that to happen. The problem is our short lifespan and God's great patience. However, when one is doing God's will, there is no question, no doubt, the way is clear. That does not mean it is easy. No, it may be fraught with danger and suffering, but the way is clear. I take it you are on a mission?"

Marco nodded eagerly.

"Are you questioning your own motives?"

"Yes, I suppose I am. There have been difficulties. Someone even died because of my interference."

Justus and Elizabeth exchanged a grieved look. "I am sorry to hear that. That would certainly cause one to question if the mission is in accordance with God's will. There is a way to test your motives if you can be honest with yourself. If God truly puts the mission in your heart then your motive for following it will be your love for God above all else. Your mission will also be a demonstration of your love for humanity, your family, or a friend, a stranger, or even for a sick or injured animal. But your motive must be for love, not greed or lust of the flesh or lust for power. Love wants nothing in return; it is unselfish. If you crave a reward in this world, then your motive is corrupt."

"If my motive is selfish then I will fail. Dionysia will remain a slave far from her family," said Marco sadly.

"Not necessarily," interjected Justus. "God will use any servant he sees fit to use. The pharaoh of Egypt refused to let the Israelites leave. In turn, God revealed amazing and terrible signs of power throughout the land. Pharaoh's motives were corrupt, yet God's will was done. Judas Iscariot's motives were corrupt, yet God's will was done. Joseph's brothers had corrupt motives when they sold him into slavery, but as always, God's will was done. I could go on and on. The point is that God can use your mission to accomplish his will despite your motivation."

Marco stopped chewing. He swallowed and lowered his spoon. "Does that mean that even if I have some selfish reasons for going to Herculaneum, I could still be doing God's will?"

"Of course, but what are you hoping to gain from this mission of yours? Gratitude? Glory? Loyalty?" Justus waited for an answer.

Marco lowered his head. "Maybe all three."

"I admire your honesty, young man, along with your excellent Hebrew. Did your father teach you?" Justus asked.

Marco nodded. "He's a good teacher. I miss our lessons."

"Can you also read Hebrew?"

"No. Unfortunately, I did not excel at that. I can only read Latin and Greek. Father can speak and read four languages. His mother and her aunt, Misha, taught him well. He said learning languages was easy for him, like it was for his mother." Marco took another bite of stew, chewed slowly, and swallowed. "Maybe I have misunderstood God's plan for me. I tried to help a runaway slave once, and it turned out that he had murdered his master and a fellow slave. Father said I was foolish for not getting the facts first. I admit I reacted without thinking. What if I'm being foolish all over again? How can I know what to do?"

Justus thought for a moment. "Try this. Imagine that your mission is successful. You return home expecting to be praised, but instead, you are denounced. You are tossed into the night, alone. If you know that will be the result, despite your success, will you still do it?"

Marco sucked in a lungful of air. "I see your point. I must think about that. My Aunt Dionysia would be reunited with her brother, Nikolaus, and she would have her freedom. They were separated twenty-two years ago. The rest of their family died in a plague on board a ship. My grandfather adopted Nikolaus, so my father is his brother, but Dionysia is the only one left to Niko from his immediate family." Marco looked from Justus to Elizabeth. "Yes, I would still do it even if my family does not understand. I feel in my heart that it is the right thing to do."

"Then why have you come alone, Marco?" asked Elizabeth. "Why aren't your father and uncle with you?"

"Because they have given up on freeing Dionysia," Marco answered with passion. "Uncle Niko tried several times to buy his sister's slavery contract, but she wouldn't leave her children. They are grown now. Uncle Niko said they are married and living in Rome."

"Surely, with the children gone, your uncle could once again make an offer to buy her freedom. Have you considered that there may be other reasons she stayed?" Justus asked.

"No, because it doesn't matter," declared Marco firmly. "I am sure that I am supposed to do this, and I pray that God will show me the way. A plan will reveal itself. I'm sure of it. Didn't God tell Abram to 'Go to the land that I will show you?' God didn't even tell him where that would be. God said start walking in that direction and I'll tell you when to stop. Right?"

"Yes, you described it pretty well," said Justus.

"That's what I'm doing. I'm going in a certain direction, at a certain time, and will do certain things when I get there. I just don't know what those things will be yet."

"It sounds like you are acting on faith."

"Yes, but faith in whom? In God? Or myself?"

"That is a question only you can answer, Marco. However, the fact that you're even asking the question is a good sign. You recognize that there may be ulterior motives in your heart. That is only honest, not evil. Perhaps only the delusional man thinks all of his motives are pure."

"Perhaps. I hope I am doing this for the right reason, because, as I said, it has already cost one life. Calais didn't deserve to be deceived to the point of taking his own life, but that's what happened. I thought I was going to help him. Instead, I set a series of events into motion that led to his suicide. I might as well have killed him myself." Marco bowed his head.

"We are sorry to hear about your friend," said Elizabeth.

"Thank you. And thank you for taking me in. I should go on out to the stables." Marco got up to leave.

Justus pointed toward the ceiling. "Take a mat up to the roof. Why sleep in a smelly stable when you can sleep under the stars? The stairs are around back."

Marco thanked them again, picked up his knapsack, and went to the door. He climbed the outside stairs to the roof and sat down cross-legged on the mat. Justus had given him much to think about. He pulled a blanket from his knapsack and made the knapsack into a pillow. Marco lay back on the mat and gazed at the black field of sky dusted with starlight. The stars, always coy in the presence of the moon, sparkled brilliantly in the absence of moonlight.

Marco wondered how far he would have to fly to see a star up close. "Probably a hundred times the distance from here to Rome," he told the night. "Maybe even a thousand. What makes you burn so bright, starry night? I bet Aquila figures it out some day."

Saying his brother's name out loud made him think about Calais. If only he had not given him the poison until it was time to use it. He still would have mistaken Aquila for Marco. "But you wouldn't have had the means to kill yourself," he whispered aloud. Anger burned in his heart to think how easily Aquila deceived Calais, without one thought of the consequences.

Marco tried again to think of some way to convince Decimus to let Dionysia go, but was too tired to stay awake. He was sleeping soundly until a noise from the stairs woke him. Something had hit the mudbrick stairs and shattered. Marco sat up and looked around. He crept over to the side of the house and peered into the darkness. He went halfway down the stairs and stepped on a piece of broken ceramic. He crouched down and felt around on the steps. There were more pieces. He hurried back to the roof and gazed about the area, trying to see if anyone was around. The door of the house across the street opened slightly and someone held up a lamp. The light revealed a shadowy figure crouched next to the door.

"Behind you!" called out Marco as he pointed. "There's a man!"

The neighbor flung the door open and stepped out into the street." What? I can't hear you."

Marco pointed again into the now darkened area behind the door. "Someone's behind you!" The man turned around and held the lamp higher. No one was there. Not wanting to take any chances, the neighbor scurried back into his house and slammed the door shut. There was a chilling sound of laughter from out of the darkness.

Marco's heart was racing. Was that Calais? He shuddered at the thought. "It can't be," he whispered to himself. "A drunken idiot threw his empty wine jug. That's all." He returned to his mat after he scanned the empty, dark streets.

Marco stared wide-eyed into the night but finally went back to sleep. He awoke just as the eastern sky was surrendering its darkness to the sun. He stretched and stood up. Then he remembered the broken pot and walked over to the stairs. The pieces of ceramic pot were gone. Marco felt his mouth go dry. He knew he had not imagined picking up a broken piece. Why would a drunken man retrieve the broken pottery? He hurried down the stairs and knocked on the door. Elizabeth called out for him to enter.

"Did you sleep well, Marco?" she asked as she prepared breakfast.

"Yes, but someone threw a jug at the stairs last night. Did you pick up the pieces?"

She blinked at him in confusion. "Justus, did you see a broken jug on the stairs?" she asked as her husband entered from the front door.

"No. Why, what happened?"

"Nothing. I must have been dreaming." Marco licked his lips nervously. He avoided Elizabeth's searching gaze. She frowned with doubt but turned back to her task. Justus gestured at a chair and invited Marco to sit.

"I've been thinking about your horse, Marco. You can stay here as long as it takes you to find passage on a ship, and when you do, you can leave your horse. I could use a pack animal and I promise he will be well treated. If you should come back this way, the horse and the saddle are yours for the taking. In the meantime, I'll use him until you return. What do you say?"

"That would be great, Sir. I would appreciate it. I've been wondering what would happen to Arrow. He's a good companion. He's slow, but dependable. I have only one condition. You keep the saddle."

Justus grinned. "It's a deal. After breakfast, I will go to the dock with you and see if we can find a ship captain you can trust."

Chapter 15

A Pursuit, a Frightening Figure, and a Disappearance

———❦———

T he next morning, Justus and Marco found a ship being loaded with kegs of olive oil, bound for Myra, the Roman capital of Lycia. Marco was disappointed that it wasn't sailing for Herculaneum, but Myra was on the way. The trip would take about seven days, and the ship would be ready to set sail in the morning. The ship's captain, a Greek named Cletus, was impressed with Marco's language skills in Hebrew and Greek. Cletus hated Latin so he hired as many Greeks as he could find. Marco, as a Roman, was a bonus since he was sailing for one of Rome's capitals. The captain offered him the clerk's job. Manifests, wage and expense sheets, and a daily log needed to be maintained. Marco's wages were agreed upon over a handshake and he and Justus started down the gangplank to leave.

Marco stopped in his tracks. He quickly turned his back to the dock and bit his lower lip. Justus looked over his shoulder and saw three men on horseback. Two coal-black stallions with muscled chests and thick flowing manes were on either side of a golden-sheened horse with black mane and tail. Justus didn't need to ask who they were. It looked like Marco was riding one of the black horses. Justus frowned and gave his head a slight shake as if to clear his vision.

"We look perfectly alike, don't we?" Marco said. "Have they seen me?"

Justus took a few moments to answer. "No, they have moved down the pier. You never mentioned you have a twin."

Marco let out a sigh of relief and ignored Justus's comment. "I can't let them find me. I'm through trying to get my father to understand why I have to do this."

Justus pursed his lips and shrugged. "You're of age now, a grown man. You have the right to make your own decisions, but are you sure it's best to not make contact? Perhaps he's changed his mind and wants to help."

"No, I need to do this on my own. Besides, I can't risk the chance that he's here to make me go home." The two men hurried across the dock to a side street. They took alleys; Marco peered around corners before stepping out into the open. He didn't relax until they were safely back in Justus's courtyard.

Marco went to the stable to check on Arrow. Adan had taught his children to talk to animals as if they understood every word. Adan instructed them, "Animals relax when you talk to them. They don't answer with words, but they do reveal their emotions. You have to pay attention to their different sounds, the positions of their ears, and even when they're swishing their tails. Hard, quick tail switching means the horse is angry, but if they swish the tail slowly, they're just trying to swat a fly. You have to pay attention or you could get hurt, usually by getting in the way."

Marco had taken the lesson to heart, even though Aquila thought it was silly to talk to Nighthawk. Marco noticed that Wingshadow would perk her ears forward and nicker a deep-throated welcome whenever she heard his voice, but paid no attention to Aquila. Marco stood in front of Arrow and placed his hands on the sides of the horse's head. Arrow blinked at him and turned his ears to face the young man.

"I can't take you with me, Arrow. I'm going on a ship, but you'll be safe here with Justus and Elizabeth. They will take good care of you. I'll come back for you." The horse let out a loud exhale and nickered, a low resonating sound of contentment. Marco rubbed Arrow's forehead. The horse blinked at him and lowered his head for a mouthful of hay. Marco found a brush and got to work. Arrow occasionally made contended grunts as he ate. It was half-an-hour before he left Arrow and went into the house.

Adan, Nikolaus, and Aquila road along the pier, hoping to catch sight of Marco or find someone who had seen him. A few of the ship captains remembered talking to Marco but did not know where he had gone after turning him away. One captain took a close look at Aquila and accused them of wasting his time with their "stupid joke." Obviously, he had talked with Marco.

"I think we need to come up with a better plan," said Adan. "Instead of trying to find him here, we should go back to Caesarea, leave the horses, and book passage on a ship for Herculaneum."

"Makes sense to me," said Nikolaus. "Pitio is going to stay and help Titus with the inn, and Gnaeus is going to take care of the flour mill. My assistants will manage the wine shops for the three to four months we'll be gone. What did your commander say?"

"I haven't taken leave in years," said Adan. "He said the decurions would probably appreciate a break from my training for a few months."

Nikolaus snorted. "Doesn't he know how well you make up for lost time? They will be sorry you were ever gone."

Adan laughed. "It was the wedding cake, right? I doubled our sparring sessions the next day after giving you that second piece of cake and you *still* remember that? It was one day."

Nikolaus laughed and shrugged his shoulders. "It was really good cake."

"Father, perhaps you and Uncle Niko can go back to Caesarea," suggested Aquila. "I'll find Marco and bring him home."

"No, I'm not going to try to bring him home," said Adan. "We have passage out of Caesarea tomorrow. I made tentative plans with the captain of the *Pegasus* in case we didn't find Marco here. Like you pointed out before, there will be no question who we're looking for if I have you with me. We don't need any false leads. I just want to shadow him in case he needs help."

Aquila made a disgruntled face. "How will you know if he needs help? Marco doesn't even know when he needs help." Adan gave him a sour look but didn't comment. They turned down a street of shops and wine bars on their way out of town. They scanned the townspeople and street venders. Still, no sign of Marco.

"Father, here's a bakery," said Aquila. "Is it all right if we buy some bread?" Adan reined in Blackfire. Aquila slid from the saddle and entered the shop. When he came out with a loaf under his arm, he saw that his father and uncle had ridden down the street, talking with merchants as they went. He walked over to Nighthawk and took the reins instead of climbing into the saddle. He led the horse to an alleyway and paused to watch the people as they conducted business.

An odd sensation made the back of his neck crawl. The feeling that someone was intently watching him was unmistakable. Aquila looked up and down the street. No one seemed to notice him. He whirled around and looked down the alley. At the far end, leaning against a courtyard wall, stood the figure of a young man. His features were in shadow. He was wearing a shabby tunic and sandals but was missing a belt. Aquila did not hail him or move, but only returned his unwavering stare. Angered at the rudeness of the stranger, Aquila started to walk toward him.

Aquila called out less than five paces from the figure, "*Ohe,* are you that slave that tried to kill yourself? It's not my fault, you know."

Aquila stepped closer and the young man slipped around the corner of the wall. Aquila rushed to the end of the alley and turned the corner. There he was, walking away. Aquila grabbed his shoulder and spun him around.

"What do you want?" demanded the boy, his brown eyes wide with alarm.

"*Ohe!* Where did that slave go?" exclaimed Aquila.

"What slave?" asked the perplexed youth.

"A young man, dark hair, green eyes, dressed like you." Aquila glanced at the boy's belt. "Except he wasn't wearing a belt. Sorry. My mistake." He swallowed hard and turned back into the alley. He walked to Nighthawk and hoisted himself into the saddle. He glanced back down the alley. No one was there.

"Aquila! Come on!" called Adan from farther up the street.

Aquila frowned and tried to dismiss the sickening feeling tightening his throat. As he neared his father, he muttered to himself, "Impossible. I don't believe it."

"Don't believe what?" asked Adan looking back at his son.

"Nothing, Father." Aquila's thoughts whirled. Had a ghost lured him into that alley?

Adan frowned at the odd look on his son's face but dismissed it.

During the ride back home, Aquila kept scanning the terrain and looking over his shoulder. Nikolaus finally asked him why he was so nervous, but Aquila only mumbled a vague answer. As the distance from Dora increased, Aquila became more and more convinced that he had imagined the encounter with Calais. Surely the stress of Marco running off again and feeling guilty for it was getting to him. When they reined their horses in at the top of the cliff road, Aquila felt relieved enough to laugh at himself for being so easily frightened.

He decided the trip to Rome would be good. He would have his father and uncle to himself without Marco competing for attention. Getting to see Grandfather Aquila would be an added bonus. Maybe the two of them would have time to try a few of the experiments they had designed together by way of letters. Maybe it wasn't so bad, after all, that Marco had run off without him.

Chapter 16

Sailing to Myra, a Scapegoat, and a Prisoner

Marco awoke early, too early. There had been no noise of shattering pottery or even someone shouting or slamming a door. He simply couldn't sleep any longer. Marco rolled onto his back and looked up at the stars. Judging by the positions of the constellations, it was about three hours before sunrise. He wondered how the stars stayed in place. How do they hold onto their patterns? Why did the planets move among the constellations but never stray from an east to west path? The wandering dots of light, the planets, changed positions over the weeks and months at different speeds, some quickly, others much slower.

Dulcibella and Adan had taught their children the names of the constellations and how to know the hours of the night by their positions. Marco liked the way some of the constellations looked like their names—Orion a man, Leo a lion, Scorpio a scorpion, and Draco a dragon with a twisting tail. Marco loved to gaze at the dusty path of diffused light that spanned the sky, especially when there was no moonlight.

The family enjoyed the nights they lay out on the roof of the villa, watching for the stars that would disappear after streaking across the black expanse of the heavens. Most enchanting of all were the rare times when one would burn for many seconds until it separated into two or three streaks of light. Sometimes they would change from yellow to orange, and even green as they neared the horizon.

One time a falling star, which was the brightest and lasted the longest they had ever seen, made a hissing sound as it burned across the sky. All of them had gasped at the thrill of such a rare event. Marco would never forget it or what Longina said when the star disappeared. She said, "Maybe that was an angel falling from heaven." Aquila scoffed at her idea and declared, "Or maybe it was a star that burned up. There's so many, it won't be missed." Always the optimist, Dulcibella ended the speculation by saying, "Whichever it is, perhaps God will make more."

Marco smiled to think of those nights. The treasured memories caused him to think, for the hundredth time, of how he would convince Decimus to let Dionysia leave. "Of course!" he said aloud. "I don't need to convince him. What I need to do is make him *want* her to leave." He sat up with excitement. People who became infected with leprosy were banished. That's it, he thought. "I just have to make Decimus think Dionysia has leprosy; he will be begging me to take her as far away from him as possible." Aquila would know how to fake the initial symptoms of the disease. Marco slumped back to the mat. Aquila would probably refuse to help even if they were together. "Maybe I can figure this out for myself."

With a working plan finally fixed in his mind, Marco slept the rest of the night. When morning greeted him, he was refreshed and eager to get to the dock. He went to the stables first. "Arrow, I want you to be a brave horse," he said as he ran his hand down the old horse's neck. Arrow shifted his weight and snorted. "You'll be fine here with Justus, and you won't have to work hard for your hay. I will keep my promise and come back for you." Marco left the stables allowing Arrow to eat his hay in peace.

"Ah, there you are," said Elizabeth as she set three plates on the table. "We will miss you, Marco. We wish you well on your quest to find your aunt."

"Thank you, Elizabeth. It was good staying with you and Justus. And thank you for keeping Arrow for me. He's old and slow but reliable."

After breakfast, Marco collected his knapsack and bade farewell to his new friends. He walked to where the ship was docked, and Captain Cletus signaled for him to come aboard.

"We'll cast off soon," the captain said. "You can stow your knapsack in the guest quarters since we have no passengers for this voyage. The cost will come out of your pay, unless you'd rather bunk with the crew."

"No," said Marco, "I'll take the guest quarters if someone will show me the way."

The crew finished loading the cargo, and the captain made his final check before casting off. Marco stood in the bow of the ship with the wind running gentle fingers through his hair and breathed a great sigh of relief. He was finally on his way. He glanced over his shoulder when a crewman shouted to someone. A solitary figure on the dock stood watching the departing ship. His dark hair framed his handsome face. He was wearing a ragged tunic without a belt. Frowning, Marco walked to the stern of the ship as he stared at the young man who remained silent and still. Marco remembered that the figure on the road to Dora was dressed the same, but his features had been in shadow. A crewman walked in front of Marco, momentarily blocking his view. When the sailor passed by, Marco searched for the figure but he was gone.

"Three times I have seen you, Calais," Marco muttered. "Three times you have disappeared. Are you alive, or is my guilty conscience tormenting me? Or are you—a ghost?"

"Did you say ghost?" exclaimed Captain Cletus who had walked up behind Marco. "Are you seeing one now? You have endangered us if you have brought a spirit of the dead onboard. If something bad happens, I will not hesitate to throw you into the sea. The ghost will follow you to the depths and leave us in peace. The sea is dangerous enough without being trapped in a haunted ship." Cletus pointed toward the shore. "Swim if you can. Leave if you have brought Death on my ship." Without waiting for a response, the captain resumed barking orders at his men as they unfurled the main sail. He glanced furtively at Marco with narrowed eyes. Marco grasped the sapphire under his tunic. Its presence reminded him of his mission and gave him assurance.

Marco knew the word from the captain would spread quickly among the crew that he may be a bad omen. Sailors were just as superstitious as soldiers when it came to survival. Sudden storms seemed to have no natural cause except to punish bad behavior of those on the ship. He knew he might be in real danger if even one crewman accused him of having an evil influence. Someone could cause a problem and lay the blame on the "wolf-eyed Roman who sees ghosts." There would be no defense for Marco. He would be tossed into the sea. The ghost of Calais could appear right in front of his face, and Marco would have to pretend nothing was there.

The other possibility was just as threatening. What if Calais had survived the effects of the poison and was determined to extract revenge? He had not witnessed Calais's cremation, and there was no way for him to know if Serapio had, as planned. Calais knew the details of his plan to free Dionysia and could easily follow him. Hadn't someone, or something, who looked like Calais done just that so far? If Calais really was alive, Marco had to convince him that it was Aquila who had feigned ignorance of their plan. To do that, Marco would have to confront Calais face to face, leaving himself open to attack.

Whether Calais was alive or not, the possibility for disaster was high. Once the captain overheard Marco talking about a ghost; he had set himself up as the scapegoat for any misadventure. It was common knowledge among sailors that someone had to be sacrificed to the waves when things went badly. He remembered Philip had told them the story of Jonas and the big fish, probably a whale shark, that had swallowed him when the crew tossed him into the sea. As soon as Jonas was gone, the storm threatening the ship subsided. Marco wondered if God would send a big fish to save him if the crew sacrificed him to the sea.

The first four days were uneventful. Marco began to relax, especially since no one appeared anywhere on the ship who looked remotely like Calais. However, on the fifth day, the wind began to confound the sail and the oarsmen had to work extra hard. They veered off course toward Cyprus to take advantage of its sheltering effect. This calmed the crewmen's nerves and the captain's temper, but caused the ship to make port in Myra a day past their schedule.

The captain approached Marco. "I do not ever want to see you on the decks of my ship again. If it had not been for the shores of Cypress protecting us, I would have tossed you to the waves. Here are your wages. Now go."

The few coins Cletus dropped in Marco's hand were only a fraction of his earnings, but he started to leave without argument. Then he thought of his mission and how his success depended on having enough money to get to Herculaneum. He needed the money for Dionysia.

Marco turned around and faced the captain. "I should tell you that the spirit I saw was that of a Greek slave who took his own life. He swore an oath to me before he died. An oath of loyalty and obedience. He upholds it to this day." Marco looked at the pitiful number of coins in his hand. "Are you sure you don't want to honor our agreement? You owe me eleven *denarii*."

The captain made a surly face. "Begone with you!"

"Fine." Marco raised his hands. "*Ca-la-isss!* I call upon you to attach yourself to this man." He pointed at the captain. "Spoil his bread with your ghostly touch. Pull the blankets off him as he sleeps. Run your fingernails down the boards of these cursed decks until the screech summons the dead from the depths of the sea. *Calais—I summon you!*"

"*Enough!*" The captain tried to dig into his coin pouch with trembling fingers. When he couldn't get it open, he unbuckled his belt and jerked the pouch away. "Here! Take the whole thing and *get off my ship!*" He threw the pouch at Marco.

It hit the deck with a loud jingle. Marco scooped it up. He opened the pouch, counted out eleven *denarii,* and dropped them in his own coin pouch. He set the captain's coin pouch back onto the deck, hefted his knapsack over a shoulder, and strolled off the ship.

He couldn't believe his playacting worked. When he was out of earshot, he laughed out loud in amazement, having never done such a thing. Aquila was the one who could playact any role. "Brother, you would have been proud of me." He whispered to himself.

Marco dodged among the dock workers and stacks of cargo but paused for one last look at the ship. He almost expected to see Calais standing there, shaking a disapproving finger at him, but he wasn't. Marco breathed a sigh of relief.

After a few rebuffs from shop owners, Marco found a seaside café that needed a dishwasher and accepted the job. He would work for his meals and a mat in the corner of the kitchen at night until he could find a ship going to Italy. After a week of trudging up and down the docks asking for work, Marco was getting discouraged. Some of the captains waved him off while others refused to speak with him. One man threatened to have him arrested. One particularly excitable man looked Marco in the eye and backed away muttering incantations of protection from the evil eye.

Marco decided to give the city of Myra one more week. If he still couldn't find a ship, he would travel westward to Patara and try there. First thing every morning before work, Marco wandered out on the dock to see if any new ships had come in during the night. A ship from Caesarea was just entering the harbor. He watched as the crewmen began to unload its cargo. A centurion came from below deck leading several men in chains. A man who kept with the prisoners, but was not in chains, left the ship with the centurion. The escort soldiers followed behind.

Marco looked at the man walking next to the centurion more closely. "Paul!" he called out. "Paul of Tarsus, is that you?"

"Ah, if it's not my friend Marco, then I'm imagining things," cried Paul.

Marco hurried to approach his friend, but the centurion blocked his way. "Halt! What business do you have with this man?"

"Centurion Julius, I know this young man," said Paul. "In fact, you may know of his father, Centurion Adan Clovius Longinus, the man King Herod tried to execute, but he survived."

Centurion Julius turned his attention on Marco. "Survived? No! You mean he came back from the dead. They say he is a werewolf. I can see why if his father has the same eyes."

Paul chuckled and slapped a hand on Marco's shoulder. "I assure you Longinus is no werewolf and neither are his sons. What are you doing here, Marco? The last time I saw you in Jerusalem you were seeking a quest. Are you still?"

"I am, Sir, only now I know what I am to do. I have to get to Herculaneum."

"I am on my way to Rome to see Caesar," said Paul. "You can travel with us when Centurion Julius finds a ship. I'm sure you can make yourself useful to pay for your passage." Marco hoped Paul was right.

Centurion Julius found an Alexandrian ship sailing for Italy. He asked the captain, a man named Gratian, if he needed a ship's clerk. Captain Gratian didn't even hesitate when he learned that Marco was fluent in Greek. The owner of his ship demanded detailed logs to be kept in Greek and Latin, a job the captain found tedious and unnecessary. He hired Marco on the spot. Marco ran back to the café to get his knapsack and joined Paul on the dock as they waited to board.

After sacks of wheat, flagons of wine, and precious sacks of salt were loaded onto the ship, the prisoners were confined in the hold. Only Paul could remain at liberty. Centurion Julius knew Paul would not try to escape since he had requested an audience with Caesar. Paul saw his request as an opportunity and faced it with anticipation. King Agrippa had proclaimed to Governor Porcius Festus, "*This man might have been set free if he had not appealed to Caesar.*"

Centurion Julius allowed Paul to visit friends in Sidon, an unprecedented show of faith since Julius would have been executed if Paul had not returned. However, Julius did not make the decision solely on faith. A story circulated among the soldiers about Paul and Silas Silvanus when they were prisoners in Philippi. A great earthquake shook the foundations of the prison and *immediately all the doors were opened and everyone's shackles were loosened.* The jailer awoke to the sight of open doors, and drew his sword to kill himself, *supposing that the prisoners had escaped. But Paul shouted, "Do not harm yourself, for we are all here."* After that, centurions eagerly volunteered to oversee Paul. Escorting him offered an easily earned bonus and pleasant companionship. After all, it wasn't only Paul and Silas who remained in the prison by choice. Paul convinced all the prisoners to stay in their cells causing the apostle to be highly respected among the Roman soldiers.

Paul pointed to the bow of the ship and laughed. "Do you see that, Marco? This ship is called *Margarita,* the Latin word for pearl. It is the largest cargo ship I have ever seen.

It must be close to one hundred cubits, if not more. Much gold was spent to build this ship, and many trees felled. *Margarita* is a ship of great price."

"Yes, like the pearl of great price. I hope it is one of great safety as well," said Marco. He reached for the front of his tunic to feel the shape of the sapphire under the cloth. He knew a pearl was a vast treasure compared to his common sapphire, but its presence was reassuring. He scanned the dock for any semblance of Calais as the ship pulled out of port. When he saw that no solitary figure stood staring after him, he let out a sigh of relief. He chided himself for being foolish. Marco knew that nothing could go wrong now. Surely, he would be under God's protection since he was traveling with Paul, one of God's great servants.

Chapter 17

The *Pegasus*, Simon, and Sharks

⸻

Marcus and Dulcibella rode to the wharf in Caesarea with Adan, Nikolaus, and Aquila to bid them farewell the next morning. Marcus had tried to talk Adan into taking a few escort soldiers with them, but he thought it was unnecessary. The ship they had booked passage on was sailing straight for the Italian coast and should take about a month with smooth sailing. After Marcus prayed for protection for the family and their safe return, they exchanged bittersweet hugs.

Dulcibella gazed into Adan's eyes. "Bring our sons home, my love."

"I will say the same thing I said to Marina when she made me promise to bring Niko home. I would rather face a raging tiger than the wrath of a woman. I promise; I will bring everyone home." They kissed one more time before the three men walked up the gangplank to board the ship. Marcus gathered the reins of Blackfire, Inventio, and Nighthawk as they waved goodbye. Dulcibella leaned against her father as he put a protective hand on her shoulder.

Marcus kissed the top of her head. "Don't worry, Bella. I've never known Adan to break a promise."

"No, he hasn't. Not intentionally. But the world is a dangerous place," she said pensively.

The oarsmen heaved to and the ship made its way out of port. The mainsail invited the wind for a chat and the ship set her sights on the horizon. A sea breeze ruffled their hair. The rolling motion of the deck was subdued as the ship glided through the dips and peaks of the dark water of the Mediterranean. The sky presented a scattering of fluffy clouds that looked like clumps of cotton floating on a field of pale blue. Shadows would race across the deck as the clouds occasionally obscured the sun.

Adan, Aquila, and Nikolaus were welcomed aboard by the captain and escorted to the guest quarters. They were on the upper deck when the only other passenger found them and introduced himself. He was a stout man of average height in his late fifty's. He had a gray beard and thick, gray-streaked, dark hair which he was proud of, considering many men were bald at his age. He wore his hair as if it was a crown of honor.

"Ah, traveling companions, how pleasant," called out the man as he approached the trio. "My name is Simon Magus of Gitta." He shook hands with them. "Of whom do I have the pleasure?"

"I am Centurion Adan Clovius Longinus. This is my son, Aquila, and my brother, Nikolaus. We are pleased to meet you, Simon."

"What, if I may be so bold, is the purpose of your journey? I, myself am traveling to the gem of the Roman Empire, the city of Pompeii. I have recently inherited property there. It is a lovely city, full of amazing architecture and beautiful frescos. However, one cannot ignore the vulgar advertisements for the brothels. You do not find such vulgarity in Samaria or Judea. But everyone knows Romans tend to be of a carnal nature. Yes?" Simon sniffed as if an offensive odor had reached his senses. "To the credit of the city, Pompeii offers benefits even for the pious. There is a cafe on every street corner offering the most lavish food and delicious wines." He fingered the many gold chains he wore around his neck as he talked.

Adan noticed that Simon had not allowed them to answer his question so he didn't have to come up with a cover story. He wasn't prepared to tell a stranger that he was following his wayward son. Nikolaus noticed that a gold, stylized fish hung from one of the chains.

"That is an interesting talisman you have there, Simon," said Nikolaus. "Does it have special meaning for you?"

"It does. It surely does," the man chuckled. "It is the symbol of the Way. Have you heard of it? We are a sect that follows the teachings of our Messiah, the great Yeshua of Nazareth. Well, we once thought he was from Nazareth. We now know that he was born in Bethlehem, just as the prophets foretold. You might have also heard of me. I am known throughout the land of Samaria, as Simon the *Magus*."

"Simon the Magician?" asked Aquila.

"I prefer Simon the Sorcerer, if you're referring to my great skills." The man beamed at Aquila. "But I am most pleased that you have heard of me."

"But I haven't. Heard of you, that is," answered Aquila. "I was only restating your title,"

Simon looked a bit dismayed at Aquila's unfriendly expression but continued. "I assure you; I am quite famous in the whole province of Samaria. No doubt, there are stories of my great abilities throughout Judea, and perhaps beyond."

Nikolaus and Aquila wanted to move out of earshot, annoyed at the man's boasting, but Adan was curious. "So, tell me, Simon. What is so special about this Yeshua of Bethlehem you speak of?" Adan ignored the startled glances of Nikolaus and Aquila.

The breeze fluttered the man's beard. He smoothed it with a bejeweled hand. "I wouldn't expect someone of your race to even ask about such a thing. You are a Gentile after all, and unclean. But since we will be traveling companions for the coming weeks,

I will indulge your curiosity. I met a man named Philip who convinced me that Yeshua was a great man of God with a special message for the people. I believed and was baptized into the Way. I saw the miracles and signs that Philip and other followers of the Way could do. I could also do great signs and wonders. Yes, very great, spectacular wonders in fact; but I admired these men, nonetheless. Then two men came from Jerusalem and joined us. Philip is a bit too meek in my opinion, and he allowed these two men, who were quite self-righteous and pompous, I might add, to basically usurp his authority."

"Really? That must have been quite annoying," said Adan.

"Very annoying, yes. Very intrusive, I should add."

"What were their names?" asked Nikolaus.

"Simon, like my name. He was surnamed Peter. His friend was named John, the son of Zebedee. They treated me harshly, which was quite unfair to someone of my stature. But Yeshua, our Lord and Savior, will set them straight when we all gather before the great throne of God. He will rebuke them as they rebuked me, you mark my words."

"What do you mean?" asked Adan.

"They have this gift of 'laying on of hands' and giving to the believer the Holy Spirit of God. Yes, it is quite real, I assure you. I see by your expression that you must have heard of it, since you're not surprised. I only wanted to join with them in the giving of the Spirit, but they rebuked me for my wish to serve God."

"For wanting to serve God?" asked Aquila with a suspicious tone.

"For that very thing," said Simon with another sniff. He ignored Aquila's sarcasm.

Adan kept his expression neutral. "I have heard of Simon Peter and John of whom you speak. I wouldn't think they would rebuke a true believer." Nikolaus caught Adan's eye and gave him a what-are-you-doing look. Adan pretended not to see.

"Ah, you doubt my word, Centurion. You should be ashamed since I am a great man of God. I would never let a single lie escape my lips. Trust me. I never lie."

Aquila snorted and started to turn away. Adan held up a hand. "I don't mean to doubt you. Please, continue with your story."

"If you insist," Simon eagerly continued. "I offered them a donation, a substantial donation, I might add, and they rebuked me for my generosity. Can you believe it? I made this offer because of my great love for God and they rejected it."

"You offered them money?" asked Aquila frowning.

Adan gave Aquila a warning look before he spoke, "That is truly disgraceful of those two men. Surely, in offering this substantial donation, you did not expect anything in return."

Simon blinked at him in surprise. "When you give something to someone, it is only polite to receive some type of compensation in return. I'm sure you agree. I saw the power they had, and I thought they would want to share it with me. The more workers you have, the more work is done, don't you think? So, I said, '*Give me this power also, that anyone on whom I lay hands may receive the Holy Spirit.*' But Peter said to me, '*Your money perish with you, because you thought that the gift of God could be purchased with money!* Then he denounced me before all of them saying, '*your heart is not right in the sight of God.*' I was too shocked to argue, and frankly, very embarrassed, very, very embarrassed. Then this Peter fellow said that they were mere humans and could not grant a gift that could only come from God. He said my offer to pay them spoke of a corrupt heart. How could a so-called man of God be so ignorant? Who else would I pay the money to? It's not as if I could hold up my gold to the sky and ask God to take it from my hand. Yes, I offered them gold. I can see by your expressions that you are impressed with my generosity."

"Wait." Adan held up a hand. "Did you offer to buy the ability to bestow the Holy Spirit on people?"

Simon started to speak but paused. He shifted his gaze to avoid eye contact. "My dear centurion, it is a matter of semantics, simple wording." He licked his lips and continued. "The truth is that after Peter's outburst, they were all staring at me as if I had done something really terrible. I could have defended myself easily, but to my credit, I refrained. What good would it have done since the other men were quite intimidated by this Peter fellow? Therefore, I apologized and begged them to pray that none of the awful things Peter predicted would happen to me. He basically cursed me as if I didn't have the purest of hearts, which I do."

"You didn't ask them to pray for you to have a change of heart?" asked Aquila.

"Change of heart? Mine? Why would I do that? As I said, my heart is pure because I only want to serve God and the Christ. Those two hypocrites need the change of heart. Just think what God could have done with my generous donation, and they rejected it! It was quite a relief when they returned to Jerusalem. Philip left as well. I was free to pursue my own interests."

"What interests would those be?" asked Adan. Aquila rolled his eyes and turned his back.

"God has been very, very good to me," assured Simon. "As I went about Samaria performing more wonders than those people have ever seen, they lavished money and offers of hospitality upon me. I, of course, express gratitude when I am given donations, unlike those two from Jerusalem. I went from town to town, revealing the great wonders of God by using my magic. The gratitude of the people was shown in such abundance, I have become a rich man, spectacularly rich, abundantly rich. Which is good since I'm sure I will need to renovate the property I have inherited to fit my taste. It has a lavish villa and the most extensive vineyards you have ever seen. The land surrounding the slopes of the mountain has the most fertile vineyards in the entire Roman Empire, maybe in the entire world."

Aquila flashed a toothy smile, but his expression was scornful. "The grapes are the size of pomegranates, right?"

This time, Simon reacted to Aquila's biting tone. "Either you jest or you're quite ignorant. Grapes cannot possibly grow that large. I imagine none of you knows how to tend vineyards and produce fine wine," said Simon with a tongue click of disapproval. A corner of Adan's mouth curved up with the irony of Simon's statement considering his father's vineyards.

Nikolaus asked him for details about his villa while Aquila turned and faced his father. He whispered in Egyptian, which Simon was not likely to understand. "How can you stand here and listen to this tripe? The man is a fraud and a pompous fool."

"Perhaps, but we should not judge him," Adan answered, also in Egyptian.

"So, we stand here and act like we believe every word? Isn't that the same as condoning the way he is slandering Peter and John? Don't we have a responsibility to the truth? They're your friends, Father. Simon Peter healed you, twice! John taught you everything he knows about Yeshua. Aren't you going to stand up for them?"

"Peter and John do not need anyone standing up for them. However, you do make a good point about our responsibility to the truth. What if I let Simon trap himself in his own words? Would you be satisfied with that?"

Aquila grinned. "Maybe. How will you do it?"

A knowing grin graced Adan's face. "Simon, I'm sorry, I was just reminded by my son about an incident that occurred some years past. You say you follow a man named Yeshua from Nazareth. What are his teachings?"

"Yes, he was a great teacher, but more importantly, he is the Messiah. He was the final blood sacrifice that established the new covenant God made with his people. You would be wise to believe in the Messiah, Centurion. I can see that you are lost, without purpose or real power. Let me teach you the Way. I would only ask for a small donation in return for my services." Simon held up a finger. "As it is written; one should not muzzle the ox as it grinds the grain. The worker is worthy of his wages. We have the entire voyage ahead of us, which is plenty of time."

"Tell me about this new Covenant. What is the purpose of it?" asked Adan.

"The forgiveness of all sin. That is the purpose. Without the shedding of blood, there can be no forgiveness. Yeshua shed his blood for the forgiveness of all sin, of all believers, from now until the end of the age."

"For all believers? Including you? Yeshua's sacrifice covered your sins as well?"

"Of course. I am pure now. I am without sin because Yeshua took my sin upon himself." Simon beamed at the three men. "Aren't my riches proof enough of God's favor with me?"

Adan ignored his question. "So Yeshua's death took away your sin?"

"His death and resurrection, Centurion. Let's not leave out the resurrection."

"Ah, *that* Yeshua," exclaimed Adan. "The one, rumor had it, who came back from the dead days after he was crucified?"

"It was no rumor, Centurion! Do not doubt my words. I assure you, Yeshua was dead, very dead and he arose from the grave Sunday morning. I see by your expression of scorn that you do not believe me. But why should you believe in God's infinite power? You're a pagan."

"I heard that he didn't actually die on the cross," said Aquila with a sidelong glance at Adan. "That he only passed out and his followers revived him."

"Lies and deception! No, no, Yeshua was quite dead. The heathen soldier thrust a spear into Yeshua's heart, and water and blood poured out. One must be dead for hours before water gushes forth when the heart is pierced. But I doubt you three are capable of belief. You are beyond saving and will most assuredly suffer in Sheol for all eternity."

Adan focused his full gaze into Simon's eyes. "Actually, we do believe you. I know for a fact that what you say is true."

"Surely, as a Roman, you are only mocking me." Simon glared at him with a curled lip.

"I do not mock you. I believe you because I carried out Yeshua's crucifixion."

Simon gasped and stepped back. He waved his hands defensively as if to ward off an attack. "You vile and wicked creature! I should have known you are a demon with your wolf eyes. You are the murderer of my Lord and Savior! You are as worthless as the bones discarded from a gutted fish. You cover your family with sin and shame. Begone from me, Satan!"

Adan took a step toward Simon. "You said Yeshua died to forgive the sins of all believers. Aren't you a believer? If no human had ever sinned, then God would not have needed to sacrifice his own Son, a part of himself. You said Yeshua's blood had to be shed to take away all sin. Yeshua took away your sin." Adan stepped closer. "Doesn't that mean *your* sin killed him as well as *mine*?"

Simon scowled with narrowed eyes. "You twist my words, Centurion! You look for fault in me to try and hide the fault in your own heart. You're just as evil as those two pompous, know-it-alls from Jerusalem. Of course, Yeshua was sacrificed to cover the sin of mankind. The shedding of his blood sealed God's new covenant with humanity. But you tortured my precious Savior to death and now you boast as if you're proud of your despicable deed. *Yahweh* will condemn you just as he will condemn Peter and John to eternal punishment. You deny guilt but you are just as guilty as Judas Iscariot, the betrayer. Both of you will burn in Sheol for eternity!"

"I deny nothing. Yeshua asked God to forgive us as he suffered on the cross. I couldn't accept it; my guilt was so great. So much so, I wanted to punish myself and leave a reminder on my hand to never execute an innocent man again. I cut this cross with my dagger." Adan held up his right hand, palm out. "The cuts became infected. They were burned with a hot iron rod, but still the infection persisted."

"See there! That was God's judgment for your heinous sin!" exclaimed Simon.

"Then why did God use Simon Peter to heal my hand the next day? I took responsibility for my actions and God forgave me. And doesn't God promise through the prophet Isaiah, '*I, even I, am He who blots out your transgressions for My own sake, and will not remember your sins.*'?"

Simon's mouth dropped open. "You deceitful trickster! You know Simon Peter, yet you feigned ignorance. You tried to trap me, but it won't work. I am innocent. As I said, you're just like those two schemers from Jerusalem."

"As for comparing me to those two schemers as you call them—the greatest compliment any man could ever say to me would be, 'Adan you're just like Peter and John.' They are men after God's own heart, and I can never equal their dedicated service and love for Yeshua. They love God above all else, even more their own lives."

Simon gasped again. "Blasphemer! You defend those hypocrites! I was wrong. You're not like them. You're worse than them!" He turned and shuffled along the deck until he came to the hatch to the lower deck. He disappeared into the bowels of the ship without looking back.

Nikolaus pursed his lips. "That was mildly amusing. Should we invite our new friend for dinner this evening?"

Aquila glared at his uncle. "How 'bout we invite our new friend to have dinner with the sharks? He can be the main course."

Adan gave Aquila a stern look. "Aquila, shame on you! I taught you better than that. How can you suggest committing such a heinous deed? It is evil to knowingly poison animals."

Nikolaus laughed outright.

Aquila snorted and shook his head. "Good one, Father."

Adan shrugged his shoulders nonchalantly but turned away before Aquila could see the grin on his face.

Chapter 18

The *Margarita*, Paul, and a
Prediction of Disaster

⸺⸺◦∞∞◦⸺⸺

arco spent most of his time in Captain Gratian's quarters transcribing the daily logs into Greek. When he wasn't working, he and Paul sat on the deck in the bow of the ship. The great expanse of the sea and the soothing touch of the soft wind were comforting. Marco quickly adjusted to the daily routine on the *Margarita*. He tried sleeping in a corner of the captain's quarters, but the man snored like a flock of honking geese. Halfway through the first night, Marco took his mat to the deck and slept in the bow of the ship. He lay on his back with his hands tucked under his head and tried to count the stars. They seemed to play a game with him, twinkling and sparkling in faint flashes of yellow, blue, or red within their white brightness. Marco loved gazing at the night sky especially with no moon to cast a veil over the gleaming stars.

The shimmering starlight soothed Marco's loneliness. Everyone he loved was far away. Separation from his family was more traumatic than he expected. He had dreamed of taking life by the horns and steering it into paths of adventure and glory. Never had he thought he would miss the soft voice and gentle touch of his mother, the comforting presence of his father, and the foundation of his family. He missed Wing-shadow's nickering welcome when he walked into the barn and pulled his saddle from the wall peg. The horse would toss her head and snort with impatience as if to say, "I'm ready! Let's go!" For the first time in his life, Marco felt the pain of a broken heart. He yearned for his family and his home, but there was no turning back now. He could not change course even if he wanted to. The ship was headed for Crete, many miles from the port of Caesarea.

The wind was gaining strength. In turn the waves crashed higher and higher against the bow of the *Margarita*. A rogue wave battered the deck, soaking Marco. He bolted upright from sleep, sputtering and gasping for air. He ran his fingers through his drenched hair and looked around. He would have to make his way back to Captain

Gratian's quarters and get out of his wet clothes. It wouldn't be easy in the dark on a wet wooden deck. He braced himself against the life rails and made his way toward the hatch. He thought of Paul down in the hold with the other prisoners and decided he would not risk waking the bad-tempered captain.

Marco found the hatch leading to the hold below and the cramped space for the prisoners. He felt his way in the dark until a voice sounded from the inky blackness.

"Is that you, Marco?" asked Paul.

"How did you know it was me?" Marco whispered as he picked his way around the slumbering prisoners.

"I could smell wet linen. I know you like to sleep on the deck, so I figured you would be the only one to get drenched in sea water in the middle of the night."

"I'm sorry," said Marco as he found a spot next to Paul. "I didn't mean to wake you."

"You didn't. I was already awake. Here, take this blanket and get that wet tunic off. And tell me what's on your mind."

Marco managed to peel off the garment and wrapped the warm blanket around his broad shoulders. "You promised back in Jerusalem that we would talk again and here we are. Can I ask you about the blue pearl? You said that my parents earned a great treasure in heaven because of what they did. What did you mean?"

"God sees everything we do, both good and bad. If we ask for forgiveness, we are forgiven for our bad deeds. Likewise, we may be rewarded for our good deeds in this life, but sometimes not. Sometimes, we have to wait until we are with God. Your parents received no recognition or reward for their extreme generosity except for the peace within their hearts. Their reward is waiting for them in heaven. What that reward will be, I haven't a clue, but I'm sure it is beyond anything our human imaginations can conceive."

"So, when we do good things for other people, even against our family's wishes, then God rewards those deeds?" asked Marco. He peered into the darkness wishing he could see Paul's expression.

"Yes, but as I told you before, you must honor your father and mother, Marco. It would not be God's will for you to do something that would dishonor them. Even if your parents were evil, God would not want you to dishonor them by doing something equally evil. That being said, it looks like you are still on your quest."

"Things happened that encouraged me to continue." Marco sighed at the memory of his brother's last words. "That is if you consider angry sarcasm a form of encouragement."

"Ah, yes. Anger. It is a double-edged sword. It can be productive, or it can be destructive. I have felt both edges. I also have used both edges."

They fell silent for a few moments, each lost in his own thoughts. Marco cleared his throat. "I need to ask something so I can understand. I know Yeshua had to be sacrificed but why in such a horrible way? Crucifixion is so appalling and agonizing."

"The reason is because sin is appalling and agonizing. Yeshua took on all the sin of the world from now until the end of the age. Yeshua became sin. The world went dark because God turned away. But God cannot die; therefore, Yeshua could not remain in death. We no longer need to shed the blood of animals for forgiveness. God shed his own blood when he allowed Yeshua to be sacrificed for the forgiveness of all sin. An individual's belief in Yeshua, as the Christ, binds that person to God's promise. Accepting the promise gives one access to God the Father."

Marco thought for a moment. "What if someone does not believe?"

"That person cannot go to God. Yeshua said many times, *'I am the way, the truth, and the life. No one comes to the Father except through Me.'* Once you believe in the Christ, nothing can snatch you from his hand except your own free will. To believe in Yeshua the Christ, and then later reject him is apostasy. Some say that the person who rejects Christ never truly believed. That is not true. One cannot lose what one never had. Apostasy is the loss of previous belief, but even that can be forgiven."

"Is executing God's Son forgivable?" whispered Marco. "Did my father fulfill God's will when he obeyed Valentius's orders?"

"It was a terrible task, but one that had to be done," said Paul sadly. "As for your first question, I know for a fact that Yeshua forgave your father. Don't you know that?"

Marco felt his face flush and was grateful that Paul could not see him. "I just wanted to be sure that . . . I was hoping . . . "

"That your father had told you the truth?" asked Paul gently.

"It shames me to admit it but, yes."

"Your father told us he suspected Yeshua was innocent of any crime, but he certainly did not know his true identity until later. I have also done terrible things in ignorance even though I was convinced that I was honoring God."

"How can I know I am doing the right thing? You were convinced you were doing the right thing when you had believers imprisoned and even killed. Then Yeshua appeared to you on the road to Damascus. You told us that Yeshua asked why you were persecuting him, and then you were blinded for three days. Nothing like that has happened to me."

"The Holy Spirit will speak to you in different ways," said Paul. "I, however, needed a dramatic confrontation to convince me of the truth. For others, the direction may come in subtle ways. Circumstances may help or hinder you. People will say or do something that speaks to your heart. But most of all, you must pray for God's guidance and he will show you the way."

"Does the message from God have to come from a believer?"

"No, God uses all of his creation to convey his will. You must be listening and watching; be ready to respond. If a message speaks to you, pray that you are hearing correctly, and if the message is from God, circumstances will open up for you."

Marco grasped the purple sapphire. "Then I believe God has spoken to me. That's why I'm here with you. I will go to Herculaneum and I will bring Dionysia home."

As they talked, light slowly began to creep into the hold of the ship. The waves continued to pound the vessel as the wind increased in intensity. They sailed under the shelter of Crete off Salmone, but the stormy weather made passing this location difficult until they reached Fair Havens near the coastal city of Lasea. It was then that Paul asked to speak with Captain Gratian and Centurion Julius.

Paul met with them on deck. He waved his hand toward the raucous sea. "*Men, I perceive that this voyage will end with disaster and much loss, not only of the cargo and ship, but also our lives.*"

"I make payments into the Maritime General Average," said the captain, "to be reimbursed for losses caused by disaster, but that is just good business. I do not make predictions of disaster that will jinx my ship. The wind will calm down. You'll see. How many ocean voyages have you taken, Paul? Six, seven, eight? I have taken hundreds. We will be fine."

"What do you think, Centurion?" asked Paul.

"I trust Captain Gratian. I'm sure he knows what's best," said Centurion Julius.

Paul raised an open hand in a gesture of regret. "Since I cannot convince you to heed my warning, I pray that God be with us."

Captain Gratian's prediction was validated the next day. A gentle south wind replaced the westerly wind, promising smooth sailing. The captain decided not to make for the harbor of Phoenix on Crete. He had planned to winter there if the bad weather persisted, but when a calm wind replaced the violent gusts, they headed for Italy.

Their good fortune would not last. A tempestuous headwind came up which the sailors called *Euroclydon*, a hurricane. They were rare on the Mediterranean, but Marco remembered the stories about a hurricane hitting the night his parents were married. Now, Marco would experience the ferocity of a hurricane from the place of greatest danger, a ship at sea. His assumption that traveling with Paul would safeguard him from danger was worse than false hope. It could cost him his life.

Chapter 19

The *Pegasus*, the Storm, and Blue Fire

A dan, Nikolaus, and Aquila spent most of their time on the main deck of the *Pegasus,* in route to Ostia. They would take a barge up the *Tiberis* River to Rome. From Rome, they would hire a carriage for the five-day journey to Herculaneum and Decimus Lentulus's villa. Having little else to do on board ship, Adan told Aquila about his experiences during the two years he served at the Antonia. His son asked a few questions but mostly he listened without interruption. For the first time, Adan described in detail what he and Lucius Octavean talked about while they were waiting to be executed in Herod's Theater. Aquila was amazed that either one of them could carry on a discussion while death drew ever closer. Adan then told his son about how he and Dulcibella gave a priceless blue pearl to Paul to use for famine relief. Aquila was shocked, not only with disbelief, but with a touch of anger.

Adan saw the flash of irritation in his son's eyes. "Aquila, would you agree that a small dose of opium is beneficial when someone has surgery?"

"Of course," answered Aquila with an impatient frown.

"But what about large doses every day? Is that also beneficial?" Adan asked.

"No. You would get addicted, and then you'd want more and more until you'd probably overdose and die."

"Exactly. Money can be just like opium. It is good to have what you need for security and a measure of comfort, but if you have much more money than you need, you risk the danger of becoming addicted to it. Then no matter how much you have; you will always want more. You will no longer control your money. It will control you. The same as too much opium."

"It's not the same, Father. You can't get addicted to money."

"You think not?" Adan snorted. "There are two things just as addictive as opium. Money and power. The more you have, the more you want. Your mother and I were very

124

careful with the pearl. We did not flaunt it. The pearl was incredibly beautiful with its soft blue glow as if it had an internal light. But it was a relief to hand it to Paul. There are some treasures not meant to be held by a single person, but to be shared among many. The blue pearl was one of those treasures."

"I don't really understand, Father," admitted Aquila. "Maybe I will someday."

Days passed in peaceful repose. The captain of the *Pegasus*, Captain Drusus, was pleased to have a Roman centurion traveling with him since he had been forced to hire a new crew. Only his first officer, a Samaritan from Caesarea, had been with him for many years. The presence of a Roman officer might make a potentially unruly crew more cautious.

They had smooth sailing until they neared Crete and encountered swirling winds that played havoc with the mainsail. The oarsmen had to work hard to keep the ship on course after they were forced to take it down. Captain Drusus, contrary to what most sea captains would have done, sailed north of the island of Crete and headed for Syracuse of Sicily. The battling winds called a truce and the heaving waves calmed. The weather cleared and the mainsail was once again deployed.

Simon Magus chose to spend most of his time in his quarters since the unpleasant conversation with Adan and Aquila. He only ventured on deck when he thought Adan and the others would not be there. When they left Crete behind, the wind grew blustery once again, and the waves were heavy with whitecaps and spray. Simon appeared on deck more often as the weather worsened. He would sulk and glare at Adan and Aquila, but mostly ignored Nikolaus. The three men tried to ignore Simon, but his intense scrutiny was disconcerting.

The crew became sullen when the sky darkened with a thick, charcoal-gray blanket of clouds. They muttered to each other and cast hostile glances at Adan and Aquila. The winds became fierce, and the waves bashed the ship, occasionally swamping the deck. Storm clouds in the west grew into massive anvil-shaped thunderheads fit for the forges of giants. Flashes of lightning ripped through the sky. It didn't take long for the low rumble of thunder to amplify into crackling explosions.

Braving the storm, Adan, Nikolaus and Aquila stayed on the deck. A Samaritan crewman shouted in panic as he clung to the rigging with one hand and gestured at the mast with the other. Brightly glowing tongues of blue flames were emanating from the top.

A Greek crewman shouted, "It's the torch of Helene! Don't be afraid! It's a sign from the gods that we will be safe." The Samaritan sailor cursed at the Greek crewman, calling him an idol worshipping pagan, but did not offer an alternative explanation for the phenomena.

"What is it, Father?" asked Aquila, fascinated with the glowing flame.

"I've never seen anything like it," said Adan.

"Look!" shouted Nikolaus as he pointed to the raised ends of the unmanned oars. When not in use, the handles of the oars were secured within the hull leaving the ends pointing upwards outside the ship. Blue orbs of light flickered from the tops of the oars and the mast.

Captain Drusus staggered across the heaving deck to Adan. "This is the first time I have seen the torch of Helene. It is told that it only happens during a severe storm and that it is a good omen. At least, that's what most seafarers say. If the *Pegasus* can make it through the Mediterranean and into the Tyrrhenian Sea, we will be safe."

Captain Drusus turned to several crewmen and ordered them to throw some of the kegs of olive oil overboard to lighten the ship. The mainsail was lowered and secured. Adan, Nikolaus, and Aquila stood in the bow of the ship, bracing themselves against the life rails, to watch the storm as long as safety allowed. They were observing the approaching storm so intently, they were unaware of the activity developing behind them.

Aquila was startled to feel a hand come down on his shoulder and across his back. It was a forceful action and it pushed him forward. He whirled around to find Simon standing behind him.

"What are you doing?" demanded Aquila angrily.

"I am so sorry, young man," exclaimed Simon with exaggerated courtesy. "I stumbled and had to catch myself."

Adan and Nikolaus turned around at the commotion and found many crewmen standing behind Simon. They glared with flinty eyes and mouths stiff with hostility.

Simon gestured at the storm clouds. "You see! Just as I have been telling you. These two," he pointed at Adan and Aquila, "are demons from Satan's horde. Look at them. Have you ever seen eyes like that? Yes, you have. They are the eyes of wolves! Demon wolves!" He pointed at the glowing blue "fire" at the tops of the oars and mast. "It is the fire of Sheol. This ship is marked for destruction along with us! I say we save ourselves before it is too late!"

Adan stepped forward. "What do you think you're doing, Simon?" he shouted loud enough for all the crewmen to hear. "It's a storm! Not a monster!"

"It is judgment, I say," he shouted to the crew. "Are you going to let the sea swallow us alive or are you going to save yourselves? Throw the two of them overboard!"

"What is the meaning of this!" shouted Captain Drusus as he pushed his way through the crewmen. "Get below and man your stations!"

"We're not going anywhere until we're safe, Captain," declared one of the men.

"We won't be safe until those demons are off this ship," shouted another man.

Several of the men surged forward to take hold of Adan and Aquila. Adan and Nikolaus stepped in front of Aquila. Adan shouted over the roar of the wind, "This man, Simon, is angry because we called out his lies and corruption. He is only using you to get revenge against us."

"This storm and the blue fire say otherwise," yelled one of the men.

"We don't care why this man accuses them," another shouted. "We can see with our own eyes. Those two are werewolves. They become beasts of prey when the moon is full!"

"Yes! Beasts of prey," chimed in Simon. "They are creatures that feed on the flesh of their victims. They hunger for your blood!"

"Why do you blame these men?" demanded Captain Drusus. "What harm have they done? It's just a storm! Stop with this foolishness!" He pointed to the glowing blue orbs of light. "The blue fire is a *good* omen! Those that see the torch of Helene always survive."

Simon pointed a shaking finger at Adan. "I tell you, that one is a murderer!" The crewmen gasped. "Yes, that's right. He even bragged to me how he crucified an innocent man. He confessed his heinous crime to me without so much as a shred of remorse. He nearly whipped the man to death, and then he nailed him on the cross! He mocked and spat upon this undeniably innocent man as he suffered the most agonizing execution."

Aquila started to deny the lies Simon had spouted about his father, but Captain Drusus pushed him aside. He pointed at Adan and faced his crew. "A murderer? Is that what you are accusing this man of—*murder*?"

Simon eagerly shouted, "Yes, yes! He confessed all of it to me!"

Drusus stared at Adan with a gaping mouth. He turned to his crewmen and burst out laughing. "*Ha!* He's a Roman soldier! They're *all* murderers! This man Simon is making fools of you. Now get back to work before I have every one of you thrown overboard without your wages!"

Threatening to throw them overboard had little effect but threatening to withhold their wages caused the crewmen to hesitate. One of the older sailors shouted, "The captain speaks the truth. I have seen the torch of Helene once before during a terrible storm. The ship and all the crew survived, unharmed. Helene will protect us."

A Roman sailor pushed his way to the front. "Perhaps the ship will be spared *because* they are on board." He pointed at Adan and Aquila. "Neptune would not want to anger Pluto by capsizing the ship and drowning his brother's children."

"I tell you; they are demons from Sheol, the domain of Satan!" exclaimed Simon. "I can prove it! Watch the young one. If he belongs to Satan, the evil one will mark him." The crewmen pressed in, eager to see what would happen.

Captain Drusus rounded on Simon. "I swear, if any harm comes to these two men, it is you who will pay the price. I am the captain of this ship and I—" A wave of seawater crashed over the bow and hit everyone closest to the life rails. Aquila was drenched.

"*See!* I told you!" shouted Simon as he pointed at Aquila. The seawater steaming from his tunic was stained blood red. It ran down his back and puddled on the wooden deck. "Satan marks his demons with the blood of their innocent victims."

The crewmen gawked and gasped with fear. "Grab them!" one of the men shouted. "Throw them overboard now before it's too late."

Captain Drusus hit the man in the face with his fist. The man crumpled at their feet. Drusus shouted at his men. "Do you not know who this Roman is? He is Centurion Longinus of the Antonia. He is the man who came back from the dead! Yes, that's right. He is that man! Five thousand soldiers watched an arrow split his heart. The

127

tribune tested for life—none. Herod's own *medicus* tested for life—none. The centurion in charge smashed his fist down on his chest to test for life—and there was none! Yet, here he stands. Are you sure you want to try to send him to his death—*again*? What will happen to you when he returns?"

The crewmen backed away. The wind screamed around them and the sea heaved the ship about like a cork. "But the storm, Captain! What about the storm?"

Adan stepped forward as he balanced on the heaving deck as best, he could. "I understand your fear. I ask for only one thing. Give us one day. By this time tomorrow, if the storm is not over, I will throw myself into the sea."

"No!" screamed Aquila. He moved to push his way in front of his father.

Nikolaus grabbed his arm and whispered, "He knows what he's doing."

The men muttered among themselves. Captain Drusus saw his first officer at the back of the crowd and signaled to him. "Take this man, Simon Magus, to his quarters. Make sure he stays there." Several of the crewmen joined the first officer in escorting Simon below deck. The captain motioned for Adan, Nikolaus, and Aquila to follow him to his quarters. Drusus posted several of his most trustworthy men outside the door. When they were inside, he slid the bolt to lock the door.

Adan turned to him with a lopsided grin. "Roman soldiers are all murderers. Really?"

Captain Drusus shrugged. "Sorry. Nothing personal. I had to say something."

"Well, it worked," said Nikolaus with a grin.

"Father, you're not really going to throw yourself overboard, are you?" wailed Aquila.

"Of course, not," said Adan calmly. "I'll throw Niko over."

"Nice," said Nikolaus. "I've always wondered what's on the bottom of the sea."

Aquila was not amused. "How can you joke about this, Father? And why did the water turn to blood?"

"Did Simon touch you in anyway?" asked Adan.

"He pushed me and slapped his hand down the whole length of my back. When I turned around, he was right behind me. He didn't look like he stumbled."

"He must have wiped some kind of chemical on your tunic," Nikolaus suggested. "I know certain types of *carbonium* will turn water red. He did say he used magic to impress the people of Samaria so I'm sure he knows how to use lots of different chemicals and potions."

Captain Drusus invited the three men to stay in his quarters while he checked on the condition of the *Pegasus*. It wasn't long before the ship ran straight into the storm, but the captain had made a wise decision to go north of Crete and head due west to Syracuse. Only the outer edge of the *Euroclydon* affected the *Pegasus*. The eye of the hurricane was approaching Malta. The oarsmen were put to work. They struggled against the wind, but they maintained their course.

The next day found calm seas. The captain ordered that the mainsail be deployed and the oarsmen were given a rest. All talk of throwing anyone overboard was silenced. Simon was allowed to leave his quarters but made no appearances on deck. He moved among the Samaritan crewmen and tried to sway them to mutiny against the captain. When that didn't work, he claimed that Adan and Aquila meant to poison them. Word of his grumblings reached the captain's ears and he suspected Simon might take matters into his own hands. When the Samaritan was caught in the ship's galley, Captain Drusus had him searched. A vial was found dropped down the front of his tunic.

"What is in this vial, Simon?" questioned Drusus.

"Nothing of any interest to you, Sir," drawled Simon. "It is my medicine. I need it on sea voyages. The motion of the ship makes me queasy."

"Then drink it." Drusus smiled when Simon sputtered an excuse. "It's poison, isn't it? You were going to make the crew sick so you could blame Longinus and his son. I've had enough of you." Drusus ordered Simon to be dragged to the top deck.

Adan, Nikolaus and Aquila were sitting in the bow watching the sunset when the men dragged Simon up the steps to the top deck. He shouted and cursed at Captain Drusus to no avail.

"Captain, what are you doing?" demanded Adan.

"I'm throwing out the trash, Centurion," replied Drusus. "I've had it with this man. I just caught him about to poison the crew's food. Apparently, he has been predicting that you three were going to poison them. He was going to make his prediction come true."

"Captain, you don't need to do that," said Adan.

Aquila frowned at his father. "Why not? This man is a menace!"

"And if he is," answered Adan, "he should face justice, but throwing him overboard is no different than murder. He deserves the same protection of the law as any man. Let a judge decide what should be done with him."

"He's not a Roman citizen, Centurion," said Drusus. "There's only one judge that matters right now and that's me. I am the captain of this ship; therefore, this vessel is a nation unto itself, in a manner of speaking. He would have emptied this vial," he held the ceramic flask up for the others to see, "into the barley as it was boiling. The whole crew would have gotten sick or worse. No, Centurion, this is my ship and I say he goes overboard."

"I have money, Captain Drusus," wailed Simon. "I can pay you double for my passage, triple, if you want. It isn't really poison. It would have only made them a little sick. Just the crewmen, not you, or," he pointed at Adan, "them."

"So, you are that well acquainted with the workings of the galley? You knew that I keep a separate food supply in my quarters for myself and my passengers, including you. How convenient. You would never knowingly make yourself sick, would you?"

Simon curled a lip in disgust. "I was only trying to protect us from them!" He pointed a finger at Adan and Aquila. "We must free ourselves of these demons."

"You see, Father," cried Aquila, "he's still trying to get us killed. Captain Drusus is right. He needs to be thrown overboard."

"No!" exclaimed Adan. "He needs to be confined to quarters and charged before a magistrate in Ostia. Let the justice of the empire deal with him. I will not have his murder on my conscience."

The crewmen looked at Drusus, then at Adan, then back to Drusus. "What are your orders, Captain?" asked the first officer. "We will do as you say."

Drusus glared at Simon, and then shot a look at Adan. "Fine. Confine him to his quarters."

"*What!*" squawked Simon. "Why don't you confine *them* to quarters?"

"They haven't done anything wrong," said the captain. "You've done nothing but make accusations and conjure cheap tricks to put suspicion on them." He held up a small ceramic jug. "Look what we found in your quarters, Simon. *Carbonium.*" He removed the cork and tapped the contents onto the deck. He took a waterskin and splashed water on the white powder. Red splashes appeared on the deck. "There's the mark of blood you so accurately predicted, Simon. You were right to suggest I search his possessions, Nikolaus. No telling what other havoc you could cause," he growled at Simon. "Why are you so intent on finding fault with them?"

Simon's face contorted with indignation. "That one," He pointed at Adan, "killed my Lord and Savior. He knew Yeshua is the Son of God and he crucified him. He is evil."

"And he proved that you are a liar," said Aquila. "You slandered our friends Peter and John. You lied about him, too. He only crucified Yeshua because those were his orders. He never did those other things you said." Aquila pointed a finger at Simon. "You tried to pay money for the Holy Spirit! *You* are the one who is evil!"

"Aquila, that's enough," said Adan gently. He turned to Simon. "I humiliated you so you're retaliating. Isn't that right?"

"I don't know what you're babbling about," hissed Simon. "You could never humiliate me. My heart is pure, very pure. I am rich because of my good deeds. My wealth is the proof of my innocence. I was only trying to save the crew from evil men like you. I had to think of some way to discredit you. Look at the chances I took to save this crew. Mark my words;" he glared around at the men, "you will all suffer because of the way you have mistreated me. The Lord God will punish you!"

"Get him out of here!" shouted Captain Drusus. "Put hourly watchmen at the door and don't let him out of his quarters." The crewmen dragged Simon down to the lower deck. He screamed curses as they went, until the first officer, a fellow Samaritan, told Simon that one more word and he would be tied to the mast for the rest of the voyage. The result was immediate silence.

Captain Drusus turned to Adan and Aquila. "I hold you responsible as well. If that man causes any more disruptions on this voyage, I will throw both of you overboard along with him." Aquila took a menacing step toward the captain as he turned his back and walked away.

"Aquila, don't make things worse," said Nikolaus under his breath. "The captain is only saving face. He won't harm us or he would have done it already."

"But he was going to throw Simon overboard," countered Aquila.

"I don't think so," said Adan. "We talked him out of it too easily. I think he just wanted to scare the man."

Aquila ran his hands through his hair. "Father, how would it be murder to throw Simon into the sea? If he's found guilty at trial, he'll be executed. Same result!" challenged Aquila.

"Same result—different process. The process of the law must be maintained. You think the action of vigilantes is justice? No, it is the action of out-of-control emotions. A vigilante often reacts to unproven accusations supported by false, misleading, or even imagined evidence. You said it yourself, '*If* he's found guilty' he would be executed. Maybe. Maybe not."

"But we know he is guilty!" said Aquila. "He didn't even deny it, and we know he put *carbonium* on my tunic to make the water red. That is real evidence."

"Yes, it is, Aquila, but what happens, if on this same voyage, someone else does something questionable, but without the same level of evidence? You saw the crewmen, even Simon's fellow Samaritans. They were ready to kill him just as easily as they would have killed us. Some men will do anything if someone in authority tells them to do it. I won't be a party to that. Not again." Adan looked at the scars of the cross on his right palm. "Not ever again."

"But this is all Simon's fault. He needs to pay," insisted Aquila.

"I have to own up to some of the fault," said Adan. "I could have ignored Simon's lies, but I chose to humiliate him instead. It is dangerous to tease a snake that might have hidden fangs."

"I only wanted you to confront Simon's lies about Peter and John. He lied about you, too. Saying you whipped Yeshua and spat upon him. I wanted you to stand up for the truth." Aquila bit his lower lip. He looked at his father with dismay. "Of course, that's exactly what you did and it only spurred Simon to do worse. Mother told me that just because something is true doesn't mean you have to say it."

Adan arched an eyebrow. "She told me the same thing. She also reminded me that the truth can stand up for itself. It finds a way, sometimes in the most unexpected moments."

Nikolaus raised an open hand. "No one was harmed. I was glad when you silenced the braggart, Adan. You shouldn't be so hard on yourself."

"Stopping someone from doing actual harm is one thing," said Adan, "but sometimes a braggart just needs to be ignored. I should have taken my own advice."

"Well, it's over now," said Nikolaus. "I doubt that Simon will cause any more problems. We can look forward to seeing Father and Janae for a few days. Let's hope Marco is there. Maybe he has changed his mind about going alone and will accept our help."

"I'm eager to see Grandfather Aquila and Grandmother Janae," said Aquila, ignoring what his uncle had said about Marco. "He'll be pleased to see how I have grown in the past three years. And I'll show Grandfather and Gregos the new device I have invented for pressing grapes for wine. They'll be amazed."

"I, too, am looking forward to seeing Father and Janae. I certainly hope Marco is there," said Adan. "But Aquila, how 'bout you and your grandfather try not to blow anything up."

Aquila's expression brightened. It was the first time he had smiled since Marco disappeared into the night.

Chapter 20

The *Margarita*, a Hurricane, and a Promise

T he *Margarita* was in trouble. The height of the waves was making it difficult for Marco to walk on the deck without being thrown against the life rails and possibly overboard. To make matters worse, the ship was in danger of running aground at Syrtis Sands, the shallow gulfs off the coast of Africa that trapped the largest ships. The crew struck sail and gave up all control to the wind and waves. On the third day of the storm, crew and passengers threw the tackle overboard to lighten the ship. Eating was out of the question since no one could keep anything down anyway. After many days of being buffeted by the wind and waves with no visible sun or stars, the men on the *Margarita* gave up any hope of surviving.

Paul gathered the men about him below deck. At first, he admonished them for not heeding his warning and then assured them there would be no loss of life even though the ship would be destroyed. Paul declared, *"For there stood by me this night an angel of the God to whom I belong and whom I serve, saying, 'Do not be afraid, Paul; you must be brought before Caesar; and indeed God has granted you all those who sail with you.' Therefore, take heart, men for I believe God that it will be just as it was told me."* He warned them that the ship, however, would run aground and be destroyed.

After the fourteenth night of the storm, the movement of the waves signaled that they were nearing land. They took soundings and determined they were in twenty fathoms of water. After a few more hours, the soundings revealed they were in fifteen fathoms of water. The crew dropped four anchors from the stern and prayed that daylight would soon come.

The sailors decided among themselves that their only chance of survival was to abandon the *Margarita* despite their captain's orders. They cut the skiff from the securing lines and began to haul it to the side of the ship to lower it down by ropes.

Paul saw what they were doing and exclaimed to Centurion Julius. *"Unless these men stay in the ship, you cannot be saved."* He knew that if Centurion Julius thought only the sailors in the skiff might be lost, he would let them do as they pleased.

The centurion turned to his *legionaries*. "Cut those ropes! Let the skiff fall into the sea!" The crewmen were powerless against the armed soldiers.

Paul knew they were afraid and spoke to them. *"I urge you to take nourishment, for this is for your survival.* Not a single one of you will lose his life in this storm."

Paul asked Marco to gather up as much bread as he could carry. It was a struggle just to get to the galley, but he found several cloth sacks and stuffed them with the stale loaves. When he handed a loaf to Paul, he broke it, and gave thanks for their lives. The men were encouraged and were able to eat after Paul said they had to for their survival. There were two hundred and seventy-six people on the ship, yet there was plenty of bread for them all. The crewmen who worked in the galley glanced at each other in surprise. They did not remember there being so much bread. After they had eaten, they lightened the ship further by throwing the cargo of wheat into the sea.

The sky gave way to daylight and revealed land nearby, but none of them recognized it. There was a bay with a wide beach where they could run the ship aground. They cut the ropes to the anchors, but also lost the rudder ropes. They could no longer steer the ship. The captain ordered to hoist sail; he let the ship be driven toward land. It struck ground with the prow rammed in so deeply it was immovable. This exposed the stern of the ship to the thrashing waves. The screaming wind tore at any loosened deck or side plank. The stern was breaking up. It was only a matter of time before the whole ship would be pummeled to splintered planks.

Marco clambered down into the hold to see what was happening to the prisoners who were still chained to posts. Two of the soldiers were eyeing the prisoners and muttering among themselves. Marco crept closer and listened.

"It doesn't matter if they drown in the storm!" shouted one of the soldiers over the screeching wind. "But if just one gets out of our custody alive, they will execute us."

"What do we do about it?" cried the other solider. "Kill them?"

"What else? We will suffer nothing if they're all dead. Only Centurion Julius will pay the price. Better for him to be executed than all of us."

Marco slipped away and told Centurion Julius. The commander was furious and hurried into the hold of the ship. He grabbed the conniving legionnaires by the front of their leather armor.

"What is the meaning of this?" Julius snarled. "You want to kill the prisoners to save your worthless hides? I should have the two of you run through with your own swords." He threw them to the floor of the ship and ordered his other *legionaries* to take their swords and haul them to the top deck. Centurion Julius unlocked the chains of the prisoners and told them to go up on deck.

Julius found Marco topside. "You did a brave thing telling me about their plan. Not only would it have cost my life, it would have cost Paul's as well. He is the only reason we have survived this long. Your father would be proud of you." Marco beamed at the praise.

Those who could swim dove into the tossing waves and made for shore. Others broke off boards from the damaged stern and used them as life rafts. Marco watched as Paul leapt into the churning sea. He started to dive into the water when an odd sensation crept up his spine. Marco looked over his shoulder as the wind screeched and the sea swamped the deck. There, standing by the mast, was a solitary figure. There was no expression on his ashen face. He was standing apparently unaffected by the gusting wind and wave-pummeled deck.

"Calais!" shouted Marco. "Is that you?"

Marco heaved himself to his feet and tried to step toward the image of the former slave, so paradoxically calm in the midst of the seething storm. As soon as he let go of the life rail, a battering wave knocked him off his feet and over the railing. He caught one last look of the figure's face before he lost sight of the spectral image. Marco managed to surface and suck air into his lungs. He looked back at the ship, but no one was there. The instinct to survive forced Marco to fight his way through the tempest to the shore. He dragged himself up the beach to join the other survivors. He lay on the sand in shock. There was no doubt that the image on the ship was Calais, but he had appeared to be impervious to the storm. A question now burned in Marco's heart. Was he to be haunted by Calais for the rest of his life? A gloating smile of pleasure appeared on the image's face just before Marco fell over the railing. He shuddered at the realization that it didn't matter if Calais was alive or a ghost. He would have his revenge on Marco one way or another.

Marco sat up and looked around. Someone was shouting for him. It was Paul, and he was signaling him to follow. They were stranded on the island of Malta, a very long way from his goal. Marco could not remember ever feeling such despair. His task seemed an impossible one, especially now that he knew Calais had doggedly tracked him as a spirit or an avenging predator. He was shipwrecked, and Calais was among them. Marco knew this because Paul had said that not a single life would be lost. That was unless Calais was already lost, a creature of the netherworld.

Chapter 21

Rome, Chains, and a Fight

Adan, Aquila, and Nikolaus enjoyed the rest of the voyage knowing Simon was confined to quarters. They passed Syracuse and headed north to Ostia. The *Pegasus* made port and the gangway was lowered to the pier. The passengers prepared to disembark in Ostia to find a cargo barge for the twenty-five-mile trek up the *Tiberis* River to Rome. Simon pushed his way ahead of Adan and the others and disembarked. He hurried to a bench at the passenger loading dock and sat to wait for his luggage to be unloaded. His hostile glare never wavered from Adan and Aquila.

Nikolaus turned to his brother and nephew. "It breaks my heart to say farewell to our endearing new friend."

"Tell your heart to mend, Uncle Niko," muttered Aquila. "I'm sure he's waiting to offer us the hospitality of his *very* grand villa and *very* extensive vineyards. I'm bubbling with anticipation."

Adan arched an eyebrow. "Aquila, do I see acid dribbling from the corner of your mouth?"

"And what of it, Father?" countered Aquila. "He deserves far worse than mere words."

"Most likely," deferred Adan. "But not from you. Leave judging to the judges."

Aquila frowned with irritation. "You just don't want to agree with me. You'd rather point out some high-and-mighty virtue I obviously lack."

Adan started to answer, but Aquila stalked down the gangway and walked out of earshot. Nikolaus looked at his brother with sympathy. "Adan, he's young and overly sensitive, but your response was just as sarcastic as his. Perhaps there's a better way to calm his anger."

Adan shot Nikolaus a disgruntled glare, but then relented. "I suppose you're right. Dulcie tells me the same thing. I am hard on my children. Sometimes I wish that Marco and Aquila could be more like their sister. Longina has always been easy to deal with.

I feel like Dulcie and I were wonderful parents when we see her with her husband and children. She is such a good wife and mother. But my sons," Adan sighed. "I think they devise new ways to challenge me every chance they get."

"I know it is tempting to compare one child to another, but I remember what my mother said to Father once. She said, 'Nicandros, would you compare the sky, to the land, and then to the sea? No? Then why are you comparing our children to each other?' I still remember the surprised look on his face."

"Did he answer her," asked Adan.

"No, but I never heard him compare one of us against the other again," said Nikolaus. Adan gave his brother a grateful glance and went to join Aquila. Nikolaus gave them some privacy before he strolled over to join them.

Captain Drusus strode up and down the deck shouting orders as the crew unloaded the cargo. He stopped in front of the trio. "Gentlemen, I can't say it was a pleasure having you on board, but it certainly wasn't boring. I thought I might mention that my cousin, Fabius, runs a salt barge on the *Tiberis* River that should be leaving this afternoon and arriving in Rome early in the morning. Tell him Cousin Dru sent you."

"Thank you, Captain," said Adan. "We'll look into it."

They found the river barge easily since there were armed guards protecting the men loading the salt. Not even a shipment of gold ore would require as many swordsmen since salt was valued more highly. Nikolaus spoke with the barge captain, making sure he mentioned Cousin Dru.

Fabius inspected them with narrowed eyes. "I only take passengers my cousin recommends. One can never be too careful with a cargo of salt. Welcome aboard, gentlemen."

They gathered their luggage and boarded the barge, but Aquila felt uneasy and glanced over his shoulder. Simon Magus stood up and moved toward the barge, watching them closely. His ugly scowl told of his festering resentment. Aquila gave him a mocking grin and raised a hand in an exaggerated gesture of farewell. Simon bristled with anger. Aquila laughed and turned his back. Simon's eyes gleamed as a slow smile crept across his face. Perhaps an opportunity would arise that would take the mocking grin away from the boy. He rubbed the palms of his hands together in anticipation.

The short journey on the *Tiberis* was refreshing. Adan and Nikolaus were certain they would find Marco at his grandfather's villa. A gentle breeze wafted about them as they sat out on the deck. The cloudless sky was a cerulean blue, indicating a lack of moisture, as if the nearby sea was holding its breath. The three men talked of past family reunions when Grandfather Aquila and Janae were able to join them. Adan recalled when Aquila stepped foot off the ship for his first visit to Caesarea. Being the *minor consul* in Rome, he expected to be greeted by at least one Roman dignitary.

Adan nudged Nikolaus with an elbow. "Do you remember what Father said?"

"No. What did he say?"

"In his most imperial voice, he announced, 'Son, did you forget to tell them I was coming?' Nikolaus and Aquila chuckled at the perfect imitation of Aquila senior's voice and manner.

The journey was over quickly after a good night's rest on the deck of the barge. They found a carriage at the river dock that morning and rode to the Longinus estate.

Nikolaus eagerly pulled on the doorbell. "Let's hope Marco is here." Adan enthusiastically agreed, but Aquila remained expressionless.

Gregos, his father's long-time servant, opened the door. "Adan! Niko! And—" He glanced behind Aquila. "Where's the other one? Come in. Come in. Such an unexpected surprise! But you've missed seeing the children. They have gone for the month to visit with Janae's parents in Volsinii. Is this Little Quila or Marco? Not so little anymore, I see. And where *is* the other one? Getting the luggage?"

Adan's expectant smile faded as soon as he saw how surprised Gregos was to see them. "We were hoping to find Marco here."

Gregos frowned with concern at the look on Adan's face. He gestured for them to come in. "What has happened to Marco? Come. Let's find your father." Gregos led them through the atrium and out to the terrace where they found Janae and Aquila senior enjoying the view of the river and the terraced rows of their lush vineyards.

Aquila and Janae turned at the sound of footsteps. They beamed with delight at the sight of their family, but their expressions sobered when Adan explained why they were there. Janae asked questions while Aquila stood in silence.

Finally, Aquila spoke. "So, my grandson Marco is off to make a name for himself. The boy has a brave heart but his venture is unwise. At least this young man," he clapped a hand on Aquila's shoulder, "has shown good sense by making himself useful."

"How is that, Grandfather?"

"Helping to find your brother. I am proud of you for joining your father and uncle. I suspect Marco will need your help before this is over. It was rash to attempt this mission alone, but I wish him success." He nodded his head once at Nikolaus. "Dionysia should be with you, Niko."

Aquila rolled his eyes impatiently. "Father and Uncle Niko have tried to buy Dionysia's slave contract several times and it never worked out. How could Marco possibly succeed?"

"Quila, just because something did not work in the past, does not mean it never will. Have faith. Where two failed, four may succeed. Now, enough of this sadness. Tell me, Quila—may I still call you Quila? You're not little Quila anymore." His grandson nodded with a smile. He loved his grandfather's nickname for him. "Good, so tell me what wonderful new inventions have you devised lately? Have you determined a better way to make water run uphill yet?"

Aquila grinned. "Working on it, Grandfather. But I could use your expertise. May I share some ideas with you?"

"Of course," said Aquila senior. "I have a few ridiculous new ideas to share with you as well. Perhaps together, we can change the ridiculous into practical."

Adan chuckled, "About those ideas of yours, could you two avoid making loud noises and sudden bright lights? I swear my ears were ringing for hours after that last experiment when you blew up the salt peter." Grandfather and grandson looked at each other and laughed.

The next day, after a hearty breakfast, Adan and his father sat down for a serious talk about Marco and other family matters. Nikolaus volunteered to introduce Aquila to the marketplace to buy a new pair of sandals.

Nikolaus and Aquila had been gone for hours, and Adan was getting worried. He was about to suggest that he take one of his father's horses and go look for them, when the front door slammed shut. Footsteps ran down the hall to the terrace where Adan and his father were sitting.

"Adan, come quickly!" shouted Nikolaus. "It's Aquila! He's been arrested."

The three of them jumped into the family carriage and Taye, an Ethiopian servant in charge of the stables, took them to the basilica in the forum. They learned that the charge was theft. They were ushered into Prisoner Holding and taken to Aquila's cell.

"Thank God you are here," cried Aquila when the three of them stood outside his cell. "Uncle Niko and I were just looking over some fruit in the marketplace when this street vendor started shouting and pointing at me. Two men grabbed me and searched me. The merchant started yelling that a little girl saw me take a bracelet. They found a bracelet down the back of my tunic. I hadn't even felt anything, but it was there. I don't know how it got there."

"How close were you to the merchant's display?" asked Aquila senior with a frown.

"I don't know, maybe, three or four paces. Why? Is that important?"

"I'm afraid it is, Quila. Was it an expensive bracelet?"

"I never saw the bracelet. The two men grabbed something from inside the back of my tunic and took it to the merchant. I hope it wasn't valuable. The higher the value, the more severe the punishment, right?"

Adan nodded. "Yes, usually. Father, will they charge him with a manifest theft?"

"Most likely. He was within five paces of the merchant when they searched him."

"What does that mean?" demanded Aquila.

"It carries the highest punishment," Aquila senior responded. "The person caught with a stolen item within five paces of the victim, is most likely the culprit and not just an accomplice or an unwitting buyer of a stolen item. Manifest means the guilt of the culprit is obvious."

"But I didn't do anything!" cried Aquila.

"I believe you, son," said Adan. "The thief saw the girl alert the merchant and point at him. He knew he was about to get caught. He must have been standing right next to you so he dropped the evidence down your tunic. Did anyone brush against you?"

"Sure, lots of people. It was crowded. I would have felt the bracelet eventually, but it all happened too quickly."

"I'm sure the child pointed at the thief," said Adan, "but since he was standing near you, the merchant thought she was pointing at you."

"That's possible. She looked frightened when they grabbed me and she ran off."

"She must have panicked when they grabbed you and not the thief." Adan turned to his father. "You know about these matters. How long will he have to stay here before his trial?"

Aquila senior turned sad eyes on his grandson. "It could take months."

"*What!*" snapped Aquila. "I was thinking hours, not months. I can't believe this is happening?"

"We'll figure this out," said Adan. "You'll be out of there in no time."

Aquila senior pulled Adan out of his grandson's hearing, "Do not make rash promises, son. This looks very bad."

"He is the son of a centurion and the grandson of *Consul* Longinus and of *Primus Pilus* Centurion Cornelius. Surely the judge will believe his story."

"And what if the judge cares nothing about family connections? What if he is impartial as a fair judge would be?"

Adan had no answer. He tilted his head toward his son. "Come on, Father, we need to make sure he knows he is not alone." They rejoined Aquila and Nikolaus. "Son, we will come every day to bring you food and stay with you as long as the guards will allow."

"Bring me food? What are you talking about?"

"They don't supply food to the prisoners, only water," said Nikolaus.

Aquila's eyes widened with surprise. "You mean it is legal to let a prisoner starve to death? Isn't that the same as murder?"

"It is considered a just punishment for being arrested," said Aquila senior. "A person is considered guilty when arrested. We have to prove that you are innocent."

"It isn't right to be punished even before a conviction," cried Aquila.

"That is true, son," said Adan. "But we have to deal with reality as it is, not how we want it to be. For now, that is the law."

"There is one thing I can do," said Aquila senior. "I will speak to the centurion in charge and request that you not be held in the pit while you await your trial. You will be safe, Quila. We will make sure of that."

"The pit! Do you mean it's possible for me to be thrown in the pit with real criminals? With the rats and roaches and whatever else comes crawling out of the walls."

"I will see to it, Quila. You will not spend one minute in the pit."

Aquila sighed deeply as his shoulders sagged in discouragement. "This can't be happening. How is it possible that someone could be debating whether to buy apples or pomegranates one minute and hauled off in chains the next?"

They did not have an answer. More assurances were spoken before Adan, Nikolaus, and Aquila senior were forced to leave. All three men looked back when they reached the outer doorway. Aquila was gripping the iron slats of his cell, staring after them. It took all the strength Adan had to turn away and walk out of his son's sight. They left Prisoner Holding and returned home after Aquila senior spoke with the centurion in charge. Janae was devastated at the news as was Gregos, and the other servants. They knew it would be impossible to prove Aquila's innocence unless they found the real thief, which looked to be equally impossible.

The following weeks dragged by like years. Adan, Nikolaus, and their father went to the garrison every morning to bring food to Aquila. The *legionaries* knew Aquila's family connections, but rules were rules—any prisoner held more than a few days was subject to hard labor. The first time he was led out of his cell in chains to work, he was ordered to scrub mold and algae from the fortress *latrinae*. He balked and talked back to the guard who thrashed him across the back with a cane made of stiffened reeds. The pain dropped Aquila to his knees. He learned very quickly that, Roman citizen or not, the overseers had the authority to discipline unruly prisoners. They were also allowed to define "unruly" which meant that rebellion in any form was never tolerated.

Day after day, Aquila was forced to work like a slave. Some days he was chained and taken alone to clean the *latrinae* of various grand villas. The pumice stones used for the cleaning left his hands scraped and blistered. On other days, he was chained together with other long-term prisoners to repair damaged masonry walls or street-paving stones that were cracked from long use. Some of the prisoners were even used as sparring partners for the new recruits at the garrison. They were given shields, but no weapons, and were often seriously injured.

A few of the guards thought Aquila needed to be more submissive and that he would make good sport in the arena. He was brought out and handed a wooden shield. His opponent was a young Egyptian who coldly studied Aquila, and then smiled. Aquila timidly stepped into the arena. One of the soldiers watching at the arena came up from behind and pushed Aquila forward. He stumbled and fell to his knees, dropping the shield. The other soldiers laughed and taunted him. Aquila looked around timidly and, picking up his shield, slowly approached his opponent. His fear was obvious as he licked his lips and panted for air.

Aquila fumbled with the shield as if he found the handle unfamiliar and cumbersome. His other hand was clenched in a fist. "Can we talk about this?" asked Aquila in Egyptian.

The soldier blinked in surprise to hear a Roman speak his native language. "So, you prefer the study of language rather than the study of combat. It shows. My sister would be more challenging than you. Don't worry. I won't hurt you too badly."

"How about you don't hurt me at all?" Aquila begged.

The soldier laughed and hefted his sword from hand to hand. Aquila moved the shield back and forth, trying to anticipate which sword hand the Egyptian would favor. Again, the spectators laughed and called out insults. The men watching from the arena winked at each other and snickered. They shouted encouragement to the Egyptian and yelled out estimates of how long it would take until the prisoner cried for mercy. No one suggested more than two minutes.

The Egyptian grinned and charged at him. Instantly, Aquila's eyes burned with deadly intent. He braced his feet and waited. When the soldier was mere feet from him, Aquila sprang forward and swung the shield. He deflected the soldier's downward swinging sword and, at the same time, threw sand into the man's eyes. It was the oldest trick in the arena, but the Egyptian had missed seeing Aquila grab a handful of dirt when the soldier pushed him to his knees. The man cried out and dropped his sword as both hands flew to his face. Aquila swung the shield and hit the man across the bridge of his nose with the edge. The soldier jerked his head back as blood gushed down his face.

Aquila dropped the shield and smashed his fist into the man's face while hooking his leg behind the soldier's knee. The man fell hard on his back. Gasping for air, he was momentarily stunned. Aquila lunged at him. The soldier threw his arms up in defense. Aquila grabbed the soldier's wrist and twisted his arm, forcing the man to roll to his stomach. Aquila dropped onto the man's back, knocking the air out of him again. He ripped the soldier's helmet off, grabbed a handful of hair, and pulled his head back. He smashed his fist into the side of the soldier's face until he cried out. Aquila planted both hands on the back of the soldier's head and pushed his face into the sand. The soldier flailed his arms and legs. He tried to grab hold of Aquila's arms, but Aquila pressed into the man's spine with his knee. The soldier was defenseless as he lay pinned face down. Aquila grabbed the soldier's sword and stood up. He yanked the man by the arm, forcing him to his back. Aquila planted a foot in the center of the man's chest and put the sword to his throat.

There was only silence as the soldiers stared with gaping mouths. Aquila moved the sword point along the man's throat leaving a thin red line. The man's eyes flared wide with terror as his face lost all color. Aquila raised the sword high with both hands. The soldier screamed in terror and covered his bloody face with his hands. Aquila thrust the blade into the sand barely missing the man's neck.

"You forgot the most important rule," Aquila snarled. "Your opponent will never be as stupid as *you!*"

Aquila turned his back on the man still sprawled on the ground and walked to the arena gate. The soldier who had pushed him to the ground opened it for him. Aquila was never brought into the arena or forced to clean a *latrinae* again. During the following weeks, his body strengthened as he worked at lifting heavy, limestone blocks for construction. It would have been gratifying work without the chains and humiliating stares and comments from bystanders. Being locked into a cage every night with no place to sleep except the rough ground was dehumanizing. Rats and scorpions hunted for food from one cell to the next. Aquila smashed the locusts and beetles that found their way into his cage, but he saw the other prisoners eating them. They told him the insects supplied good protein and it was better to eat them since the smashed moths, beetles and cicadids attracted the rats. He found that if he held his nose, he could eat just about anything.

Seeing his family every day was all that kept Aquila from losing hope, but he saw the pain in their eyes as they passed food to him through the iron slats. They brought him more than enough to keep him from starving, but he didn't tell them that he was sharing his food with some of the other prisoners, behind the guards' backs. He knew his family would bring more, but the guards would confiscate the extra food for themselves. Also, no one, even centurions or politicians, was allowed to give food to non-family members. Aquila was on his own if he wanted to help a few of the other prisoners. At first, he had tried to ignore their suffering, but he found that the pain of a guilty conscience was worse than the pain of hunger. He was surprised at his own willingness to endure distress for the good of total strangers.

Nikolaus could hardly bear to look his nephew in the eye. He knew how it felt to be chained and locked in a cage. He had been chained the entire voyage from Rome to Jerusalem when Tribune Salvitto bought him.

His grandfather's eyes burned with anguish to see his grandson treated this way, but he was powerless to demand any changes other than to keep him out of the pit.

Adan would have immediately traded places with his son if it had been allowed. Since he couldn't, he went to the basilica after each visit and kept up a steady demand for the trial to be scheduled. His efforts paid off when the trial was moved up a month simply because the clerks complained about Adan's daily badgering. Finally, after being incarcerated three months, the trial date was set. Adan, Aquila, and Nikolaus hurried back to the garrison to tell Aquila the good news.

"That is a relief to hear, but I'm worried," said Aquila. "The guards tell me that my Roman citizenship only protects me from crucifixion in this case. Conviction of a manifest theft is punished with flogging, slavery, or even death if I have a harsh judge."

"Aquila, all of those options are unlikely," said his grandfather. "The judge might allow us to pay a fine to the merchant of three or four times the value of the bracelet. I'm sure the man would rather have the payment than seeing you flogged."

Aquila felt encouraged. "Hopefully, the very best thing will happen, and I will be found innocent." He turned sad eyes on his uncle. "There is one thing I have learned in here."

"What is that?" asked Nikolaus.

"I understand a little of what you went through, Uncle Niko, and what Calais wanted to escape. I hope Calais is alive. I hope he won't be able to find Marco and will come after me so I can beg for his forgiveness. No one should be forced into slavery." Adan smiled at Aquila proudly and nodded agreement.

Aquila thought for a moment. "Father, about Marco. You should go on to Herculaneum. He must have gotten there months ago. He may be in trouble and you're stuck here with me. Grandfather and Uncle Niko can bring me food."

"I'm not leaving you, Aquila," said Adan. "I know they will take care of you, but still, I will not desert you. When we leave, we will all go together."

Aquila's expression relaxed with relief. He reached through the iron slats. Adan grasped his son's hand. Father and son looked into each other's eyes and saw the strength of a loving bond far more powerful than iron chains or cages.

Chapter 22

Malta, Rocks, and the *Twin Brothers*

⬦

M arco and the survivors from the *Margarita* made it safely to the shores of
Malta. Everyone was exhausted and half starving. Marco was so exhausted,
he would have been perfectly content to lay in the wet sand all day and night,
with the torrential rain pouring down on him. The stress of dealing with the continuing
storm and fear of capsizing had taken its toll. Marco wanted to believe Paul when he
said not a single life would be lost, but his fear had latched onto him like ticks on a dog.
Ironically, it was the very fulfillment of Paul's prediction that now gave him pause. Calais
would survive the storm if he was a living, breathing human. Marco would be trapped
on Malta with him. If the images of Calais were the ghostly spirit of a dead man, he could
be haunted for the rest of his life.

Marco dragged himself up from the sand and followed Paul into a large, central
meeting place built by the Maltese. It was a covered structure with a raised, dirt floor
which gave some protection from the rain. The craggy, white limestone cliffs and escarpments defined an area that had once been completely submerged by the sea. Modest but
well-made homes were scattered over the landscape. The inhabitants did a little farming
for their own needs, but high-quality olives and olive oil exports were their main source
of income. They had everything they needed and more; therefore, they welcomed the
shipwrecked crew of the *Margarita* without duplicity. The people were accustomed to
peaceful living and were willing to share their bounty.

The sky was still drab shades of gray, and the cold wind chilled the survivors
through their wet clothes. They were led into the enclosure, and fires were lit to provide
warmth and light. Marco helped Paul collect a few broken branches to add to the fire.
When Paul laid some of the sticks onto a pile, a viper leapt out and fastened on his hand.
He shook it off into the fire.

The Maltese observers agreed with the assessment of one of their own. *"Surely this
man is a murderer. Though he has escaped from the sea, justice does not allow him to live."*

They watched Paul closely and waited. Hours passed, but when his hand did not swell and he showed no signs of illness, the natives decided he must be a god. They bowed to him and chanted praises, but Paul would have none of their adoration. He showed them where the snake's fangs had penetrated his hand and reminded them that his hand had bled just like any mortal's would. Paul's insistence that he was only human made them believe even more that he was a god.

The leader of the Maltese, a man named Publius, made special provision for the survivors over a three-day period, allowing them to regain their strength with ample food and rest. While they were convalescing under Publius's care, Marco did not see Calais, but he often felt the unnerving presence of watchful eyes.

Paul was keeping busy administering to the Maltese. He learned that the father of Publius was very ill with a high fever and dysentery. He was in danger of suffering fatal dehydration. Paul went to the man *and prayed, and he laid his hands on him and healed him. So when this was done, the rest of those on the island who had diseases also came and were healed.* The Maltese honored Paul and the other survivors by continuing to provide food and shelter. They even entertained the survivors in the evenings with song and storytelling.

Paul wanted to keep a journal of their time on the island but needed help. He explained his disability to Marco. "I cannot see my own handwriting very well unless I write very large letters, which wastes the papyrus. Your handwriting is small and precise. Would you mind spending a few hours each day taking dictation?"

"I would be glad to help," said Marco. "My father would approve. He says I should practice my Greek every chance I get."

"Then we are in agreement," declared Paul happily. "And in exchange for your services, I'll teach you how to make the best tents for all types of weather."

The time Marco spent with Paul made the days pass quickly. Their bond of friendship strengthened. Marco began to think he could be happy staying on the island for years rather than months, but then strange things began to happen.

Marco was walking along the beach one afternoon, as he often did, and saw a curious sight. A series of pebbles had been arranged in a pattern. Marco approached the stones and recoiled with fright when he realized that the pebbles spelled out the Greek word *prodotes,* traitor. He looked up and down the beach. There were only a few fishermen sorting their catch, as well as a group of children searching for seashells. They paid no attention to him and were too far away to hear him if he called out. Marco dropped to his knees to touch the pebbles. Just as he did, a rock sailed over his head, brushing his scalp as it passed. If he had not dropped down, the rock would have hit him hard. He spun around to see who threw the stone. No one was there.

Marco stood and scanned the sand dunes and low scrub bushes scattered along the hills and ravines. He saw no tall trees, no large boulders, no nearby structures to hide behind. Without warning, a painful punch to the back knocked him down. He sprawled on the ground and rolled to his back. Another thrown rock lay next to him. It had come from the direction of the sea, but no one was standing in the water. He looked out over the gently cresting waves. If someone was hiding under the water, he would soon have to surface. No one did.

Smash! Another rock sailed through the air and hit Marco on the shoulder. It came from the direction he had been looking, but no one was there. It seemed that his assailant was invisible. He slapped a hand to his coin pouch and thought about Calais's wooden owl. Perhaps that's what he wanted—to have Sofi back. Marco thought about leaving the figurine in the sand when he glanced down at the pebbles spelling 'traitor.' He had promised to keep the little owl safe. He would be a traitor if he broke his promise. Another rock landed at his feet. Again, no one was in sight. Panic seized Marco. He ran as fast as he could, despite the futility of escaping a ghost.

Unexplainable things kept happening over the following weeks. Tools Marco used would go missing. He would wake up the next morning holding the missing item in his hand. The thought that someone, or something, had placed it in his hand while he slept was more than disturbing. At other times, he would catch a glimpse of someone watching him from the shadows, but he never managed to see the figure walk away. It would just disappear.

Marco was sitting by a fire one night, mesmerized by the flames and lost in thought. A voice hissed right next to him, "Traitor! You will feed on poison in Tartarus." Marco gasped and jumped to his feet. No one was there. There was no sound of running footsteps. It was the voice of Calais. Marco wanted to scream into the night, but others would think he had lost his mind. He caught a whimper in his throat as he peered into the darkness. He felt the unseen presence watching him. Was it coming closer? Reaching for him? Would a cold hand of death brush his face? Then he heard a soft, gloating laugh from out of the black void. Marco turned and ran. From that night on, he was possessed with an unrelenting dread of the ghostly appearances.

It was three months before another Alexandrian ship, *the Twin Brothers, which had wintered at the island* was ready to leave. The name of the ship reminded Marco of his and Aquila's habit of calling each other Brother when they were separated. People outside the family would not know which twin he or she was talking to. The brothers would smile at the different ways people tried to discern their identity because they were too embarrassed to ask. It was a game for the twins; it was uncomfortable for everyone else. Despite his anger at Aquila, Marco missed his brother more than anyone else in the family. They were two very different people, but at the same time, very much alike. Yet how could he and Aquila ever be close again?

During the four months since Marco found Calais's body in the Antonia stables, he reflected on the events leading up to that moment. When he allowed himself to be honest, he knew that what he had set in motion was wrong. He decided to confess his actions to Paul. Once they left Malta and set sail on the *Twin Brothers*, he would tell Paul everything.

The money Marco had earned as the captain's clerk on the *Margarita*, would not last long once he reached Rome. He would still have to make his way to Herculaneum, well over a hundred miles from Rome. It was a shame that the ship would not be docking in Herculaneum before moving north to Ostia. Marco decided that he would not try to see Grandfather Aquila and Grandmother Janae until he came back from Herculaneum with Dionysia. They might try to talk him out of going. He couldn't risk the chance that he might submit to their persuasion.

Marco voiced his anxiety to Paul. "It's been four months. My family must think I'm dead. If only I could have sent them a letter. I have an idea on how to get Decimus to send Dionysia away, but I don't know if I can make it work." An uncomfortable thought had been gnawing at Marco and he finally voiced it. "What if she refuses to leave and I have to return home alone? No one in my family will ever respect me again." He gave Paul an anxious look.

"What did you expect, Marco?" asked Paul. "You set out on this venture without a thought of danger or delays. Did you think your mission would be easy?"

Marco thought for a moment. "Yes, I think I did when I was hired to work on a ship with you. Since you're a great man of God, I thought nothing bad would happen."

Paul chuckled softly and eyed Marco with affection. "And why would you think I could be your good luck talisman? Should I show you my scars from the beatings with whips and canes and stones? This old talisman is marred from head to foot, and my suffering is far from over. I do not believe I will leave Rome alive, but I will have my say first. All of Rome will hear of it. The time I have spent on Malta has been the most peaceful for me since I lived with Philip in Caesarea. I taught the Way to your parents and grandparents there. I enjoy nothing more than sharing my love of God and teaching the Way of Yeshua. I miss those days."

Marco hung his head. "I'm sorry, Paul. I have only thought of myself. I didn't even think about what you will have to face."

"Don't apologize, young man. I understand your frustration," said Paul. "Just remember, with God there is a reason for everything, and it is done at the proper time. You must have faith that things will work out as they should. Even when someone is taken from this world by the evil of others, that soul goes to God and eternal peace."

"I'm sure you're right, but it doesn't make it any easier. Patience is not my best virtue."

When Paul, Marco, Centurion Julius, and the soldiers boarded the *Twin Brothers*, Marco glanced around, worried he would find Calais only to see him disappear. Just as concerning, he might not disappear. He realized that leaving Aquila behind had been a terrible mistake. If Aquila had been with him, he would never have given the poison to Calais. Aquila would have talked him out of it and probably would have offered a better plan. Marco finally surrendered to the truth. Pride and self-interest had kept him from inviting Aquila on his quest. As a result, he was tormented by Calais's unexplainable appearances.

The loneliness for his family threatened to overwhelm Marco. He pulled the sapphire out from under his tunic and looked at the etched faces of the hexagonal crystal. It gave him comfort somehow. He could not give up faith in his mission now. Encouraged at the touch of the stone, he stopped looking for Calais. If he was on the ship, then so be it.

They sailed northeast for Syracuse on the island of Sicily where they stayed for three days. Some of the survivors of the *Margarita* did not return to the ship but stayed in Syracuse. Again, Marco caught himself scanning for Calais among the men leaving the ship and those who re-boarded. From Syracuse, the *Twin Brothers* circled around and sailed past the shores of Rhegium where a brisk south wind filled the mainsail.

Marco decided it was a good time to tell Paul everything that happened in Jerusalem. Paul listened without interruption. "Marco, I will not try to tell you what to do or pass judgment on you. We must leave judgment to God. I don't even judge myself. However, there are some things you must consider before you continue this quest. You must honor God first and then your family. You believe that it is God's will for you to free your Aunt Dionysia. You believe you do this for the good of your family. Yet you have excluded the involvement of your family, which contradicts the motive you claim. There is a remedy for this paradox. You should go to your grandparents in Rome. If they offer help, you should accept it."

Marco pressed his lips tightly together. "But what if they refuse to help and try to talk me out of going? I don't think I can take that chance."

"You think that if you do not bring your aunt to your family, your efforts will have been in vain?" asked Paul.

"Of course." Marco frowned in confusion.

"If you have learned anything good about the reality of this life or come to the aid of any person, then your efforts have not been in vain. The events may not have followed your plans, but I assure you, they have followed God's plan. Consider going to your grandparents, Marco. It is your decision, but I suspect it will determine whether you succeed or not."

Paul's advice gave Marco much to think about as they sailed ever closer to Ostia. The next day they reached Puteoli on the western shore of Italy. Paul had friends there, and Centurion Julius allowed him to stay with them for seven days while the ship's cargo was delivered and a new shipment was loaded. Marco went with Paul and was fascinated by the discussions he had with his friends. He was glad that his father had taught him Hebrew. The men were impressed with Marco's command of the language.

More of Paul's friends heard about their arrival and came to meet with him from as far as Appii Forum and Three Inns, nearly fifty miles away. Paul was greatly encouraged by their presence. When they finally reached Rome, Centurion Julius *delivered Paul and the other prisoners to the captain of the guard, but Paul was permitted to dwell by himself with the soldier who guarded him.* Marco was invited to stay with him until he could secure travel to Herculaneum. He finally began to relax. Calais had not made an appearance since they left the island of Malta.

Chapter 23

Rome, the Trial, and an Unexpected Revelation

T he day of Aquila's trial finally arrived. The family's best hope was that the merchant would not appear in court. The charge of theft would be dropped. The worst outcome would be a guilty verdict and a sentence of death by beheading. When the merchant entered the courtroom, the Longinus family's hopes were dashed. Nikolaus and Aquila senior, sitting on either side of Adan, whispered encouragement. When Aquila was escorted into the courtroom in chains and secured to the railing of the defendant's box, Adan had to look away. He felt Aquila's shame and fear. His dread for his son's fate was worse than what he had felt the day of his own execution in Herod's theater. If there were any way Adan could have taken his son's place, he would have.

Adan and the others initially sat in the spectators' section of the courtroom. The judge recognized Aquila senior and moved them to the witness holding area. The court scribe stood at the judge's signal and read the charge and the name of the defendant.

"How do you plead, Aquila Clovius Longinus?" demanded the judge.

"Not guilty, Sir," called out Aquila in a clear voice.

"Enter the plea, Scribe," ordered the judge. "Is the plaintiff present in the courtroom?"

"I am," said a man in the witness holding box as he came to his feet.

"Proceed. Tell us what happened," directed the judge.

"Yes, Sir. I was showing my wares to a man and his wife when a young girl pulled on my sleeve. She told me that someone had just stolen a bracelet and pointed at him," he stabbed a finger at Aquila, "and sure enough, the bracelet was in his tunic. I did not see him take it even though the display stand was right next to me. But he was within *three paces*, Judge!"

"Scribe, make note," said the judge. "This crime shall be recorded as a manifest theft due to the closeness of the accused to the scene of the crime. If the accused is found guilty, he may receive the maximum punishment under the law."

Adan expected this ruling, but it was still devastating to hear. Nikolaus and Aquila senior exchanged anxious glances over Adan's bowed head.

"Proceed, plaintiff. What did you do next?" asked the judge.

"I ordered my two sons to apprehend the thief and search him. The bracelet was found hidden down the back of his tunic. His belt, of course, prevented the jewelry from falling away. It is a common practice among thieves to drop the item down the back rather than the front."

"You may sit. Defendant Longinus, tell me your version of the events," said the judge.

Aquila lifted his chin and looked directly at the judge. "I was standing at a fruit cart debating with my uncle on what I should buy when two men grabbed me and searched me. They found something down the back of my tunic, but I did not put it there. I did not steal this man's property and I do not know who did. He claimed I stole a bracelet, but I never even saw it."

Aquila senior came to his feet. "Judge, if I may speak." The judge waved permission. "My grandson has no need to steal nor does he have need of a woman's bracelet. However, someone stole the merchandise and used my grandson as a hiding place. The chance of our finding the real thief is next to impossible. Even though the merchant recovered his stolen property, he has been inconvenienced. I offer to pay this man the usual fine of three times the value of the bracelet."

The merchant pursed his lips and looked at Aquila senior. "I have lost valuable time coming here to court. If you will pay me four times the value of the bracelet, which will compensate me for my time spent here, that will be acceptable."

"I agree. Is that acceptable to the court?" asked Aquila.

"If the accused will change his plea to guilty," announced the judge, "I will rule that the accused was convicted and a fine of four times the value of the stolen item shall be paid."

"No!" exclaimed Aquila. "I will not change my plea to guilty because I am *not* guilty. I will not dishonor my family with a conviction for something I did not do. Grandfather, it is not fair for you to pay for the crime that some stranger committed. I did not steal the bracelet. I do not accept this ruling. I never even saw what I am accused of stealing. How can we know that this man," he pointed at the merchant, "isn't lying? Perhaps nothing at all was stolen. I never felt anything being dropped down the back of my tunic. Isn't it possible that he has faked this crime knowing he could make four times as much money? His own sons searched me! One of them could have held the bracelet in his hand and pretended to find it on me."

"You make a good point," said the judge.

The merchant came to his feet and asked to speak. The judge gestured for him to proceed. "To answer this accusation of fraud, the couple I was dealing with at the time of the crime saw one of my sons take the jewelry from the thief's possession. They can also testify that the child saw him take the bracelet and pointed him out. I do not know their names, but my wife is acquainted with the woman."

"How do you know the child actually saw the accused take the bracelet?" asked the judge.

"She pulled on my sleeve and said, 'That man took a bracelet.' She pointed at the accused."

"And he was already across the street inspecting fruit with his uncle?" questioned the judge. "Why did she wait so long to tell you about the theft if she actually saw it happen?"

"I don't know, Sir. Only she can tell you."

"Why isn't this child here today to testify?" asked the judge.

"She ran away and did not come back. I've never seen her before."

"Very well. I see no need for additional testimony in this case. Sit down, Sir," ordered the judge. "Let the record show that I rule in favor of the agreed upon fine and a plea of . . . "

"Judge, may I speak," called a gentleman who had just slipped into the courtroom. "I wish to address the court before you make your ruling."

"Who are you, Sir?"

"I am Simon Magus of Gitta of the Province of Samaria. I now reside in Pompeii. I have a villa there and extensive vineyards. My grapes produce the best wine available in Pompeii. As a property owner, may I ask the court a question about this case before you rule?"

"What is *he* doing here?" Adan hissed.

Nikolaus frowned anxiously, "I have no idea, but it can't be good."

"Do you know this man?" asked Aquila senior seeing the concern of his sons.

"He's the man we told you about on the voyage here," whispered Adan.

Aquila's eyes narrowed with suspicion. "Why *is* he here?"

While the judge asked Simon for a few introductory details, Adan gestured to the scribe to approach and spoke to him quickly. "We know this man of Gitta. We had difficulty with him on a recent voyage." Adan told him several details. The scribe approached the judge and conferred with him. The judge arched an eyebrow as he looked at Simon and listened to the scribe.

"Simon Magus, I grant you permission to speak," declared the judge.

Adan frowned that the judge was still going to let the man speak even after telling the scribe about Simon's murderous intentions on the *Pegasus*. He tried to think of a reason to interrupt, but he was too distracted by his concern for his son.

"Thank you, Sir," said Simon as he stepped out into the aisle. "It seems clear to me that the accused is guilty and only feigns disagreement with his grandfather to deceive you. Therefore, I ask, does wealth supersede obedience to the law? Does power supersede obedience to the law? And what of politics?" he gave Aquila senior a sidelong glance. "Should this accused boy be released without punishment by letting his grandfather suffer the fine? The accused will not even lose a single coin. Should we allow a victim, this law-abiding merchant, who was robbed and is losing valuable business time, be paid off with," he struggled for the right word, "with this bribe? The stolen item may be nothing more than an ordinary copper bracelet, but the law must be respected. Principles must be upheld in a civilized society such as our own. Shouldn't we demand that this thief pay for his crime? If he gets away with theft now, what will he do next?"

Spectators muttered among themselves. "He's right," said one.

"A year of slavery will teach the brat not to steal," said another.

"He should be flogged," said a man sitting on the front row.

"I say execute him," said another spectator, "before he murders somebody." Several others muttered agreement with bobbing heads and pinched expressions.

Aquila senior came to his feet. "Judge, may I speak?" The judge granted him permission. "Thank you, Sir. Tell me, Simon Magus, were you a witness to the crime?"

"Most certainly not, Sir," answered Simon in a clear voice. "As I said, I live in Pompeii. I am only here to see the next trial. No harm in being early."

"Have you discussed the crime with any of the witnesses, or with the merchant who was robbed, or with his sons?" asked Aquila senior.

"Of course not! Why should I do that? I care nothing about the crimes of your grandson."

"Are you acquainted with the accused and his father and his uncle?"

Simon only hesitated for a moment. "What does that have to do with your grandson's crime?"

"Answer the question, Sir," demanded the judge.

"Barely acquainted, if you could call it that. We sailed from Caesarea on the *Pegasus*," said Simon. He raised his chin defiantly. "Since you mention it, I recall that they were most unruly and stirred up the crew to mutiny against the captain."

The spectators gasped and gaped at Aquila and Adan with suspicious eyes.

"Simon Magus, you will confine your comments to the case at hand," ordered the judge. "Continue Longinus."

Aquila nodded. "Thank you, Judge. Tell me Simon, have you ever seen the stolen item?"

Simon sighed in exasperation. "How could I have seen it? As I told you, I was not at the scene of the crime."

"If you were not at the scene of the crime, and you did not discuss the matter with any witnesses, and you did not see the stolen item—how did you know that the bracelet was made of copper?"

Simon started to answer and stopped. The crowd murmured with surprise. The judge focused on Simon. "That is a very good question. I distinctly heard you describe the stolen item as 'an ordinary copper bracelet,' did you not?"

Simon swallowed hard and glanced around at the others in the court room. "It was only a guess, an obvious attempt to simplify the matter. Many bracelets are made of copper."

"True, but you said it with confidence," stated the judge. "Tell me something Simon Magus, while you were in Samaria, what did you do for a living? I warn you to answer truthfully. You are not a Roman citizen, and therefore are not protected from severe punishment."

Simon blinked at him wide eyed. "I—I was a healer."

"Is that all?" asked the judge. "I understand that you are known as Simon the Sorcerer. I have a friend who does tricks by sleight of hand to amuse his children. Did you employ sleight of hand when you earned your reputation as a sorcerer?"

"I am just a simple healer, Judge."

"Yet, according to what Centurion Longinus has told my scribe, you announced on the voyage from Caesarea that you are famous throughout Samaria as a great sorcerer. Do you wish for me to direct him to testify under oath?"

Simon glanced at Adan. He knew who the judge would believe. "That is not necessary, Judge, but I see no connection to my activities in Samaria to this case of theft by this young man standing before you in chains."

"Do you now admit that you are skilled in sleight of hand as a sorcerer?"

Simon knew what Adan and Nikolaus would testify to under oath. "It was only a slip of memory, Judge. I have not employed those techniques in many years."

The judge smiled. "You forgot that you have these skills? Yet when faced with testimony from these men," he gestured at Adan and Nikolaus, "you suddenly remember? Interesting. You, Sir, knew that the bracelet was made of copper. Not once, has it been mentioned by anyone in this court today that the stolen item was made of copper. Using your skill, you could have stolen the bracelet yourself and dropped it down the back of the accused's tunic. How else would you have known it was a plain copper bracelet? You then questioned my judgment for considering terms that are approved by law and agreeable to the plaintiff. You claimed to have *forgotten* that you are skilled in sleight of hand. Then there is your accusation that these men encouraged the crew of a ship to mutiny against the captain. If I bring the captain of the *Pegasus* into this court, will he support your accusation?"

Simon blanched. He knew Captain Drusus would tell the judge about the poison he tried to use to make the crew sick. "I-I am sure the captain was much too busy with the foul weather to be aware of the crew's misgivings about those three." He pretended to cough to give himself time to think. "We all wondered about the reason for the sudden storm. The three of them," he pointed at Adan, "seemed to enjoy the stormy weather and even stayed on deck. Perhaps you should ask them about that, Judge."

The spectators murmured and nodded at Simon in agreement. They knew that storms were caused by the misdeeds of someone, other than themselves, of course.

The judge angrily pointed a finger at Simon. "You don't tell me how to run my court! You dodged my question when all I needed was a simple yes or no, which tells me that the captain will not support your accusation. You knew the stolen bracelet was made of copper. You object to a lawful fine being paid for a crime in which you claim to have no interest. You, Sir, have much to explain. Guards! Take this man!" He pointed at Simon. "I want him interrogated."

Simon threw his hands up and backed away. "No! I don't know anything about this case. It was only a guess about the bracelet, just a guess," cried Simon. "And I might have misunderstood a few crew members when they were grumbling about the poor weather conditions. Would you interrogate a man for listening to gossip?"

"Yes! Since you chose to repeat that gossip in my court!" cried the judge.

"Judge, may I speak," asked Adan as he came to his feet. "I do not wish to bring accusation on our behalf against this man."

"Are you sure, Centurion? It is clear that Simon Magus may be guilty of several crimes. If he is guilty and I let him leave, then I am derelict in my duty as a judge. I have a responsibility to uphold the law for the greater good of the many."

"I do believe in upholding the law," said Adan, "but let it be known that we will not bring accusation against him. We live in Caesarea in Judea and do not wish to be burdened with giving testimony here in Rome."

"Do you therefore have complete faith in my verdict on this matter?" asked the judge.

"I do," said Adan. "We submit to your judgment."

"And if I determine that charges, unrelated to you directly, should be brought against Simon Magus, will you give your testimony? The people deserve justice against all criminals. Surely, as a centurion, you have executed punishment upon many criminals."

"I have, Judge," answered Adan, "but can anyone guarantee that every single man who appears to be guilty, is actually guilty? My son is innocent of theft, yet there he stands in chains. We have been delayed for three months while he was subjected to slave labor and confinement, despite his innocence. We only wish to return to Caesarea unhindered."

The judge studied Adan for a moment. "So be it! The charge of theft is dismissed. Release the prisoner. Simon Magus of Gitta! You are free to go, but I warn you against coming before me ever again." The guards removed the chains from Aquila's wrists. He hurried to his family and they hugged each other, gratefully relieved that the ordeal was finally over.

An angry voice boomed behind them. Simon stood with arms crossed. "So, you think I should be grateful because you have shown me mercy? I disdain your false show of piety. There is only One who shows true mercy and that is Yeshua, the Christ, who you murdered by your own hand. Again, I say you are vile, and I abhor you. My God will deal with you, and your wolf-eyed son. God will judge you, and I will watch you kneel to him in despair!" Simon turned on his heel and left the courtroom.

Aquila glared after the man. "I have been worked like a slave these past three months because of him. Why shouldn't he be interrogated? They use torture, don't they? He deserves nothing less. It's obvious he stole the bracelet and planted it on me. The judge certainly suspects it. Why else would he question Simon about sleight of hand abilities?"

"I'm sure you're right, Aquila. He, undoubtedly, would admit guilt under torture, but there would still be a trial. The judge could order us to stay in Rome to testify. We have to leave Simon in God's hands and put the needs of your brother first. We've already been delayed three months. No telling where Marco is now or what his situation is. We need to get to Herculaneum."

"It turns my stomach to think he will get away with this." Aquila paused and looked his father in the eye. "Tell me, did you ever think I might be guilty?"

"Of course not!" said Adan. "How can you even ask me such a thing? I know you would never stoop so low to steal a copper bracelet. You're much too smart for that. If you were going to steal something, you'd go for nothing less than gold."

Aquila's eyes widened in shock until he saw a slow, lopsided grin brighten his father's face. "You had me going for a minute, Father."

"You had me going, Aquila," said Nikolaus, "when you refused to change your plea to guilty. I think the hard labor you've been forced to do has warped your brain. Why in the world would you sacrifice yourself to protect the honor of your family's name?" Nikolaus clicked his tongue with exaggerated disapproval. "Somebody might think you have integrity, or something. What's wrong with you?"

"I'm sorry, Uncle," Aquila said with a broad grin. "I'll make sure to cheat, lie, and harbor malicious thoughts to the best of my despicable ability—from now on."

"That's my boy!" said Nikolaus with an affectionate slap on the back.

"Enough of this foolish talk," growled Grandfather Aquila. "Let's get out of here before they arrest all four of us."

"On what charge?" demanded Adan.

"For theft of—everyone's sanity."

"Grandfather! Did you just make a joke?" asked Aquila incredulously.

"I don't think so, Quila. Well, maybe. What *exactly* is a joke?" He looked at them with straight-faced seriousness. They stared back. "What? I was only asking for clarification." He turned and strode from the courtroom before they could see the smile on his face.

Chapter 24

Road to Herculaneum, Camilla, and a Hornet

⸙

Marco knew he had delayed long enough. After thanking Paul for his guidance, he slung his knapsack over his shoulder and set off into the heart of Rome. He had a decision to make. Should he follow Paul's advice and go to Grandfather Aquila's villa or find a public carriage house and try to hire someone to drive him to Herculaneum. Marco had rarely seen his grandfather, and thought he was strict and aloof. His brother had a close relationship with Grandfather Aquila due to their frequent correspondence, which consisted of experiment designs, scientific discussions, and observations of the natural world. Aquila and his grandfather were bonded by their common interests. Marco had no such bond.

Marco's impression of his grandfather was modeled after the stories Adan told of his childhood. Also, Aquila senior rarely smiled and never joked with the family like his father and uncle often did. Adan and Nikolaus would get into "pun contests" and the family would be laughing so hard, tears would run down their faces. Grandfather Aquila would reluctantly surrender a smile. When asked if he thought a joke or a pun was funny, he would reply, "It was mildly amusing." Adan and Nikolaus would roll their eyes and grin at each other. Janae would snicker and Dulcibella would sigh with patient affection.

Marco loved both of his grandfathers, but he knew Grandfather Marcus like he knew his own heart. He loved to spend time with Marcus who was always available once he retired from the army. They would talk for hours when they went for long walks. Marcus was interested in anything Marco wanted to share. If Marcus had been in Rome, Marco would not have hesitated to go to him and ask for help. Grandfather Aquila gave him pause. He was intimidated by Aquila's pale blue eyes that could be ice cold in an instant. His deep voice was one of authority. When Aquila spoke, there was no question whether he would be obeyed or not. Marco was afraid that his grandfather would forbid him to go any further, and he would have to obey. He decided that he simply could not take that chance. He would head straight for a public carriage house.

The trip to Herculaneum in a carriage would cost him a good portion of his earnings, but it would be cheaper than buying a horse and quicker than walking, which would take four to five days. He spoke with drivers who might take him to Herculaneum, but they demanded more money than he could spend. Marco was considering taking a barge back to Ostia and finding a ship that would dock in Herculaneum. If he hired out as an oarsman on the voyage, he would earn some money and still reach his destination. However, it would take longer due to cargo loading delays.

Marco was debating his options and didn't notice the woman in the open carriage across the street from the carriage depot. She was in her late thirties, past the stage of prime beauty, but still attractive. Her driver waited patiently for his mistress to give him instructions. He was used to waiting. He knew she was looking over the "selection" of young men trying to hire a carriage.

"That one, Nonus," said Camilla as she pointed a bejeweled finger at Marco. "Go ask him if he wants a ride."

Nonus climbed down from the driver's bench. Marco saw the man approaching and frowned. "Young man, my mistress sees that you are having no success in hiring a driver. She wants to know where you are going."

Marco glanced at Camilla and nodded. She arranged her face in her most enchanting smile. "I need to go to Herculaneum," said Marco. "I have some money, but not enough."

Nonus walked back to the carriage and repeated to Camilla what Marco had said. She gestured at Marco to approach. "What is your name?"

"Marcus Clovius Longinus, but everyone calls me Marco."

"You may call me Camilla. I'm vacationing and just happen to be going to Herculaneum as well. You can ride with me. The pleasure of your company will pay your passage."

Marco glanced at Nonus and back at Camilla. "I have limited funds, but I can still pay you. I can sleep in the carriage when you stop for the night. I'll keep guard over it and your horse."

She patted the space next to her on the carriage seat. "No need, Marco. As I said, your companionship is enough. Nonus will stay with the carriage at night. Perhaps there will be jobs for you at the inns to pay for your bed." Her eyes glittered invitingly. Again, she patted the seat. "Come sit with me."

Marco smiled at his good fortune and climbed into the carriage. He noticed that the only luggage was a small satchel under the carriage seat. He decided that she must travel light even on vacation. A gentle breeze blew through his hair as the driver pulled out into the traffic of the cobblestone street. The roofless carriage would not offer protection from the autumn sun, but the days were getting shorter and the air was crisp with the nip of October weather.

Marco began to doubt his good fortune when hour after hour was filled with Camilla's droning voice. She rarely stopped talking long enough for Marco to even answer her questions. She often touched him, her hand lingering too long. He even dozed off once and jerked awake when they hit a pothole. He started to apologize for falling asleep until he realized Camilla had not noticed.

Marco planned to work for his room at the inn when they stopped for the night. Camilla watched closely as he discussed the matter with the innkeeper. She made a disgruntled face when the two reached an agreement. She was hoping Marco would be at her mercy with no way to pay for his own room. On the last day of the journey, Camilla invited Marco to go with her after she left Herculaneum.

"Tell me, Marco," purred Camilla, "why do you wish to stay in a sleepy little town like Herculaneum? Wouldn't you rather go to Pompeii which has so much more to offer? Or perhaps go back with me to Rome. I could go to either city. It makes no difference to me. Why don't you choose? It'll be fun. There must be at least a hundred and fifty bars and cafes in Pompeii, a city of pleasure I'm sure. Rome has the colosseum and the games. I especially love the *gladiator* contests. They're so entertaining. You're not afraid of a little entertainment, are you?"

Marco hesitated at the odd tone of her voice. She had made him feel uncomfortable all day. "I have family in Rome and in Herculaneum. I wanted to surprise my aunt with a visit."

The smile faded from Camilla's face. "You have family? I see." She glanced away to hide her annoyance. Her irritation did not last. Marco was handsome with the most unusual eyes she had ever seen. She liked his polite, shy manner. His inexperience with women was obvious, and she had no doubt she could convince him to stay. If he did rebuff her advances, she would find another passenger the next morning. She never wasted her time with unresponsive young men.

Camilla began to describe her exciting life of travel and luxury ever since her husband passed away and left her a fortune. She said she was unencumbered with children and had a villa full of slaves to see to her every whim. Marco listened with increasing distaste. Hours plodded along as slowly as the pace of the carriage horse. On and on she chattered about herself. Marco struggled to not fall asleep again. When they hit a rut in the road, forcing the carriage to tip, she fell against him and steadied herself with a hand on his thigh. When he looked over at her, she was smiling up at him and did not move away.

"Do you think I am pretty, Marco?" she whispered. He glanced at Nonus's broad back. "*Ohe*, don't look at him." She touched his jaw and coaxed him to look back at her. "He won't bother us. He knows better than to turn around." She lifted her face toward Marco.

"I—I'm not sure I'm the one to answer your question," said Marco as he tried to move away from her.

"Why not? You do like women, don't you, Marco? I'm a woman. What problem could there possibly be?" She widened her eyes at him and smiled.

"Uh, would it be possible for your driver to stop here for a moment? I seem to need the cover of those trees for a quick, you know, nature call."

She laughed and waved a dismissive hand. "By all means, Marco. One can never be too prepared for whatever may come. Nonus, stop the carriage over there. Marco needs to go for a bit of a walk." She giggled and coyly dipped her chin toward a shoulder.

Marco hopped out of the carriage and hurried to the trees. He did, in fact, need to answer the call of nature but wasn't sure what to do next. Slowly, he walked back to the carriage. He was dismayed to find Camilla sitting in the middle of the carriage seat. Marco was nervously blinking up at her when the horse squealed and reared. It side-stepped and tried to shake something from its neck. Marco rushed to the head of the horse and found a hornet stinging the poor animal. Again, the horse reared. Nonus raised his whip and slashed it down on the horse's back.

"*Stop it!* You'll only make her panic!" shouted Marco. He picked up a flat, fist-sized rock and scrapped it down the horse's neck, crushing the hornet. The horse tried to back up and squealed again. Marco saw Nonus raise the whip. Without thinking, he threw the rock, smashed hornet and all, at the man. It hit him in the chest. He cried out in pain and dropped the whip.

"You filthy creature!" he shouted. "I should thrash you for that!" He rubbed his chest and started to climb down from the carriage.

Camilla beat him to it. She had jumped out of the carriage and grabbed the whip. "How dare you assault my slave!" She raised the whip and slashed at Marco. He stumbled back and tripped. She raised the whip again and Marco held up his hands to ward off the blows. The whip cut into the undersides of his forearms. The pain spurred him to get to his feet and he backed away. Still, she came at him, but he ducked, avoiding most of the blows. He held up an arm to protect his face and reached out with the other hand. He grasped the whip and jerked it out of her hand. He took hold of the handle and raised the whip. Camilla screamed and ran back to the carriage.

She shouted at Nonus as she scrambled into the carriage. *"Go!"* Nonus flicked the reins and the horse took off at a gallop. Marco's knapsack sailed in the air from the back of the carriage. They raced down the road in a cloud of dust. He looked at the whip and then threw it as far as he could into the scrub oaks along the road. He picked up his knapsack and stared after them until they disappeared.

How did everything go so badly, so quickly? Marco looked up and down the road. He was alone. He felt something warm running down his arms and saw that the whip had raised welts and cut into his skin. The lacerations weren't deep but would leave scars. "Florinus, I should introduce you to Camilla," he muttered to himself. "You two would either fall in love or kill each other." Marco was dismayed that the people he thought God had sent to help him, had both turned on him. He had to admit that doing something heroic was proving to be much more complicated and dangerous than he thought it would be, especially after being shipwrecked and haunted by a ghost.

Marco considered his options. What should he do now? He was only a few hours away from Herculaneum, but the closer he got, the more anxiety he felt. Finally, near his goal, he realized that his chances of success would be significantly lower if he continued without assistance. He should have taken Paul's advice. Perhaps he had unfairly dismissed the idea that his grandfather would help him. The more Marco thought about it, the more he realized he had been shortsighted not to give Grandfather Aquila a chance. Or was he stalling to avoid the actual confrontation with Decimus since he had come so close and only now decided to seek out his grandfather?

"All right," he said out loud. "I'll go back. But, Grandfather, don't try to pressure me out of going." He felt silly for trying to sound brave when he knew what the real problem was. In truth, he had always been afraid of Grandfather Aquila. Marco had heard that even men equal to his grandfather's status would sometimes wilt in the face of his displeasure.

A new thought occurred to Marco; he was looking at the situation from the wrong angle. If he was afraid of Grandfather Aquila, maybe Decimus would be as well. The man had ruled in the highest elected position in Rome for many years. He had power and knew how to wield it. Aquila Clovius Longinus would be a formidable ally.

Marco felt a smile grow across his face. He turned around and stepped into a brisk walk back to Rome. A few days on the road would help him clear his mind. The refreshing October breeze lifted his spirits as his prospects for success seemed to improve with every step that took him away from Herculaneum. Or was it relief that energized his spirit because he had put off the dreaded moment of facing Decimus?

With a glad heart, Marco studied the hills and escarpments covered with vegetation of varying shades and textures of green. The trees of dark green foliage gave an artistic contrast with the greens of the wildflowers' leaves and grasses. He knew there was no hurry to get to Herculaneum since he had time on his side. Marco turned his attention back to the road and stopped in his tracks. Someone was standing there, once again, quite motionless. The lone figure was all too familiar and unwelcome.

"*Calais*," Marco hissed under his breath.

Chapter 25

Rome, Vindication, and Family Secrets

Simon was pleased with Aquila's arrest and fervently prayed for a conviction. Execution was an unlikely outcome, but possible. He traveled to Rome for the trial. When the judge indicated that he was going to accept terms of the standard fine in exchange for a guilty plea, Simon couldn't let it go. A slip of the tongue nearly resulted in an interrogation under torture, but ironically, he was more distraught over Longinus's refusal to testify against him. The centurion's lack of vindictiveness was contrary to Simon's condemnation of him. Why didn't Longinus seek revenge for his son's arrest and the false accusations Simon brought against them on board the *Pegasus*? In short, why was he being so passive?

Simon would never forget those yellow eyes looking at him without a hint of guilt when he admitted to killing Yeshua. Shouldn't the centurion suffer the loss of his own son, just as he had taken the life of God's Son? Simon viewed himself as an instrument of judgment dedicated to serving God. He only preyed upon the worst of sinners, which included everyone except himself.

Unfortunately, the Longinus family slipped out of his trap, despite his cleverness. Simon felt that he could still succeed if he persisted. The only reason the boy's case was dismissed was because Simon had overplayed his hand. He would be more careful next time. He returned to Pompeii to devise his next plan of attack.

* * *

The Longinus men returned to the villa and were greeted with cheers and hugs. Janae took one look at her grandson and burst into tears of joy. Adan saw Gregos duck his head and wipe at his face with the back of his hand. He muttered something about needing to tell his wife the good news. However, their joy was a bit tempered when they got a better look at Aquila. He had lost weight, despite the daily manual labor. His wrists were scarred from the chains he had been forced to wear every day. Working outdoors left him deeply tanned which glaringly revealed scars along his arms and hands from hewing limestone blocks and fitting them into place. There was a troubling distraction in his expression that had not been there before he was arrested.

Aquila's joy at being released did not last long. He now knew Simon Magus had stolen the bracelet to implicate him. While in prison, anger over the unfairness of the situation was amplified with each humiliation or taunt from his guards or passing observers. He was understandably frustrated at being falsely accused. Then to learn that his arrest was deliberately orchestrated by a virtual stranger, out of spite, was more than Aquila could accept. He believed Simon wanted payback for being openly ridiculed, but he was only partly correct. He was dangerously underestimating the sorcerer's delusional self-righteousness.

Aquila was free from imprisonment, but not from the trauma. The scars on his wrists were a constant reminder of his ordeal. Even though the chains were gone, he could still feel the weight of them. He was haunted with nightmares of being dragged through the city streets by a mob that ridiculed him with laughter and insults. They were led by the sorcerer who towered over the townspeople. His gray-steaked dark hair and shaggy beard framed his leering face. His dark eyes glittered with hatred. None of his family ever appeared in the nightmares. He was always alone. He would jerk awake, sweating and shaking night after night.

Try as he might, Aquila could not rid himself of his anger at Marco for running off without him. He understood why his father refused to submit charges against Simon, but it only fueled his resentment. Once again, Marco's needs took priority over Aquila's.

Adan was eager to get to Herculaneum now that Aquila was free, but Aquila senior asked for a day's delay. He told Adan they needed to discuss some family business and document signing. After the issues were in order, Aquila asked his son to walk with him in the vineyards.

"Son, there are things you should know," said Aquila, "my promise of silence to your mother is no longer in anyone's best interests. When you first came here after I received that horrible letter from Salvitto about the executions, you had questions about her. Gregos told you how your mother and I met, but he doesn't know everything. I told you Marsetina didn't want you to see her as a sickly invalid. That was a lie. I'm sorry, Adan. I just couldn't talk about these things all those years ago because the true reason is much more disturbing."

"Father, you don't owe me an explanation."

"But I do, Adan. I am done with keeping secrets from the ones who most deserve the truth."

Aquila gestured to the gazebo. They sat on the bench and looked out over the landscape of terraced grapevines. The *Tiberis* River flowed across the landscape below them.

The ribbon of water looked like liquid silver in the sunlight. Adan took a deep breath of the chilled air and waited for his father to speak.

"I think Gregos told you that your mother's name was not always Marsetina. It was Masika. You know that her parents, Colaxis and Zahra, gave her to a Parthian warlord to take the place of a diseased slave woman Colaxis sold to him. Since the woman showed no signs of disease when he sold her, Colaxis was unaware that she had contracted *variola,* the spotted disease."

Adan was shocked. "*Smallpox?* No wonder the warlord threatened to crucify Colaxis."

"Marsetina learned that the warlord actually bought the woman to reward his favorite general. When the warlord learned that the woman was infected, he ordered the execution of everyone who had been in contact with her. He was furious for being forced to kill his own men, especially this most trusted general. Giving Marsetina to the warlord was even more heinous because Colaxis thought the warlord had bought the diseased woman for himself."

"If he had, Mother could have also been infected. Gregos did not tell me this."

"He doesn't know. Tina never told him."

Adan understood. "She waited until she learned Latin to tell you."

"Yes, Gregos had to translate for us for months since they both spoke Greek. Parthian was your mother's native language, but she had a gift for languages. Like you." Aquila looked toward the river. His face was lined with sorrow. "Gregos doesn't know my Tina had a child by the warlord. A daughter, Pantea, named after one of the greatest female warriors that Babylon ever knew. In Parthian, the name Pantea means strong which is sad considering how things turned out. Your mother loved that child. She was her only comfort besides her Aunt Misha. The warlord saw her affection toward the baby and grew jealous. Tina, of course, never looked at him with any semblance of love. He grew hateful toward Pantea and treated her harshly until one day he threatened to kill her. Then Tina became ill, and the warlord took Pantea away from her, saying that the baby would become sick as well. Tina cried day and night to be reunited with Pantea. Her illness was not contagious and the warlord knew it." Aquila fell silent and gazed at the ground with unfocused eyes. Adan waited in silence.

Aquila squared his shoulders and continued, "The warlord brought Pantea back. Tina was overjoyed to hold the child in her arms once again. The warlord watched her with growing resentment." Again, Aquila fell silent.

"Father," said Adan gently, "did the child die?"

Aquila slowly nodded. "The next morning Tina woke up with Pantea lying next to her—dead. Suffocated. There was bruising around the little one's mouth and nose. It was then that Tina decided to betray the warlord at any cost. She risked her life to learn that he was going to violate the truce with Rome and ambush us. She told Misha to tell only General Livius Longinus and that they would be attacked in the valley of the lake. Fortunately, my father believed her."

Aquila wiped at his forehead with the back of his hand. "Pantea had eyes the same color as yours, as did your grandfather, Colaxis. Tina was convinced that you were a reincarnation of Pantea because of this shared trait. You cannot blame yourself, Adan, but when you enlisted, Tina believed Pantea's reincarnation in you was completed. Once you became a soldier, the ghost of the warlord would be able to find you because he would think you were Pantea, alive once again. It didn't matter how I tried to reason with her; Tina was convinced."

"Father, I am so sorry." Adan bowed his head in sadness. "That's why you tried so hard to keep me out of the army."

"That is true, but I also had reasons of my own. I saw first-hand what war does to a man's soul. You have your mother's loving heart. Being forced to destroy lives can turn the heart to stone. However, it was meant to be." Aquila waved a hand of acceptance and continued, "Tina believed the warlord's ghost would avenge her betrayal. She swore she could feel his presence when she became ill. The warlord didn't kill Pantea until she was in Marsetina's presence. Your mother believed his ghost had to follow the same condition. You would be safe as long as you were far away from her. She had lost two children, Pantea and your little brother, Martialis. She refused to endanger you despite how desperately she wanted to see you."

"If only I could have been with her, she would have known her fear was unfounded."

"No, your presence would have only made it worse," insisted Aquila. "Her fear of that man was so traumatic she never once spoke his name, thinking it would empower his ghost. She refused to answer your letter because she believed just her words in your hands might summon his spirit. As I told you before, she died before your second letter arrived. Your mother suffered from a despair that never healed. She had irrational fears and even knew they were irrational. In fact, that is why she swore me to silence about her real reason for not sending for you. She didn't want you to know how twisted her mind was when it came to that warlord. However, she told me that our love for each other gave her a reason to live. Her love for us, you and me, gave her purpose. If only she could have freed herself from the bondage of the past."

Aquila lowered his head and took a ragged breath. "When your mother died, *I* wanted to die. If Gregos had not forced me to attend Janae's estate sale, I would have died." He nodded his head in gratitude. "Janae and Gregos saved my life."

"I am so sorry that Mother was forced to bear so much tragedy at such a young age, and you suffered because of it, too, Father. Nothing equals the pain of losing a child." Adan thought for a moment while Aquila gazed at the terraces of grapevines. "Were you present when Misha warned Grandfather Livius . . . "

"Don't call him Grandfather," snapped Aquila. "He rejected that privilege when he ordered my execution."

Adan stared in shock. "*What?* He wanted you *executed*?"

"He did. I find it barbaric that all Roman fathers have the right to kill any of their children for any reason. My father ordered my death for disobeying his wishes. One of his centurions warned me. I told Gregos that Father banished me and that we had to leave immediately. I didn't tell your mother the truth until much later. We never did tell Misha."

Adan asked in disbelief, "He was that cruel? But didn't your father send you to rescue Mother after Misha told him about the ambush?"

Aquila gave Adan a sour look. "No, he didn't. I took Gregos and went on my own. I know for a fact that he never ordered anyone to rescue her. Even Gregos thinks my father sent us and he also doesn't know about the order to execute me. I see no need to tell him now."

"Father, I am so sorry both your parents rejected you," lamented Adan. "The legality of murdering one's own child, without legal oversight, should be abolished. In Mosaic Law parents can present a disobedient son to the people and request that he be stoned to death. However, the parents must prove their case and the people must consent to the killing."

They were silent for a moment, lost in their own thoughts. Adan placed a hand on Aquila's shoulder. "Father, the hate of Livius and the warlord didn't defeat you and Mother. You loved each other and your children. As long as someone can love others, he or she has the greater power."

"You are right to give honor to her love. If we focus on the bad then evil wins."

Adan smiled with a pensive sigh. "Mother was so hard on me, making me do the servants' work if I was disrespectful. Yeshua's followers pointed out how different I am, in the best of ways. If Mother had not loved our servants as she did me, I would have turned out very differently."

"You were a challenge," said Aquila, his expression eased with amusement.

Adan laughed. "Sorry, Father."

Aquila smiled. "But I knew you would turn out all right, for which I can take no credit."

"Not true," said Adan, his expression serious once again. "I owe much to you, Father. *I* had to suffer before I understood that."

Father and son looked at each other. Appreciation passed between them.

"Thank you, Adan. Believe me, it is good to hear you say that, but I'm not sure you would have made it without Serapio and Marcus Cornelius. They took up the slack after my failings."

"I have a confession, Father. When you investigated the incident of that man holding his family hostage and Marcus saved the family, I thought you were trying to get him in trouble."

"I can match your confession," said Aquila. "I *was* trying to get him in trouble. I began to see as I investigated, that I should be praising Marcus, not condemning him. That's why I sponsored his promotion to *Primus Pilus Centurio*."

Aquila smiled pensively. "Also, Serapio paid me a visit. He told me about his son and how he died. He reminded me that none of us knows how much time we have. He said that the two of us, you and I, were acting like stone walls, deaf and immovable. Then when I got Salvitto's letter about your execution, I was furious with myself for dismissing what Serapio had tried to tell me. I couldn't sleep, couldn't eat. It was the same terrible despair I felt when my Tina died. I still can't believe I got a second chance to make things right with you. It is the greatest blessing of my life next to the years I shared with your mother. Did Serapio tell you about coming to see me?"

"Not a word."

"That was good of him. So, how are Serapio and his family?"

"They're doing well. Did I tell you Nebetka and his wife just had their fifth child? *Ohe,* what's wrong with me! I forgot to tell you that Serapio is no longer half blind."

Aquila's eyebrows went up. "Really! Did Simon Peter heal him?"

"No, but God did, through Peter."

"I understand. I am glad for Serapio. Perhaps more than just his eye was healed as well."

Adan leaned his elbows on his knees. "When Serapio came to talk to you, did he tell you about my weapons? How he commissioned them and had 'Loyalty Above All. Son of the Father, Longinus' inscribed on the scabbards?"

"Serapio paid for your weapons? I never knew that. I thought you bought them yourself. I never noticed the etchings. I guess I didn't want to look too closely. I have always felt guilty for not supplying your weapons as a father normally would do."

"Stop berating yourself. You adopted Niko because I asked you to. And you bought that ruby ring with the initials NK just because I liked it even though I could never use it. Niko wears the ring with pride, and you were the one who bought it as a father would do for a son. Ultimately, buying that ring was the first step toward giving me a brother, which is a far greater gift than a set of weapons."

Aquila smiled with satisfaction. "I felt so strongly that I should buy that ring."

"Yes. I was quite surprised when you didn't even hesitate. It was the initials NK that caused me reach out to him when I learned his name."

The two men smiled into each other's eyes, savoring the moment.

"Tell me Father, was it true what you told me about Mother's reason for not telling me that Misha was her aunt, my great aunt?"

"Yes, that was true. Binding the curse, when she burned her parents' written names in the fire, required keeping the family connection to Misha a secret. Otherwise, in her mind, both you and Misha would be in danger. I have never put stock in curses, but your mother certainly did. When I left with Marsetina, my father assumed I would come back without her and Misha. He told me that when I returned, I was to enlist in the army. He used to call me his *Parvus Legatus.*"

"Little Commander. That must have been quite a burden for a child."

"It was. He never asked me what I wanted. He always told me, 'You will make me proud when you become a great soldier.' However, when I came back with Tina as my wife, I could no longer enlist, since *legionaries* cannot be married. Then my father said,

'You are the greatest disappointment in my life. You're a sorry excuse for a son.' Those words are burned in my soul."

"His harsh words made both of us suffer."

"Yes, you told me what my father, Livius, said to Valentius. That he was a sorry excuse for a centurion and a man. That seems to have been his favorite phrase."

"Father, you need to let go of those words. You are only doing yourself harm by holding on to them. I learned something from a woman named Pomona, Valentius's daughter. She said Valentius originally brushed the harsh words aside. He said they were only the rantings of a miserable old man. But over time, the hurt festered, eventually causing Valentius to believe you had his son, Aurelius, murdered to open a position for me at the Antonia."

"The tongue can be a deadly weapon," said Aquila. "Words matter."

"Speaking of words—you did a wonderful thing for your grandson today. I wasn't listening when Simon described the bracelet. I was trying to think of a good reason for the judge to expel him from the court. As it was, Simon's own words were his undoing, despite how good he is at verbal misdirection. You saved Aquila from a false conviction and undeserved punishment. I only hope he will come to terms with his bitterness."

"Adan, he suffered a great deal while in custody, but he will recover."

"I hope you're right," said Adan as he came to his feet. He put a hand down for his father. He gripped his son's wrist and stood up.

He looked Adan in the eye. "If Aquila had been sentenced to a physical punishment or even death, were you going to ask the judge to let you take his place?" Adan nodded. "I would not have allowed that, son. As the elder member of the family, my request would be heard first. I would never let Quila or you die if I could stop it."

"I believe you, Father. I will treasure those words."

A slow smile curved Aquila's lip. "Yes, there are some words that should be safely locked into one's heart, never to be forgotten. I have many treasures of your mother, right here." He patted his chest. "When I grieve for her, I think upon those treasures and I feel comfort."

Adan's eyes brightened with a warm smile. "I am glad to hear that, Father."

Chapter 26

Captain Egnatian, the Prophecy Box, and a Sighting

The next morning was a busy one as the travelers prepared for their journey to Herculaneum. Adan had no way of knowing if Marco was already there, on his way, or nowhere near Italy. Aquila had his driver, Taye, ready the carriage and told him to take his son, Jemel, along on the trip as well. The two Ethiopians were formidable swordsmen, which would come in handy if they were ambushed by robbers. They had once been slaves, as had all of Aquila's servants, and their loyalty to *Consul* Longinus ran deep. Adan knew he could depend on them.

Aquila senior and Janae watched as the open carriage moved down the lane and into the street. They already missed their sons and grandson and were sorry their children would not get to see them.

Adan tried to get Aquila involved in conversation, but he made only monosyllable responses. Nikolaus eyed his brother with sympathy when Aquila curled up on one of the carriage benches and appeared to fall asleep. The brothers fell silent. They stared absently at the thick vegetation of olive, pine, myrtle, and juniper trees along with the occasional oak. The air was sharp with an unusual dryness and scented with the autumn wildflowers that bordered the road. The rhythm of the horses' hooves striking the dirt road was soothing. A fly lit on Aquila's arm. He flicked it off with a hand. Adan and Nikolaus exchanged glances.

Adan mouthed the words, "He's awake." Nikolaus shrugged.

"You know, I was thinking about Valentius," said Adan. "Do you remember how angry I was after we escaped from Jerusalem and got back to Caesarea?"

"Remember it? How can I forget? That would be like forgetting I have feet," said Nikolaus.

"I was alive, and grateful for that, but in order to protect our family, I would have been forced to give up almost everything. You remember. I wasn't even sure if I would

169

ever see my father again. I hated Valentius with a passion I didn't think was possible. He endangered my life every chance he got for two years. And to think, Valentius's hatred for me started with something my grandfather said before I was even born. That is truly pathetic." Adan took a long, slow breath. "Simon Peter came to my rescue."

"You mean from the belladonna?"

"No, I'm talking about what Peter said after the healing. He said my anger was giving Valentius permission to sabotage my happiness. He said even if the man were dead, he would always poison my heart, even without the belladonna, unless I did one thing."

"What was that?"

"Forgive him."

Nikolaus recalled a memory. "I remember when we encountered Valentius outside of Jerusalem on our way to confront Herod. You had your sword on Valentius's neck, and the guards did nothing to stop you. I thought you were going to kill him."

"I was. I wanted so badly to kill him it was nearly overwhelming. I was just about to slice his neck open, when I saw it," said Adan.

"Saw what?"

"A corner of his mouth curved up. Then his face seemed to brighten with, I don't know, hope, maybe. I realized that he *wanted* me to kill him, to spare him from Roman justice. So, I put my sword away and I did what I thought would be impossible. I forgave him."

"You're kidding! I never knew that," said Niko. "Why didn't you tell me?"

"I told Dulcie. I thought you heard. After that, I didn't want to talk about all that stuff anymore. In fact, I haven't even told my children any of this. I probably should."

"What did Valentius do when you forgave him?"

"He was furious. He spat on the ground and said, 'That's what I think of your pathetic forgiveness.' Then he said the vilest things anyone has ever said to my face. He was so enraged; I thought his head would explode."

"He was angry because you forgave him! That must have made *you* angry."

"No, well, it was annoying." Adan laughed softly. "Maybe a little more than annoying. The truth is, Niko, it didn't matter how Valentius reacted. He was still responsible for his crimes, would still be punished by Roman law, and still had to face God, whether I forgave him or not. I forgave him for me, for my own happiness. Peter was right. As soon as I forgave that broken man, his power over me vanished. Now I rarely think about that awful time in my life. Those two years in Jerusalem would have been unbearable if it hadn't been for you, Serapio, Fabiana, Nebetka, even Salvitto. As it turned out, being in Jerusalem was the best thing that ever happened to me."

Nikolaus smiled. "Yeshua."

Adan nodded. "Yeshua. And you, Peter, and John, Yeshua's mother and his followers. Sometimes we have to be thrown to the ground before we can fly like an eagle."

"Don't I know it!" declared Nikolaus. "I was sold into slavery after being a pampered, privileged child. Captain Egnatian made sure of that."

"Egnatian? That was his name? I don't remember you ever saying his name before."

"I probably haven't. I couldn't say it without getting nauseous. Egnatian tried to ruin our lives twenty-three years ago, but it feels like yesterday. I hated that loathsome man, but I was also angry at Dionysia."

"Because she refused to marry Egnatian?"

Nikolaus nodded. "Egnatian was obsessed with Dionysia. I thought it was strange. His crew believed she was a demon from the Underworld because of her being an albino. She tried to hide it by dying her hair red with henna. But that didn't make any difference. One crewman told me they believed she colored her hair with the blood of her victims."

"Unbelievable!" Adan exclaimed. "Where did they get that idea?"

"*Ohe*, it got worse when the crew started getting sick. Naturally, they blamed her. After the first crewman died, they demanded she be thrown overboard. Then my whole family got sick. That calmed things down, until another crewman died. An oarsman dragged Dionysia to the upper deck to throw her into the sea. She was screaming and I tried to intervene, but some of the crew grabbed me. I was screaming and fighting but there were too many of them. Then suddenly Egnatian was there. He knifed the man in the back and tossed him overboard like he was trash. I was grateful Egnatian saved her life, of course, but I didn't know it would come with such a high price."

"Niko, you never told me these details before. I'm so sorry," said Adan.

Nikolaus ran his hand across his forehead. "I haven't let myself think about it. Killing that oarsman didn't stop their fear. The crew still wanted her off the ship, but they feared the captain more than her. The next morning, my whole family was dead except for Dionysia. The disease killed so quickly I lost my parents, my brother, and four sisters in one night. The crew left us alone after that."

"Are you saying that seven members of your family died all on the same night?"

"It was awful. I was so overwhelmed with grief; I wanted to die. If it hadn't been for Dionysia, well, I probably wouldn't be alive today."

"I am so sorry you and your sister had to endure such a terrible loss," said Adan. He felt for his brother but he also wondered about the likelihood of seven members of the same family dying at the same time from illness. Yet, Adan could not think of any possible motive for foul play. "That must have been a very contagious disease. Did your family eat with the crew? Is that how the illness spread?"

"No, passengers were kept separate from the crew, but we ate the same food. There was one common water supply, of course. Occasionally, the captain offered us wine. Dionysia and I didn't like it, but Father told us to accept it and be grateful. I remember once, Egnatian seemed really drunk, and he made a big show of pouring wine for each of us. The idiot spilled most of Dionysia's wine and tried to make a joke about it, but none of us laughed. I poured most of mine out when Egnatian wasn't looking. I can't believe I can talk about this now."

"It's good that you can," said Adan with sympathy.

Nikolaus pursed his lips in thought. "Perhaps."

"How long were you and Dionysia sick?"

"We recovered quickly after the ship's doctor treated us. We had nausea and headache, but that's all."

Nikolaus paused in thought. "I remember the last night before our family died. Dionysia and I went on deck to look at the stars. It was a beautiful night. When we returned below deck, they had taken a bad turn, especially father. He died first. It was horrible to watch. There was nothing I could do to stop it." Nikolaus looked at Adan with sadness. "Just like when you were in Herod's theater."

"That is an awful memory for both for us," Adan said in a subdued voice.

Nikolaus wiped at his eyes with the back of his hand. "The doctor thought the illness might be malaria, but I think he was guessing. In all, nine people died, including the two crewmen. They became paralyzed, and finally, couldn't breathe. They . . . it was so . . . " He swallowed hard.

Nikolaus was silent for a few moments and then continued. "You know what I think now? I think Egnatian wanted Dionysia *because* they thought she was a demon. He was depraved. I've never known anyone who oozed evil like he did. He even wore a talisman of Orcus."

Adan frowned. "Orcus! The god of eternal torture? You can't be serious. Some parents tell their children Orcus will torment them and kill their pets if they misbehave."

"Maybe Egnatian thought he and Orcus would be great pals in Hades." Nikolaus waved a dismissive hand. "After our family died, the ship's doctor offered me an apprenticeship to pay our debt to him and give me a livelihood. It was then that Egnatian claimed Father hadn't paid our passage yet and demanded that we be sold as slaves to cover the cost. He said that if Dionysia would agree to marry him, he would drop the charges. It took a long time, but I was finally able to forgive her for not marrying him. I had been the son of a world-famous architect, a member of high society, and surrounded by a close family. Suddenly, I was a slave on the auction block. I actually don't know how I survived."

"Do you think you can ever forgive Egnatian, Niko?"

"What! You mean try to find that monster?"

"No, you don't need to find him. You forgive someone for your own happiness, not theirs."

"I'm perfectly happy now. I have grown comfortable with my anger toward Egnatian. Why should I let it go? Egnatian was more than evil. Did I tell you he even confiscated our luggage? Dionysia and I only had Father's ruby ring and Mother's purple sapphire, which we had to sell, of course. I still can't believe Decimus tracked down the sapphire and bought it back for her. That was a generous thing for a master to do for his slave. But all of Father's scrolls, a papyrus book of architectural designs, and," Nikolaus's eyes went wide with alarm. "And the box! What happened to that box?"

"What box?" asked Adan, startled at the panicked expression on his brother's face.

"How could I have forgotten it? I was fascinated with it. It had disks, and dials, and rods on the front, and three round-shaped gemstones, also on the front. One at each top corner and one in the center at the bottom. I found Father with it quite by accident. I was trying to hide from my brother so I slipped into the room Father used as his private study and hid in a cabinet. Father came in. I could see him through the slats of the cabinet door. He put the box on his desk and started working the dials. I crept out and stood behind him for a long time, watching, fascinated with the way the rods were moving around the center disk. He must have sensed me standing there because he looked over his shoulder. I thought he was going to collapse; he was so unnerved." Nikolaus paused, trying to remember every detail.

"Then what happened?"

Nikolaus hesitated. "Now things get blurry. He was so angry. I guess I don't want to remember that part. The only thing I remember is he called it the Prophecy Box."

"The Prophecy Box? That is certainly intriguing. What kind of gemstones were on it?"

"I've never seen anything like the stones set in the top corners. They were rounded like opals. No facets. One was reddish that blended into pale yellow with silvery tones. It was in the top right corner. The one at the top left was in shades of iridescent pale blue, indigo, and turquoise, also with silvery tones. The colors seemed to blend and shift as if a light inside the stone moved as the observer moved. The stone at the bottom center looked like sand dunes on one half with a solid colored sky at the top. They call it picture jasper. The hills were shades of reddish-brown and ivory with dark-brown outlines, while the sky was kind of dull green with white specks that looked like stars or snowflakes. I've seen other picture jaspers before, but this one looked exactly like a miniature landscape under a starry night. All three stones were beautiful."

"Did the corner gemstones look like Ethiopian opals?"

Nikolaus frowned in concentration. "No. The colors seemed to shift inside the stone. But that may just be my memory playing tricks on me. What I do remember, very clearly, is that Father told me his life depended on the box remaining a secret. He said it was the only one in existence and that no one else knew he had it. He said the men who invented it had died a long time ago. He said the box would be mine someday, but until then, I was to forget about it. Obviously, I took his command to heart since I did forget about it until now. Egnatian must have found it when he confiscated our luggage."

"This is a very curious story," said Adan. "How could a box generate prophecies? And how did Nicandros come to own it?"

"I wish I knew, Adan. I asked him where he got it. He made the oddest expression, like something between guilt and relief, and then pulled his hands away from it. He wiped his hands on his tunic as if they'd gotten dirty or wet. He wouldn't look me in the eye. Then he took me by the shoulders and made me swear to never breathe a word of it to anyone, not even our family, including my mother. He said his life depended on keeping the box a secret because others would kill both of us to get it. I wonder if Dionysia ever saw it."

"Maybe Nicandros was just being dramatic," said Adan, "to make an impression on you."

"Father was not the dramatic type. He was calculating and methodical. I can't remember him ever raising his voice even in anger. But I remember when he told me to keep it secret, I saw terror in his eyes for the first time, the only time. It really scared me."

"How old were you?"

Nikolaus pressed his lips in thought. "Seven. We moved from that house just before I turned eight and we only lived there a year. We moved around a lot."

"Just to different houses or different cities?"

"Different cities." Nikolaus frowned. "I remember asking Mother why we had to move so often. She rarely gave me a straight answer. Maybe *she* didn't even know." Nikolaus scanned the clouds that had thickened as they talked.

Adan considered his next words carefully. "Could anyone else have discovered that Nicandros had the box?"

"I suppose it is possible, but not from me. Why?"

Adan wasn't prepared to share his growing suspicions about the deaths of Nikolaus's family. "No reason. Just curious."

The two brothers were silent for a while, deep in their own thoughts. Large, scattered raindrops began to fall. The breeze fell away causing the rain to fall straight down.

Nikolaus broke the silence. "Egnatian still haunts my thoughts. I have nightmares about him. Marina says sometimes I talk in my sleep and I sound panicked. It's always the same nightmare with Egnatian trying to stab Dionysia and—"

"Stop it!" cried Aquila as he sat up. "You two can stop ganging up on me now. I know what you're trying to do. You think I'm feeling sorry for myself and I need to get over it." He blinked angrily and wiped at the rain on his face.

Nikolaus and Adan looked at each other and back at Aquila. Adan asked with a subdued tone, "I take it you've been awake for a while?"

"Of course, I've been awake," grumbled Aquila. "How can anyone sleep with this carriage finding every single pothole in the road? And now, it looks like we're going to get soaked."

"We were only talking, Aquila. Apparently, there are things Niko and I have never discussed."

"I know you both have gone through some really terrible things, but so have I. And before you both start lecturing me, let me save you some trouble. I'm not about to forgive that loathsome Samaritan. Not ever."

"Even if holding on to your bitterness makes you miserable?" asked Adan.

"I'm not miserable!" growled Aquila. "I'm just angry. I have every right to be angry."

"You know who has the only right to be angry? God!" said Adan. "We humans hate and abuse and kill each other for the worst reasons. Still, God told Isaiah, *'I am He who blots out your transgressions for My own sake; and I will not remember your sins.'* If God forgives us for his own sake, then we should do the same."

"I don't want to talk about it anymore," cried Aquila. "Let me out of this carriage."

Adan called out to Taye, "How about we stop here for a while."

"Yes, Centurion," answered Taye. "Perhaps we should take shelter under the trees while it rains. It won't last long." Taye reined the horses over to the side of the road.

Aquila stalked off through the rain-soaked grasses and shrubs scattered across the landscape. Nikolaus watched with a sad heart. Simon Magus, the Sorcerer, was Aquila's first encounter with a vindictive malcontent. He knew Simon would not be the last.

Aquila didn't want to hear anymore lectures. He could feel, and think anything he wanted to, and didn't want to be told what to do. He also wanted to think about the Prophecy Box that Nikolaus's father had owned. Why was Nicandros so terrified of anyone knowing he had it? Could the box truly reveal the future? And what kind of gemstones could change colors? Aquila didn't know how he could find the answers, but the challenge only made him more determined. Marco wouldn't be the only one to bring a great "treasure" home to Uncle Niko if he could find the box.

Adan wanted to clear his head and walked up the road far enough to work the soreness out of his legs. He ducked his head to protect his face from the pelting rain. However, the sharp coolness of the precipitation was refreshing. The rain cloud was surrounded by a smattering of lace-like clouds which allowed bands of sunlight to glide across the landscape. Adan approached a bend in the road as he prayed for God's help to find Marco. If he found Marco, they could confront Decimus Lentulus as a family. Adan followed the curve of the road. A solitary figure was walking ahead of him toward Herculaneum. Adan wiped at the rain in his eyes with the back of his hand. He stiffened at the familiar rhythm of the gait and motion of the arms. He increased his pace, keeping his attention on the distant figure. It was a young man with a knapsack over his shoulder, dressed in the knee-length tunic and belt of a freeman. His dark hair was still wavy despite the soaking rain.

"*Marco!* Is that you!" cried Adan. He looked over his shoulder and shouted at Nikolaus, "He's here. It's Marco!" Overjoyed at finding his son, Adan looked back up the road. His stomach lurched with shock when the figure turned around. It wasn't Marco. It was Calais.

Chapter 27

Herculaneum, Dionysia, and a Dagger

⊗⊗⊗

M arco was heading back to Rome until he looked up to find Calais standing dead center in the road, once again. He didn't dare take his eyes from the solitary figure. "What do you want from me?" Marco shouted. There was no answer. "Are you a ghost then?"

Marco started to move toward the image of Calais. An unseen rock in the road snagged his sandal and he tripped. In his effort to keep his balance, he dropped his knapsack but managed to right himself. He leaned down to retrieve the knapsack. When he looked up, Calais was gone.

Marco cried out, "Are you trying to drive me crazy, Calais? It's *not* going to work!" It was working. "I'm going back to Rome." No, he wouldn't. "You can't stop me!" Yes, he could.

Marco clenched his teeth in exasperation. What was he supposed to do? What if seeing Calais was an omen. Maybe he appeared when Marco was going the wrong direction. Or maybe he was supposed to return to Rome and Calais was trying to sabotage his efforts.

Marco was confused. There were too many factors to consider and too few facts to make a logical decision. He walked a short way until he found a comfortable spot under the shade of a myrtle tree. He swallowed hard and realized he was getting thirsty. Camilla had not thrown his waterskin off the carriage along with his knapsack. Herculaneum was only a mile away, an easy twenty-minute walk. The nearest inn in the other direction would take at least six hours to reach. He got up and headed back toward Herculaneum. He told himself it had nothing to do with Calais. He just needed water.

* * *

A short time later, less than a mile outside of Herculaneum, Adan shouted at Nikolaus. "He's here! It's Marco!" When he looked back, the solitary figure was facing him. It was not Marco. "Calais! *How!*" blurted Adan as he tried to wipe the rain from his face. When he looked again, the figure was gone.

Aquila joined Nikolaus after hearing his father shouting and they ran up the road to find him standing with his open palms raised in exasperation.

"Where is he?" exclaimed Nikolaus.

"He was right there!" Adan pointed up the road. "But it wasn't Marco. It was Calais. He's alive. Serapio was right to warn us."

"So, where is he?" asked Aquila, scanning the landscape.

Adan felt a chill creep down his neck. "He couldn't have run away." He scanned the road ahead that ran straight a good way before it curved. "The trees are too far from the road. He couldn't have run to them before I'd see him." Adan hung his head in bitter disappointment. "I really thought it was Marco, but then he stepped into the sunlight. Then he just disappeared. I know it was Calais, but how did he disappear?"

"Uh, Father, Uncle Niko, there's something I should have told you." Aquila bit his lip as they stared at him expectedly. "I've seen Calais, too, in Dora."

"*What!*" Adan and Nikolaus exclaimed in unison.

"I'm sorry. I chased him down an alley, and he turned a corner. I followed him, but he was nowhere in sight. I thought I was losing my mind. I should have told you."

"It doesn't matter," said Adan. "What would we have done about it, anyway?"

Aquila looked at his father with relief. "You're not mad at me?"

"No. It was understandable."

"This is a problem," said Nikolaus, "how did he disappear both times?"

Adan shot a look at Nikolaus. "What are you saying? He's a ghost?"

Nikolaus and Aquila stared at him in silence. This was a question in which all the answers were equally unpleasant.

Adan headed back to the carriage. He called out to Taye and Jemel. Jemel gave water to the horses and Taye took up the reins. Adan, Nikolaus, and Aquila scanned the trees and rolling terrain as they went down the road, but saw no one watching from the shadows.

They came across a middle-aged woman in a carriage on the outskirts of Herculaneum, headed toward Rome. Her driver, a large, older man of Roman appearance glared at them as they approached. The woman was talking to a young man with a waterskin hanging from a shoulder. He was handsome with blonde, curly hair and bright-blue eyes. He was smiling when he took the woman's offered hand and started to climb into the carriage. As Adan's carriage drew even with the woman, she glanced over and saw the three passengers. She gasped with surprise as she stared at Aquila. Then her eyes fell on Adan, his weapons, and the belt of a centurion. Her eyes darted back to Aquila. The woman let go of the blonde man's hand and pushed him back. She shouted at her driver to go, and the big Roman flicked the reins. The carriage sped off leaving the young man staring after her.

"What was that all about?" said Aquila looking from his father to his uncle.

"Really? You can't guess?" said Nikolaus.

"Marco?"

"Yes, I think she has met your brother," said Adan, "but it seems that it was not a positive experience. She was frightened about something. That's troubling."

"He probably tried to talk her driver into running away with him," grumbled Aquila.

Adan threw him an aggravated glare. Aquila lowered his gaze.

"Marco must be ahead of us," said Nikolaus, hoping to deflect Adan's irritation. "He must already be in town. Decimus's villa won't be hard for him to find in a town this small."

"What are we going to tell Decimus if Marco isn't there?" asked Nikolaus.

Aquila snorted. "What are we going to say if he's come and gone? 'Decimus, what do you mean Marco stole your slave and kidnapped your children? He would *never* do that! Are you sure you haven't misplaced them?' We'll be lucky if he doesn't have us arrested."

"Aquila!" growled Adan. "Enough."

Nikolaus coughed and drew Adan's attention. "Brother, I think the truth will be our only option. It usually is the best one in the long run."

They rode down the streets, past the bars, cafes, and the brothels with graphically advertised mosaics on the walls. They arrived at the villa of Decimus Lentulus in an upscale residential area. Adan pulled the bell hanging outside the door of the villa. He tried to temper his eagerness, knowing that Marco may not be there.

The door opened and Decimus's eyes went wide with delighted surprise. "You've come! How wonderful! But how did you hear so quickly? Dion's letter must have been carried by the wing-footed Mercury himself. Come in! Come in! Your visit could not have been better timed." Decimus eagerly shook hands with the three men, but then looked out the door. "Where is—" He glanced at Aquila. "the other one? Where is Dulcibella? Didn't they want to come?"

Adan and Nikolaus's faces fell with disappointment. Adan said, "So, Marco is not here. We were hoping he was."

"*Ohe*, why did you expect him to be here?" Decimus frowned in confusion. "Come. Let's sit on the terrace and we can trade news, even though I suspect mine is much better than yours." Decimus ushered them down the hall and out to the terrace. He waved a hand at the chairs. "Please have a seat. Let my slaves bring you refreshment." He clapped his hands and a woman appeared in a doorway. He gave her instructions and she hurried away. "Now, tell me how you heard our news so quickly." He studied the unhappy expressions on their faces. "You're not here to celebrate with us, are you?"

"We hoped that Marco would be here," said Adan. "He took off on a wild scheme to come see Dionysia and, well, to rescue her."

"Rescue her? *Ohe*, that's unexpected. I am sorry he's not here," said Decimus. "But we do have good news. Let me get Dion and she can tell you." As he walked toward the door, the same slave appeared carrying a tray of cups filled with wine and bread with a bowl of herbed olive oil.

Adan and Nikolaus exchanged curious looks. "It must be very good news" volunteered Nikolaus. "And I don't ever remember hearing Decimus call her Dion."

A cry of delighted surprise came from an open doorway. They turned to see Dionysia hurrying across the terrace. Nikolaus jumped to his feet as she threw her arms over his shoulders. They hugged each other with joy.

"Niko, you rascal! How did you get here so quickly?"

Nikolaus gave a confused look. "Quickly, for what?"

"Then you haven't received my letter! Deci's wife divorced him. She just packed up one morning and said she was moving back to Rome and handed him a divorce decree." She reached for Decimus's hand. "Deci and I were married a week later." They beamed at each other.

"The truth is," said Decimus, "Dion and I have been in love for many years. There was no love lost between Viola and me. Her only desire was to have children. When she couldn't conceive, I brought Dion into the family. All was well as long as the children were young. When the youngest reached twelve, Viola lost interest in all of us. Truth be told, they admitted that they never thought of Viola as their mother. They knew who really loved them. Now, tell us about Marco. Why are you looking for him?"

Aquila laughed, but it was without amusement. "Unbelievable! Marco takes off and wanders around God only knows where. I get falsely arrested and do slave labor for three months. We finally get here and find out that you two are married. And we still don't know what he has been doing for the last four months. So much for his quest. I think I'll pass out from the sheer delight of this wonderful waste of time!"

Aquila's tirade was met with concern from Decimus and Dionysia and embarrassment from Adan and Nikolaus. No one spoke. Aquila felt his face flush and strode across the terrace to the balustrade.

"Well, that answers our question," said Decimus in a small voice. "You must stay here until Marco shows up."

"We appreciate that," said Adan. "And forgive us not saying sooner, congratulations on your marriage!" Nikolaus added his own best wishes.

"Are you going back to Rome when you find Marco?" asked Decimus.

"Yes, my father and Janae want to see him," said Adan.

"In that case," said Decimus. "Dion and I were planning to take a trip to Rome sometime this month to see the children. Did you hire a carriage?"

"No, I have my father's carriage and his servants," said Adan.

"You can send them back and ride with us. My carriage will seat eight people comfortably and I have a team of four horses that will make quick work of our journey."

"That's a good plan, Decimus," said Adan. "I will send Taye and Jemel to the *Consolari* Inn that I saw along the way so they and the horses can rest. They can leave in the morning."

"No need, Adan. They can stay here. We have plenty of room." Decimus clapped his hands again and the same woman appeared. He gave her the additional instructions.

"There is one thing I need to attend to in town," said Adan. "We passed the basilica in the forum along the way. Aquila and I will go there and ask if anyone who looks like him has managed to get himself in trouble. Won't we, Aquila?" Adan called out. Aquila turned from the balustrade and joined his father.

Father and son left the villa and walked through the streets in silence. Adan could feel the resentment billowing from Aquila like smoke from a wildfire. He knew there was nothing he could say to temper his son's anger. Adan would have to be patient and let Aquila work through his emotions on his own. Adan couldn't decide which was more difficult, trying to think of something to say or not saying anything at all.

They turned down the last street and headed for the surprisingly white limestone of the basilica. It looked new since the stone had not yellowed yet. Adan stepped around an elderly woman when Aquila stopped so abruptly, Adan bumped into him. Aquila was staring straight ahead. His face reddened. Adan looked to see who he was staring at so angrily.

"*Marco*, don't run off!" Adan stepped in front of Aquila.

Marco saw the depth of compassion in his father's eyes, but he also saw his brother's rage.

Suddenly, a hand holding a dagger appeared above Marco's right shoulder.

Adan saw the face of Calais. "*Marcus! Behind you!*"

Marco spun around. Less than a pace behind him stood Calais, his arm raised, a small dagger clenched in his fist. Marco sidestepped and nearly tripped, throwing himself off balance. Calais's face was twisted with hate as he moved forward. Adan lunged for his son revealing Aquila who stood staring at the dagger. Calais's jaw dropped in shock. He was looking at a second Marco. Adan grabbed Marco's arm and jerked him aside. Calais slowly lowered his arm.

"It was me, Calais," said Aquila. "It was me who betrayed you at the Antonia, not my brother. Marco would never do that. Please. Believe me."

Calais's eyes darted from Aquila to Marco, back and forth. He turned and ran.

Adan grasped his son in a hug that even Serapio would have envied. "Are you all right? Are you hurt?" He let go and held his son out by the shoulders. Adan saw the cuts and welts on Marco's arms. "Who did this?"

"It's nothing, Father. I threw a rock at a woman's driver and she objected."

"Marco don't *ever* run off like that again! Your mother was frantic with worry."

Marco hung his head. "I was afraid you would not let me go. I had to do this. I have to save Uncle Niko's sister." He clasped the sapphire through his tunic. "God sent me a message."

Adan hugged him again. "We're together now. We'll get this figured out."

Marco felt cold eyes on him. "Aquila, I'm sorry I couldn't take you with me."

"Are we going to talk about what just happened?" Aquila blurted, ignoring Marco. "In case no one noticed, that was Calais. He had a dagger. He was going to kill you, Marco. So, I guess we have the answer to our little mystery. Calais is very much alive, but he's in a really bad mood."

"Aquila, the least you can do is be glad we have found your brother," said Adan.

"Be glad? None of us would have even been upset if he hadn't deserted us in the middle of the night. Why should I be glad now? I just want to go home." Aquila stalked around them. "I'm going back to the villa." He stopped and turned slowly. "I promise not to go missing, Father." He turned again and rushed away.

Marco sighed and bowed his head.

Adan started after Aquila and gestured for Marco to follow. "Come on, son, we need to settle this." Marco hesitated. Adan softened his tone. "I know you're afraid to talk things over with your brother, but you'll get through it."

"I'm not afraid of talking with Aquila," said Marco despondently. "It's the cold silence that will follow that scares me."

Chapter 28

Anger, a Truce, and a Covenant

———⊗⊗⊗———

Adan and Marco caught up with Aquila. The three of them walked the last few blocks back to the villa in silence. When they stepped into the courtyard, Aquila turned around to face them. "Why did you let that crazy slave get away, Father? He's going to keep coming and . . . "

The ground began to shake. Grinding and cracking sounds could be heard over the low rumble that verberated through the air. It lasted only a few seconds but seemed to last much longer.

"This is the second earthquake since I've been here" said Marco. "What does it mean?"

"I don't know," exclaimed Adan, glancing at the overhead balconies and awnings. anxiously. "Come on! It's not safe here." The three of them continued to the villa amid people gawking at the new cracks in their homes and shops. They stood about shaking their heads and cursing the gods for allowing Vulcan to pound his forge so violently. Marco stopped and pointed at the mountain dominating the horizon. It's cone-shaped top was silhouetted against a blue translucent sky. Wisps of smoke hovered over the top of the mountain.

"Father, didn't you say the best wine comes from that mountain. What do they call it?"

"*Vesuvio*. They call it *Monte Vesuvio*," answered Adan.

"Looks like some of the vineyards are on fire," Marco said. "Will they send soldiers to put it out?"

Aquila whirled around. "Shut up about the stupid mountain, Marco. That was Calais with a dagger aimed at your back. It would have been me if he had come from the other direction."

"But he didn't," snapped Adan. "He nearly killed your brother. You could be grateful that he didn't succeed instead of thinking of yourself." He signaled for his sons to follow him into a side street where they could talk. "I'm relieved that Calais is alive and his attempted suicide will no longer haunt our conscience." Adan glared at Aquila. "But the uncomfortable truth is that he has been following you, Marco. Now he knows there are two of you, but that might not pacify him. I'm afraid the damage is done, thanks to the three of us, including me. I should have checked his vital signs more carefully when I thought he was dead."

"You said the three of us. I didn't do anything wrong," declared Marco. "I was trying to help him."

"By stealing another man's property! Whether you like it or not, Calais belonged to Commander Lysias. You could have offered to buy his contract, not deceive Lysias. You gave Calais a deadly poison not knowing how he would be affected. By using deception, you endangered his life. You would also make him feel obligated to you."

"Obligated? How? It worked; he's free again," countered Marco.

"If your original plan had worked, and only you knew the truth, he would have to trust in your silence. That would enslave him to you in exchange for your silence. When you proposed your plan, what did you want him to do?"

"I only asked him to go with me to find Dionysia," admitted Marco.

"Please!" barked Aquila. "Was he in a position to politely excuse himself from your suggestion of servitude? You may have phrased it like an invitation, but you expected him to follow you, groveling and bowing with gratitude. I wasn't good enough for you so you found yourself a slave."

Adan threw Aquila a warning glare. "How would you have reacted, Marco, if your plan succeeded, but Calais disappeared? Would you be angry? Would you think he had deserted you?"

Marco looked away without answering.

Aquila sneered at his brother. "Yes, and yes. Since you can't admit it, I'll do it for you."

Marco gave his brother a surly look but said nothing.

"Aquila, that's enough," declared Adan. "Come on. We'll finish this later."

They left the alley and retraced their steps toward the villa. Dodging foot traffic and the occasional donkey or horse-drawn wagon slowed their progress. They saw bits of roof tiles lying shattered in the streets as they walked. A few walls of some of the houses and courtyards revealed cracks wide enough to see through. Some of the cobblestones that paved the streets were thrust higher than other stones causing wagons to jolt and rattle.

When they reached Decimus's front door, Marco balked. "Father, I—I don't know what to say. You've already told them why I came here, haven't you?"

"I didn't need to, Marco," said Adan impatiently. "Once again, you've jumped into the boat without checking for leaks. You didn't need to take off without telling us."

"You did, Father! You took off without telling your parents."

"I joined the army, Marco. I went into training with men who knew what to expect in this world. I had a plan and a reasonable way to achieve it. I took care of sick and injured and pregnant horses. Trust me, it wasn't glorious or heroic. It was hard, messy, bloody work."

"I didn't leave home for glory," Marco grumbled. "I left to save Dionysia."

"Then where have you been all these months?" demanded Aquila. "Hopping from one resort town to the next? Enjoying plays in the theater and cinnamon-spiced wine in the bars?"

Marco ignored the sarcasm. "No, for three months I was shipwrecked with Paul on Malta."

"Shipwrecked? As in almost drowned?" asked Adan with dismay. "You were with Paul?"

"Yes. Calais was there, too, but I didn't know it until I got washed overboard. The ship was breaking apart. He was just standing there, watching me. Just before I went over the railing, I saw that his lips were peeled back from his teeth in a hideous grin, but his eyes looked dead."

"*Ohe,* that's terrible," declared Aquila with an exaggerated tone. "You haven't asked about us, but I was having a lovely time in Rome. I even have the scars to prove it. What did you endure? Were you tortured with boredom? Basking on the beach can be so traumatic."

"Aquila. Not another word." Adan spoke softly, but his voice was edged like a blade as he stared his son down. Aquila dropped his gaze, but a red flush of anger and embarrassment crossed his face. Adan turned to Marco. "Thracius told us about the purple sapphire he bought for you. Was that really why you decided to find Dionysia?"

Marco clutched the sapphire under his tunic. "Let me show you."

Aquila jerked the cord for the doorbell. It only took a moment before steps could be heard running to the door and it flew open. Nikolaus threw his arms out when he saw Marco. He reached for his nephew and hugged him with relief. Dionysia came running and hugged Marco for the first time ever. Even though Adan and Nikolaus had made two trips to secure Dionysia's freedom, they had never brought their children.

Marco was stunned by her unique beauty. Her soft alabaster skin, reddish hair, and crystalline sky-blue eyes were not like any features he had ever seen. He glanced at his brother to see if he was reacting with the same appreciation. Aquila was staring at him, not Dionysia, and it was not a good look. Marco looked away quickly.

Decimus soon joined them and herded the family out to the terrace. The huge oak trees offered shade and cooled the sweet-scented breeze that stirred the leaves. The balustrade surrounding the terrace topped a gentle slope that dropped down to the street below. Across the street were more villas. However, the villas were not what offered the most spectacular view from the terrace. The velveteen dark-blue water of the Tyrrhenian Sea filled the western horizon with beautiful mystery.

"Let's all sit down," said Adan. "Dionysia, please tell Marco your good news."

Dionysia thanked him for trying so hard to free her. She explained to Marco how Decimus first granted her freedom and then proposed marriage. She was now protected by law as a Roman citizen and married to the man she loved. "What made you decide to find me, Marco? Was it dramatic? Like a vision or a dream?"

"Nothing like that. It wasn't dramatic at all." He pulled on the leather cord around his neck and removed the necklace. "See the crystal? It's a purple sapphire, just like the one you have. Well, it's not carved like yours, but it's a purple sapphire."

Adan glanced at the gemstone. "Centurion Thracius said a street vendor talked you into it with wild promises of treasure. You didn't really believe any of that, did you Marco?"

"Of course, not, Father. I knew he was making that stuff up to get me interested. But I believed what he said about the man who once owned this necklace. He was born blind and then Yeshua healed him and he could see. The stone has a message on it, but the words are in Tamil, a language of India." He gestured impatiently. "None of that matters. What's important is that God used the merchant and this crystal to send me to you, Dionysia." Marco offered the necklace to his father. Adan glanced at it but didn't take it. Aquila snatched the necklace from Marco's hand.

"It just looks like the crystal is scratched up. Too bad." He tossed it back at Marco. He turned his back on his brother and walked to the edge of the terrace.

"I think the merchant lied about there being a message on the stone," said Adan, "It was damaged so he made up a ridiculous story."

Marco groaned in frustration. "It was not a coincidence that the merchant had a sapphire of the same rare color as Dionysia's sapphire. I prayed to Yeshua for guidance and there was the sapphire. I felt that Yeshua had answered my prayer."

Decimus looked from one to the other. "Who is this Yeshua you speak of?"

"He is the man I crucified," said Adan. "I split his heart with my spear. On the third day after his death, he greeted me with a smile in the garden where he had been buried. He's been with me ever since."

Decimus gaped at him. "You are haunted by his ghost?" He glanced around fearfully. "Is he here now?"

Adan smiled. "Perhaps I should start at the beginning. Let's go for a walk." The two men headed for the gate that opened to a path that circled the property.

Nikolaus took Dionysia by the hand. They followed Adan through the gate. "I need to ask you something, Sister. Did you ever see Father with a wooden box about the length of your forearm and about as wide as my hand?" He held his open hand up. "It had a metal disk on the front with cogs and dials and rods protruding from under the disc."

Dionysia blinked at him. "A wooden box? Not that I can remember. Why?"

"Just wondering. I had forgotten about it until now. It was real. I touched it. Father jerked my hand away. He said I was never to touch it again and never tell anyone about it. He called it The Prophecy Box. Does that sound familiar?"

"No. I'm sorry, Niko. I never saw it. But I wonder," her voice trailed off.

"What? Did you think of something?" Nikolaus eagerly asked.

"I remember something that happened when Father started getting more commissions and we had moved into that huge house in Corinth. We were outside having a birthday party for a neighbor next door. I went into the house to get something and heard Father in his study. He was shouting at a man I had never seen before, or since. The man started shouting at Father. He said, "If you don't give us the box, Nicandros, you will pay dearly!" It scared me and I gasped. They heard me and saw me standing there. I'll never forget the look of dread on Father's face. Do you think they were talking about, what did you call it?"

"The Prophecy Box."

"Yes, the Prophecy Box. I never saw that awful man again. I wish I knew more."

"Me, too," said Nikolaus pensively. "I have a feeling it was very important. A terrible secret, perhaps. But we'll never know now."

"That's another mystery in our family," said Dionysia. "So many mysteries."

"What do you mean?" asked Nikolaus, frowning.

"You were probably too young to remember. Father was having difficulties getting commissions for his building designs. No one wanted to employ someone so young and untested. Then all of a sudden, he was in great demand and had more than enough projects. His fame spread even to Emperor Tiberius. Mother and I were shocked when Father announced we were moving to Rome. Even at fifteen, I wondered why Tiberius would go to such expense to move us from Greece to Rome. There were plenty of excellent architects already there. Why spend so much money to hire Father? There were other things I never understood. Father could be very secretive at times." Nikolaus nodded agreement.

Marco watched as his aunt and uncle walked away. He wanted to follow, but he needed to confront Aquila. He stared at his brother's back until he couldn't stand the silence any longer. He put the necklace back around his neck and dropped the crystal under his tunic. Cautiously, he approached.

"I know you are very angry with me, Aquila," said Marco.

Aquila snorted. "Why should I be angry with you? I don't care what you do."

Marco bit his lower lip at the coldness in his brother's voice. "I had to do this on my own, Aquila. I wanted to take you with me, but that would have defeated the whole purpose. For once I wanted to solve a problem on my own. When I made arrangements to travel with that merchant, I had to act quickly. I didn't have time to discuss it with you."

"What do you mean?" blurted Aquila. "You had plenty of time to invite me into your little conspiracy. You wrote that letter long before . . . ," Aquila went silent. He had not meant to reveal what he knew.

"How do you know when I wrote it?" Marco demanded. "The noise I heard in your room, just before I left. You *were* awake. You already knew I was leaving, didn't you?"

Aquila didn't answer. He gazed out over the sea; his face was rigid with tension.

"Answer me, Aquila!"

His brother spun around. "All right! Yes, I found the letter. I thought it was just wishful thinking. I didn't think you would really leave."

"I had to leave. God put this on my heart, and I had no choice."

"God selected you to be his champion!" growled Aquila. "What does that make me, leftover rubbish?"

"I don't know why I had to do this. I only know that it was the right thing to do." Marco watched his brother apprehensively. "And God doesn't think you're rubbish."

Aquila glared at his brother. "Really? How do you know that? Did God tell you that in a dream. Did he say, 'Aquila is a fine young man, but he's not up to this task. I need a hero and that's you, the great and wonderful Marco, the savior of the downtrodden!'"

"Aquila, that's not fair! You can do amazing things. You look at a problem and this perfect solution materializes right out of your head. I don't know how you do it. I don't understand how we can be so different since we're identical in every other way, but I can't begin to do the things you can do. God has other tasks for you, Aquila, you just don't know what they are yet."

Aquila curled a lip. "Other tasks? Like what? Should I figure out how to make the wheels on a wagon turn without a horse to pull it? That would be useful, right? Wagons could go spinning around on their own and crash into each other."

"Now you're talking crazy." Marco clenched his teeth in frustration. He thought back to the night he first left. "When I was still in the house, I called out to you. You must have heard me. Why didn't you say anything?" The hurt in Marco's voice was unmistakable.

"I don't know," admitted Aquila. "I guess I wanted to see if you would really leave without me. It was childish, but I was hoping you would go back to your room if—"

"—if you pretended to be asleep?"

Aquila nodded. "I didn't want you to go, but if you did, I wanted to be included."

"I thought I was doing everyone a favor by not taking you with me," said Marco. "it would have been a double shock to Mother and Father if both of us left. And then you would have been second guessing me on every decision. You would have taken over and I would have been useless."

"Doing everyone a favor? By sneaking away in the night? You scared Mother and Father to death. Yes, that was such a wonderful favor you did for the whole family. Do I have to remind you that you ran off twice? Were you doing everyone a favor when you left me, again, on the road to the garrison? The family can do without your favors."

"You wanted me to run off! You pushed me into it," accused Marco.

"What are you talking about? I didn't do anything to you," growled Aquila.

"Let me think," grumbled Marco. "How does this sound? 'We have to drag you home with nothing to show for all your false bravado. The whole family will be so impressed.' What else was I supposed to do after hearing that? Hang my head in shame and crawl home like a beaten dog?"

A painful silence fell between the brothers. Marco walked across the terrace to distance himself from Aquila. The pain of the humiliating words pushed them apart like an iron wedge. Aquila regretted his harsh words but could not bring himself to apologize.

Aquila called out, "What did you say before about me criticizing you every minute? What were you talking about?"

Marco frowned in confusion. "You would have found fault with everything I did like you always do. You didn't really want to come with me. You're just mad because I did something brave without you."

Aquila threw his hands up in frustration. "Of course, I wanted to go. Do you remember who you're talking to? I'm the one everyone pats on the head and says, 'Tell Aquila to do it. He always does what he's told.' Yes, like a trained monkey. Do you think I just love being the dependable little boy all the time?"

Marco blinked at him. "I thought so. Apparently, I was wrong."

Aquila's eyes glinted as he laughed. It was a bitter sound. "Yes, I'm thrilled to be the puppet dangling from Father's strings. Your keen sense of perception astounds me."

"Aquila, I hate it when you do that."

"Do what?"

"Say all those sarcastic things."

"Why? Because you know it's true?"

"No. Because it's the only cowardly thing you do." Marco turned his back and walked a few paces along the balustrade.

Aquila looked away as his face flushed with embarrassment. The brothers stood apart, both unwilling to break the silence. Finally, Aquila sighed, his anger spent. "Don't you see how it is, Marco? Father is so hard on you. He's always dragging you around with him, showing you how to do things, making you do stuff over and over until you get it right. He chews you out every time you slack off. He doesn't let you get away with anything, ever!"

"You're saying that as if it's good thing. I'm confused."

"You don't get it!" exclaimed Aquila. "I just wish Father would . . ." He turned away with a shake of his head.

Marco watched his brother for a moment. "Are you jealous?"

"Yes! Don't you understand. You get all his attention. He spends all his energy on you. He's with you ten times more than he is with me."

"Aquila, that's not true. He likes to see your experiments and asks how you came up with your ideas. He gives you jobs to do and doesn't look twice to see if you've done them. He knows you'll do them perfectly. He trusts you. He depends on you. Don't *you* get it? I was jealous of you. Why do you think I felt like I needed to prove myself?"

"You know," Aquila said, "we could both be loathsome tax collectors and Mother would still love us. She might not like us much, but she would still love us. I've never felt in competition with you for Mother's attention. I don't know what it is with Father, but I've always been envious of your time with him."

"This is unbelievable, Aquila," said Marco. "I'm jealous of you because Father has *complete* confidence in you. And you're jealous of me because Father has *zero* confidence in me. What is wrong with us?"

The two brothers walked to the bench under the shade of the largest tree and sat. They were silent as each tried to think how the other one must be feeling. They were two people born from one conception. One embryo split into two human beings with very different likes and dislikes, talents, and interests, yet they shared the exact same genetic foundation. It was a mystery.

Aquila cleared his throat. "I think I'm beginning to understand something. I've always thought that Father would like me more if I were like you. You're amazing with animals and healing and calming them down when they're hurt or scared—like he is. Maybe even more so."

"And I've always thought," said Marco, "that Father would like me more if I were good with reasoning and problem solving, like you. He's good with all that stuff, too. I think you might be better at it than he is. It's as if each of us inherited only a part of Father, but that part is amplified. Do you know what I mean?"

"I think I do. I never saw it that way before." Aquila thought for a moment. "I assumed Father thought I was useless with healing. That's why he gave you Wingshadow."

"He gave you Nighthawk," pointed out Marco. "What's the difference?"

"There's a huge difference, which proves my point," said Aquila. "Nighthawk was perfect when he was born. No problems. But your horse, Wingshadow, was sick. She was weak and might not have lived. Father trusted you with Wingshadow because he knew you could heal her and make her strong. That's exactly what you did. Wingshadow was a sickly foal, but now she's a magnificent mare. Father knew I couldn't handle healing a mouse much less a horse."

"Father gave you that copper and iron smelting *furnus* and those tools for making your own molds," said Marco. "He showed you how to use them and you made all kinds of useful things. Mother and Cook still use those tongs you made for taking pots out of the kitchen *furnus*. I was so jealous when Father took those tongs to the garrison to show everyone what you had invented."

"I was jealous when he rode Wingshadow to the garrison and explained to his decurions how you took a sickly horse and nurtured her into perfect health."

Aquila took a deep breath and slowly exhaled. "I know what's wrong with us."

"Me, too," said Marco.

"What do you think it is?"

"We're both stupid and selfish and—did I say stupid?" asked Marco with a lopsided-grin.

"You did," said Aquila with a nod.

"Should I say it again?"

"Probably."

"We're both stupid."

"Now I think we've got it covered," said Aquila. "What do we do about it?"

"Well," said Marco, "we've spent our whole lives sitting around the comfort of our home, hearing stories about our family's adventures. We need to have our own adventure, together. Something without Father's or Uncle Niko's help. We need to prove ourselves, not to them, but to each other." Marco glanced at his arms. He looked at Aquila's arms and frowned. "Looks like we've left our formerly pampered lives behind, and have the scars to prove it. However, being the victim of a crazy woman's horsewhip was not what I had in mind."

"You're right. We need to be warriors. We need to use our talents together," said Aquila, "You're a magician when it comes to animals. You have a gift. You walk in the stables and every horse looks up and points its ears at you. They do that low, rumbly nicker in their throats and move around to face you. The dogs follow you everywhere. When you get up and leave, they follow you. You whistle and they come running. There must be some way we can use that."

Marco didn't respond at first, surprised to hear his brother's praise. "You understand scientific things and you invent things. You find a problem and you know how to fix it, just like that." He snapped his fingers. "We can use that as well."

The compliment pleased Aquila but he tried not to show it. He gave his brother a sidelong look. "You nearly scared Father to death when Calais almost stabbed you. He called you Marcus."

"*Ohe,* that's true. He usually only calls me that when I've broken something."

Marco picked up a chunk of limestone on the other side of the balustrade. He hefted it down the slope and watched it cascade down the cliff face. "First, let's clear up a few things. What happened with Calais? Why did you deceive him? You had to have known how devastated he would feel. Now he wants to kill me or at least he did. Hopefully, not anymore."

"I was wrong to do that," admitted Aquila. "I thought you were going to run away with him. The two of you would have been caught in hours, probably. No telling what they would have done to you. Father, no doubt, would have tried to take your punishment. I think he was planning on doing the same for me if things had gone badly in Rome."

"What are you talking about?" asked Marco with a frown. "Does it have to do with your new scars?" He studied his brother's arms more closely. "What happened?"

Aquila gestured impatiently. "I'll tell you later. As for Calais, I am really sorry, Marco. I won't ever pretend to be you again, unless you ask me."

"Can I trust you, Aquila? What if you do it again on impulse. It'll be too late to take back."

"How can I trust you to never keep a secret from me again? Trusting each other goes both ways, Marco." Aquila considered the problem. "I know something we could do. We could swear a blood covenant."

"I'm not cutting some poor animal in half!" Marco exclaimed.

Aquila made a face. "Well, there is that. Disgusting doesn't even cover it."

"How do you know about a blood covenant?" asked Marco

"Father told me."

"Why didn't he tell me?"

"Really? You have to ask? Who has the special bond with animals? So, who told you?"

"Some friends of Paul's brought it up. They said Yeshua was the final blood covenant. They said that in essence God took mankind by the hand and walked through Yeshua's blood to seal his promise of eternal life."

Aquila looked out over the sea. "How fitting. God shed his *own* blood to seal the new covenant. Father said it had to be a perfect creature of pure innocence. What could be more perfect than God's own Son?"

Marco didn't answer but picked up another rock and tossed it. It clattered down the cliff side and disappeared into a clump of scrub oaks. "Maybe we don't need some type of ritual or blood sacrifice," suggested Marco. "Maybe we just need to make up our minds that we will never again use deception against each other."

Aquila looked doubtful. "Easy to say, hard to do."

"Slicing an animal in half would do it for you?" Marco eyed his brother with distaste. "I'll pass if you can't trust me on my word of honor. Did Father and Uncle Niko walk through blood before they trusted each other?"

Aquila considered the question. "In a way. Through Yeshua's blood."

"Then so have we," said Marco. "Which means no more blood needs to be shed."

"That's true. Then let's make the bloodshed symbolic," suggested Aquila. "I want you to swear on something that you treasure. Something that would kill you if it were taken from you."

"What will you swear on?" asked Marco. "I know what I can pledge. Not counting our family, the one thing I love above all else is Wingshadow. You can take her away from me if I break the oath."

Aquila pursed his lips. "You're going to laugh when I tell you what I can pledge."

"Why would I laugh?"

"Because it's not alive," said Aquila. "It's the book I'm writing. Grandfather Aquila gave me a papyrus book with blank pages. It cost him a fortune, but he said he knew I would use it wisely. I've been recording and drawing diagrams of all my inventions and almost-inventions and invention ideas. I've described all my experiments, successes, and failures, including those I did with Grandfather Aquila. I've been working on it for eight years now. It would kill me, as you said, if something happened to it."

"You could write all that stuff down again," said Marco.

"And you could buy another horse," countered Aquila.

"Fair enough. Then let's do it." Marco put his left hand out.

The brothers put their hands atop each other's until all four were pressed together. "I'll go first since I ran off," said Marco. "If I should ever break my oath of truth to you, Aquila, you can take Wingshadow away from me and do with her as you please."

Aquila nodded approval. "If I should ever break my oath of truth to you, Marco, you can take my book of inventions away from me and do with it as you please."

"What if I choose to give it back to you?" asked Marco.

Aquila studied his brother for a moment. "That is a choice we both are free to make."

The brothers looked into each other's eyes. "It is done," they said in unison, and pulled their hands away. They smiled at each other. The covenant was sealed.

"In that case," said Aquila, "I guess I'd better tell you something."

"What's that?"

"I have an idea for our first adventure together. I want to go to Pompeii and find a man named Simon Magus of Gitta. I have a score to settle with him. If we put our talents together, I bet we can come up with a perfect plan. I have more than enough money to handle everything we'll need."

"You don't want to hurt this man, do you?"

"Of course, I want to hurt him! But I'm not going to. I want him to confess. I want him to admit to my face what he did and why he did it."

"Tell me what happened."

Aquila told Marco everything.

Chapter 29

Memories of a Ghost

───────◦∞∞◦───────

Calais was in shock. He ran around a corner and ducked down an alley. He needed to think about what just happened. He had never seen a set of twins that looked so perfectly identical. He thought he was hallucinating when he saw a copy of Marco appear from behind Centurion Longinus. The second Marco looked at him intently, but there was no empathy in his expression as there was in the Marco he knew. There was, however, something else in those pale golden eyes that he had not seen in Marco. It was guilt. Calais realized the truth of the situation. The betrayal had been perpetrated by Marco's twin brother for reasons he could only guess.

As painful as the memory was, Calais made himself replay the scene at the Antonia when the other twin, who he thought was Marco, denied even knowing who he was. Marco's brown horse was not there, but Centurion Longinus's black stallion was there, along with Nikolaus's gelding and another black stallion that was nearly identical to the centurion's horse. When he approached the twin brother, he was standing by the second black horse. Now the memory made sense. The other twin owned the second black stallion.

Calais pushed his memories aside and stepped into the first bakery he could find. It was busy with customers buying their bread for the day, and no one noticed the dark-haired, deeply tanned Greek with the olive-green eyes. He bought a loaf of bread and slipped out onto the street. He hurried along the streets until, after a few wrong turns, he found his inn. The woman who owned the inn smiled when she saw the young man. His behavior was rough around the edges, but he was handsome. If she had to rent to the lower classes, she might as well enjoy the "view."

Calais nodded at her as he went past. She informed him that dinner would be served in an hour. He thanked her and retreated to his room. Calais opened the lattice and sat down on the window seat. He needed to think.

* * *

193

The memory of waking up in a cart in a dank, little barn haunted Calais. He could hardly think of anything else. He thought about when he first awoke and realized he was not dead, not in Hades, and not at the Antonia, but where? He was cold, even though a tarp was over him and it was nearly July. His back ached from lying on the hard, wood surface of something that was not a bed. It was dark and he had no idea where he was or how he got there. He reached out a hand tentatively and felt wooden slats. He pushed the tarp aside. A horse sneezed and shook its head. There was also a donkey, but it didn't move. He could smell the familiar odors of horse sweat, urine, feces, and hay. He sat up and tried to see where he was. His head ached with a dull pain. His eyes felt dry and scratchy. Slowly, carefully, he crawled out of the cart. He found the water tank in the barn and splashed his face. Then he drank deeply. His mouth felt like it was lined with bird feathers. He was hungry. Feeling his way around the barn, he found a bag of oats. He scooped out a handful and walked back to the water tank. He mixed the oats with water into a thick paste of oatmeal and licked it from his hand. He ate until the hunger pangs subsided.

The horse stomped a hoof and snorted. He went to the horse and ran his hand down the animal's neck. A section of the mane was missing. "What happened to you? Did your master cut burrs out of your mane?" The horse exhaled a deep breath of contentment.

He had to get out of there. Slowly, the truth of his situation began to make sense. He had drunk the poison Marco had given him. All of it. He remembered the cruel look in the boy's eyes when he asked if it was time to act and saw confusion and then anger. Marco had not only reneged on their plan; he had walked directly over to the guards outside of Prisoner Holding and talked while pointing in his direction. He had run into the stables in panic. He couldn't understand why Marco double-crossed him. Why would the son of Centurion Longinus, the only man he had ever trusted at the Antonia, go to such lengths to talk him into escaping, give him poison to fake his death, and then betray him? This treachery was worse than his mother's selling him into slavery. At least, her motive had been to keep him from starving to death.

He remembered carefully sliding the bar out of the door brackets and opening the barn door. The night breeze chilled him to shivers. He untied his belt and threw it on the floor. He knelt down and smoothed the belt flat to display the name Lysias. He spat on the name, stood up, and stomped on the stitching so violently, he became dizzy. He threw a hand to the cart to steady himself and stood panting until his vision cleared. The horse shifted its back hooves, and he could hear the sound of water hitting the dirt floor. He snatched the belt up and threw it under the horse's stream of urine. A mirthless laugh escaped his lips as he waited for the horse to finish. He picked the belt up by a corner and draped it over the side of the cart. "Now, your name suits you, Lysias."

Slowly, he made his way out of the stable. He paid no attention to which streets he wandered down. He was trying to clear his head so he could devise a plan. One thing was certain, despite the betrayal, the plan had worked. Commander Lysias must think he was dead. He was free, but there was no celebration in his heart. He was homeless and without money. Worst of all, he was still in Jerusalem which was patrolled by soldiers who could identify him.

He staggered along the streets for hours until the sun rose and shop owners began opening their doors. He stopped at a bakery and tried to talk the owner into letting him clean out his stable for a loaf of bread. The man eyed him as if he were sick from something contagious. The baker gave him a loaf of bread, probably to get rid of him. He did not thank the man, but instead said something about bread of stone and breaking teeth. He was surprised to hear his own voice since he had not meant to speak out loud. He gulped down the bread as if it would be his last morsel of food. Thirst drove him to the nearest public water fountain. He saw a young man collapsed across the retaining wall of the fountain. He pulled the body off the wall and let it drop to the stone pavement. The belt and coin pouch were missing. He cursed his bad luck. Someone else had beat him to the young man's money. He was drinking from the fountain when loud voices startled him. A group of soldiers with a cart came around a corner, and he had to scurry into a pedestrian alleyway to hide. He watched as the soldiers loaded the body into the cart and left. His legs folded beneath him as he collapsed in the narrow alley. That dead body could have been his.

In despair, he sat with his head in his hands, trying to decide what to do. Then he heard a deep voice. He looked around the corner of the alley and saw Serapio, the furniture maker, talking with a woman. She gestured toward the fountain and Serapio nodded understanding. The man urged his horse into a plodding walk and paused at the fountain to let the horse drink, and then moved on. Watching from the alley, he gasped in recognition of the horse. It was missing a section of its mane just like the horse in the barn. It must have been Serapio's barn, and now, the man was probably looking for him. But why? Did Serapio want to turn him over to Commander Lysias for a reward? He would have to follow the furniture maker to discover his intentions. If the man went to the Antonia, all was lost.

He kept his distance since it was easy to follow the big man on the slow horse. Serapio left the city and continued on the road that led to the crematory. When Serapio entered the walled compound of the crematory, he waited outside the entrance, trying to boost his courage. The smell of rotting and burnt flesh was overwhelming, but he finally managed to force himself into the crematory.

Once inside the compound, he watched from behind a building as Serapio stood gazing down into a pit that must have been set afire only a few minutes earlier. The smoke billowed into the sky as the flames grew higher. The furniture maker backed away, mounted his horse, and left.

He walked over to the pit where Serapio had stood. All he could see were charred bodies. He looked more closely and saw that several bodies closest to where Serapio had been were not burned yet. Then he saw him. It was the dead man who was missing his belt. Calais glanced down at his own waist. The realization of the situation sank in. The furniture maker must believe that the dead man in the pit was him. No one would be looking for him just as Marco had said. He realized that he was truly free and elation filled his heart, but not for long. The plan only worked because he had tried to kill himself. It was Marco's fault that he had nearly died. The desire for revenge crushed the joy he had felt only seconds ago.

He had to know Serapio's intentions. He hurried from the crematory and spotted the former *gladiator* on horseback. He was vulnerable if Serapio should look over a shoulder, but he had to know where the furniture maker was going. The man entered the city gate closest to the Antonia. He bit his lower lip and nearly drew blood. He steeled himself and entered the city. He watched from the gateway to see if Serapio would enter the garrison. Serapio never even glanced at the garrison gates or watchtowers. He rode slowly past and turned the corner onto Commerce Road and out of sight. Encouraged, he hurried to the intersection and peered around the corner as Serapio paused at the next intersection of Commerce Road and Sheep Gate Street. He dismounted and led his horse into the barn at the back of Serapio's *Suppelex*.

Relief washed over him like a cool, misting waterfall. If Serapio was going to inform Commander Lysias that his slave might be alive, he would have done it on his way back from the crematory. He swayed where he stood as the full impact of his new-found freedom overcame him. The reality of the garrison walls and watchtowers sobered his momentary happiness. He dodged carts and pedestrians down one street after another to get as far from the Antonia as he could. He found his way to the largest flour mill and hid there the rest of the day. That evening when the night watchman fell asleep, he quietly approached and drank from the guard's waterskin and found a loaf of bread in his knapsack. He stepped away as quietly as possible, and he wriggled into the back of a delivery wagon marked with the symbol for Caesarea's garrison. It was already loaded with sacks of barley and covered with a tarp. Marco lived in Caesarea, and that was where he wanted to go. He ate the bread and fell asleep.

He woke up when a wheel hit a pothole. He peered out of the back of the wagon from under the tarp to get his bearings. Judging by the position of the sun, he knew they were going in the right direction. He and his father had traveled to Caesarea once and he would never forget the way. When they neared a fork in the road, he knew the merchant would take the road to the garrison. He climbed out of the wagon and headed west on the road to Caesarea. Just after passing a second fork in the road, he heard a horse snort some distance behind him. He stopped and faced the rider. It was Marco, riding that old pack horse. He didn't know what to do. He froze and stared at the figure on horseback. Marco looked up, reined in his horse, and shouted to him. Marco didn't recognize him at first. In a panic, he couldn't move, but when Marco looked away, he dove into the tall weeds and grass growing alongside the road. He belly-crawled through the vegetation until he reached a stand of trees. If Marco had approached the trees, he would have found him huddled behind a tree trunk, but he didn't. Instead, Marco spun his horse around, returned to the fork in the road and galloped north toward Dora.

The horse must have slowed to a walk quickly. He only had to run a short distance before he caught up with Marco and followed him into town. He watched from around corners of buildings as Marco tried to find lodging. When a man, a Galilean judging by his clothes, opened his gate to Marco, he made note of the location. That night he returned to the house. He watched as Marco came out with a rolled mat under his arm and disappeared around the corner of the house. Within a few minutes, the boy appeared on the roof. He waited in the dark for hours until he was sure Marco was asleep. Picking up a cracked ceramic vase left on the street, he crept up the stairs. He approached Marco asleep on the mat. He raised the vase and was about to throw it down on Marco's head when an owl swooped in and landed on the roof wall. It hooted at him and folded its wings. He lowered the vase. Surely, Athena was sending him a message by her pet owl.

The presence of the owl had stopped him from smashing the vase on Marco's head. A quick death was not the way to punish his treachery. The boy must see it coming and be afraid. He stepped back from where Marco lay. "Thank you, Athena," he whispered to the owl. The bird spread its wings and silently took flight. He thought of searching Marco for Sofi, but the little wooden owl was probably in Marco's knapsack, which he was using as a pillow. Instead, he descended the stairs. He turned and threw the vase as hard as he could. It crashed into pieces and the broken shards clattered down the steps. He fled to the house across the street and turned to watch. The door of the house opened and a man held out a lamp through the narrow opening. Out of sight of the man, he crouched next to the door, but was in full view of Marco who appeared at the roof wall. The boy pointed and called out to the man. He stepped out into the street, opening the door farther. Marco repeated his warning and pointed at the now darkened area behind the door. In the darkness, he slipped out of sight. The man turned and scurried back into his house. From around the corner of the house, he laughed to see Marco all alone and afraid.

It was the next day when the other twin nearly caught him, but he managed to dodge into a shop just as his pursuer came tearing around the corner. He laughed to himself at the memory of seeing the twin spin a Greek boy around by the shoulder. Then he thought he had lost Marco when he spotted him aboard a ship just leaving port in Dora. But someone told him the ship was going to Myra, so he hired on as an oarsman on the next ship sailing for Myra. It wasn't hard to find the boy in Myra.

He remembered how lucky he felt to see Marco board a ship called the *Margarita*. He approached the hiring clerk and asked if he needed any more oarsmen. The man took one look at him and hired him on the spot. He saw the look in the clerk's eyes and knew what the man was thinking. He had seen that vile smirk many times. He wanted to walk away but caught a glimpse of Marco talking with a centurion in charge of some prisoners. He clenched his fists at the memory of how badly he had wanted to smash his fist in the clerk's leering face. Instead, he had stepped aboard and hurried below deck before Marco could see him.

He never stepped foot above deck until the ship grounded on the sandbar off the island of Malta. The storm waves and wind acted like a battering ram as they tore the stern of the ship to pieces. The wind screamed in his ears. The pummeling of the waves knocked him off his feet so many times he lost count. He was about to be washed overboard when he grabbed for the rigging tangled around the mast. Through the blur of cascading waves and shrieking wind, he saw the centurion's son. The waves had just slammed Marco against the life rails. Did the boy know how to swim? He thought it would be interesting to find out. He started to move toward Marco and tripped on deck planking that had separated and was half broken. He hooked his feet under the planking which kept him steady in the gusting wind. He clamped his arms tightly against his sides which held his clothes in place. It looked as if the wind had no effect on him. The expression of terror on Marco's face was thrilling to see. He remembered the feel of a leering smile pulling his lips back from his teeth. Marco thrust out a hand as if to ward him off, but a violent wave hit the boy so hard, he fell over the railing and into the churning sea.

He went to the railing and watched as Marco plummeted beneath the waves. He remembered the expression of despair on Marco's face when he hit the water. Another huge wave crashed onto the deck throwing him back from the railing. It carried him across the deck and slammed him against the other side. The next thing he knew, he was underwater struggling to reach the surface. He finally broke through the waves and gulped for air.

His father had taught him how to swim in the Jordan River. The gentle patience of the man had calmed his fear of the water. His father had taken him into only a few feet of the river and taught him how to float before encouraging him to explore deeper water. The praise his father quietly spoke to him as he attempted longer and longer distances sounded in his memory even then, so many years after his father was dead and buried.

A wave smacked him in the face, and he went under again. When he kicked his way to the surface, he looked toward the shore. His father was standing on the beach, motioning for him to swim toward him, to fight the storm, and live. "I'm coming, Father!" he managed to shout, and he began to swim. He reached the shore and struggled onto the beach until he was above the reach of the storm waves. The torrential rain scoured his body in gusts, but he was alive. He shielded his eyes from the slashing rain and saw his father walking toward him. Two strong hands gripped his arms and hauled him to his feet. Powerful arms supported him as they trudged away from the crashing waves.

"Come on before you drown out here," shouted the man. It was the helmsman, a man called Xavier who looked out for him aboard the ship. Xavier told him when they first met, "I have a younger brother who looks very much like you, Calais. He's my favorite brother." When the helmsman caught the hiring clerk trying to bait him into a fight, Xavier grabbed the man's wrist and twisted his arm behind his back. He smashed the man against a bulkhead. The hiring clerk collapsed in a heap. The helmsman told the clerk that he would beat him within a breath of his life if he ever harassed his "little brother" again. The man stood up slowly on wobbly legs but managed to walk away. He was never a problem after that.

He remembered that over the next three months, he and the other two hundred and seventy-five survivors were well treated. He was provided with shelter, food, and new clothing, including a freeman's leather belt. He found himself drawn to Xavier who found work for the two of them. Distracted by the companionship of his protector, he almost gave up his vendetta against Marco. However, when he saw the boy laughing with Paul and others, Marco's obvious enjoyment of island life rekindled his bitterness.

He noticed that Marco often walked along the beach. It was the only time Marco was alone. He also noticed that some of the sand dunes looked shallow from the beach but there was room to hide, not evident from the shoreline. There was also a small barrier island close to the shoreline that could be easily reached from the dunes or from under the waves. He could slip in and out of the sea from the tiny island without being seen from the beach. He devised a plan, practiced his maneuvers, then waited for an opportunity. He tried out his technique of throwing rocks when several Maltese children were playing on the beach. He didn't try to hit the children; he just wanted to see if his plan could work. It did. They ran away in terror.

The idea of spelling the word "traitor" in Greek with stones added to the sinister effect. He was rewarded for his efforts when Marco saw the word *prodotis* and was forced to dodge the rocks thrown from an "invisible" hand. He grinned, remembering how seeing Marco running in fear soothed his bitter grudge. He stole the boy's tools and placed them in his hand during the night. He stalked Marco, allowing himself to be seen, but keeping too far away to be confronted.

He noticed that Marco liked to sit by a fire, alone, late at night. He practiced speaking into a ceramic vase to amplify his voice and make it sound much closer to a listener. Then he waited for an opportunity to use his new skill. One moonless night, when no one else was nearby and the boy was distracted by the hypnotizing flames, he slithered on his stomach under a dark-colored blanket and got as close as he dared. He uttered hissing words that made the boy jump up and stagger back. He remained perfectly still under the blanket, watching the terror unfold. He couldn't stop the low, menacing laugh that escaped his lips. He watched Marco turn and run in panic. Savoring the moment, he inched away from the ring of firelight and melted into the darkness.

When he learned that Marco would take passage on the *Twin Brothers*, he hired on as an oarsman. He grinned at the memory of seeing the hiring clerk decline the captain's offer of a job when Xavier boarded the same ship. The voyage went smoothly, and they eventually arrived in the port of Ostia. He thought about staying with his protector and abandoning his plan of revenge, but Xavier left without a word. Bitterness rekindled in his heart. When he thought of the ways he would make Marco regret his betrayal, his grief eased over the loss of his protector, once again. It was better to stoke his anger than to collapse into despair.

It was easy to follow Marco along the dock until he boarded a cargo ship. He didn't need to ask where the ship was headed. They all went to Rome. However, once they both arrived in Rome, tracking Marco would be harder. It was a huge metropolis and he had never been in a city bigger than Jerusalem. Then he remembered something Nikolaus had said while he was a slave about the father of Centurion Longinus being the *minor consul* in Rome. Even though Longinus was retired from politics, he reasoned that many shop owners and street vendors would know the address of the former *consul*. The second merchant he asked told him what he wanted to know.

He staked out the villa and was soon rewarded. Marco showed up but he was with the centurion and Nikolaus. He didn't know he was watching Aquila instead of Marco. He was concerned that Marco was no longer alone. Despite the complication, he decided to go on to Herculaneum since he knew that was Marco's destination.

For a few copper coins, a merchant heading for Herculaneum let him ride in the back of his wagon loaded with sacks of barley. Several days passed without incident. Near the outskirts of Herculaneum, the merchant pulled off the road to take a nap. Since there was only a short distance left, he set off walking. He was about to round a bend in the road that was hidden by a stand of trees, when he heard a horse squeal in pain. He ran around the curve in time to see Marco throw a rock at the driver of a carriage. He was mystified that Marco was ahead of him and no longer with the centurion and Nikolaus. When the woman riding in the carriage jumped out with a whip in her hand, he watched with glee as she lashed at Marco over and over. Eventually, the carriage took off leaving the boy behind. He waited until he knew Marco would not see him following. He knew where Marco was going, and in such a small town he would not be difficult to find, especially with his unusual eye color. After giving his prey a head start, he stepped back onto the road and started walking. He was deep in thought when someone shouted at him from behind.

"*Marco, is that you?*" He stopped and spun around.

The memory of his shock at turning around to find Centurion Longinus still made him anxious. When the centurion shouted over his shoulder, he dove into the underbrush. He was getting very good at crawling on his belly. From the cover of tangled vegetation, he took a shortcut to a section of road ahead and once again started toward Herculaneum. Why was Centurion Longinus behind him, but Marco was ahead of him? Again, he wondered why they weren't together as they had been at the villa in Rome. Perhaps they had gotten in a fight.

He was in for another surprise when he looked up to find Marco heading right for him. He had turned around to go back to Rome. They both stopped and stared at each other. The boy shouted at him, then tripped, losing sight of him. He dove for a clump of bushes, and hid but he could see Marco sitting under a tree with his head in his hands. Finally, the boy got up and, once again, headed for Herculaneum. He knew the centurion's carriage wouldn't be far behind. He hurried after Marco, and finally reached

Herculaneum. He was exhausted, but at least he had money to rent a room at a cheap inn. He would rest first and then find Marco.

It was easy to locate Marco since he had checked into an inn only a few blocks from his hotel. He felt sure that now was the time to take his revenge. He planned to follow Marco along the streets and then strike when there was a large enough crowd milling around; then he would blend in with the shocked onlookers. He found a shopkeeper selling daggers and other metal works. He selected the cheapest dagger the merchant offered. It was battered and bent, but he needed to use it only once.

He ran the fateful scene with Marco, the centurion, and the other twin through his mind. Armed, and shaking with anticipation, he waited outside Marco's inn. He followed him at a safe distance when the boy left the courtyard gate. Marco started up a busy street; he decided to make his move. He came up closer and closer until he was only two paces behind the one who had promised him freedom and instead betrayed him. He closed the gap to one pace. His heart was racing as his target unexpectedly stopped in his tracks. "Good," he thought, "he's making it easy for me."

He raised his dagger and focused on Marco's back. Someone ahead shouted a warning. He looked past Marco's shoulder and saw Centurion Longinus reaching for his son in panic. As he did, the person who had been behind him was revealed. It was Marco! But Marco's back was to him and then he spun around. He lowered the dagger as he gaped at two Marcos. Twins!

"Marco would never turn on anyone," said one of the twins. "This was my fault. Please. Don't take it out on him."

He remembered how he turned and blindly ran in confusion. He didn't stop running until he got to his hotel. He raced through the courtyard and reached the door of his room. When he got inside, he slammed the door and slid the bolt. The memory of this day would forever be etched on his heart. It was the day he nearly made the worst mistake of his life.

❋ ❋ ❋

Calais threw the dagger on the floor. It clattered across the tile. "There are two of them!" he cried aloud. "I have ruined everything!"

Calais's life was in shambles. He thought that maybe he should have died from the poison, after all. He reached for the dagger and thought a wave of dizziness had thrown him off balance until he realized that the floor was shaking. The walls of the room were shaking as well. The lattice screen in the window rattled. Calais went to the door. He fumbled with the bolt until he could finally slide it back. When he stepped out into the courtyard, a few roof tiles crashed to the ground. He looked around at the other frightened guests who had come out of their rooms as well. Oddly, the landlord who was sitting on a bench looked around with mild interest but showed no concern.

One of the guests threw her hand to her chest and looked around. "What will it do this time? Will the roof of my room collapse?"

A gray-haired man sitting with the landlord grumbled with contempt. "Don't be foolish, woman. This happens all the time and it has for years. It's just the gods having a disagreement."

"Do they have to disagree so violently? Why doesn't Hercules tell them to leave his city alone," she exclaimed. "I thought this place was under his protection."

By the time the two men assured the woman that Hercules would surely object if his city was damaged, the shaking had stopped. Calais went back to his room. What would he do now? His motive for taking revenge against Marco was now irrelevant. Calais didn't know what motivated the other twin to deceive him, but it didn't matter anymore. What did matter was that Calais was afraid Centurion Longinus would hate him. He had tried to kill his son right in front of him. He might even report him to the slave hunters.

Calais began to pace the floor. He thought of several plans but discarded each one. Perhaps he should go to the boat docks in the morning and see if he could hire out as an oarsman again. He could go back to Rome and blend in with the crowds. Then he thought of Pompeii. It was bigger than Herculaneum, but much smaller than Rome. Perhaps he could go there and start a new life.

Calais found the wheat bread and apple he had bought earlier in the day. He ate slowly, enjoying the taste of good food after eighteen years of barley bread and raw vegetables. The night wore on until he blew out his lamp and lay down on the bed. He thought of his parents as he did every night. He remembered how his father would come to his corner of the one-room house and speak softly with him. He would say, "Sleep well, son. Tomorrow will be a new day." Then his mother would sing him to sleep. And he would sleep soundly, unafraid, and secure.

More than anything else, Calais missed hearing their voices. If only tomorrow really could be a new day. His eyes shot open with a sudden thought. If he threw himself on the centurion's mercy, would he forgive him. A sad, terrible laugh crept into the corners of the room. How could he be so foolhardy to think that any father would forgive someone for trying to murder his son? But Centurion Longinus wasn't just anyone.

Calais made his decision. He would trail the centurion and his sons. He would watch and wait for an opportunity. When the time was right, he would confront them. Surprised at his lack of fear, Calais decided that he would let the centurion do as he pleased. Better to die facing the spear than to live cowering in the shadows.

Chapter 30

Pompeii, Gossip, and a Ruined Villa

⊰⊱

A quila and Marco were determined to set off for Pompeii in pursuit of Simon Magus. They found a bit of papyrus, a pen, and ink. They wrote a note for Adan and Nikolaus and set it outside on the terrace table under a rock to prevent it from blowing away. Aquila went back into the house to get their knapsacks; but Marco hesitated at the table. He pulled his necklace from around his neck, wound the cord around the sapphire, and set it next to the rock on top of the note. Aquila came out of the villa carrying their knapsacks and joined Marco. They hurried along the path skirting the villa until they reached the stone-paved walkway to the street.

Adan, Decimus, Nikolaus, and Dionysia were deep in conversation until they realized they had not seen the twins in some time. When they didn't find them in the house, they went out on the terrace. Adan saw the rock and coiled necklace sitting on the table. "Not again!" he strode over to the table and snatched up the note. With a groan of frustration, he shoved the note at his brother.

Nikolaus read it to them. "Father, Uncle Niko, please don't be angry with us. We have gone to Pompeii and will be back in a few days. Do not worry about us. We can take care of ourselves. Aquila wants to settle a score and I want to help him. Please do not follow us. We promise not to break any laws. Marco and Aquila."

Adan threw his hands in the air. "I can't believe this! I swear those two are determined to drive me insane."

"At least they did what you ordered them to do, Adan," said Nikolaus. "They settled their differences." Amusement twinkled in his eyes. "And they promised not to break any laws."

"Ah, that makes me feel so much better," Adan retorted. "No telling what mayhem those two will conjure up together." He thought for a moment and then started laughing. Nikolaus stared at him in confusion. His expression cleared, and he started laughing as well.

"I fail to see the humor in this, gentlemen," said Decimus. "How is this amusing?"

"I know my sons," said Adan. "Aquila loves to explode things that make loud noises and lots of smoke. He and my father think it is great fun. As for Marco, even I can't train a dog to do the kind of tricks he can. I think we should start praying."

"For Aquila and Marco?" asked Dionysia.

"For Simon," said Adan and Nikolaus in unison.

Marco and Aquila hurried along the streets of Herculaneum. They decided not to rent a carriage since they would need to use their money to rent a room for a few days and buy supplies. It was about ten miles to Pompeii, but it gave them time to form a plan as they walked. First, they needed to locate the villa of Simon Magus. Second, they would need to find a few shops with specialty merchandise. It should be easier to find what they needed in Pompeii since it was a much larger city than Herculaneum. Then they would need to round up a few stray dogs willing to "work" for food, which would basically be every stray dog in Pompeii.

The brothers reached Pompeii late in the morning. They walked along the raised sides of the paved roads to stay out of the way of carts, horses, and excrement. Streets lined with shops looked promising, and they stopped at a few to get the ingredients Aquila would need. When the smell of fish grilling over coals hit their senses, they stopped for lunch.

After their meal, they wandered up and down streets looking for an inn with affordable rooms. They asked for suggestions from some of the shop keepers and were pointed in the direction of a street lined with inns and cafes. The brothers selected an inn that looked well-kept but was not too expensive. The innkeeper was a wizened old Egyptian who looked the brothers in the eye and hesitated. He stated a much higher price than the standard rate. Marco began haggling with the old man in Egyptian. The innkeeper's eyebrows shot up in surprise. He offered Marco a discount, saying he was "much more polite than the average Roman." Marco accepted. Then he asked the man if he knew the location of the grand villa and vineyards of Simon Magus of Gitta. The old man gurgled with laughter. He got up from his bench and motioned for the brothers to follow him into the courtyard. Using a stick, he drew a map in the dirt. Marco and Aquila didn't understand why the old gentleman thought their request was funny. However, they followed the directions and soon found the address.

"This must be a mistake," said Marco. "Could there be two streets called *Via de Monte*?"

Aquila looked across from the ruined building with the crumbling walls. "Let's ask the people that live across the street. They must know something."

They crossed the street and pulled the bell cord. A woman in her late sixties opened the door and peeked out. "Whatever you're selling, I don't want it." She started to shut the door.

Aquila held up a *dupondius*. "How about we pay you instead. We only want information." The woman inched the door open wider. Aquila pointed across the street. "Does Simon Magus live there?"

The woman snickered, holding her hand over her mouth to hide her missing tooth. "Simon lives in the guest house behind the ruins." She looked the twins up and down. "Do you know about the big earthquake? It hit on February 5, seventeen years ago. My husband and I will never forget that day. Much of Pompeii was destroyed and some of the damage still has not been repaired. The man who lived in that villa was killed when it collapsed on him but his wife survived. His name was Maximus. He was the tax collector for this district. His wife lived in the guest house until she died last year. Simon moved into the guest house about three months ago." She pointed at the crumbling sandstone walls of the villa. "The gods smiled on us when they struck down Maximus, the old scoundrel. A few of us went through the ruins of his house and found the money he had overcharged for taxes. You could say the earthquake reimbursed us for the extortion that Rome calls tax collecting."

"The earthquake reimbursed you?" questioned Aquila with a sneer. "Don't you mean the earthquake helped you steal money from a dead man?"

The woman sniffed piously. "He stole it from us first. We had every right. We were able to rebuild our tavern with that money. We make a good living and pay our taxes on time. We only took what was rightfully ours."

Aquila snorted. "Rightfully yours, by *your* calculation, of course."

The woman resentfully narrowed her eyes at Aquila. Marco coughed and nudged his brother with an elbow.

"Don't think we got off easy, young man," the woman chided him. "We work hard to earn a living. Besides, the gods no longer smile on us. Ever since that terrible quake all those years ago, the ground often shakes and damages our houses. We heard that some villages on the coast had to be evacuated when the land sank into the sea." She shrugged. "But that's not our concern."

"Did Maximus or his wife have relatives in Samaria, by any chance?" asked Aquila.

The woman answered eagerly, enjoying the chance to share gossip. "As a matter of fact, they did. Maximus's wife told me she would leave the property to her nephew who lived in Samaria. Simon told me the nephew gave it to him as payment for curing his daughter. I haven't seen a single architect or laborer set foot there, which means Simon doesn't have the money to rebuild the villa." She put her hand out for the copper coin. "Is that enough information for you? You owe me a *dupondius*."

Aquila started to drop it in her open palm but allowed the coin to slip through his fingers. He watched it hit the ground and turned his back to walk away. The woman glared at him but bent to pick up the coin. Marco reached for it first.

"Sorry," he said as he placed the coin in her hand.

The woman pressed her lips together in contempt and slammed her door shut. Marco quickly followed Aquila. The brothers walked back across the street and found their way around the crumbling villa to the guest house behind it.

"Now I can see why the innkeeper was laughing," said Aquila, "when we asked about Simon's villa. Since when is a guesthouse a grand villa? I rather like the extensive vineyards as well. Those eight grape vines really do put Grandfather Aquila's thousands to shame."

Marco took in the ruins without comment.

"This makes me wonder about something," said Aquila.

"I know what you're thinking," said Marco. "If the people of Samaria were knocking each other over to give their money to Simon, why hasn't he rebuilt the villa?"

"Because he was lying," answered Aquila. "He's broke."

The front door of the house opened and Simon stepped out. The brothers hid within the ruins of the villa and watched. Simon walked through his courtyard and turned down the street. Marco and Aquila waited until he was out of sight. The brothers approached the guesthouse and tried to open the door but it was locked. They looked through the lattice in the window openings and discovered everything they needed to know.

Back on the street, Marco stopped to get his bearings. "I need to find a stray dog or two. Smart dogs. They have to be smart for this to work."

The brothers began searching the streets. Marco bought dried meat at a curbside shop and kept an eye out for any large, stray dogs. They spied many strays roaming the streets, but they were too small or too skittish. Marco was getting discouraged until he glanced down an alley and saw two big dogs rummaging through trash dumped from a second-story balcony. Both dogs were of the *cane lupino* type, a wolf-like breed popular among Romans. They had long, thick, dark-brown and gray fur, with white markings on their chests and bellies. They had short, stand-up ears, and long, slender muzzles. Yellow eyes completed the wolf image of their breed.

Marco approached the dogs with a low whistle. When they looked up, the brothers grinned at each other. "I think we've found our co-conspirators," said Marco with satisfaction. He sat on the ground and the dogs cautiously approached him. He talked softly to them and they tilted their heads from side to side as they listened. Aquila backed away to the head of the alley to discourage anyone from entering it. Almost immediately, both dogs took turns eating dried meat from Marco's hand. Within thirty minutes, the dogs sat on command. In less than an hour, both dogs lay down sphinx-style and jumped to their feet with whistle commands.

"You," Marco pointed at the male, "I will call you Deimos. And you," he pointed at the female, "I will name you Phobos."

Aquila chuckled. "The twin gods, Dread and Panic, the children of Ares, the Greek god of war. You're not afraid of insulting Mars? I mean, we are Romans, are we not?" he asked with feigned concern. "You could name them Romulus and Remus after the children of Mars."

"True, but Phobos and Deimos sound scary, and Simon is a Samaritan; he won't care about Roman gods. But if he knows Greek, he'll know what these names mean."

"Good point," said Aquila. "They look healthy. They haven't been strays for long."

Marco instructed the dogs to follow him. Aquila smiled to himself knowing that the dogs would obey. Dogs always obeyed Marco. The brothers wandered the streets until nearly dusk, feeding the dogs treats as they went. When they got back to the inn, Aquila distracted the innkeeper long enough for Marco to sneak the dogs into their room.

Marco immediately started teaching more difficult tasks to Phobos and Deimos. It would take that evening and the next day, but he was sure the dogs would be ready for the big event at Simon the Sorcerer's house. While Marco worked with the dogs, Aquila prepared his ingredients and built his contraptions. The devices were small, since they needed to fit in the palms of their hands, but their construction was complicated. Several times while they worked, the brothers looked up and smiled at each other.

Aquila woke the next morning to find Marco curled up on a blanket on the tile floor. He had his knapsack stuffed under his head. Phobos was nestled against Marco's back and Deimos was curled against his chest. Aquila smiled at the sight. He got out of bed and tiptoed quietly to the door. Both dogs raised their heads to look at him but remained with Marco. Aquila slipped out and found a curbside café offering bread, olive oil, and smoked fish. He bought enough for their breakfast, including enough for the dogs. Marco was awake when he returned. He was sitting cross-legged on the floor talking to their new pets. They sat in front of him, looking as if they were memorizing his every word.

All four of them enjoyed breakfast. Marco sneaked the dogs out for a walk. They stayed close on either side of him as they walked the streets until Marco found a wooded area to run them through their recently learned behaviors.

On their way back to the inn, Marco kept up a steady stream of conversation. Occasionally, someone would turn and glare after him, thinking he was talking to himself. Marco didn't notice; he was too focused on the dogs. No one accosted him, however, seeing the size of the dogs and their obvious obedience to him.

Marco was unaware that he was being followed. The figure paused when Marco stopped to look over the merchandise in a shop or offered by a street vendor, and continued when Marco moved on. He lingered at a three-story building to admire the intricate mosaics decorating the walls. He wondered if it was someone's home or an office building. He was looking at the top balcony when the earth suddenly heaved. He felt the ground ripple beneath his feet. The people passing by did not seem to be concerned. They just stepped off the cobble-stone sidewalk curbs into the lower center reserved for carts and wagons. They looked up at roofs and extended balconies as if the shaking was a normal occurrence and kept walking. However, when cracking sandstone blocks and mortar gave way to the stress, everyone stopped and blinked up at roof overhangs and balconies. Fear tightened their expressions. This quake was far worse than usual.

Phobos and Deimos whined with their tails pressed between their legs. People came out of the shops and their homes to stand, swaying in the street. Still, there was no panic.

Marco shouted at the dogs to move away from a building just as he caught a blur of motion from the corner of his eye. Someone knocked him two paces from where he was standing. The man threw Marco to the ground and covered him with his own body. A loud crashing sound made Marco look back as he was slammed to the ground. A section of a balcony, three stories up, had collapsed into the street where he had been standing. Shattered pieces of brick and plaster pelted them. Terracotta tiles slid from the edge of the roof and smashed into pieces on the stone paving below. The shaking stopped; people looked around, nervously laughed, and shrugged their shoulders. They went back to their previous activity as if nothing unusual had happened. The man who had pushed Marco out of the way of the falling debris stood up and dusted himself off.

Phobos and Deimos spun around and rushed at Marco. They were snarling and growling, but they weren't looking at Marco. They slunk into a crouch and barked at Marco's rescuer as he turned to walk away. Even before he got off the ground, Marco knew it was Calais.

Marco signaled the dogs with an open palm. "Stop. It's all right, Phobos. It's all right, Deimos. Come. Good Phobos. Good Deimos." He reached for the dogs and they obediently approached him. He signaled for them to sit and praised them again. He wiped the street dust off his tunic and arms. Calais was walking away.

"Calais! Please, listen to me," begged Marco. "I am so sorry about what happened to you. I never meant for you to think that your life wasn't worth living. I really did want to help you."

Calais turned and approached him. He looked into Marco's eyes. "So, which one are you?"

"I'm Marco. My brother's name is Aquila."

He studied Marco's face and then the partially healed cuts and fading welts on his arms. "Looks like you had an argument with a horse whip. I think the whip won."

He held his arms up. "Yes, it was a horse whip. But better for it to hit me rather than an over-worked horse."

Calais tilted his head. "Did the whip belong to a lecherous woman in an open carriage? And the horse an old, red mare that has seen better days?"

"I guess you saw her," said Marco.

"Did she offer you a ride?" Calais asked.

"Yes, from Rome to Herculaneum. It was fortunate since she asked for nothing in return."

Calais snorted. "You must be a fool. Of course, she wanted something. Or did you know exactly what she wanted and that's why you accepted her offer?"

"I don't know what you mean," Marco set his jaw defiantly. "She only offered me a ride. I thought she was being kind."

"Did you keep her company at night in the inns?"

Marco blushed, but anger quickly replaced his embarrassment. "I worked off the cost of my own room every night. Camilla only wanted someone to talk to on the road."

"You really are naive," grumbled Calais. "When someone looks at you like you're a piece of meat, they have only one goal in mind; their own pleasure at your expense."

Marco focused on the debris in the street. "You saved my life. Why did you do that?"

Calais sniffed. "Now we're even. I didn't even care which twin you are. No matter what your intentions were or why your brother deceived me, the plan worked. I am free. So, I figure we're even now. The only problem is that your family will always be a threat to me. You know who I am. Centurion Longinus, you, or your charming brother, could turn me over to Commander Lysias. But now I have saved your life. That makes us even." Calais turned his back and started to walk away.

"Calais, we would never turn you in. You could go back with us to Caesarea. You could work with Andreas and his sons and have a good life."

Calais turned to face him. "Caesarea? You think I'd be safe there? It would take only one soldier from the five thousand at the Antonia to get transferred to Caesarea. One soldier, and my life would be forfeit."

Marco lowered his head in acceptance. "You're probably right. Where will you go?"

"Some place you'll never look." Calais turned and walked away. Marco watched him make his way down the street, stepping around fallen chunks of buildings and roof tiles. He reflectively scratched the dogs' heads as they sat on either side of him.

He turned his attention to the minor damage of the buildings around him. This quake seemed to be stronger and last longer than the two in Herculaneum. He wondered what it meant, and why the people here seemed so unconcerned. He gave a low whistle and the dogs jumped to their feet. "Let's get back to Aquila."

When he returned to the inn, he found Aquila standing in the courtyard. The innkeeper was nowhere in sight. Aquila looked around hurriedly and motioned for his brother to follow him. They went into their room and locked the door.

"Where have you been for so long," demanded Aquila. "I was getting worried."

"Did you feel the quake? Was anything damaged here at the inn?" Marco glanced around at the walls but he wasn't sure if the cracks in the plaster were new.

"Of course, I felt it." Aquila eyed his brother suspiciously. "You didn't answer me."

Marco told Aquila about the collapsed balcony and Calais pushing him out of the way. Aquila was grateful that Calais had saved his brother, but he hoped he would never have to face the young man again.

"Calais will be all right," declared Aquila. "He's nine years older than we are and we're doing just fine on our own. He will, too. Now we need to concentrate on Simon. One more day and we'll be ready. Tomorrow after sunset, I will have a confession from that pompous braggart even if it's the last thing I ever do."

Chapter 31

Simon, a Demon, and Glowing Wolves

A quila checked the supplies he and Marco had collected. "I hope that's enough flour. I did a few tests while you were gone to be sure everything worked. The copper ore was a bit trickier, and I had to grind it down a little. It was too coarse. The sulfur worked the first time."

"How about the vials? Did they break easily enough?" asked Marco.

"They shattered with little effort. You only need to drop them to the floor. But we'll need to practice slipping an ember in the mouth of the vials to be sure the contents ignite properly. We want the flour to burst into flame in one big whoosh. The copper powder makes green fire and the sulfur makes blue. I couldn't believe our good luck when we found the *phosphoro*. That's really going to do the trick."

"Are you sure the phosphorous won't burn their skin?" asked Marco as he massaged the dogs' necks. They lay on either side of him as he sat on the floor.

"Your children will be fine. I'll lightly dust their hair, just enough to give them a shimmering glow. It'll show up in the dark very nicely. I made finger protectors from almond shells so we can handle bits of embers to light the vials. I made small, wide-mouthed pots to carry the embers. We can hang the pots and vials from the fish hooks I sewed inside the robes. We'll go to the river harbor when we're done, and the dogs can romp in the water to wash the phosphorous off. By the way, what are you going to do with them when we go back to Herculaneum?"

"I'm keeping them," said Marco. "Father won't mind. They'll be good company for us on the voyage home. No one will mess with Dread and Panic or us."

"Let's hope so," said Aquila. "You never know what can happen. I learned something from Simon. He proved how easily some people can be manipulated into doing just about anything."

"Well, I better practice some of my own manipulation if the children are going to do their part." Marco turned his attention to the dogs and they perked up their ears.

"Right," said Aquila, "show me what you've got. I'll need to know what to expect."

The brothers rehearsed their plan with the dogs. Then Aquila took two ceramic jars and filled them with small glowing embers from the fireplace. This would be the most difficult part of their plan. They would need to remove an ember and place it in the top of each vial of flour and chemicals. After practicing with the finger protectors and pebbles, the brothers were satisfied with their work. They donned the long, black robes fitted with the hidden vials and small ember jars. They left the inn with the dogs.

"Our timing has to be perfect, Marco." Aquila glanced to the west. "The sun is just about to set. It'll be dark in less than an hour. I'll need about half an hour to prepare the dogs before we make our move." Marco nodded.

The brothers navigated the streets, taking as many alleys as they could. A few pedestrians stared after them as they walked past. It was rare to see twins, but twins dressed in identical long, black wool robes was extraordinary. Birds began to roost among the trees, and shop owners were taking in their display carts of merchandise or farm produce. The debris that fell during the quake had been cleared away. The residents were settling in for the night.

Aquila's heart was pounding with excitement and anxiety. He knew many things could go wrong and jeopardize their scheme. His greatest fear was that Simon might not confess.

Aquila was convinced the man was guilty, but what if he was wrong? What if Simon was innocent, and he really had only guessed that the bracelet was made of copper? What if he had come into court just to gloat, having heard that Aquila was on trial? What if the merchant really had faked the theft? If Simon did not admit to stealing the bracelet, he and his brother could find themselves in serious trouble and it would be Aquila's fault. For an uncomfortable moment, he debated the pros and cons in his mind.

He tried to soothe his doubts by reasoning that Simon was guilty of trying to get him and his father thrown overboard and had attempted to poison the crew of the *Pegasus*. Those crimes alone were enough to warrant what they were about to do. Or were they? Aquila's conscience was giving him second thoughts.

Marco paused and raised a hand to stop Aquila. "We're almost there, Brother. Whatever happens, no matter if Simon confesses or not, I'm with you."

Aquila's doubts evaporated in the face of his brother's courage. "Let's do this."

The brothers drew near to the ruined villa in front of Simon's house. Their biggest concern was that Simon would not be alone. Aquila signaled for Marco to wait inside the ruins of the crumbling villa while he checked for horses or a carriage. Aquila cursed under his breath in frustration when he saw two saddled horses tethered to the post by the front door. If the visitors stayed too long, the embers in the ceramic pots might burn out. Aquila returned to Marco to inform him. They sat down to debate whether they should try the next night.

"By the way," said Aquila, "Grandfather Aquila told me about a resort city called Baiae, across the bay from Herculaneum. There are tunnels under the city that the residents believe lead to the Gates of Hades. They say the Oracle of the Dead is there. People brave the hot tunnels to ask the oracle about their future. If you hear me say something about the Gate to Hades, you should say something about it as well."

"How did Grandfather know about the tunnels?" Marco asked.

"He walked down them once when he was young. His father had taken him to Baiae and left him to entertain himself while he attended a meeting. Grandfather said it got hotter and the smell of sulfur got stronger the deeper he went. Grandfather and I think it must be layers of coal burning underground and that's why the water in the mineral springs at Baiae is hot."

"How does the coal catch on fire?"

"Probably lightning. Grandfather told me about finding a fulgurite once."

"What's a fulgurite?"

"It's a channel of melted sand or dirt caused by lightning going into the ground."

"How did he know the lightning melted the sand?"

"He saw it. He said it struck a tree first, split the trunk into splinters, and then went into the ground right in front of the tree. Grandfather said it was amazing. I wish I had been there to see it."

While they were talking, they heard farewells exchanged and horses trotting past. Marco and Aquila looked at each other as they mirrored sly grins. They checked the supplies hanging inside their robes and stepped out into the growing darkness.

"There's one more thing to do," said Aquila. He pulled two black wool shawls from his knapsack. He handed one to Marco. "Wrap this around your head and pull the front out to shadow your face." Marco watched Aquila fashion his makeshift hood and did the same.

Marco grinned at his brother. "We look like demons of death." Aquila snorted and smiled.

Aquila went to the front door and pulled the bell. He braced himself and waited. The door opened. Simon started talking before he looked through the opening. "Did you forget something?" He blanched with alarm when he saw Aquila. "What are *you* doing here?"

Aquila pushed the door open. Simon stumbled back sputtering and protesting. "How dare you break in like this!"

"You opened the door," answered Aquila calmly. "How have I broken in?"

"Wh-what do you want?" Simon nervously backed into the entryway. Aquila followed him and pushed the door shut.

"I have come to confess." Aquila's lips smiled but his eyes gleamed with malice.

"You're going to confess to me?" Simon frowned in confusion.

"Yes. You see, you were quite right about me and my father. He works very hard to control his, should I say, preferred state, but I have grown tired of hiding my true nature."

"Do you mean your sinful nature?" demanded Simon eagerly.

"I'm talking about the compulsion to change into my true form. You accused us enough times on the voyage. Why do you stare at me with such confusion? Don't you remember?"

Simon's mouth fell open. "I—I don't know what you mean."

Aquila slowly walked toward Simon forcing him to backup into the central atrium. Aquila slowly padded around the room until Simon's back was to the front door. The oil lamps placed on pedestal tables near every doorway flickered as Aquila passed them. He almost seemed to float across the room. Virtually no moonlight streamed through the *compluvium,* the open skylight in the center of the atrium's roof. The *impluvium,* a low-walled cistern designed to catch rainwater from the skylight, reflected soft light from the lamps. The front door inched open behind Simon. Aquila laughed loudly as he took in the sparse furnishings of the atrium. The sound covered the opening of the door as Marco and the dogs slipped inside.

In most Roman houses, the central atrium was accessible from all rooms of the house and the rooms were also connected to each other by doorways. The skylight and latticed windows in each room allowed sunlight and fresh air to access the entire villa. The atrium in Simon's house was large but held only a smattering of benches and several pedestal tables along the walls. Potted plants were placed on the tiled enclosure of the cistern.

Aquila snatched a lamp off a table and shone the light along the plants. He recognized nightshade, snakeroot, oleander, tobacco, belladonna, and larkspur. They were poisonous to humans if ingested and could be fatal. The larkspur was the poison his brother had given Calais. He set the lamp back on the table.

Simon trotted after Aquila. "What true nature are you babbling about, then? I don't know what you mean! I already know you're a sinner of the worst kind. Get out of my home!"

Aquila smiled and began to rearrange the folds of his robe. His pale-amber eyes shined like polished gold in the lamplight. He walked over to a lamp and snuffed it out with his "bare" fingers. Simon gasped when Aquila smiled, obviously feeling no discomfort.

"Don't know what I mean?" mocked Aquila. "Of course, you do. You claimed we were werewolves and should be drowned in the sea. In fact, you convinced the crew of the *Pegasus* to demand our deaths." Aquila padded around the atrium and crossed to the opposite doorway. He bent down by the lamp and shot a look at Simon, knowing the light would make his eyes appear more yellow, before he snuffed the wick out with his fingers. Simon glanced around nervously. The near darkness was unnerving.

"That's what I have come to confess. You were right. We are werewolves!" Aquila raised his hands in a dramatic gesture and muttered an incantation. He dropped his hands and a column of green and blue fire erupted from the floor. It whooshed into the air in a radiant blaze of unnatural flames. They both felt the heat of it and the air reeked of sulfur.

Simon screamed and threw his hands up as he staggered backward. He had never seen supernatural fire burst from a man's hand. The crux of his sorcery was "predicting" events that Simon had actually caused and "summoning" long-dead loved ones to comfort the living. He knew certain tricks and illusions could fool the foolish, but all the trickery in the world could not give someone yellow wolf eyes. The creature that stood before him must truly be a demon from the Underworld.

The creature gestured as if to throw something in Simon's face. He defensively threw his hand up and turned his face away, but only for an instant. Afraid of what the creature may do, he quickly looked back. The werewolf was gone. Instantly, a voice rang out behind him from a doorway on the opposite side of the atrium. Simon spun around and saw that the werewolf was across the room in the skip of a heartbeat.

"You don't know what you've done, Simon Magus of Gitta," said the diabolical creature. "Forcing me to do slave labor those three months in prison broke down my resolve to deny my cravings. The ill treatment I suffered caused an overwhelming desire to indulge my natural appetite. I thought it only fitting that I should start with you since it is your fault that I hunger for it."

"No! No! This can't be happening!" Simon turned to run. Low growling stopped him in his tracks. Two glowing, wolf-like creatures stepped out from a doorway. Their lips were pulled back from their teeth as they snarled. The light of the last two lamps reflected red in their eyes. Their bodies glimmered in the darkened room as they advanced.

"You see, Simon; I have brought my cousins. I have called them up from the tunnels."

"Tunnels? What tunnels," cried Simon, eyeing the creatures.

"Surely, you know of the tunnels under the city of Baiae where the Oracle of the Dead can be found. The Oracle summons spirits of the dead to commune with the living." He waved a hand at the wolf-like creatures. "They come up from the tunnels when I call them. They fly through the night to come to my aid. Let me introduce Deimos and Phobos, wolves of the dead from the Underworld. They hunger for human flesh just as I do. See how they glow? Only the Hounds of Hades carry the light of the moon upon them. It is the full moon that gives them their greatest strength."

"There—there's only a quarter moon tonight," wailed Simon. "Doesn't that weaken them?"

The werewolf gave him a mocking snicker. "No, it just makes them peevish. Demons can be so cranky when they're hungry for human blood."

Simon cried out to the werewolf. "Call them off! I beg you!"

"Face me, Simon Magus. Look upon the power of the Underworld." Again, the werewolf raised his hands and waved them about in a ritualistic gesture. He spoke an incantation and dropped his hands. Again, the flames shot into the air, flashing in blue and green waves of incandescent fire. Within seconds, the werewolf was gone.

Immediately, the werewolf's voice sounded from the far corner of the room opposite from where he had stood only a second before. "Simon, do you smell the brimstone of Hades? The tunnel of Baiae reeks of it. You should go there. I find the fumes particularly delightful, don't you?" The werewolf laughed. "I can send you there. Phobos! Deimos! Bring the man!"

Simon turned to face the dogs. They dropped to their bellies and slunk on the floor toward him. Slowly, the crouching demons inched closer, their glowing red eyes focused on their prey.

Simon turned back to his tormentor. "No! No! Call them off. I'll do anything you ask. There must be something that you want! I have money, gold and silver!"

"We want your flesh, Simon. We want your blood. Why should I deny myself that pleasure?" He gestured at the creatures. "Or them? You did not deny yourself the pleasure of seeing me in chains when you appeared in the courtroom. You could have stayed away. Your scheme had already caused me much suffering. Yet, that wasn't enough for you."

"I—I was there on other business, I swear!" cried Simon. He glanced back at Phobos and Deimos. "Don't let them eat me! Please! There must be something I can do for you!"

"You can tell me the truth! Only that will save you, Simon Magus of Gitta! But if you lie to me, you will surely feel our fangs." The blue and green fire erupted again. Before Simon could blink, the voice of the werewolf spoke from behind him. He jerked around to find himself face to face with the man who had been across the opposite side of the room only an instant before.

Simon threw his hands up and dropped to the floor. His flailing arms knocked over several of the potted flowers. The dogs snarled and snapped their jaws at him as they stalked toward him with the fluid gait of a predator's imminent attack.

"The truth, Simon. If I don't hear the truth from you now, Deimos and Phobos will taste your blood."

Simon's hands trembled in front of his face as he tried to scoot away from the dogs. "All right, I'll tell you. Just make them stop!"

"Phobos, sit. Deimos, sit." The dogs obediently sat. "Speak!" shouted the werewolf.

"You were right. I did try to pay money for the gift of the Holy Spirit. I wanted to impress the people the way Peter and John did. I wanted the power that they had. I wanted the villagers to respect me, too. I thought they would sell it to me if I just offered enough money. But you and your father made sport of me as if you had the right. How dare *you* judge *me*! Your evil father murdered God's Son!"

"We all killed God's Son," exclaimed the werewolf. "Our sin killed Yeshua!"

Simon blinked in confusion to hear a demonic creature say such a thing. He stood up. The dogs jumped to their feet, barking and snapping their jaws. Simon cried out. He looked back at the werewolf, but he was gone.

"Behind you Simon. I'm right behind you." There was a short, sharp whistle and the dogs licked their lips and sat on their haunches. "You're right about my father. He did kill Yeshua. Just like I will let Phobos and Deimos kill you if you don't confess your sin to me. *Did you steal the bracelet?*"

Simon dropped to his knees and clasped his hands in front of his chest. "Yes! Yes, I stole it. I put it down your tunic. I told the little girl that you had stolen a bracelet and that the merchant would reward her if she told him."

"She was afraid when she ran off. What did you say to her?"

Simon swallowed hard. "I told her that you saw what she did and would be angry with her." His tone sharpened. "But what does it matter? My plan worked. That's all I cared about. I wanted the judge to sentence you to death. I wanted to take you away from your father just like he took Yeshua away from God. Yeshua is my Lord and Savior and your father murdered him!"

Aquila's mouth dropped open in shock. "You think you were doing God *a service*?"

"Yes, and I'm proud of it!" exclaimed Simon. "I did it for God. I don't understand why you were set free, but who am I to question my Lord. He must have something worse planned for you. He only let you come into my home to test my resolve. I am not afraid. God will protect me!" he declared as he shot a look of terror at the dogs.

"You must have had more reasons than that!" exclaimed Aquila in disbelief.

Simon dropped his gaze and cowered. He knew the demon would know if he lied.

"What else motivated you?" demanded the creature.

"I have every right to punish you and your father. I am a servant of God. When you mistreat the servant, you mistreat the Master of that servant. Therefore, both of you dishonored God by dishonoring me. I didn't deserve to be humiliated by pagans. So I have every right *and duty* to avenge my Lord Yeshua."

A long whistle sounded behind Simon and the dogs leapt at him, knocking him flat on his back. They stood with their front paws on his chest, snapping and snarling in his face. Simon could see the feverish desire in their eyes. He could feel the hot breath of Hell on his arms when he tried to cover his face.

"Get them off! Get them off!" Simon screamed.

The werewolf's voice sounded in his ear. "If you ever come after me or my family again, Deimos and Phobos will find you. They will come up from the Gate of Hades and find you. They will tear your limbs apart. God will deal with us as he pleases without your help. For now, he lets us roam the earth, but we will see judgment. Beware, Simon, or these demons of death will come for you in the night."

A high-pitched whistle sounded and the dogs pushed off from their captive and ran. The werewolf extinguished the lamps, smothering the flame in his fingers. The front door slammed shut.

Simon the Sorcerer looked around. He was alone in the dark. He sat up and patted himself. He was uninjured. Had he really had an encounter with a werewolf and his demon wolves? It wasn't possible. Then why did the room smell of brimstone?

Chapter 32

Festival of Vulcanalia,
Broken Cages, Jova, and Cato

<hr>

Aquila and Marco hurried from the house of Simon the Sorcerer. If anyone had seen them, they would have run in fright at the sight of two huge, glowing dogs. The brothers removed the ember pots, then took off their robes, and rolled them up, fishhooks and all. They found their way to the river harbor and walked out to the end of a boat ramp. Aquila threw the ember pots into the river. Marco took off his sandals and stepped into the river up to his knees. He whistled two sharp chirps and both dogs bounded into the water. He splashed them to wash the phosphorous off. He whistled three sharp chirps and the dogs climbed out of the water. They shook as hard as they could. Water flew in all directions. The brothers laughed when the spray soaked their tunics.

The dogs lay on either side of Marco and rested their heads on outstretched paws. Neither brother spoke for a while. The October night was edged with a chill. The quarter moon's white glow had morphed to yellow as it hovered above the western horizon. Wispy clouds wove themselves among the stars as if they were vines growing among sparkling flowers. Marco thought the night sky looked magnificent. Aquila studied the clouds.

"Marco, have you ever wondered why clouds float in the air? They hold huge amounts of water when they pour down rain. Water is heavy, yet clouds hang suspended in air. Why is that?"

"I have no idea, Aquila. Let me know when you figure it out." He looked over at his brother. "You got your confession. Do you feel better now?"

When Aquila didn't answer, Marco peered at him, trying to read his expression in the soft darkness. Finally, Aquila cleared his throat. "No. I'm trying to, but it's not happening."

"What do you mean? Simon admitted stealing the bracelet. Isn't that what you wanted?"

"Yes, I wanted him to own up to his crimes, but that's just it. He doesn't think they were crimes. He admitted to everything except guilt. You heard him; he thinks he was doing God's will. He's convinced that lying, and stealing, and attempted murder were the right things to do. We think he's evil, and he thinks we're evil. That's not what I had in mind."

"Aquila, he tried to buy the power to bestow the Holy Spirit on people for his own glory. That's as evil as someone offering to pay Yeshua to sacrifice himself on the cross. Simon's heart is corrupt. That makes his thoughts and actions corrupt as well. You can't change his corrupt heart or his flawed reasoning. We certainly can't do it with deception."

"Deception? What do you mean?" asked Aquila.

"We fooled him into believing we were a werewolf from the depths of Hell. His false accusations against us have been confirmed—by us. He'll also believe he was justified in trying to get you and Father thrown into the sea. Now he thinks he is a victim of Satan's demons."

Aquila sighed with frustration. "If you think what we did was wrong, why did you participate? You trained the dogs. You practiced over and over with me. You had plenty of time to change your mind."

"I took an oath. Where you go; I go. I accept the consequences. Aquila, I will never turn my back on you again. I didn't care if it was wrong or right. I cared about you."

Aquila stared at Marco open mouthed. "Then you felt this was wrong from the beginning?"

"Pretty much," said Marco. "I also knew that you would not understand if I told you how I felt. You would have thought that I was trying to weasel out of helping you. No, I was determined to see this through. Are you going to tell Father what we did?"

"Yes," Aquila declared. A slow grin spread across his face. "When he's too old to do anything about it."

Marco looked at Aquila. Aquila looked at Marco. The brothers laughed until tears ran down their faces. Phobos and Deimos pranced about, eager to share the emotional moment. They excitedly smacked their tails against their flanks. The brothers threw their arms around the dogs' necks, not minding the wet-dog smell, and accepted their enthusiastic face licking.

Aquila eyed his brother. "Since we have agreed to stick together, with no secrets, there is something I need to tell you. Father and Uncle Niko were talking about something that could be dangerous and most likely impossible to find, but we have to try."

"What is it?" asked Marco, intrigued by the excitement in Aquila's voice.

"It's a Prophecy Box. Uncle Niko said it belonged to his father, but it disappeared just before he and Dionysia were sold into slavery." Aquila told Marco the details.

Marco was fascinated. "How are we going to explain this mission to our family?"

"I haven't figured that out yet," admitted Aquila. "I'm working on it."

Marco grinned. "We'll figure it out together."

It was Aquila's turn to grin. "Deal!"

The brothers headed back to the inn. They didn't want to meet any crime-minded residents of Pompeii lurking about the dark streets or alleys. At one intersection, both dogs stopped and growled a warning. They warily approached the corner of a courtyard wall and barked. Footsteps ran away from the other side of the corner. Marco peered down the street in time to see a shadowy figure hurrying away in the dark. He praised their "bodyguards," and they moved on. They entered their room at the inn and collapsed into chairs with relief that their task was successful. Marco gave the dogs fresh water, and they curled up at his feet.

Aquila has just taken an ember from the fireplace to light the oil lamps when the floor started shaking. Even the walls of the room began to shake. Aquila instinctively flattened himself against a wall and looked around with wide eyes.

"Get over here, Marco! If the ceiling collapses it will be from the middle." Marco signaled to the dogs and hurried to join his brother. Plaster dust filtered down through the air. An oil lamp toppled over. Aquila ran to the other lamp and snatched it just as it wobbled toward the edge of the table. The air smelled of lime as more whitewashed plaster dropped from the walls, and dust filtered down from the spaces between the wooden roof beams. Slammed doors could be heard from the courtyard as guests rushed from their rooms.

"Maybe we should get out of here," suggested Aquila.

"I'm not leaving the dogs."

"So, it's better getting crushed by a collapsing roof than being fined for having dogs?"

Marco didn't answer. The shaking stopped. Both brothers sighed in relief. The dogs looked up at Marco as if waiting for an explanation for the bouncing room. He sat on the floor and signaled for the dogs to sit together facing him. He talked to them about the upcoming ship voyage and about their new home in Caesarea. Aquila couldn't keep from smiling and shaking his head. He was used to Marco talking to animals, but he had never seen them listen so attentively. Marco raised an open hand, palm facing the floor and slowly lowered it, then rotated his hand. Both dogs lay down and rolled to their sides. He praised them and scratched behind their ears and necks.

"How do you that?" asked Aquila.

"Do what?" Marco looked up as Aquila sat down on the bed.

"Make them do what you want?"

"I can't *make* them do anything. I only ask them to show me what they're willing to do."

The brothers eventually fell asleep, but woke as soon as the sun neared the horizon. They took to the streets and were surprised to find a festive atmosphere, with throngs of shoppers and street corner musicians playing lutes and singing. Marco kept an eye on the dogs to be sure they followed closely. Wagons loaded with rough-cut wood trailed along the main streets, heading in the direction of the amphitheater. People were grouped in the streets laughing and gesturing as the wagons lumbered by. The twins passed several shops nearly overrun with young girls buying necklaces of bright-blue, ceramic tiles of squares, ovals, and disks strung on leather or woven cords. Overcome with curiosity, Aquila stopped where bundles of twigs were offered for sale.

"Sir!" called Aquila to the owner, "why are they taking wood to the amphitheater? Is there some type of celebration going on?"

The man's eyebrows shot up in surprise. "Were you born yesterday, boy? What is wrong with you? It's for the Festival of *Vulcanalia*. Do you not worship Vulcan, the god of fire? We honor him so he won't vent his anger on our city. Everyone knows Vulcan might steal Jupiter's thunderbolts to set our homes and vineyards ablaze when his wife, Venus, rouses his jealousy. The goddess of love is not the goddess of loyalty. If we honor Vulcan, his temper will cool."

A group of young girls pushed past the twins, laughing and jostling each other. They all wore the blue-tile necklaces. One of the girls lost her balance and tried to steady herself by grabbing hold of Marco's arm. Deimos and Phobos growled, warning her off. She scampered closer to her friends, and they moved away.

Aquila asked the shop owner, "Why are the girls wearing those blue necklaces?"

"By the look of your eyes and your ignorance, your family must be a pack of wolves. Do you not know the story of Vulcan and how his mother, Juno, threw him into the sea because of his ugliness, breaking his leg in the process? The water nymph, Thetis, took pity on him and raised him as her own. In gratitude, he crafted a magnificent silver and sapphire necklace on his fiery forge, just for her. Juno saw it and was overcome with jealousy. Imagine her shock when she learned that Vulcan was the craftsman. The very son she had rejected and crippled."

When Marco heard the man mention a sapphire necklace, he slapped his hand over his heart. He frowned when he remembered he had left the sapphire behind.

"The shops selling the necklaces must make a lot of money," observed Aquila. "Why aren't you selling them as well?"

The shop owner waved a hand at the people standing in line to buy the bundles of sticks. "Only the women buy the necklaces, but everyone buys the wood. It is bad luck not to throw your own little flame into the bonfires we will have in the amphitheater tonight. My slaves collect the twigs and sticks throughout the year for this one night. I will make enough today to pay my yearly taxes with money to spare. Tonight, I will eat and drink in celebration to the great Vulcan, but tomorrow I will stay home and count my gold." He grinned in anticipation.

Marco wandered down the street to see what other vendors were selling. He found a shop offering tiny cages with a single mouse, baby chicken, sparrow, or dove, and even baby rabbits. Several other shops were selling small, open-mouthed jars full of water holding a single live fish. Marco returned to the shop where Aquila was still talking with the owner.

"Why are they selling these animals," Marco asked.

"To throw into the bonfires to make sacrifice to Vulcan, of course," replied the shop owner.

Marco was horrified. "You throw them into the fire *alive*?"

The shop owner shrugged. "Why not? If living sacrifices appease Vulcan, then for all I care, dogs and cats could be thrown into the bonfires. Better to sacrifice useless animals than to see our vineyards and fields ablaze."

Marco was speechless with rage. He looked at Phobos and Deimos and back at the shop owner. Aquila saw Marco clench his hands into fists as he took a step toward the merchant.

"Marco!" cried Aquila. "Why don't you go down the street and see if you can bump into any friends of yours." Marco turned blazing eyes on his brother but blinked in surprise when Aquila looked at him with wide eyes and winked.

"What?" Marco saw the gesture but didn't comprehend.

"Friends. You might *bump* into a few." He tilted his head toward the tables loaded with the flimsy little cages.

A slow smile extinguished the anger in Marco's eyes. When he turned to walk away, Aquila looked back at the shop owner.

"What happens if Vulcan isn't pleased with your sacrifices?" asked Aquila with a smirk. "Will he pitch a tantrum and rain fire down on the city?"

"*Ohe*, don't let Vulcan hear such things. When Venus is unfaithful to him, he beats his forge in madness. Flames come from *Monte Vulcano, Aetna* and *Lipara*. The people of Sicily watch and weep. When Vulcan discovers the treachery of Venus," he threw his hands into the air. "Boom! The mountains in the sea explode. Fortunately for us, there is no flaming mountain near Pompeii. We are safe from Vulcan's fiery temper."

"Why throw live animals into bonfires if you're so safe?" asked Aquila. "Lightning sets the fields on fire anyway. You're wasting your money on bonfires and sacrifices."

The shop keeper scornfully eyed Aquila. "Do you wish to deny us a chance to make an honest *denarius*? We have families to feed and taxes to pay. We breed the birds, mice, and rabbits for this one day a year. That's the only purpose they serve. Begone with you, wolf-eyes. Do you begrudge us our livelihood?"

Aquila spun on his heel and moved down the street to catch up with Marco. They watched as slaves brought more of the tiny cages from the back of the shop. Aquila whispered in Marco's ear and he nodded. They waited until one of the larger wagons loaded with wood drew even with the longest table piled with cages. Marco pointed at the top of the wagon and shouted to a group of women, "Look out!" When they looked up startled, Marco and Aquila knocked against the table overturning it. The women and others gathered around the table screamed and scrambled out of the way in confusion, also knocking against the table. It tumbled over on its side, tossing the fragile cages to the ground. Most of them broke open. Animals scampered in every direction, and the young birds took flight. The twins managed to "accidently" break the rest of the cages as they tried to help the slaves retrieve the spilled merchandise.

The shop owner uselessly shouted and gestured in frustration. Deimos and Phobos snapped at the escaping animals, but they got away. The dogs' frantic efforts added to the melee. People jostled each other trying to get out of the way. More tables were upset causing more cages to break when they hit the ground. Aquila looked to see if Marco was watching, but he had his back turned as he knelt over another table just before a cascade of cages hit the stone pavement.

Aquila grabbed the wrist of the panicking shop owner and pressed several gold *aureuii* in his palm. "Does that help?" Aquila asked the man.

The merchant gaped at the gold coins, and then clenched his hand shut. He shouted at his slaves, "Leave it!" Without a word to Aquila, he retreated into the shadows of his shop. The slaves stopped and stared after him in amazement. Marco and Aquila hurried away with the dogs. They dodged into an alley and laughed until their sides hurt.

"Good job Phobos! Good job Deimos!" Marco rubbed the dogs' necks as he looked at his brother with pride. "We make a good team, Brother."

"We do. I wish we could have freed all of them but, at least, most got away."

"I guess we better think about getting out of here, especially now," said Marco. "That merchant is probably reporting us to a patrol this very minute."

Aquila smiled. "Perhaps not, but we *would* have to pick today to get back to Herculaneum, right in the middle of the biggest festival of the year. Who is going to leave the festivities behind to drive us to Decimus's villa?"

"I would say our timing is bad," Marco declared, "except for all the animals we rescued."

Aquila nodded agreement. "Come on. Let's go find a carriage."

The brothers eventually found a driver willing to take them to Herculaneum. He hesitated when he learned that the dogs were included, especially after he realized the twins' eyes were the same color. However, a gold *aureus* pressed into his palm, with the promise of another at the end of the trip, was enough to ease his anxiety. The driver cast nervous looks at the dogs until they went to sleep, curled up on the floor of the carriage. The travelers stopped occasionally to stretch their legs, and Marco tossed sticks for the dogs to retrieve. A whistle was all they needed to race back with anything Marco tossed for them.

When the carriage pulled to a stop in front of Decimus's villa, Aquila and Marco paid the promised fee and prepared themselves for a tongue lashing from the entire family. Aquila pulled the bell at the door.

The door opened. Adan looked out at them. "Good. You're alive. I won't have to tell your mother that I managed to lose both of you." He turned and walked down the hall. The brothers looked at each other with wide eyes and followed their father as he strode out to the terrace where Dionysia and Nikolaus were sitting.

Dionysia jumped up to hug the brothers. "Deci will be sorry he missed your homecoming. He had to go into the city to oversee deliveries in preparation for the *Vulcanalia* Festival. He supplies wine to many of the bars and cafés in the city."

Nikolaus gave them a shake of his head and a slow grin. "What are we going to do with you two?" The dogs stepped out of the doorway to the terrace. "*Ohe*, I mean, the four of you. Have you adopted them, or did they adopt you?"

Adan looked at the dogs. A slow smile relaxed the lines of tension in his face. He knelt on a knee and extended a hand. The dogs walked to him with their heads lowered and their tails wagging. They sniffed his hand and then his knee and shin. "They're beautiful. They're from the *cane lupino* breed, the dog-wolf. They're probably from the same litter."

"That's what we thought, too," said Marco.

Adan ruffled the dogs' ears and stood up. "I'll get them some water. They're probably thirsty." Aquila and Marco exchanged amused glances. Adan had not offered *them* anything.

"You might as well sit down and tell us all about your adventures," said Nikolaus.

"Aren't you going to yell at us?" asked Aquila.

"Should we?" asked Nikolaus.

Marco and Aquila exchanged startled glances. "It's what we expected," said Aquila.

"The two of you are of age. You can make your own decisions. You had your own money. I might add, you both proved your resourcefulness. I have one question. Did you keep your promise and not break any laws?"

"Yes, Sir," exclaimed the brothers in unison. Aquila added, "He opened the door and stepped back. That's an invitation to come in, right?"

"Who opened what door?" asked Adan as he returned. He set a bowl of water down for the dogs and they eagerly made use of it. The brothers told them everything that had occurred in Pompeii including the encounter with Calais. Adan and Nikolaus asked a few questions, but mostly listened in silence.

Dionysia listened without interrupting until the twins had finished their entire explanation. She then reached for a hand of each brother. "Do you really think that there is true justice in this world? To force an admission of guilt from the offender will not make the crime go away. It will not alter the memory of despair, or grief, or humiliation. It certainly will not inspire the offender to be a better person. What do you think you have accomplished by tricking this man into admitting he stole the bracelet?"

"We got the truth out of him," stated Aquila.

"You have also perpetrated a lie," said Adan. "He probably believes he was justified in assuming the worst about us. After your prank, he might even be more inclined to take deadly action against someone who looks different. Dionysia has also suffered because of false assumptions. The crew of their ship wanted to kill her. They thought she was a demon from Hades because of her pale coloring and red hair. Simon now believes that werewolves are real, and he'll spread that belief to other ignorant people."

Aquila gave Marco a quick look of guilt. "Somebody else pointed that out to me."

"What you did is understandable, son," said Adan. "You were unjustly imprisoned and forced to do hard labor. I suppose the three of us could go back to Pompeii and confront Simon with the truth. However, very few people are willing to relinquish long-time beliefs despite the facts. Old beliefs are familiar, and therefore, seem to offer security. New ideas are usually met with suspicion and fear. Simon is not likely to ever change his mind now. The damage is done."

Adan pointed to the terrace table. "Marco, you might want to retrieve your amulet. Nobody has touched it since you left it there."

Marco picked up the necklace and put it around his neck. "Thank you for keeping an eye on it, Father."

Aquila frowned. "Why didn't you wear it to Pompeii."

"I wanted Father to know I would come back with you." Marco closed his hand over the gemstone. The sapphire felt warm despite the cool October air.

No one spoke for a while, each lost in his or her own thoughts. Marco gave a soft whistle and the dogs came to him. They sat facing him expectantly. He ran his fingers through their fur along their necks and behind their ears.

"Father, can I keep them," asked Marco. "I'll take good care of them."

"I know you will, but I have one request. Would you consider changing their names? I'm not sure we need Dread and Panic in our home."

Marco grinned at his father as the others laughed. "I can do that. How about Cato for the brother and Jova for the sister?"

"Much better, but you should ask them. Try it out and see what they do," suggested Adan.

Marco pointed at Phobos and gestured for her to sit. "Jova, sit." The dog tilted her head at Marco then sat on her haunches. Marco pointed at Deimos and gestured. "Cato, sit." The dog hesitated for only a moment and sat. "Jova, come." She rose, walked to Marco, and laid her chin on his knee. "Cato, come." He did the same and laid his chin on Marco's other knee.

"Well, that answers that. I think they like their new names," said Dionysia.

"I think Marco could call them Mudslop and Swampgas and they'd still obey his every command," said Aquila with pride. Marco smiled at the rare compliment. "You should have seen them in Simon's house. They performed perfectly. You'd think they understood every word."

"How do you know they didn't?" asked Adan. "Doesn't a mute understand every word you say? He just can't answer with speech."

"But you can tell them to do certain things and they won't do it," countered Aquila.

"Maybe that's because they don't want to, not because they don't understand," said Adan. "How would you know the difference? Let's test it out." Adan signaled for the dogs to sit in front of him. They obeyed. "Jova, Cato, go to Nikolaus." The dogs tilted their heads. Adan repeated the command. The dogs glanced at Dionysia and Nikolaus but didn't move. "Jova, Cato go to Marco." They stood up and eagerly returned to Marco.

"Do you think they would come to me if I had dried mutton in my hand?" asked Nikolaus.

"Of course, they would. Even dogs can be bribed," said Adan. Cato and Jova looked at Adan and barked.

"I think they took offense, Father," said Marco. "You should apologize."

Adan chuckled. "I suppose I should. Cato, Jova, I humbly apologize for insulting your integrity." The dogs perked up their ears and sat. They swished their tails over the tile.

"Ah, apology accepted," said Nikolaus. They laughed as the dogs jumped to their feet and pranced from one to other, accepting all ear ruffling and head patting.

Chapter 33

Herculaneum, a Premonition, and Vesuvio Awakens

———◦◦◦◦◦———

Decimus was relieved to find that Marco and Aquila had returned when he came home that evening. He suggested that they go to Herculaneum's amphitheater to celebrate the Festival of Vulcanalia. He had bought bundles of sticks for them to light and toss into the bonfire. When no one expressed any interest in the festival, Decimus called to his slaves, a married couple he had bought before he brought Dionysia into his household.

"Festus, why don't you and Eunice go to the amphitheater tonight," said Decimus. "Take the sticks for Vulcan's bonfire and light one for each of us. I wouldn't want to insult the god of fire and tempt him to set my vineyards ablaze. Be back before the moon sets."

Festus and Eunice happily thanked him. In essence, he was giving them the night off from their duties, something that rarely happened. As they turned to leave the room, Marco handed Festus several *denarii*.

"Get yourselves something good to eat at the food stands," Marco told the man. Festus glanced quickly at Decimus for permission to accept the money. When he nodded, Festus extended his hand with a smile. He and his wife thanked Marco and left the room.

Dinner was a celebration, but not for the festival of Vulcan. Nikolaus was especially happy to see Dionysia at peace with her new life as a free citizen, married to the man she loved and who loved her. Also, Marco's quest was over, and the reunited family would soon be traveling back to Caesarea. Yet, Marco was quiet throughout the meal. After dinner, Adan asked him if he would take a walk with him. They left the terrace and headed for the gardens surrounding the villa.

"What is troubling you, Marco?" asked Adan.

He pressed his hand on the sapphire over his heart. "I can't shake this feeling that we still need to do something. For Dionysia. I know she's happy. I can see they are deeply in love, but something is wrong. I wish I knew what it was."

"Could it be that you think your mission was unnecessary? You must feel confused because Dionysia is no longer a slave and is quite happy here."

"I am confused," admitted Marco. "How could I have been so wrong? I put you and Mother through so much grief. I nearly got Calais killed. I nearly drowned after getting shipwrecked. Calais almost killed me. Aquila got arrested and was worked like a slave. I could have lost my brother if he had been executed. He was so angry with me, I nearly lost him anyway. And for what? Nothing!" Marco grumbled in frustration. "I should have stayed home."

"Perhaps," said Adan. "But you and Aquila have both learned valuable lessons during this time. I have, too. This time has not been wasted. Besides, we're not home yet."

The family sat on the terrace enjoying the evening together until time to call it a day. For the first night in months, Adan and the others slept soundly, but not for long. The quiet contentment of the night was shattered when everyone was violently shaken in their beds. The furniture hopped across the floor as the entire villa shook. The dogs jumped to their feet, whining and whimpering, as the floor vibrated and the walls flexed. There were cracking sounds, and thin lines appeared in the wall plaster. The smell of plaster dust filled the air. Adan was already in the atrium calling to the others by the time they managed to get out of bed and stumble to the central room. Marble and limestone statues decorating the villa and terrace toppled over. Arms and heads broke off as they hit the tile and flagstone floors.

The family hurried out to the terrace along with the two slaves, Festus and Eunice. They huddled by the balustrade away from the villa.

"I don't understand," cried Decimus. "The quakes are never this bad. We've been having them for years and they've only been a nuisance until now."

"When did they start?" asked Nikolaus.

Dionysia tried to remember. "I've lost count of the years, but the quakes have become much more frequent in the last few months. Before that, we had a few each year, except for that awful one seventeen years ago. I'll never forget how terrified I was." She and Decimus exchanged a long look. "That was the first time I knew you truly cared about me, Deci. You came for me even though part of the roof collapsed. You snatched me out of bed and carried me outside away from the house." She turned back to the others. "The quake destroyed parts of the cities near *Vesuvio,* and they had to be rebuilt. That's why much of Herculaneum looks new. The basilica had to be rebuilt, along with much of the forum, many homes, and shops."

"The villa on Simon's property was destroyed by that earthquake," said Aquila. "A tax collector named Maximus was the original owner, but he was killed in the quake. At least, that's what his neighbor told us. Apparently, Simon doesn't have enough money to rebuild it so he lives in the guest house behind it."

"Father, could this be why I'm here?" asked Marco. "Perhaps something really bad is going to happen. I think we need to leave for Rome tomorrow. We should not wait even for a few days. Maybe you need to leave permanently," he said to Decimus.

"Leave Herculaneum?" exclaimed Decimus. "Why would we do that? Nothing bad is going to happen. Like I said, we have these quakes all the time. This one was the worst we've felt in some time, but certainly there is no reason to leave. Besides, how would I pack up my vineyards and stuff them into my knapsack?" He laughed and the others smiled, but Marco did not.

"Marco could be right," said Aquila. "Perhaps a quake as bad as the one seventeen years ago is going to happen. Maybe even worse. You were going to take a vacation to Rome anyway. Why not leave tomorrow. You can always come back whenever you want."

"My sons are right, Decimus," said Adan. "I think it would be wise to err on the side of caution. Why don't we leave as soon as possible, just to be safe? Consider it a vacation. You can . . . "

The earth jolted again. This time the shaking was much worse. Rocks tumbled down the slope outside the balustrade. A few tiles slid off the roof and crashed onto the terrace flagstones. More cracking sounds came from the block masonry and wooden beams of the roof. This tremor seemed to last longer. Aquila counted the seconds.

"One thousand one, one thousand two, one thousand three, one thousand four . . . " his voice trailed off as he counted in silence and the shaking went on. Finally, it stopped after eighteen seconds. It was odd how it felt like it went on for much longer.

"What is that smell?" demanded Marco.

"Sulfur," said Aquila. "Why is that?" He gazed over the landscape with concern. "Is something burning?" They looked about but saw no fires.

A sliver of brilliant sun crept above the horizon and spread a soft light across the landscape. As the sky slowly brightened, they could see into the grounds of neighboring villas. A few carved stone cornices and decorative motifs had fallen to the ground and shattered. Statues had toppled. Some lay across stone terraces, broken at the neck or arms. Heads had rolled away from the bodies of marble and limestone.

"We need to leave, Decimus," said Adan.

"I agree," said Nikolaus. "The quakes are becoming more frequent and severe. That must mean something. Why not leave this morning? It's as good a time as any."

"I understand that these tremors may have unnerved you since you're not used to them like we are," said Decimus. "There really is no danger. We'll need to plaster over a few cracks. We've been doing that for years." He chuckled at their concerned expressions. "You're overreacting; I assure you. We can take today and tomorrow to pack and leave at our leisure. No rush."

Adan saw the anxiety in Marco's eyes and felt the same. Short of physically forcing Decimus, there was nothing they could do to convince him of the danger. An odd sensation seemed to press against his chest as dread gripped his heart. Something was very wrong.

Marco moved to stand by Adan. "Father, I have the worst feeling. It's as if my stomach is in a clamp."

"I know. I feel it, too."

"Isn't that beautiful!" called out Dionysia. She had moved away from the others and stood facing east. There was a narrow gap between their villa and another villa across the street where the sun hovered above the horizon. Dense, crimson-and-gold clouds shrouded the opening, but glowing light had slipped through the clouds and streamed out like spokes on a wheel.

Adan looked over at her, curious to see what had drawn her attention. She turned to face him. The rays of the sun framed Dionysia, setting her red hair ablaze with a golden sheen. The memory of his hallucination before he "died" in Herod's theater seemed to have taken shape before him. Dionysia reached for Adan, concerned at the shock on his face. She looked like the vision of the fire-haired girl with the violin who had danced on the wind. He remembered the enchanting music and the beautiful white bird she sent to him. He remembered his grief, while he waited to die, thinking he would never see Dulcibella again. Yet, the bird had told him not to despair. Death had tried to take him but had failed. It was not a coincidence that Dionysia appeared to be the dancing fire-haired girl. This was a warning.

"Father!" exclaimed Marco as he grasped Adan's arm. "Are you all right?"

Adan turned to the others. "We have to get out of here. Now!"

"Adan, you're panicking for no reason," said Decimus with annoyance. "Nothing will happen. I'm telling you; we have earthquakes all the time."

A column of gray smoke shot into the air from the summit of *Vesuvio.* About twenty seconds later they were hit with a low booming sound. The column rose thousands of feet into the air. Gravel-like particles pelted down onto the slopes while the smoke column hovered in the air. Sounds like the snorting of an enraged bull came from the summit. They stared, frozen in shock, as the huge white and gray cloud of smoke began to drift in a southern direction toward the metropolitan city of Pompeii.

"Per—perhaps we sh—should go to the harbor and find a ship," sputtered Decimus. He turned to his slaves and told them to pack enough belongings for a few weeks. They rushed into the house to comply. Adan and the others did likewise. They grabbed a hasty breakfast of fruit and bread to take with them. Decimus loaded his gold and silver coins into a leather shoulder bag. He left the copper and bronze.

When they were ready to leave, Marco signaled for the dogs to sit and knelt in front of them. They tilted their heads attentively. "Jova, Cato, come with me. Stay close. If you run off, I won't be able to save you." Both dogs stood and wagged their tails.

Chapter 34

Complacency, Chaos, and
the *Child of the Ocean*

———⌾———

Adan and the others hurried to the street. Many people were standing around, staring at the mountain, but when nothing else happened, some went back into their homes and businesses. Those who continued to stare at the unprecedented sight were ordered to get out of the way as wagon and cart drivers tried to move past on the narrow, one-way streets. A few people came from their homes carrying knapsacks and baskets. They told their neighbors it was a good day for a picnic away from the city. The others smirked and laughed, gesturing at the mountain and shaking their heads. They thought anyone leaving the city because of a few puffs of smoke must be hopelessly foolish.

Curbside shops were open for business as usual, and customers were buying food and wine while keeping a curious eye on the mountain. The normally sleepy-eyed, early morning risers were wide awake. Birdsong usually filled the air with every sunrise but not this morning. Not a single bird was in sight. A slight whiff of sulfur blanketed the city like an invisible shroud. The gray billows of smoke lost their bulbous shapes and crept down the mountain slopes like a dirty fog. The atmosphere held a disconcerting silence as if Mother Nature was holding her breath.

A lone runner occasionally passed Adan's group, intent on some unknown destination. People glanced above their heads as they made their way through the streets lined with two- or three-story villas, multi-family tenements, and businesses. Many citizens of Herculaneum stood on their balconies watching with bored, amused, or curious expressions. Others called out to the few people hurrying through the streets carrying household items, accusing them of overreacting.

One man shouted from his balcony, "Run, run little rabbits! It is only Vulcan pounding his forge!" He laughed with contempt when a few looked up at him with obscene gestures and catcalls. Again, the earth shook, stopped, then started shaking again. There was no rumbling sound, but the shaking was becoming more frequent by the hour.

When Adan's group reached the cliff above the harbor, they stopped to survey the situation. Ships were moored at the pier where crewmen loaded or unloaded cargo. Some families stood on the gangplanks asking for passage, but not as many as Adan expected. The casual demeanor of most indicated they may have already been planning a trip and would have been there anyway. Many of the ship captains shook their heads at the passage seekers, claiming they only had room for cargo. A few signaled for a small family or a single man to come aboard but halted the entry of any others who attempted to follow. Adan and his family hurried down the limestone steps from the cliff to the beach below.

Adan turned to his sons. "Marco, Aquila, you boys start on opposite ends of the harbor and ask every captain for passage no matter how bad the ship looks. Tell them we can pay double the standard rate. Niko and I will start in the middle and work our way out."

"I'll stay here with Dion and guard our belongings," said Decimus. He instructed his slaves to watch for opportunistic, fleet-footed thieves.

The brothers ran along the harbor in opposite directions, asking for passage. One captain after another turned them away. Adan and Niko were having no better luck. Most ships had only one or two quarters for guests, but more money could be made if cargo filled these rooms. Captains would ask high fees to compensate, but they still preferred cargo over passengers.

Marco approached the largest ship and hailed the helmsman. The captain had turned away and walked toward the mast to supervise the unfurling of the mainsail.

"Sir!" cried Marco to the helmsman, "We request passage on your ship. There are eight of us. We can pay double the standard rate." Marco looked down at Jova and Cato. "Well, make that ten. I have to bring my dogs as well."

"Your dogs," scoffed the helmsman, "since when are wolves called dogs? You must be touched in the head, boy. Go away! I see you have their eyes. We don't need your kind on board."

"Please, sir, my father is a centurion and his father was the *minor consul* in Rome. We can pay more than double."

The helmsman was about to rebuff Marco with curses when the captain reappeared. He stared at Marco. "Did you say your father is a centurion? What is his name?"

"Adan Clovius Longinus, Sir. My grandfather is Aquila Clovius Longinus."

The captain eyed him in silence. Marco was about to offer even more money when the captain gestured toward the harbor. "Out of all the ships, you choose this one? Why?"

"You're the last one, Sir. No one else will take us."

The captain peered into Marco's golden eyes. "Go get them. You have passage."

Marco thanked the man and took off down the harbor calling to the others. They hurried up the gangplank and came aboard. Marco looked around for the captain but he had turned his back and walked away. A crewman led them below deck to the guest quarters, but Adan stayed on deck. They were preparing to shove off when a lone figure ran up the gangplank.

"Centurion!" Calais shouted.

Adan spun around and rushed to the life rail. "Calais, you must come with us. Come on. I will pay your passage."

"No! I only wanted to tell you that I am sorry," exclaimed Calais. "I'm not asking for forgiveness. I only wanted to tell you that I am truly sorry for how things turned out. I didn't want your last memory of me to be the man who nearly killed your son."

"You must come with us," pleaded Adan. "I don't think you'll survive if you stay here."

"Why? It is only a few earthquakes." He looked over at the mountain looming in the near distance. "It's just smoke, probably a fire. It doesn't mean anything."

"I think it does," cried Adan. "Do you see any flames? And what was that loud boom all of us heard? A fire doesn't behave this way. Don't you smell brimstone? Something else is happening. You must come with us."

"No! You might hand me over to Commander Lysias."

"I promise no harm will come to you. You are a free man now. Lysias left you for dead. As far as the law is concerned, you *are* dead. Please! Come with us!"

"Why should I?" exclaimed Calais. "You might keep your word, but what of your son, the one who deceived me. Can I trust you to defend me if your son turns against me?"

Marco and Aquila came up from below deck with the dogs close behind. The twins saw their father talking and gesturing to someone on the gangplank. They hurried to Adan's side.

"Calais!" cried Marco, "Come with us!"

The earth shook again more violently than ever. The posts holding up the pier cracked and snapped. The wood planks at the end of the pier behind Calais splintered and broke apart. Still Calais refused to move. He could still leap across the broken section to get back on shore. If the shaking became more severe, he could retreat to the limestone vaults built into the cliff that faced the harbor. A few women and children already huddled under the archways of the vaults. They were sturdy arched structures built of limestone blocks and reinforced with concrete to house the boats of the wealthiest in the area. They were confident that even a severe quake would not collapse the vaults.

"Calais, I left you behind twice before," exclaimed Adan. "I will not do it a third time. You must come with us. Something terrible is going to happen. I know it."

Calais gestured defensively. "I can never go back to slavery. I would rather die than be another man's property again."

"Then come with us and be free. You have your whole life ahead of you."

The helmsman approached Adan. "Centurion, we can wait no longer. We must shove off. The sea is getting unsettled."

Adan acknowledged the warning and looked back at Calais. "If you will not come with me, then I will stay with you." He stepped off the ship onto the gangplank. Marco and Aquila looked at each other. Marco slapped a hand to his chest and felt the purple sapphire under his tunic. The feel of the crystal gave him reassurance. He looked at Aquila and a silent determination passed between them. They stepped off the ship to stand by their father's side. Cato and Jova pranced and whined at the life rail. They put their front paws up on the rail and whimpered. When Marco did not turn around, they barked and tried to jump the rails. Marco turned and signaled for the dogs to sit. They hesitated and then sat but continued to whimper and anxiously wag their tails.

"If you will not come with us," said Marco. "Then we will stay with you as well."

Calais stared in astonishment. "What are you doing? Go, and take your sons, Centurion. You can't stay here. Your wife and daughter are in Caesarea. Yes, I know all about your family. I will not go with you. There is nothing for me in Judea."

"We're staying with you," said Adan calmly. Aquila and Marco remained on either side of their father.

The earth trembled. Waves sloshed over the gangplank. Families on the beach began to separate as the men told the women and children to join the others already under the shelter of the limestone vaults. The men continued to beg and haggle with the ship captains for passage.

Marco pointed at the mountain. "It's doing it again!"

Aquila and Adan looked where he pointed. Calais saw that every man on deck stopped what they were doing and stared in the direction Marco and others were pointing. Calais turned and stood transfixed with amazement. Jova and Cato frantically jumped to their feet and put their front paws over the life rails again. They furiously barked at Marco. They would have jumped over the railing, but several sailors held them back.

Another, but larger, writhing, black, gray, and white monstrosity shot into the sky from the top of *Vesuvio*. The smoke billowed and mushroomed into blossoms of ever-changing shapes. There was an odd silence, as if all the sound in the world had been sucked into oblivion. No one moved. Instinctively, everyone seemed to be expecting something more.

A colossal explosion resounded from the mountain. The faces of the youngest children twisted in pain as they clamped their hands over their ears. The adults grimaced but withstood the sound without as much discomfort. Startled, the dogs whined in pain. The women and children in the vaults huddled deeper into the dark recesses. The men trying to secure passage paused to stare at *Vesuvio*. Again, pumice and ash pelted the slopes of the mountain while smoke hovered over the summit. Once more, the sky above the mountain turned to gray as the ash fanned out across the horizon and began to drift downwind toward Pompeii.

The people muttered anxiously one to another, "What is happening? Why is the mountain making thunder and smoke?" They speculated that the vineyards flanking the mountain were on fire, but no flames were visible. Others said the billowing smoke was a show of displeasure by an insulted goddess or god. They discussed how a mountain could only explode if manipulated by the gods. The startling suggestion was voiced that *Vesuvio* must be a *flammas et vaporem cructans,* a flaming mountain, such as *Aetna, Vulcano,* and *Lipara.* The people of Herculaneum pleaded to their gods and goddesses for mercy.

Calais watched as the column of gray and black smoke rapidly morphed into a billowing mushroom cloud. Light-tan debris pelted the slopes like flour sifted from a sieve. The top of the cloud grew white as the dark smoke sank within the column. Jagged, gray and black boulders flew out from the sides of the cloud. They hit the flanks of the mountain; some rolled down the slope, some lay where they landed. Calais looked at the ship, then Adan and his sons. They made no move to leave him.

"You're really going to stay here with me, and that?" He pointed at the convulsing smoke.

Nikolaus appeared at the life rail. He had been below deck with Dionysia and Decimus but came up at the sound of the explosion. He stared at the mountain in shock, and then stepped off the ship to stand with Adan, and the twins.

"Do you really want to stay here," said Nikolaus, "and see what happens next, Calais? What if this is only the beginning of whatever is happening? Is it best for the five of us to die here, or should we take our chances with the sea? Stop thinking like a slave. You are free to live your own life now, but that," he pointed at the mountain, "looks like death!"

The earth shook so violently they were nearly thrown off the gangplank. Adan and Nikolaus grabbed hold of Aquila and Marco. Calais went down on a knee. Crewmen pushed the ship away from the pier with their oars as they prepared to shove off.

"Centurion, we are leaving!" shouted the helmsman. "With or without you!"

Adan and the others made no attempt to move. Marco opened his coin pouch and pulled out the little wooden owl. He held it up. "Calais! What do you want me to do with Sofi?"

Calais looked at the little owl with longing and then at Adan and the others. He saw they were willing to risk their lives for him. He stood up. "All right! I'll go with you!" He ran to join them as they turned toward the ship, but the last tremor had torn the gangplank away. Crewmen came to the life rails, gesturing and shouting for them to jump. The five of them took a running start and leaped with all their strength. They barely cleared enough distance to grab hold of the life rails. Hands grabbed arms, the backs of belts, and handfuls of tunics as they hauled the men over the side onto the ship's deck. Jova and Cato jumped on Marco before he could stand up and eagerly licked his face and neck. He laughed and hugged the two dogs as they happily whipped the air with their tails. He reached down inside his tunic where he had dropped the wooden owl to free his hands. He handed the owl to Calais.

"You kept her safe, as you promised," Calais said as he gripped the figurine in his fist.

Marco thought of the times he had almost thrown the little owl away, but something had always stayed his hand. He gave Calais a sheepish glance and turned away.

The captain bellowed, "*Heave to men!* Put your backs into it!" The oars rose and sliced through the water in a synchronized cadence. The sea waves slammed against the ship. The wind filled the mainsail. The sail bellowed out and caught hold. The ship gained speed and left the confines of the harbor. They looked back at the shore. More families were coming down the limestone steps to the pier. Men trotted from one gangplank to another as more women and children crowded into the vaults. Considering Herculaneum had about four thousand residents, very few seemed to think the smoking mountain was a threat.

Adan walked to Calais's side. "This ship is going to Ostia to unload her cargo. From there we will take a barge to Rome to let my father know we have found his wayward grandson. Then we return to Caesarea. You are welcome to stay with us as far as you wish to go. We will let you off at any port along the way. It is your choice."

Calais nodded, but wouldn't look Adan in the eye. He turned away and headed for the stern to watch the mountain and its mysterious activity.

Adan looked around for Marco. "All right, son, introduce me to this captain before the whole mountain explodes and sinks us to the depths."

Marco looked around. "He's over there." Marco and Adan headed for the ship's wheel. The captain had his back to them.

"Captain, I am Centurion Longinus. I wish to thank you for taking us on board."

The captain turned to face them. "So, we meet again, Longinus."

"Aurelius! Aurelius Julius? Is that you?"

"I am Captain Hadrian" the man said with a look of feigned bewilderment. "Aurelius Hadrian. Aurelius Pomponius Julius drowned in the shipwreck of the *Scarlet Jade.* It was a mere coincidence that we shared the same *praenomen.*"

Adan eagerly shook hands with the captain. "Yes, I remember. The son of Centurion Felix Valentius drowned in the sea, along with his name. You were also on board the *Scarlet Jade,* were you not?"

"I was." Aurelius said, enjoying Adan's "confirmation" of his secret. "I escaped with my life and my surprisingly water-proof cedar chest. Crewmen found it floating near the beach. The name Hadrian was carved into the lid and they identified me as the owner. I didn't want to belittle their honest efforts so I offered no argument. I have been Aurelius Julius Hadrian ever since."

Adan nodded approvingly. "What was in the trunk? Tools of the trade?"

Aurelius laughed. "Could be. I've never looked. It's locked and the sea swallowed the key along with the man. But I keep it with me. Someday, the lock will give way and I'll take a look."

"Curiosity would get the best of me. I'd break the lock," countered Adan.

The captain's expression become solemn. "The trunk is a dead man's grave. It holds the only thing left of his life. If I open it, will it free his ghost?"

"It has been over twenty years. Hadrian's death was accidental drowning. Not your fault."

Aurelius looked at Adan with sadness. "True. I only took his name but I do not wish to take his privacy. You told me once that I had a second chance at life and not to waste it. I took your advice. I hired on as a ship's clerk and worked my way up to captain. Then I bought my first ship, worked a few years, and saved my money. Sold it and bought a bigger ship. I was satisfied until I encountered this magnificent beauty." He gazed along the length of his ship. "When I saw her name, I knew she had to be mine."

"I didn't see the name," admitted Adan. "I was a bit distracted." He glanced back at the mountain as the blossoming, gray smoke gradually flattened out across the sky.

At first Aurelius didn't speak. He glanced over his shoulder at the mountain, but then returned his attention to the open sea ahead. "The name is somewhat unique among ship names. It is *Child of the Ocean,* and it could not be more appropriate for me. I left my former identity in the sea and I was given a new life. In a way, *I* am the child of the ocean. Besides, this is a grand ship with a reinforced hull. The width is perfectly balanced with her length and depth. She cuts through water like the wind through the trees. Nothing slows her down. I have always loved the water. My father used to say, 'You swim better than a shark. They must be jealous.' I can't imagine living on land now. I will die a happy man on the deck of this ship." He tilted his head back toward the mountain. "But hopefully, not today."

"I am glad that you have found your way to success, Aurelius," said Adan. "Your father would be proud."

The captain smiled at the compliment but made no comment. He looked over at the twins. "Those two with the dogs, are they your sons?"

"Yes, Marco is instructing his four-legged children on how to behave aboard ship, and Aquila is making sure Marco doesn't leave any rules out. You remember Nikolaus? He's standing by the life rail with them. The man and woman with us are Nikolaus's sister, Dionysia, and her husband Decimus Lentulus. The two slaves belong to him."

Slowly, the outline of *Vesuvio* became more distinct as the shroud of smoke moved away to darken the southeastern sky. Adan hoped the mysterious eruptions would not be repeated and that the people of Herculaneum would be safe. However, he saw that Pompeii was shrouded in smoke.

"Centurion, there is something I need to tell you. Do you remember I told you I saw my father just before he was executed?" When Adan nodded, he continued. "I didn't tell you everything that passed between us. He gave me a task which I failed to do, twice. I passed up the opportunity when I saw you and Nikolaus at court in Rome and again when I introduced myself to you in Ostia. He asked me to give you a message."

"Do I really want to hear this?" Adan asked doubtfully.

"Yes. You do. You have to understand, Centurion," said Aurelius. "I couldn't bring myself to say it before. I felt guilty for letting Father think I was dead. I went to all that trouble to find you and then I couldn't say it." Aurelius squared his shoulders. "Just before Father was executed, when I stepped out of the shadows and he saw me, he was the happiest I've ever seen him. I realized that he was content to lose his life knowing that I had not lost mine. He said that he had always loved me even when he hated himself."

"I remember you told me that."

"What I didn't tell you was this; he said that if you had killed him when you had the chance, he would never have known that I was alive. Father said he baited you with every ugly insult he could think of to avoid the possibility of crucifixion and it almost worked. You had your sword on his neck, but then you stopped. He said, 'Tell Longinus I am grateful to him for not taking my life.'"

Adan leaned against the life rail. "Thank you for telling me. I have to admit; it surprises me how glad I am to hear it. Doing the right thing is much more gratifying when others recognize its worth. I'm glad that your father demanded to be sent to the emperor. Herod would have sentenced him to crucifixion. My father explained that Emperor Caligula sentenced your father to beheading instead of crucifixion for personal reasons."

"That might have been the only merciful thing Caligula ever did for anyone."

"There's something I need to tell you." Adan looked over at Aurelius. "You have a sister. Her name is Pomona and she lives in Jerusalem."

Aurelius met Adan's gaze. "A sister? What are you talking about?"

Adan told him the story Pomona had related to him. "Eliana has died, but Pomona would welcome you if you should ever go to Jerusalem."

"A sister. Interesting. You say she would welcome me into her home?"

"Yes, she said she doesn't expect you would want to see her since her mother was your father's mistress, but if you accept her, she would welcome you. She knows of no other family."

"You have given me much to think about. After we drop our cargo in Ostia and pick up the next load, we will be sailing for the coast of Judea. Perhaps I will take a few days' leave from my mistress, the sea, and go to Jerusalem."

"Since I suspect you have saved our lives," said Adan as he looked back at *Vesuvio,* "it would be most ungracious of me if I didn't volunteer to escort you to her home."

Captain Aurelius Hadrian smiled. "Offer accepted."

"There is something else you might want to do while you're in Jerusalem," said Adan. "If it has not been discovered—there is that letter you wrote to Demitre somewhere in the repository at the Antonia. Tribune Salvitto couldn't remember the name of the sender, so it may still be there buried under other scrolls."

"*Ohe*, I had forgotten about that. I sent it under the *nomen* Julius. I would be executed for desertion if that letter got into the wrong hands."

"Then we better retrieve it so you can destroy it."

"We?" Aurelius looked questioningly at Adan.

"Yes. We. I would hate to see the 'child of the ocean' dragged from the sea in chains."

Aurelius reached out to Adan. They clasped wrists and smiled into each other's eyes.

Chapter 35

Escape, Explosions, and the Green Sun

⸺∞∞∞⸺

The *Child of the Ocean* made good progress toward Ostia. *Vesuvio* continued to erupt ash and smoke high into the sky every two to three hours. The charcoal-gray column of volcanic glass particles hung suspended in the air as if held by a magical force, invisible and unrelenting. Adan and the others watched as lightning flickered within the column, but the crew and passengers were too far away to hear the thunder that reverberated down the mountain. For every additional mile between the ship and *Vesuvio*, five more seconds would lapse between an eruption of ash and the explosive boom that followed. It was eerie to see the mountain erupt in silence, and then hear the explosion many seconds later. Aquila faithfully watched the mountain and counted after each eruption. Everyone began to relax as he was able to count longer after each eruption.

The shore gradually disappeared until only the summit of *Vesuvio* could be seen above the sea in the southeast. The winds died down and the oarsmen were put back into service, but the current slowed their progress. An hour after the sun slipped below the watery horizon, the oarsmen were done for the day, and the anchor was dropped for the night. Decimus and Dionysia went to the guest quarters, but as usual, Adan and the others stayed on the deck where they would eventually sleep. Jova and Cato lay down on either side of Marco.

They talked of mundane things for hours as they watched the clouds drift across the path of the stars. It was a moonless night and the Milky Way spread a dazzling path above them until it reached the southeastern skies over Herculaneum and Pompeii. Ominously, no stars were visible near *Vesuvio*. However, the mountain seemed to have expelled its burden of smoke and ash. The lightning no longer lashed at the sky and there were no more boisterous explosions.

"I'm glad that's over," said Nikolaus. "Decimus's villa will need some cleaning and possibly repairs, but I'm sure it won't take long. They should be able to go home after their visit in Rome."

"How long have we been gone?" asked Aquila.

"I left in June," said Marco. "The 11th, I think."

"We've been gone over four months," said Adan.

"Has it been that short?" grumbled Aquila. "It feels like four years, not months."

"Judging by the stars," said Adan. "I'd say we're past midnight so it's October 25th. We should be home in time to celebrate your mother's birthday in December, with time to spare."

"I can't believe we're finally going home," said Marco. "I just wish Aunt Dionysia and Uncle Decimus were going to Caesarea with us."

"Amen to that," said Nikolaus. He smiled to hear Marco call him Uncle Decimus.

A comfortable silence fell over the men as the gentle motion of the ship began to lull them asleep. The night air had a chilled bite to it, but they had plenty of blankets and thick mats to shield them from the hard wood deck. Marco had extra warmth since the dogs usually huddled against him as they slept, but a peaceful night was not to be.

A colossal column of fire ripped the black veil of the night. The top of *Vesuvio* shattered as boiling smoke and ash shot into the sky lit by blood-red, yellow, and white flames. It writhed and billowed as jagged lightning lashed out from the top of the mountain. The flames had a solid look as if they were a molten statue of incandescent metal that climbed ever higher within the shape-shifting smoke giant.

A full minute-and-a-half passed in silence after the smoke and ash burst, clawing and flailing, out of the mountaintop. Then it happened. An explosion shattered the silence as blistering hot air reeking of sulfur smashed into them. They clapped their hands over their ears as their lungs compressed. They struggled to breathe. They looked around in fright and confusion until they regained their bearings. Those below deck were spared the initial impact of the heat blast, but everyone was cringing with pain from the deafening noise.

Sound became muffled. Frightened crewmen seemed to be mouthing words no one could hear. The roiling monster of smoke stretched into the sky, across the horizon, and then hovered. The top spread out as if the rising column of darkness had hit an invisible barrier. Slowly, at first, then accelerating, the thick smoke collapsed back to earth and sped down the sides of *Vesuvio* in an avalanche of ash, incandescent mud, and pumice. The darkness contrasted with the fiery image of the mountain.

None of them knew that this type of volcanic eruption was a pyroclastic surge, the most cataclysmic and deadly of all volcanic activity. It engulfed the vineyards that once clothed the fertile grounds of the mountain. The surge of boiling mud hit Herculaneum with the speed of a hurricane. Molten two-thousand-degree lava spewed from the summit as if the Gates of Hades were flung wide open.

In Herculaneum, men slept on the beach at the harbor to make room for the women and children who slept clustered together in the limestone enclaves. A few women with no children preferred to stay on the beach with their husbands. The colossal explosion woke the harbor sleepers instantly. They jerked awake in sudden terror to see the mountain covered in billowing, burning clouds of ash cascading down the slopes toward their little town.

Several observers recovered their senses quicker than most and headed for the enclaves and the shelter they offered. They never made it. They only had time to see the flames blast from the mountain and gasp in terror before the nine-hundred-degree heat killed them. Their hands and feet contracted with the heat blast. Their lungs were seared from the inside. The water content of their internal organs boiled within seconds. Skulls shattered from the pressure of the brain instantly swelling. Muscles and organs were burned away in a matter of minutes. The blood was vaporized and bone was stained as if it had rusted. The women and children who were huddled in the limestone vaults died a second later. The unimaginable heat killed every living thing within the city and the surrounding area. The people of Herculaneum never felt the pain of death. They died before they even knew they were in danger.

A little over an hour later, glowing, red flames shot from the mountain a second time. It was the second of the six pyroclastic surges to come. Again, the sound of the explosion reached the people on Captain Hadrian's ship a minute-and-a-half after the flames were clearly visible. It was followed by another wave of near-scorching hot air. The eruption of fire from the mountain's summit continued for hours, and then died down. Time passed and the mountain rumbled with a few quakes, but no more fire burst from the summit.

Some had been frightened enough to leave Herculaneum and head for Neapolis in the northwest after the first eruption of ash. They survived. Those who fled late in the day were killed by the blast of heat, no matter what direction they took. The ones who evacuated early and headed for Pompeii did not survive the incandescent ash and pumice which would eventually bury the city. The people of Pompeii, being further away from the volcano than the people of Herculaneum, did not die instantly. They suffered for hours, inhaling ash and toxic gases until the fourth pyroclastic surge hit them with heat of about four hundred degrees. The people of Pompeii who headed southwest for Stabiae met the same fate. Those that reached the more distant city of Nuceria, in the southeast, survived if they left in time.

From the first minor eruption of ash to the sixth pyroclastic eruption, the wind blew from *Vesuvio* toward Pompeii, a common pattern for the autumn months, showering the city with ash and pumice. Of the 20,000 residents of Pompeii, those who left immediately after the first minor eruption survived. There were eighteen hours of falling ash before the first deadly pyroclastic surge strafed the living with incandescent mud, ash, pumice, and fiery heat. The people had nearly a full day to escape.

The warning of imminent danger was clear. The morning sky turned as dark as night even before the second eruption of ash the afternoon of October 24th. A third eruption in the early evening dropped gravel-sized pumice and blackened, fist-sized rocks over the city. Fine particles of gray ash enveloped the people as they fled. The ash filtered into their clothes and irritated their skin. They choked on the sulfate gases. Those who inhaled the ash gagged and coughed. They didn't know the ash was actually fine particles of glass. Occasionally, pumice became mixed with the ash and pelted them as they ran.

The people cried aloud to their gods and begged for salvation, but their pleas were useless. They cried for mercy from the violent temper of Vulcan, the ugly god with the perpetually broken, twisted leg. They begged for Venus, the wife of Vulcan, to ask his forgiveness for her unfaithfulness and appease his fiery wrath. The statues of their gods and goddesses stood mute, covered in ash, or broken into pieces on the ground.

The people didn't understand that the earth was healing by ridding itself of an overabundance of stored heat and pressure. Without the shifting of the earth's crustal plates, which causes earthquakes, volcanoes, and slow mountain building, there would be no dry land. All land erodes into rivers, which run to the sea. Plate tectonic processes cause the eroded land to be replaced. Although initially destructive, volcanic events also replenish fresh water in the form of steam, and essential minerals for plant growth, from deep in the earth.

The third pyroclastic surge exploded from the mountain. The torrent blossomed and rolled like a mass of cancerous tumors intent on consuming everything within reach. The superheated mixture of pulverized pumice, poisonous gases and pyroclastic debris buried Herculaneum. The skeletons from the first pyroclastic surge were now blanketed under a death shroud of ash and volcanic mud. Their scorched bones lay preserved as if time itself were buried with them.

Ash and pumice continued to fall from the sky hour after hour. The people, the animals, and the land were decorated with nature's unmindful handiwork. To try and protect themselves from the rocks falling from the sky, the people tied pillows on their heads. The good and the evil, the kind and the cruel, the innocent and the guilty, suffered together. Some died along the way. Family members cried out in grief, but eventually moved on. The people coming after them stepped around the fallen bodies without a thought. Survival mode triggered the need to deny sympathy or sorrow. There was only a mindless urgency to keep walking; to try and survive.

The hot ash was accumulating on the roofs in Pompeii. Some homes had collapsed from the weight, crushing the people who huddled inside, too sick or too old to flee. Those who delayed evacuating until after the second and third pyroclastic surges would succumb to a more deadly, fourth eruption an hour-and-a-half after sunrise. Ash and dust raced toward the people in Pompeii and on the surrounding roads. The debris and four-hundred-degree heat seared their lungs from the inside. Even though many people were escaping the rising levels of pumice and gravel up until then, there was no escaping the fourth surge of ash, sulfuric gas, and heat. Thousands were killed and their bodies were encased in ash.

About two hours after sunrise, a fifth surge of volcanic debris and heat swept the entire area from Herculaneum to Pompeii and to Stabiae on the coast.

The monstrous eruptions stretched and yawned, coming awake from deep within the molten inner chambers of the earth. It took just over a minute for each explosive soundwave to slam into the few remaining survivors who fled from Pompeii before the fourth surge. Ruptured eardrums bled freely. Breathing was a torment. Thirst clawed at the throats of the people huddled inside any shelter they could find. Masters and slaves clung to each other in their final hours of life. Whole families died together.

Many centuries later, bodies were discovered in the streets with door keys found near their hands or waists where a pouch had been. They expected to return home. The body of one man was found still clutching his trove of gold coins. Perhaps he was the shopkeeper who sold stick bundles to the holiday revelers planning to toss their bit of flame for good luck into Vulcan's bonfire. One body was preserved sitting, knees drawn to the chest, hands over the face. A child's remains were found clutching her little dog while her mother shielded both of them with her body. A soldier's remains were found with his sword. Modern technology would reveal the features of his face and the anguish of his last breath. He died alone, evidently running down a street. A girl, too young to be a mother, clutched the skeleton of a baby adorned with gold jewelry. The girl was a slave, evident by the poor condition of her teeth and deep wear patterns on her bones from extreme physical labor. The bodies of slaves were found with the mold of their thick slave belts around their waists. Most died alone, ordered to stay in the house to ward off intruders. In the limestone enclaves, the rich and the destitute died together. Death is truly blind to status, being an equal opportunity provider.

An incandescent cloud of noxious gases and volcanic ash continued to rain down. Eventually, the city and its dead were sealed in a monstrous coffin of volcanic debris. People who were exposed to the burning air suffocated within minutes. Those who huddled inside thick-walled rooms lived long enough to know that death waited, but not patiently. The weight of the volcanic ash overwhelmed the scorched, wooden, roof beams of a few houses, and the roofs collapsed upon the people inside. Their bodies lay crumpled and were sealed forever in the final postures of their death. Yet, most of the dead suffered no external injuries. They died from asphyxiation. Their gaping-mouthed expressions of terror, as they struggled for air, would forever be preserved. Others accepted their fate and clung to their loved ones or even strangers, feeling a small semblance of comfort in not dying alone.

And still *Vesuvio* wasn't finished. The sixth, and final surge of cataclysmic destruction was the most monstrous of them all. The smoke giant had morphed into a colossal fire-breathing dragon. The last eruption discharged ash and debris twenty-one miles into the sky. The air, filled with particles of volcanic glass, dust and sulfides, raced down the mountain slopes with the force of a cyclone. Every second, 10,000 tons of ash, burning rock, and pumice spewed from the volcano. People still alive within thirty miles of the blast suffered ruptured eardrums when the explosion of the final eruption reached them. The explosions were heard over two thousand miles away. Every living thing within a three-hundred-square mile vicinity of *Vesuvio* died.

The sixth surge of ash and pyroclastic debris didn't stop at the shoreline. The terrible dragon of *Vesuvio* took wing and reached out to sea. Since pumice is composed of solidified volcanic ash infused with gases, it floats on water. The incandescent ash and pumice spread out across the surface of the sea for at least eighteen miles. Ships within the area were engulfed in superheated air and pumice. The gale-force wind capsized ships moments after everyone on board died from asphyxiation. Any wood that remained on the surface burst into flames before sinking into the sea.

Many of the inhabitants living in the shadow of *Vesuvio* had grown accustomed to the shaking earth and ever-changing sea levels. They became the "frogs" in tepid water that is slowly heated, until the complacent creatures are boiled alive. To ignore nature's anguished voice is to invite disaster. Refusal to heed the signs of a natural world out of balance is to suffer the resulting consequences when the balance is catastrophically adjusted. Nature has always adjusted. An asteroid can crash into the earth and devastate the planet, yet life survives. A super volcano erupts, wiping out nearly every human being, animal and plant, yet life survives. Ice ages come and go, yet life survives. With or without life, the Earth, itself, will always comply with the physics of its own nature by slow, cumulative processes or violent catastrophes. Yet, life was designed to always find a way to survive and replenish the earth.

* * *

Far away from the eruptions of *Vesuvio,* no one knew of the apocalypse taking place in Italy. Across the sea in Caesarea, nature was celebrating a peaceful day with a clear, deep-blue sky and a comforting breeze. Dulcibella sat on the terrace under the shade of her ancient friend, the oak tree, with the rising sun at her back. She noticed an ominous smudge in the western sky that had the appearance of a vast windstorm of dark-gray dust. She thought of her family so far away in Italy and prayed that they were safe. She wondered if the ominous cloud was connected somehow to the two loud, booming noises she had heard in the night. Both had awakened her and left her anxious before she could fall back asleep.

She thought about her most recent letter from Adan, which was troubling. Aquila had been arrested for theft. They were waiting for the trial and had no way of knowing if he would be released. Adan also reported that they had lost track of Marco, but still believed he would go to Herculaneum. Dulcibella prayed that Aquila had already been released by the time she received the letter. Perhaps they had also found Marco at the villa of Decimus Lentulus and were on their way home.

As she scanned the sky, a seagull floated in and landed on the balustrade. Dulcibella smiled and watched the bird jerk his head around as he took in the situation. Then without any perceivable cause, the sound of another explosion resonated across the sea. It was louder than the two that had awoken her during the night. The bird squawked in fright and flew away. Dulcibella frowned and looked around. What was that sound? She got up to find her parents, but they had already come out of the kitchen door and met her on the terrace.

"Did you hear it, too?" Dulcibella asked.

"We did," answered her father. "It sounded like a barrage of rocks hitting a city wall all at once. What has happened?"

"Perhaps you should inquire at the garrison," suggested Iovita.

"My thought exactly," said Marcus as he headed for the stables.

Dulcibella and Iovita walked to the balustrade to gaze out at sea.

"I have a bad feeling about this, Mother."

The two women sat on the bench under the oak and waited to see if anything else would happen. After a few minutes, they went back into the house.

About an hour later, a much louder explosion reached their ears. There were two more explosions before they stopped, the last one being the loudest. Even though the sounds were disconcerting, nothing else happened until a few days later. Dulcibella came out of the cottage to find a layer of gray dust covering every surface. Her parents' villa, the terrace, the leaves of the trees, even the grass was covered in gray "snow." She ran into the main house to find her parents. They came out and looked around.

Marcus touched the dust with his finger and rubbed it against his thumb.

"What is that stuff?" asked Dulcibella.

Marcus frowned in confusion. "I'm not sure. It feels like powder or fine silt. But I've never seen anything like this, not even after a windstorm."

"What do you think it means?" asked Iovita.

"Something terrible." Marcus looked out over the sea toward Italy.

The three of them held each other and whispered prayers of protection for the family that was so far away. Where were Adan, Niko, and the twins? If only they could be certain their loved ones were safe, but they could only hope and wait.

That evening, Dulcibella took a scroll and went to the terrace to read. It was a copy of the account Luke wrote for Theo Salvitto. Luke had allowed Titus to make a copy for the family. She sat on the bench reading as the sun dipped into the western sky. Intent on the scroll, Dulcibella had not looked up until she realized the landscape had taken on a pinkish tint. She raised her eyes to behold a breathtaking sunset of iridescent deep-rose, blazing shades of scarlet and golds and something else. The scroll dropped from her hand. She raced into the house to find Marcus and Iovita. They ran with her to the terrace along with the house servants. They stood at the balustrade, hands over their mouths in alarm.

The entire sky was aflame with brilliant colors, but that was not the source of their fear. It was the sun. It was green.

Chapter 36

Pompeii, Simon, and Cecilia

⸺⸺⸺ ◦∞◦ ⸺⸺⸺

S imon Magus stood frozen with fear in his darkened house. Was the werewolf about to leap at him from the darkness as the hellish hounds had done? When the front door slammed shut, and nothing else happened, Simon hoped the torment was over. He felt his way to the door and slid the bolt. There was an ember container by the door. He felt for the ceramic lid and tongs. Armed with a glowing ember, he relit his oil lamps and gazed around the atrium. He placed the ember back in the jar, shuffled to a bench, and sat down. He ran his shaking hands through his hair and tried to calm his breathing. He mulled over the details of what had just happened. The memory of a trick he saw once as a child came back to him. A magician from Macedonia had thrown a pale powder into a fire and the air instantly ignited. Also, he once saw a traveling band of magicians from the Far East wave certain rocks through flame to change the color of the fire. Simon had to admit that he had never seen a magician throw unnaturally colored flame from his hand. Simon frowned in concentration. Could the frightening phenomena have been trickery?

Still, Simon could not explain the sudden vanishing and reappearing of the werewolf. Neither could he explain the vicious, glowing wolves that obeyed the werewolf's every command. Surely, they were demons from the Underworld.

Simon gave up trying to understand and went into his bedroom carrying two oil lamps. He would let them burn themselves out during the night to avoid staring into a black void while he lay wide awake. The room began to shake. He glanced around anxiously, but when the shaking stopped within a few seconds, he set the lamps on a table and got into bed. His sleep was troubled, interrupted by tossing and turning until blessed sunlight began to slip into the bedroom from the atrium's open skylight. Simon stayed indoors, not wishing to venture out among the *Vulcanalia* festivities and intoxicated revelers. Instead he watched from his windows, pacing and muttering to himself. When the day ended without incident, he slept much better that night and awoke the following morning refreshed. He was confident that his tormentor was gone for good until someone pulled the bell at his door. His panic subsided when he saw his neighbor peek through the window lattice. He opened the door. The woman from across the street was peering up at him with wide, blinking eyes. He knew what that meant. She wanted something.

"Good morning, Simon," the woman cooed. "I hope I didn't wake you. I was wondering if you might have a bit of black pepper I could borrow. I know it is hard to come by, being from the Far East, but I'll pay you back."

He stared at her barely able to hide his irritation. "I have black pepper, but it will cost you. I prefer to sell my wares, not give them away. Two *denarii*. No less."

"I have silver if that's what you want," she said with a curl of her lip, "but I could buy a couple of donkeys with that amount. Your prices are high, even for black pepper."

Without inviting the woman to enter, Simon retreated into the kitchen and took a small ceramic jar from a cabinet. He returned to the door. She looked around him, trying to see inside the atrium. "So did your friends find you the other day?" she asked as she took the jar and handed Simon two *denarii*.

"You know they did. Their horses were tethered to the post for hours," retorted Simon.

"Not those men. I mean the boys."

Simon stared at her. "What boys?"

"Why, the twins, of course," she said with a click of her tongue. "I've seen a few identical twins, but those two were perfect copies of each other. Their voices were even the same. And they had the strangest eyes I've ever seen. Looked like the eyes of a wolf or a lion. Those two were very interested in you. Didn't you see them?"

Simon stepped back and slammed the door in her face. She cursed at him through the window lattice and hurried to tell her husband of their neighbor's rudeness. Simon went to the kitchen and sat down at the table. He buried his face in his hands, processing the information. He looked up, threw his head back and howled with mirthless laughter. The sorcerer had been outsmarted by a couple of teenagers. He didn't know how the twins made the dogs glow, but that didn't matter anymore. They had mocked him and he was going to get even.

Simon changed to his most expensive tunic and robe. He would go to the Forum and find the magistrate in charge of his district to demand the arrest of the two trespassers. It wouldn't be hard to track the twins down, since they would be memorable even to the most casual observer. Simon snatched up his discarded tunic along with other soiled garments. He would drop the clothing off at his favorite laundry house on the way. He slung the strap of an empty wineskin across a shoulder, locked his front door, and dropped the key in his coin pouch. He left the garments with the freedman who owned the laundry house and headed for his favorite café on *Via Consolare*. Mt. Vesuvio loomed straight ahead, in line with the street. Simon studied the mountain and frowned. Wisps of smoke were rising from the summit, and he wondered if vineyards on the far slopes were on fire. He grunted with annoyance. The price of wine would surely go up. He reached his destination and entered the café.

The owner of the café was in a talkative mood. "Did you feel that earthquake early this morning? Practically knocked me and the wife right out of bed."

Simon muttered a noncommittal response. "I need to fill my wineskin. How much will it cost me?" He eyed the meager selection of grilled fish the owner had just set out on display.

"Eight *dupondii* to fill it with half wine, half water." The merchant saw the scowl on Simon's face. "I'm sorry. The cost of wine has jumped since so many of the vines have dried up on *Vesuvio*. Even water is going to cost you. Wells all over town are going dry. People are wondering if we're heading for a drought."

"But we have had our normal amount of rain. How can there be a drought?" Simon handed the wineskin to the merchant and watched him fill it.

The merchant shrugged. "Do I look like I should know? Care for breakfast? You better get these fish while you can. The supply has been down for the past few weeks. Fishermen are complaining that they're finding dead and rotting fish in their nets."

"I suppose the fish will cost me extra as well." Simon glared at the man.

"Sorry. Supply goes down; cost goes up. I have to make a living."

"Fine. Give me two loaves of bread and four fish," ordered Simon.

The man selected two loaves, broke them open and stuffed two fish into each loaf. "That'll be eighteen *dupondii* altogether. Or you can give me a *denarius* if you've got it."

"You overcharge," complained Simon, but he took the food and handed over a silver coin. "You won't stay in business with prices like—"

The loud boom of an explosion interrupted Simon.

"What was that?" cried the café owner.

The two men scurried outside to find people staring at *Vesuvio*. Clouds of white and gray smoke were bursting into the sky from the summit. Light brown powder dusted the slopes as the cloud blossomed into a mushroom formation. Others watched in shocked silence.

"What is the meaning of this?" asked a man standing nearby.

The café owner recovered quickly. "It means nothing. It's just a fire. *Bacchus* has gotten drunk on too much of his own wine and knocked over Vulcan's forge, no doubt. I should increase my alms in the temple. That might pacify their tempers."

Simon clicked his tongue in disapproval. "Only the one, true God can shake the earth or make smoke come from a mountain. Don't waste your alms on useless gods; pray for the true God to forgive your sins."

"Yes, yes, I'll get right on that." The merchant smirked and went back into his café.

Simon stood on the street long enough to see that the cloud over the mountain was thinning out. "Just a fire, nothing more," he heard a woman tell her companion.

Simon was tempted to point out that there were no flames, but he had reached his destination. He was about to step through the open door of the magistrate's office when the earth jolted and knocked him off his feet. He tumbled to the sidewalk in an undignified heap. Glancing around furtively and hoping no one saw the embarrassing moment, Simon struggled to his feet. He hastily gathered up the loaves of bread he had dropped and entered the building. Simon told a slave girl sitting on a bench in the center of the room that he needed to see the magistrate. The girl was anxiously glancing around the room, checking for falling debris. Simon set his loaves on a bench by the wall and clapped his hands in her face. He repeated his demand. Still frightened, the girl asked his name and trotted out of the room. Simon sat on the bench she had vacated. The slave girl returned and sat on the floor against the wall. At first, Simon was content to sit and watch people pass by the open door. He got up and looked out the window which faced the mountain to see if there was more smoke. It was hovering above the mountain like a plume of dust and was drifting toward Pompeii. He sat down again, but he has growing impatient.

Simon eyed the slave suspiciously. "Did you tell the magistrate that Simon Magus of Gitta demands his audience?"

"Yes, Sir," replied the young girl. "He is busy with a very important person right now."

"I am very important, too!" retorted Simon. "Go tell him again."

The slave started for the door of her master's inner office when the earth shook violently, as if in the throes of a seizure. Plaster dust and cracking sounds filled the air. Simon coughed and choked as his eyes darted about the ceiling and walls. The shaking grew worse, and a low rumbling could be heard emanating from the bowels of the earth. A section of the roof crumbled and fell, blocking the way to the magistrate's office. Eyes wide with terror, the slave girl ran for the open door when a balcony over the door collapsed into the street blocking that way as well. The quake went on for many seconds. Simon felt like it would never stop.

Simon started to move toward a wall, concerned that the ceiling could collapse, when he realized the slave girl was standing under the center of the roof. He took her by the arm and retreated to the bench by the wall. Suddenly, the loudest sound Simon had ever heard crashed upon his senses so violently he clapped his hands over his ears in pain. The slave girl cried out and did the same. When nothing else happened, they cautiously lowered their hands. Screams from people in the street were muffled, almost inaudible. The slave girl dropped from the bench. She began sobbing and curled into a ball on the floor.

Simon knew this explosion signaled something far worse than a vineyard fire. He got up, stepped around chunks of plaster, and looked out the window. Something was very wrong with *Monte Vesuvio*. The previously symmetrical, cone-shaped top was now distorted. A huge column of gray and white and black smoke was billowing up into the sky. A fountain of fire burst into the column along with smaller, glowing red spouts near the summit. Flashes of lightning ripped through the boiling mass of smoke. He watched in shock. How could a mountain explode? What was going to happen next? What did it mean? He looked more closely. Gray dust was falling out of the sky. It was from the smoke caused by the first explosion. He put his hand out the window to catch some but then thought better of it and snatched his hand back inside.

"Why is this happening?" Simon muttered to himself. Again, the earth shook. There were more sounds of cracking masonry and shifting wooden beams. Simon could hear more screams of people in the streets. The gray "snow" falling from the sky was like nothing he had ever seen. "What will happen to me?" he whispered.

Sadness and regret overshadowed Simon as completely as the column of ash and pumice overshadowed the mountain. He would have been safe if he had stayed in Samaria. Simon thought of how he had acquired the property in Pompeii. It was his first success at sorcery. The wealthiest family in all of the province of Samaria lived in Antipatris. They had only one child, a little girl they doted on. Simon saw an opportunity. He had learned everything he could about poisonous plants and how much would make a person sick or die.

Simon introduced himself to the father of the young girl. They invited him to stay with them while he was in Antipatris. At dinner that evening, Simon distracted the family's attention and slipped some ground tobacco leaf into the girl's stew. When she vomited, began to sweat profusely, and started drooling, Simon declared that a demon had possessed her. The parents prayed to God, but the child's symptoms worsened. When a seizure overcame the child, Simon declared that God was punishing her parents for their sins. He prayed aloud that God would use him to heal the child and banish the demon. When she did not improve, Simon began to worry that he had given her too much of the tobacco. The parents confessed their sins, yet the child showed no improvement.

The timing of Simon's visit and the child's illness began to spur whispers of suspicion. "Perhaps the demon came with Simon." Others whispered, "Maybe Simon is in league with the demon." He knew he would be put to death by stoning if she died. Realizing his life might be at stake, Simon made a potion from mandrake root and coaxed the child to take it. Within hours, her symptoms eased.

When the girl improved significantly by the next day, the parents were convinced that Simon was a great healer. The father impulsively promised to award him a piece of property he was due to inherit in Pompeii if his child was completely well by the end of the day. Simon knew the poison would wear off by that time. Instead of rejoicing that the child's suffering was over, he thought only about himself and the success of his scheme.

The people of Samaria bowed in respect as he passed by and offered him the use of their homes. They begged him to return from Gitta as often as he could. Several of the men offered him money to bless their children. Simon eagerly complied with their requests, proclaiming that he was in service to God as he slipped the money into his coin pouch. His fame spread throughout the province of Samaria.

The father of the child kept his word. A promissory document was registered and given to Simon. Years later, when the man inherited the property, he tried to talk Simon into selling it back to him. Simon refused. When the man tried to cancel the document,

Simon took the man to court and won. By this time, Simon's popularity in Samaria had waned. People were noticing that demons seemed to follow him wherever he traveled. It was a good time to leave Samaria.

"Am I getting what I deserve?" Simon asked out loud. He considered the idea and then dismissed the thought. "I healed in your name, Lord, all those that were afflicted."

He remembered a quote from The Book of Psalms. *"The wicked man writhes in pain of iniquity; he has conceived mischief and brought forth falsehood."* Simon could not deny that he had intentionally sickened many people for financial gain.

"Lord, I sought to punish the centurion who cruelly murdered your Son. I did this for you."

Words from the Book of Leviticus came to Simon. *"You shall not hate your brother in your heart. You shall not take vengeance, nor bear any grudge against the children of your people, but you shall love your neighbor as yourself: I am the Lord."*

"But the Roman and his son are not the children of my people. I tried to send them to the bottom of the sea to face your judgment. Why did you spare their lives?"

The Book of Exodus answered Simon. *"I will be gracious to whom I will be gracious, and I will have compassion on whom I will have compassion."*

As soon as these words ran through Simon's mind, he remembered something John once told him. While Yeshua was dying on the cross he prayed, *"Father, forgive them, for they do not know what they do."* Yeshua had forgiven his executioners.

"But Lord God, you sent Yeshua to offer salvation to Israel. The centurion and his son are Gentiles. Why would you forgive them?"

Simon remembered what Isaiah had written of the Messiah. *"I will also give You as a light to the Gentiles, that You should be My salvation to the ends of the earth. In Him the Gentiles shall hope."*

Simon thought of his reason for coming to see the magistrate. He wanted to retaliate against the brothers who had coerced a confession from him, even though it was the truth. The charge would only result in a fine, at the worst, but he would save face and return a small measure of humiliation on them. He wanted to get the last word.

Words from The Book of Leviticus answered him. *"You shall do no injustice in judgment. You shall not hate your brother in your heart."*

"Father God," Simon declared out loud, "why have you put your words in my heart now that it is too late for me to repent? Surely, my life is coming to an end. *Vesuvio* must be a flaming mountain. Who knew it could be such a thing?"

Simon had convinced himself that only unrighteous people would believe his lies. He believed his poisons would only sicken evil sinners, thus they deserved it. A truly righteous person would be healed directly by God through prayer and repentance. In that case, Simon's healing potions and prayers would not be needed. The poison would wear off quickly on its own or not work at all. He reasoned that punishing sinners caused them to turn to God. He was also paid handsomely for "healing" his victims, which further validated his belief in his own self-righteous endeavors. He rationalized that poisoning innocent young children was the price their sinful parents had to suffer.

"Would I have become so rich if God had not approved of my methods?" Simon asked himself.

The teachings of the Way sprang into his mind. *"Take heed and beware of covetousness. For a man's life does not consist in the abundance of his possessions. For the love of money is a root of all kinds of evil, for which some have strayed from the faith in their greediness and pierced themselves through with many sorrows."* Simon had not only been rich; he loved being rich. He had coveted the wealth of others. The fallacy of trusting in wealth was quickly becoming obvious. No amount of money could bribe Death to look the other way.

Simon thought of his attempts to get Longinus and his son thrown into the sea. He wanted the crew to do the killing, making his actions not only malicious, but cowardly. He wanted to be able to tell himself that he, personally, had never committed murder. He understood the power of suggestion and how easily some people could be convinced that speculation was fact. He preyed on the weak-minded and turned them against those who questioned his authority. He had always reasoned that God would not have given him such talents if he wasn't supposed to use them. Looking at the mountain and the hovering darkness spreading across the city, Simon thought, for the first time, that he might have abused his talents.

"Please Father God, help me to understand before it is too late," he whispered.

When the sky grew as dark as night, Simon knew he may have only hours to live. The rationalizing and denials he had stored in his heart for decades became meaningless. Everything that Peter, John, and Philip had taught him about Yeshua finally made sense. Simon bowed his head and whispered a prayer. "Please Lord God, forgive me."

The words of the Psalmist spoke to Simon, *"The Lord is near to those who have a broken heart, and saves such as have a contrite spirit. The Lord redeems the soul of His servants, and none of those who trust in Him shall be condemned."*

"Father God, I promise to put your teachings first in my heart," uttered Simon as he looked at the mountain. "I will never poison anyone again. I will sell my property and give all of the profit to the poor. I promise. Just let me live."

The sound of a whimper reached his ears. He turned and peered into the gloom of the battered building. The young slave girl sat with her back against the wall and her knees up to her chin. She was crying but nearly in silence. She was accustomed to keeping her grief well hidden.

Simon's vanity dissolved. His need for approval from others was forgotten. His desire for prestige and wealth became meaningless. Simon knew, without a touch of doubt that he was about to die, despite his prayers attempting to bargain with God for his life. Somehow, instinctively, he knew that everyone in the city was about to die. His bitterness and jealousies became irrelevant. The teachings of Yeshua finally turned his heart of stone into an instrument of belief. To love God and all others was the greatest thing any human could do, but Simon had never done that. His heart ached with remorse. It was too late. He would never be able to put Yeshua's teachings into practice.

Or was it too late? Simon looked over at the slave girl still cowering on the floor. He thought of that first little girl he had poisoned. The Samaritan child was loved and pampered. This slave girl was used like a mindless beast of burden. If he could show kindness toward the lowest being in human society, with no regard for himself, might that show a change of heart?

The child trembled as she held her hands over her face. Simon knelt and helped her to her feet. He coaxed her to sit with him on the bench by the wall.

"What is your name, child?" he asked gently.

"Ce—Cecilia. My—my name is Cecilia."

"My name is Simon. I am going to stay with you, Cecilia."

She looked at him and blinked tears from her eyes. The earth shook again and the center part of the roof finally collapsed. Wood beams fell and splintered where they landed. Simon and Cecilia were now cut off from the windows in the building and the doorways to the other rooms. The child screamed and cowered against him. He leaned over her, shielding her from falling plaster. Male voices cried out from another room, but their screams suddenly stopped as another section of the roof collapsed.

"Are we going to die?" she cried.

"We'll be fine, Cecilia. We'll stay here a little while and then we'll leave together. I promise. You won't be alone. I'll be with you."

Cecilia sobbed for a moment, but then her crying subsided. She reached over and took his plump hand with her frail, calloused fingers. "You really promise to stay with me?"

"Yes. We will stay together," assured Simon. "I have wine for when we get thirsty, and bread and fish if we get hungry. I will share with you."

She blinked at him in surprise. "I am only a slave, Sir."

"Not anymore, Cecilia. You are free now. Free to decide for yourself what you will do, or think, or believe. Do you know about Yeshua from the land of Judea? He is a great man, a great healer, and he loves you even though you have not met him."

She cringed in sorrow. "How can anyone love me? I have no family."

"I have no family either. Why don't we be family to each other? The two of us."

Cecilia wiped at her eyes. "That would be nice. I don't remember ever having a family."

"I am sorry to hear that, Cecilia. But you do have a heavenly Father who loves you. He sent his Son to show his love for you and for me. May I tell you about him? It is a wonderful story—a true story—one that you will like."

Cecilia nodded. She wanted to hear Simon's voice. It was comforting to her. Simon told her about Yeshua and the beautiful gift of salvation offered to all humanity. The rest of the day and into the night, they huddled together, trapped in the ruin of the magistrate's office.

Simon had told Cecilia everything he knew about Yeshua when *Vesuvio* ejected the fourth pyroclastic surge early in the morning of the second day. The people and animals well past Pompeii were overwhelmed with four-hundred-degree heat, and ash, and death. Simon Magus, the Samaritan, and Cecilia, the Roman slave girl, breathed their last and died together, clinging to each other. In the end, both Simon and Cecilia believed in the eternal promise of Yeshua, the Son of God.

Chapter 37

Tsunami, an Ocean of Ash, and a Red Halo

---⬯⬯⬯---

Adan and the others finally fell asleep from sheer exhaustion after a second blast of fire erupted from the mountain. But nothing could have prepared them for the sunrise that greeted them. The sky was ablaze from horizon to horizon with the most dazzling display of color any of them had ever seen. Shades of vermillion and citrine blended into dazzling shades of rose and deep golden hues over the land and sea. Adan and the others sat speechless with awe as they surveyed the unprecedented sight.

"Perhaps it is a sign," suggested Adan. "Maybe this signals the end of the explosions."

"Or it's a result of the explosions," said Aquila. "The colors are the most brilliant toward Pompeii, the same direction the smoke was blowing yesterday."

Vesuvio blasted another column of rolling ash and fire and lightning into the sky.

"Cover your ears!" shouted Adan.

They pressed their hands over their ears. Just over a minute later, a crushing sound wave hit them again. Around the second hour, there was a fourth eruption of a pyroclastic surge. Again, they covered their ears and waited for the blast of the explosion to reach them. Just after the third hour, a fifth surge erupted. By now, the southeastern sky was as black as pitch. The shroud of ash engulfed the cities of Pompeii, Oplontis, and Stabiae. Herculaneum was already submerged from the first pyroclastic surge. The oarsmen maintained a steady pull and the wind kept the mainsail full. The ship was making good progress away from *Vesuvio*.

Adan walked over to Aurelius Hadrian where he stood next to the helmsman. "Have you ever seen anything like this before?" asked Adan.

"No, but we were discussing something we've heard from other sailors. They say the sea can rise up near the shore after severe earthquakes, but there's no danger to ships in deep water. So far, we have been fortunate, but the explosions seem to be getting worse."

Aurelius turned to his helmsman. "Take us due west. The farther we get from land, the deeper the water." The helmsman made the adjustments and the ship turned straight out to sea. Everyone began to feel more confident as the shoreline disappeared and the mountain appeared to sink into the sea.

It was a wise decision. At the fourth hour, when Adan and the others thought they were safely out of reach, there was a sixth and final eruption demolishing what was left of *Vesuvio's* summit. Even at their great distance, the sound of the explosion slammed into them like a sledgehammer. They knew what to expect and clapped their hands over their ears before the shock wave hit them a minute and a half later, but still, all sound instantly became muffled. They groaned in pain even as their held their hands over their ears. Their lungs couldn't function, and they gasped for air. Within seconds, the compression of energy passed and they could breathe. They were left with an uncomfortable ringing in their ears. A few of the crewmen missed the warning to cover their ears and suffered burst eardrums.

The writhing ash giant reached higher into the sky than ever before. The molten rock shooting from the volcano looked like a colossal fountain of incandescent blood. Lightning constantly slashed the ash giant as it roiled and billowed into bulbous appendages. When the blast of heat hit the men on the deck, their skin turned bright red. They turned their faces away to protect their eyes. They were alarmed at the intensity of the heat and the caustic smell of brimstone. Only the briefness of the heatwave spared the men on deck. They felt as if the depths of the Earth were turning inside out. They watched in horror as the gray mass of swirling ash plummeted from the sky and hit the slopes of the mountain. The bulging ash cloud crossed the land and raced across the sea like a monstrous avalanche of gray snow.

The oarsmen rowed as hard as they could, desperately trying to outdistance the grasping wave of ash. The surging, hot wind filled the mainsail and helped the ship cut a path to safety. Everyone on deck watched in horrified fascination as the boiling wave of ash and pumice swept across the water, rising in height as it drew closer and closer. It seemed to be unstoppable.

A crewman standing in the bow of the ship shouted. Everyone on deck turned to look where he was pointing. A huge wave was speeding at them from the open sea. The helmsman aimed the ship directly into the coming wave. The deck tilted upwards at a terrifying angle as the ship struggled toward the crest of the wave.

"Hold on!" shouted Captain Hadrian.

Marco dove to the deck and threw his arms around Jova and Cato. Aquila grabbed hold of Marco as Adan and Nikolaus held on to both of them and any rigging they could grasp. The bow of the ship tilted ever higher until it leveled out at the crest of the wave. The stern began to lift as the bow of the ship loomed over the trough of the giant wave. Adan and the others peered down into the very depths of the sea. The ship plummeted into the trough. Water crashed over the bow. Marco was shocked to hear men screaming until he realized that he was one of them. The ship began to level out, only to be met by more swollen waves, one after another, until the energy of the cataclysm was spent.

The huge waves crested and slammed the shoreline. The surging cloud of pumice and ash reached for the ship as it rode the surface of the waves. Nature seemed to be determined to overwhelm the *Child of the Ocean*, caught in between the battling forces of *Vesuvio* and the sea.

Gradually, the billowing, gray layer of pumice and ash grew thinner and thinner until it flattened out completely. The water behind them looked like frothy, gray chalk, as if the ocean had turned into rippling concrete. Captain Hadrian ordered his helmsman to head in a northeastly direction to regain the sight of land. Once they spotted the shoreline, they continued north.

Vesuvio released the violence of its molten nature on the people of Italy for twenty hours. What was left of the volcano lay spent of energy. When no further eruptions occurred, Adan and the family held an impromptu meeting.

"Decimus, we'll be docking in Ostia soon," said Adan. "Hadrian said he'll spend a week for maintenance on the ship and loading a new cargo. Then he'll set sail for the Judean coast. During that week, Niko, the twins, and I will go to Rome, visit my father and Janae, and then head back to Ostia. The captain said we can sail with him. What do you and Dionysia plan to do?"

Decimus glanced at Dionysia and she nodded. "We'll visit our children and the grandchildren. They will hear of this devastation and be worried. We'll stay with them while you visit your father. Then we'll sail with you as far as Herculaneum. I'm sure we'll have some repairs to make on the villa, but it shouldn't be too bad."

"I wonder if anyone was killed," said Dionysia sadly.

"I'm sure there must have been a few deaths," said Nikolaus. He looked at his sister with sympathy. "I hope your friends and neighbors are all right."

"But what would make a mountain explode like that?" asked Aquila. "Grandfather and I have put certain chemicals together to make them explode but we have to throw them in a fire. Is there a fire at the heart of this mountain? If so, why hasn't it exploded before?"

"Maybe it has," said Dionysia.

"Maybe it did in ancient times," suggested Decimus.

Marco bit his lower lip and stared at the floor. Adan looked at him, "What is it, Marco?"

"I was thinking about Simon Magus. I wonder what happened to him."

"He's probably inventing new ways to con money from his victims," grumbled Aquila.

"Or he's dead under a collapsed roof," said Marco.

"If he died, he got what he deserved," said Aquila.

Adan snorted. "We'd all be dead if we got what we deserved."

Aquila frowned with contempt. "Not me. I never tried to murder anyone or get anyone arrested, but *he* did both."

"Then I should be the first to die according to you," said Adan. "I actually did murder someone—the most innocent Man that ever lived only because someone told me to do it." He turned away and walked to the bow of the ship.

Marco shot Aquila a withering look. "What is the matter with you? It was bad enough that *I* threw that in his face. Why did you do the same thing?"

"I just want Simon Magus to suffer like he made me suffer," muttered Aquila.

Marco didn't have a response. He was grieved for his brother but, didn't know how to help him. Dionysia whispered something to Decimus and Nikolaus. They nodded and Nikolaus signaled for Marco to go with them. They left Dionysia with Aquila.

"Aquila, may I speak with you?" asked Dionysia.

"I guess so," he said with a glance at the others, but returned his attention to her.

"I could have spared Niko four years of slavery if I had consented to marry Captain Egnatian. Some would say it was evil of me to think of myself first and reject a man we knew would retaliate. Should Niko seek revenge against me?"

Aquila made a face. "No, of course not."

"Why not?" asked Dionysia.

"Because it worked out for the best. Uncle Niko met my father, who freed him, and then Grandfather Aquila adopted him. You and Decimus are married. You have children you love, and you're a free Roman citizen now, like Uncle Niko."

"So, the happy ending eliminates the desire for revenge?" asked Dionysia.

"Of course. Isn't that obvious?"

"Only if you already know the end result, but what if Niko had escaped and decided to take revenge against me before he met Adan?"

Aquila clamped his lips into a tight line and said nothing.

"And what if I took revenge against Deci because he bought me as a slave? My whole world was destroyed when my family died. I wanted to lash out. Would I have been justified then? What I'm trying to say is that you never know how things will turn out. Our enemy from the past may become our friend in the future."

"The reverse can also happen," pointed out Aquila.

"Unfortunately, yes," agreed Dionysia. "But in your case, Simon was never your friend. You say that you want him to suffer. Remember this; revenge is a two-edged sword. To use that sword is to risk injuring yourself with the same blade."

"That's fine to say," retorted Aquila, "but I will never see justice done on Simon Magus. What am I supposed to do, let it go?"

Dionysia smiled. "It would be the best thing you could do for yourself."

"Easy for you to say. You weren't the one falsely accused and imprisoned."

Dionysia's eyes sparked with anger. "Easy for me? I lost my family. Niko and I *were* falsely accused and imprisoned. Niko and I were put on the auction block in chains. How is that *easy*?"

Aquila looked away. "I'm sorry. That was a stupid thing to say."

There was a tense silence while Dionysia struggled to calm her emotions. She pressed her hand to her heart and took a few deep breaths. "Aquila, I understand your frustration. But tell me, does your bitterness give you comfort? Would it please Simon to know he is still tormenting you? I wonder how he would feel if you were to dismiss him from your mind like shooing a fly from a flower. You would forget about the fly and have a flower to enjoy."

"The only *flower* I want to enjoy looks very much like a cage and Simon is in it."

"And when you have him in that cage, Aquila, will it wipe out the memory of the injustice done to you?" asked Dionysia.

"At least he will know how it feels to be treated like an animal," said Aquila.

"Then will you forget what it felt like? Will his pain erase your pain?" Dionysia watched Aquila with sad eyes. "All I am saying is that you cannot force yourself to forget your ordeal. You do have a choice, however, as to what you do with that memory. Will you let Simon ruin your happiness? By all means, Aquila, hand him a wonderful gift. Forfeit your joy to him."

Aquila stared out over the sea. His expression was tense with irritation. "Captain Hadrian said he will go up the *Sarnus* River to the harbor at Pompeii to drop off some cargo. I'll have time to pay one last visit to Simon Magus. I won't be the one to forfeit anything. If I had my way, Simon would forfeit his freedom for three months, like I did."

Dionysia sighed with sorrow. She knew there was nothing else she could say.

"I know you want to help," muttered Aquila, "but I need to do this my way." He turned away and walked to the stern of the ship, avoiding the rest of the family.

Marco watched his brother walk away and then looked at his father. "Father, are you all right?" asked Marco.

"I'm fine." He spoke in a clipped manner, but then softened his tone. "I'm better than fine now that I'm not worrying about you."

Marco smiled.

Father and son fell silent as they watched a pod of dolphins racing ahead of the ship as if they were playing a game of tag. When the dolphins abruptly turned away, Adan and Marco instinctively looked back at *Vesuvio,* afraid the creatures had sensed danger. A gray haze still hung in the southeastern sky.

"If we can still see it this far out to sea," asked Marco, "what must it be like for the people near the mountain?"

"Pretty bad, I'm sure. Like being caught in the worst dust storm ever, I imagine."

That evening the sunset once again filled the sky with luminous reds, purples, and golds. The Longinus family bedded down on deck as was their habit. When sleep eluded Adan, he got up to go to the stern of the ship. Jova and Cato, who were curled against Marco, lifted their heads. Their tails gently swept the deck as Adan knelt to rub the dogs' necks. He spoke softly to them and they laid their heads down again. Adan found Calais lying on the deck at the stern, with his arms folded behind his head. He sat up when Adan approached.

"May I join you?" asked Adan.

"Of course, Centurion. I couldn't sleep anyway. I wanted some fresh air and the stars have always comforted me. They are so beautiful and bright. They twinkle like the eyes of elves."

Adan sat next to him, their backs against the life rails. He spotted his favorite constellations, Scorpius, Cygnus, Pegasus, and Ursa Major, and pointed them out to Calais. The young man told Adan that Draco was his favorite. He liked the way the Dragon wrapped his tail around Ursa Major, the Big Bear.

"What about that one between Cygnus and Sagittarius," said Calais as he pointed, "isn't that one a favorite, too?"

"Yes, but I wasn't going to mention it," Adan said with grin. "I wasn't sure you would be interested in discussing a constellation named Aquila."

"I hold nothing against the name. It is only a collection of stars. I hold nothing against your son either, even though he may resent me."

"I doubt it. He seems to be concentrating all of his resentment against Simon Magus."

"I heard about that. Nikolaus told me a little of what happened," said Calais. "I am sorry that Aquila was arrested, but at least it only lasted three months. Perhaps I should tell you that Captain Hadrian has hired me as an oarsman. I will work for him until he stops in Crete on his way to Judea. He said he would make port in Phoenix, on Crete."

"Do you know anyone in Phoenix?" asked Adan.

"No, I won't stay there. I want to go home. My mother might still be alive."

"Where is home?"

"Patmos, the island of Patmos. Even if she is not there, I will see if my brothers and sisters are. But I want you to know where I will be. I hope you won't mind receiving a letter from me now and again. I will no longer go by the name of Calais once I get to Patmos. I will stay in contact with you by my new name if you are agreeable to receiving my letters. I just want to have some kind of anchor in case I cannot find any of my family."

"I would be honored," said Adan with genuine pleasure.

"I appreciate that, Centurion. I was wondering if you could inform me if you hear anything about Commander Lysias. I will always be looking over my shoulder as long as he lives. If you should hear any news of him, would you send me a letter?"

"Of course. As a centurion I should be able to track his assignments or transfers. What name have you chosen for yourself?"

"I haven't decided yet, but I will tell you before we part in Phoenix."

"I wish you well, Calais."

They were silent for a few moments. The gentle motion of the ship and the cold, crisp darkness of the night were relaxing. The stress of trying to find Marco was finally giving way to the anticipation of going home.

Adan raised a hand and pointed. "There are Mars and Jupiter."

"Yes, they're easy to spot."

"Where is *Lucifer*? It should be the easiest to find since it is the brightest."

"We call it Venus. But I don't see it. Wait, is that it?" Calais pointed at the planet.

Both men looked as their eyes widened with concern, then fright. There was something very wrong with Venus—there was a red halo around the bright white disk of light.

Chapter 38

Herculaneum, Pompeii, and the Vanishing

———◦◦◦◦———

The rest of the voyage for the *Child of the Ocean* was uneventful. They made port in Ostia next to the barge that would haul cargo to Rome. The captain of the barge joined Aurelius, Adan, and the others on the deck, but kept watch on his crew as the cargo was transferred.

"Captain Hadrian, are you coming from the harbor of Herculaneum?" asked the barge captain. "What happened? The sky turned black to the south of us. People are saying that Vulcan set *Vesuvio* ablaze. Is that true? Ever since the explosions, the sunrises and sunsets are the most amazing I have ever seen. They're beautiful, but their brilliance is unnerving as well. What is the meaning of all this?"

"The meaning is beyond me," said Aurelius. He described the eruptions, the giant sea waves, and floating volcanic debris that nearly swamped the ship. "The explosions seem to have stopped, now but I lost count of the blasts."

"I didn't," said Aquila. "There were nine eruptions if I count the one when we were still at the villa. I think that was the smallest one. The next two were not much bigger. But the next six were different and terrible."

"Is it safe to go to the coastal harbors?" asked the barge captain.

"I'm sure it is," said Aurelius. "I'm stopping in Herculaneum and Pompeii on my way to Crete and Judea. But other captains may have more news."

Adan and his group transferred to the barge. They reached Rome later in the day and took a public carriage to the villa of Aquila and Janae. Gregos was overjoyed, especially when he saw Marco. He hugged Marco first and then knelt to pet the dogs. Adan's father and Janae hurried from the atrium and greeted everyone with hugs, as well as back slapping for the men. Grandfather Aquila was so happy to see Marco, he hugged him as even Serapio would have approved. Janae cooed over both twins, demanding to know all about their adventures. She asked the names of the dogs and made sure they had bowls of water and food. Nikolaus introduced Dionysia and Decimus. Aquila senior was soon deep in conversation with Decimus about their mutual business of wine production. Janae took Dionysia by the hand and the two women went to the terrace to get acquainted.

Marco showed the purple sapphire to his grandparents and told them the story of how the previous owner was healed by Yeshua.

"Purple is a rare color for a sapphire," Grandfather Aquila said to Marco. "I wonder how the man first acquired the gem. And why a purple one? There are certainly more common stones like tourmaline and quartz that form crystals useful for amulets."

"Perhaps because purple is the color of royalty," said Marco. "Maybe he planned to give it to Yeshua, the King of kings, to show gratitude for giving him sight."

Adan added to the theory. "Peter and John told me about God's instructions for building a temple. He told them to use the colors scarlet, purple and blue for ornamentation. Peter explained that blue is the color of God because God covers us like the sky. Scarlet is the color of humanity because our life blood is scarlet. And purple, a combination of scarlet and blue, is Yeshua's color since he is both God and human. Maybe Marco is correct. The man may have intended to give the necklace to Yeshua."

"I wish I could read the words," said Marco. "But they are in Tamil."

Over the next several days, the family enjoyed the marketplace and a play in one of the theaters, including elaborate dinners and late nights gazing at the stars. Then Marco had a suggestion, and the family agreed. They brought an elaborate dinner to Paul of Tarsus at the home in which he was imprisoned while he waited for an audience with Emperor Nero. He was saddened to hear about the unexplainable events wrought by *Vesuvio*, but rejoiced that the family was safe. They talked late into the night. It was difficult to say goodbye when they had to leave.

Over the next few days, the conversation never ventured far from speculating on the eruptions of *Vesuvio*. Aquila and his grandfather discussed the possibility that an ancient deposit of brimstone, hidden under the topsoil must have caught fire somehow. No one could explain why there would be so many separate explosions. Janae suggested that there could have been multiple chambers of brimstone that were ignited, one after the other. Their speculation turned to the phenomenal sunrises and sunsets. It seemed odd that such beauty could happen at the same time as the frightening explosions.

One morning, Adan pulled his father aside and asked if they could take a walk in the vineyards. Aquila turned to his son. "What do you need to tell me that you don't want the others to hear?"

Adan smiled. "You always could read me like a scroll, Father. Yes, there is something I need to ask. Do you remember when Emperor Tiberius declared that Nicandros Kokinos would be his chief architect?"

"I do," answered Aquila emphatically. "It caused quite a stir. I would never say anything to Niko, but there were some hard feelings among the Roman architects, and rumored suspicions."

"Like what?" Adan watched his father's expression closely.

"Nicandros was very good, but there were others who, I feel, were superior in their designs and innovations. Why do you ask?"

"I don't have any proof, but I think Niko's family was murdered, and I think the motive came from a certain wooden box he possessed. Would you say that Emperor Tiberius was interested in the occult?"

"Very much so. If it could ever be said that Tiberius worshipped anything other than himself, it would be the gift of prophecy." Aquila was startled at the look on his son's face. "Why do you look so worried?"

"Perhaps I'm overreacting. Niko was twelve when his family died, and that was twenty-three years ago. But if they were murdered, I'm afraid it was to gain possession of an object Nicandros called The Prophecy Box. If it is missing, someone may think Niko got it back and has used it."

"What kind of prophecy? How could a box tell the future?"

"I don't have any answers, only suspicions. Niko is quite wealthy, but it took years for his wealth to be as evident as it is now. If anyone is keeping him under watch, it's possible that they believe his prosperity is linked to the same object that may have brought success to Nicandros. News travels slowly and might have to go a far distance. The passage of time does not guarantee his or Dionysia's safety."

"Keep me informed as best you can," said Aquila. "I'll see what I can learn, if anything."

On the morning of their departure, Adan and the others were in good spirits. They were eager to get home. Farewells and hugs were exchanged, and they set off for a barge back to Ostia.

At the port of Ostia, Aurelius welcomed them aboard the *Child of the Ocean* while the crew was loading supplies. "We'll cast off in an hour. Make yourselves comfortable. Our next stop will be Herculaneum."

The weather was good and the wind blew briskly enough to give the oarsmen a break during much of the day. Adan did not see Calais, but Aurelius confirmed that he was on board. As they approached the harbor of Herculaneum, the helmsman called out that they would be docking soon. Adan and Nikolaus stood in the bow of the ship. Marco and Aquila soon joined them, along with Cato and Jova who barked at the occasional seagull that flew past.

"Something is wrong," Adan said as he peered at the shore. "Where are all the trees?"

"Trees?" Nikolaus swallowed hard. "Where are the houses?"

Marco's voice was restrained with shock. "Where are the docks and ships?"

"Everything is gone," declared Aquila. "And what is all this brownish gray stuff. It looks like concrete has completely engulfed the city."

They stared in silence as the ship drew closer to the shoreline. Aurelius joined them. "I'm seeing the same thing you are seeing, but I don't understand it. Is the city under this blanket of, whatever it is?"

Adan rubbed his chin nervously. "I think the whole city is—gone. They're all gone, underneath that," he pointed at *Vesuvio*. "The whole top of the mountain and some of the side is gone. What if those columns of smoke weren't smoke at all? What if they were blasts of the mountain, itself, like a huge storm of pulverized rock?"

"Remember the blasts of heat?" said Aquila. "They were painful and we were a great distance away. What if it was three, four or maybe even five times hotter in Herculaneum. That falling rock and dust would be really hot as well. Could it have been hot enough to kill people?"

"I think it was," said Marco. "Dionysia, Decimus, and Calais would have died." They turned to look at him. Realization broke through their horror as they looked back at the shore.

"Marco! You saved their lives!" exclaimed Nikolaus.

"God saved them and Decimus's slaves, too," said Marco. "I was just the messenger." Marco turned to his brother. "Aquila, if you hadn't said what you did on the road to the garrison in Caesarea, I would have gone home with you. I would have given up."

Aquila eyed his brother. "So, for once, my cowardly sarcasm was a good thing?"

"Well, maybe just that once." Marco returned his gaze to the demolished harbor.

The observers remained staring out over the devastation of what once was the thriving, resort city of Herculaneum. Captain Hadrian saw no reason to approach any closer especially after they took depth soundings. The water was significantly shallower than it should be. He ordered the helmsman to steer them toward the mouth of the *Sarnus* River that would take them to Pompeii.

"Father, I've been thinking about Simon," muttered Aquila. "Perhaps it won't be safe to pay him that one last visit like I planned."

"You were going to see him again?" asked Adan

Aquila nodded. "I'm not sure why. I guess I just wanted to confront him. Maybe tell him what Marco and I did to trick him. Let him know that we made a fool of him."

"Didn't making a fool of him, in the first place, motivate him to get you arrested? Don't you see, Aquila, every time you retaliate against this man, he will retaliate against you. When will it stop? Feuds have been perpetrated for generations for this same reason."

"I can't help it, Father," cried Aquila. "I can't stand the thought of his getting away with what he did. I had to fight a soldier in the arena while I was a prisoner. I acted like a terrified imbecile to throw him off guard and then attacked the way you and Serapio taught me. It wouldn't have mattered what sentence I might have been given; I could have died right there." Aquila clenched his fists at the memory of the soldiers laughing at him and his opponent baiting him with insults. "I was so angry; I wanted to kill the man. I almost did. I'm not even sure what stopped me." He looked out to sea to avoid the desolation of the once beautiful city.

"Your regard for human life stopped you, Aquila," said Adan. "You're a stronger man than you realize. You have heart, a good heart. I am proud of you."

Aquila's head snapped around and he looked into his father's eyes. "You are?"

"Yes, very much so."

Aquila smiled with heartfelt pleasure. "I'm glad."

The ship sailed down the coast until they reached the mouth of the *Sarnus* River. It was no longer a river but a trickle of charcoal-colored sludge. The surrounding area was nothing but gray devastation, more like the surface of the moon than of earth.

"What has happened here?" whispered Marco to himself. He didn't expect an answer. He knelt next to the dogs and they huddled close to him. Their tails hung down between their legs. They sniffed the air and whimpered. "What is it, Cato? What do you smell, Jova?" They sneezed and wiped at their noses with a paw.

"They smell the sulfur," said Aquila. "I smell it, too."

"If the brimstone smells this strong offshore," said Nikolaus, "what was it like for the people in the city? It must have been deadly."

They stood together and scanned the shoreline. There wasn't a single tree in sight except for a few bare, twisted scorched branches. Pompeii lay buried with no visible buildings except for a few roof tops. Many of the roofs of homes and shops collapsed under the weight of the ash and pumice that dropped from the sky. More roofs would collapse in the future after rainstorms soaked the ash, increasing its weight. The once proud city of twenty thousand residents was now a cemetery for the dead, entombed in volcanic ash. Pompeii was not subjected to the full force of the volcanic heat like the residents of Herculaneum. However, being downwind from the volcanic blasts, most of the ash from the eruptions settled on Pompeii, Oplontis, and Stabiae. The finest particles were carried in the upper atmosphere and fell down over the surrounding lands of Crete, Macedonia, Greece, Judea, and areas even farther away. The ash hung in the air, carried aloft by upper wind currents and the jet stream, making the sun appear to be blue or even green for some observers, and causing the red halo that appeared around the planet Venus for weeks. The waning moon glowed with a bluish halo for many days when it rose above the eastern horizon.

"I wonder if Simon left the city in time," said Aquila.

"Whether he did or not, he suffered or is suffering," said Adan. "It is clear that no one could survive this devastation. If he left in time, his home is destroyed and he has nowhere to go. However, I feel that he did not survive, except in your wounded heart, Aquila. Ghosts may not exist, but he will haunt you just the same if you let him."

Marco put a light hand on his brother's shoulder but made no comment. He didn't need to.

Chapter 39

Crete, Antipas, and a New Beginning

⸻⸙⸻

Captain Aurelius Hadrian knew he would never be exchanging cargo in Pompeii or Herculaneum again. He ordered the helmsman to take them out to sea far enough to avoid any possible new shallows, but kept the shore in sight until they rounded the toe of Italy and slipped past the island of *Sicilia*. They reached Crete and the port of Phoenix to pick up a shipment of cypress wood and unload a shipment of wine.

It was time for Calais to leave. He picked up his knapsack and went up on deck. He looked around and spotted Adan standing alone, looking toward the east.

"Centurion, I am leaving the ship as I told you. I hope you have a safe voyage home."

"Thank you. I wish the best for you as well," said Adan, accepting Calais's offered handshake. "I hope you find a ship that will stop at Patmos."

"It might take a few days, but I'm not concerned. Captain Hadrian paid a good wage. I have enough money to get by."

"You are free from slavery, Calais," said Adan. He hesitated but then continued, "but you are not truly free, not yet."

"I am no longer another man's property. What else is there?"

"True freedom," replied Adan.

"What are you talking about?" Calais demanded.

"Setting your heart and mind free. The freedom offered by God."

Calais snorted with contempt. "Are you talking about the Hebrew God?"

"No. I'm talking about the God of everyone. The God who created everything."

"If I remember correctly, Centurion, didn't you crucify the Son of this God?"

"I did. But I didn't take his life. Yeshua gave his life so that we can live forever with God."

Calais glanced impatiently at the gangplank. "I don't need your God. I just need to find my family."

"And if you don't?" Adan asked gently.

"I'll make my own way. When we lived in Patmos, we ran a bakery for the miners. If Rome uses Patmos as a place of banishment for sorcerers and prophets, they might pay me to run a bakery for the guards and their families. If Patmos doesn't work out, I'll try Pergamon. My father had family in Pergamon."

"Have you decided on a new name?"

"My surname is Antipas. I have decided to keep it. That name is the only thing I have left of my family. Calais Antipas. It feels right. I'm not going to worry about Commander Lysias. He has probably forgotten my name, anyway. He always called me *servus*."

"He called you slave, as if it was your name? Then you're probably right. Let's not use his name as well. Should we call him *stupidus*. That will be our code name for him."

A broad grin spread across the young man's face. "Stupid? Yes, that's a good name for him. Farewell, Centurion." Calais turned to leave when Aquila, Marco and Nikolaus emerged from below deck. They joined Adan to bid Calais good-bye.

"I am sorry to see you leave. I wish you well," said Marco.

Calais deliberately eyed Marco. "I nearly killed you—twice. Do you still wish me well?"

Marco frowned anxiously. *"Twice?"*

"Sofi, in the form of a real owl, saved your life the first time. In Dora, I meant to break that vase over your head, not the stairs. An owl landed on the wall of the roof and hooted at me as if to say, 'No, not this way.' Then the owl took flight as soon as I lowered the vase."

"I always did like owls," muttered Marco. "But whatever happened, I still wish you well."

Nikolaus extended his hand. Calais only hesitated a moment before he shook it. "If you should ever need assistance or a job, you will always find both at the Ocean View Inn in Caesarea. It might be safe for you to return to Judea someday."

"That is generous of you, Nikolaus. I will not forget the offer. I swore I would never step foot in Judea again, but one never knows how things will turn out."

Calais, again, turned to leave but Aquila stopped him. "Calais, there is something I need to tell you." He paused and glanced at Marco. "I owe both of you an apology."

"Aquila, we've been over this," said Marco.

"No, Calais needs to hear this. Our Grandmother Marsetina freed every slave she could afford to buy. Grandfather Aquila freed the slaves of his second wife, Janae. When I knew Marco was doing the same thing, without me, I was jealous. But now I know what it feels like to be enslaved, physically and emotionally. I am truly sorry I deceived you." He glanced at Marco. "And letting you take the blame." Marco's eyes brightened as he smiled at his brother.

Calais considered Aquila's words. "It helps to hear you say that. I think you mean it. Perhaps what happened was for the best." He smiled, hoisted his knapsack over a shoulder, and walked down the gangplank to the dock. He never looked back.

Epilogue

Retrieval, Caesarea, and the Welcoming

———⌾———

Thge sun awakened the Longinus family to the welcome sight of the Judean shores. Captain Hadrian announced that they would dock for a few hours in the port of Dora to deliver a special cargo of glass figurines from Rome. The *Child of the Ocean* would then take on supplies and fresh water and be on its way to Caesarea.

"Father, we have a favor to ask," said Marco as they stood on the deck watching the workers carry kegs of water aboard.

"Why do I have the feeling I'm not going to like this?" said Adan as he eyed his sons.

"It's not a big favor. We'd like to get off here and walk to Caesarea. There's something here I need to retrieve."

"And you're going with him, Aquila?"

Aquila nodded. "I promise not to let him out of my sight."

Adan sighed and looked at Nikolaus. "Should I even ask why?"

"Probably not," said Nikolaus with a grin at his nephews.

"Fine. Don't make me regret this."

The brothers bounded off the ship with Jova and Cato excitedly swishing their tails. They walked down one street after the other, turning at a few crossroads and going straight at others. Marco knew the way. They stopped in front of a modest home, and Marco opened the gate to the courtyard. He pulled the bell at the door. When the door opened, a happy exclamation from Elizabeth greeted them. She clapped her hands then started to hug Aquila, stopped short, and gasped in disbelief.

"There are two Marcos! Which one is our Marco?" she laughed and gestured toward the stable behind the house. "Justus will be so happy to see you, both of you. Come on." She led them out to the stable as Justus was headed toward the house. He greeted the brothers eagerly and laughed as Elizabeth had done to see the two of them. Marco introduced Aquila and then slipped away. Aquila stayed to get acquainted.

Marco stepped into the stables. He whistled and called out, "Arrow! Arrow, do you remember me?"

The old pack horse jerked his head up, ears set forward, and nickered with a full-throated rumble of joy. He turned in his stall to face Marco and tossed his head. Marco grinned happily and rubbed his hands down Arrow's neck. He scratched behind the horse's ears and rubbed the blaze down his forehead. The horse pressed his forehead against Marco's chest.

"I'm so happy to see you, old friend. How have you been? Are you ready to go home with me?"

Jova and Cato approached slowly and lifted their noses to the horse. Arrow leaned down to them and sniffed. The dogs sat down and looked at Marco as if to say, "Aren't you going to introduce us?"

Marco laughed. "Arrow, I'd like you to meet Cato and Jova." Marco bridled Arrow and led the old horse out of the stall to join Justus, Elizabeth and Aquila.

"Justus, the saddle is yours, as we agreed. You have taken good care of him," said Marco.

"Thank you, I will put it to good use. I will miss this old horse. He worked diligently for his hay," said Justus.

They talked some more, especially about the odd dusting of gray ash that had settled over the town and the magnificent sunsets and sunrises. Neither brother wanted to mention the devastated cities buried under the volcanic debris of the mountain. The brothers were eager to get home and see the family. They said their farewells and found the road that led to Caesarea. It took less than two hours to reach the cliff road leading to the Cornelius villa and the Longinus cottage.

The brothers ascended the cliff road only a few paces before they heard shouts of joy. They looked up to find hands waving to them. Dulcibella ran from the terrace to meet them. The brothers threw out their arms, and Dulcibella hugged them both at the same time. Marcus and Iovita gathered all three in their arms. Even the servants, including Andreas, came out to join in the celebration.

Dulcibella was so overjoyed, tears of relief flowed down her face. They held each other as Jova and Cato pranced around excitedly.

"I prayed for you both every day," said Dulcibella in between sniffs. "I did not understand why you had to leave, Marco, but I accepted it. I am so glad that Dionysia and Decimus are safe. However, if either one of you should feel the need to save the world again, will you take me and your father with you?"

Adan joined in. "You know, she's not kidding. She'll probably have a word with Wingshadow and Nighthawk and you'll never get out of here again without them tattling on you."

"Thank you for sticking to your mission, Marco," said Nikolaus, wiping at his watering eyes. "Aquila, I'm grateful you were with us. There's something I've been meaning to point out to both of you. As difficult as it was for you to endure imprisonment, Aquila, it delayed us. If you had never been arrested, we would have gone to Herculaneum while Marco was on Malta Island. We would have thought we were wrong about his destination and gone home."

Nikolaus turned to Marco. "If you hadn't been shipwrecked on Malta—same result. We would have arrived in Herculaneum too soon."

"Niko is right," said Decimus. "We are alive because of what you two endured. We are most grateful."

The brothers were not accustomed to adamant praise, and blushed slightly despite enjoying the sound of it. Marco glanced down at his forearms, scarred from Camilla's whip and looked over at Aquila's equally scarred arms from the masonry work he was forced to do. He shook his head at the irony of the situation. Different experiences, different emotions and motivations, but they were still identical twins.

Marco and Aquila looked at each other and smiled. Another round of hugging followed as the family rejoiced and made their way inside the villa. Marco walked toward the stables leading Arrow, and Aquila joined him.

Marco whistled as he stepped inside the barn. Wingshadow's head jerked up with ears forward and let out a low rumbling nicker of welcome. Marco quickly opened the gate and threw his arms around the horse's neck. He buried his face in the thick, wavy mane. Wingshadow rubbed her head against Marco's side.

Aquila stood back and watched, smiling, and sighed with satisfaction. All was as it should be. He draped Arrow's reins over a stall railing and walked to Nighthawk's stall. The horse turned to him and nickered softly. Aquila went into the stall and greeted his horse. "I think I should start talking to you, my friend." Nighthawk lowered his head to Aquila. He patted the horse's neck. "It is good to see you, Nighthawk."

Dulcibella found Marco on the terrace later that evening watching the sea waves chase each other to the shore. The sunset was still unusually beautiful, as if someone had thrown buckets of brightly colored paint across the sky. He turned to her when she sat on the bench next to him.

"Mother, I'm glad you're here," said Marco. "I was feeling lonesome."

"And I am very glad you're here as well," said Dulcibella. "I missed you terribly these past months. How are you feeling now that you are home and your mission has been accomplished?"

"I feel good, really good. There were so many times when I thought I was going crazy for taking off like I did." He pressed his hand over the sapphire which he now wore outside his tunic. "I don't know what would have happened if I had not seen the merchant who sold me this necklace." He pulled it off over his head. "Centurion Thracius paid for it with a gold *aureus* and wouldn't let me pay him back. I don't think I would have thought of finding Dionysia if it had not been for this stone. I wish I knew what is written on it, but it's in Tamil."

"Who have you shown it to?"

"Everybody."

Dulcibella put her hand out. "May I see it." She inspected the crystal faces, slowly rotating the hexagonal stone. Her eyes widened with wonder as her mouth dropped open. She put a hand over her mouth as she raised her eyes to meet her son's gaze.

"Mother, what is it? You look stunned."

"I am more than stunned. I am amazed. You have said that the stone gave you comfort, but you didn't know why."

"Yes, I thought it was because the sapphire gave me direction."

"It did. More than you know. I have read the words on it."

"What?" cried Marco. "You can read Tamil?"

"No, I can't. It's Hebrew. Perhaps the merchant lied to you or he really didn't know." Dulcibella pointed to one of the flat surfaces. "There is one word on each side. If you start with this one as the first word, it reads: *Follow—Yeshua—To—Receive—Eternal—Life.*"

Marco laughed with delight. "The merchant was telling the truth, despite his intentions. Centurion Thracius doubted the message could lead to a great treasure because the man who etched the crystal died without money for his burial. But as the merchant said, 'What one may treasure, another may cast away.' I've got to show this to Father. He'll be so surprised, and sorry that he didn't look at it more closely."

Dulcibella handed the necklace back. "While you're looking for your father, if you find Aquila, would you send him to me?"

"Of course, Mother." Marco trotted across the terrace. "Thanks for deciphering the message!" he called over his shoulder.

"You're welcome. And don't make your father feel too bad. He did try to teach you to read Hebrew." Marco laughed and hurried up the path that led to their cottage.

Dulcibella stood and leaned against the ancient oak tree, feeling the texture of the ridged bark. She sighed with contentment as she looked out over the sea and the magnificent splash of colors at the horizon. She heard footsteps and turned to find Aquila walking across the terrace.

"Marco said you wanted to talk to me," he called out.

"Yes, let's sit." She sat on the bench and patted the space next to her.

Aquila asked, "Are you going to Jerusalem with Father when he takes Captain Hadrian to meet his sister? Did you know that Aurelius is alive?"

"To answer your second question. No. I did see him once in Ostia, but I didn't know who he was at the time. Your father talked with him while we were waiting to board a ship to go home after our honeymoon. I asked Adan if he was an old friend. He only said, 'No, not really, but I knew his father.' Your father is very good at keeping secrets that need to be kept. And to answer your first question. Yes, I'm going to Jerusalem."

"I'm glad. I know this long separation has been hard on both of you," said Aquila.

"Your father and I swore that once we were married, we would never be apart again. Even when Adan was gone from me physically, he was never apart from me. I would not have known this if Marco had never left. When we became betrothed, we traded hearts that day and have never traded back. Do you understand what that means?"

"Of course, Mother, you and Father love each other," said Aquila, annoyed at the question.

"It is much more complicated than that. When we traded hearts, we made the decision to hold each other in love and respect. It represents an attitude. Whatever you put into your heart will determine how you live in this world. If you nurture hate, it will twist in your heart like a venomous snake. Honey never comes from the fangs of a snake."

"You're talking about Simon Magus," said Aquila. He mimicked a sing-song tone. "I know, you want me to forgive him so I can move on and be all hugs and grins and giggles. Yes, yes, I know. But it's not that easy. And I know Uncle Niko and Decimus meant well when they pointed out that my arrest made the timing right. But couldn't God have delayed us a different way? God is supposed to love us. How was it love to throw me in prison to live like a caged animal?"

"Let's talk about that first," said Dulcibella gently. "God did not throw you in prison. The law accused you and the law threw you in prison."

"Fine. So, why did God allow the law to throw me in prison?"

"Because God created each one of us with the will to make our own decisions independent from his interference. God could have stopped Simon from framing you for theft, but that would have interfered with Simon's free will. We can either have free will and face the consequences of our decisions or we can lose the ability to make any decisions and face no consequences, ever. You cannot have the ability to make decisions and never have any consequences. Therein lies the rub—every person on earth has the ability to make decisions which may result in messy, painful, or terrible consequences."

Aquila clamped his lips tightly together as he processed his mother's words. "Meaning, we are not slaves to God the master. We are free individuals."

"Exactly." Dulcibella smiled. "When consequences impact innocent victims, then God will take the tragedy, the death, the war, or imprisonment, and turn it to something good. We may not be aware of the good, or we may not live long enough to see it for ourselves, but it happens. If you are honest with yourself, is there anything good that came of your experience, anything good for you personally?"

"Something good?" He couldn't keep the disgust out of his voice. "Do you have any idea what I went through?"

"Tell me. Tell me everything," Dulcibella said gently.

Aquila described all that occurred during the months of his ordeal. He explained what he had to do to survive the fight in the arena, the aggression of other prisoners and the intimidations of the guards. He told her the insults people would shout at him even though he had done nothing to warrant their hostility. He was vulnerable and could do nothing in retaliation. His chains brought out the cowardice and cruelty of others. Dulcibella listened without interruption.

When he finished, she looked into his eyes with compassion. "Aquila, I am so sorry you went through this torment. It breaks my heart to know that my child was being abused and dehumanized. If you could erase all those painful memories from your mind, is there anything you would want to remember, anything at all?"

Aquila looked at his mother in dismal silence. She looked back at him with empathy.

"You think God was teaching me a lesson?"

"Do you?"

He grimaced and looked away. "Couldn't he have just handed me a scroll or something? There are easier ways to learn a lesson."

"There are," admitted Dulcibella. "Are easy lessons easily forgotten?"

"You think I'm feeling sorry for myself?"

"Are you?"

"You weren't there, Mother. You didn't feel what I felt. I don't expect you to understand."

"That's good because it's not possible. Even if we had been together in chains in that cage, I would still not know how you felt. I would only know what I could feel."

Aquila thought in silence while Dulcibella waited. He sighed and the stiffness in his posture eased. "Perhaps there is one thing I want to remember. I will never look at another prisoner the same way again. I always assumed they were guilty of something and deserved to be punished. It is easy to judge by appearances, but much harder to know the truth. You have to search for it."

"Then your imprisonment taught you something that some men never learn even if they live to old age. The truth is not always obvious. Please, Aquila, learn from this. Let this Simon Magus rest in peace in your heart. Being in prison made you powerless. Yes? Do you want to know real power?"

"What do you mean?" Aquila frowned.

"The most powerful thing you can do is to love someone who is *un*lovable and to forgive the *un*forgivable. When you forgive someone, you make the choice to do so. No one controls you. The power of forgiveness is in the giving of it. It doesn't matter whether it is asked for or accepted. When you expect nothing in return, then you are in complete control. No one else can take that power away from you. You choose to relinquish that power when you let hatred take over."

"I heard Father telling Uncle Niko about forgiving Felix Valentius instead of killing him," said Aquila softly. "Father realized Valentius wanted to die so he refused to kill him. Do you mean like that?"

"That is only half the story," said Dulcibella gently. "Adan didn't know the whole story, himself, until later. When you forgive someone, even if they reject your forgiveness as Valentius did, at first, the memory is still there. When Valentius was about to be executed and saw Aurelius step out of the shadows, he was overjoyed to see that his son was alive. He realized that because Adan forgave him instead of killing him, he lived long enough to see Aurelius. Valentius was able to tell him for the first time, 'I love you, son. I always have even when I hated myself.' That one sentence changed the rest of Aurelius's life."

Aquila suddenly realized something. "Because Father forgave Valentius, and Valentius was able to tell Aurelius that he loved him, Aurelius took us on his ship, which saved our lives."

"Yes. You understand." She took his hand gently and smiled. "As I said, Valentius initially rejected Adan's forgiveness, but in the end, he remembered. Forgiveness freed Valentius to do something good for his son, and ultimately, for our whole family. When you forgive someone, Aquila, you hand that person over to God. Leave your enemies in God's hands. Wonderful things may happen. But rest assured that whatever does happen will be made right in the end."

Dulcibella placed a light hand on Aquila's shoulder. "Leave Simon to God. Come home, Aquila, truly home. Not just physically, but emotionally as well. I have explained how your father and I traded hearts. But it is not only the heart that can be given to another person. The mind is just as controlling as the heart. You believe Simon planned and manipulated others to cause you and your father harm. Yes?"

"He absolutely did! He even admitted it."

"His actions were the results of his mind?"

"Yes, of course."

"Have you imagined getting even with him? Didn't he think he was getting even with you?"

Aquila blinked at her in silence.

Dulcibella looked at her son with sympathy. "Have you traded minds with Simon? Are you now thinking of him the same way he thought of you?" She paused, watching emotions play across her son's face. "Where the mind and the heart go, your life will follow."

Footsteps sounded softly behind them and Adan sat down next to Dulcibella. "I thought I'd find you two out here. Marco showed me what is written on the sapphire. I feel like an idiot for not looking at the thing more closely. You two look like you're deep in thought. Have you solved the problems of the world?"

Aquila smiled. "No Father. Just the problem of my world. I am home now. As they say, 'Home is where the heart is,' and now my heart is right here." He patted his chest.

"Where was it before?"

"In a prison in Rome, and the jailer was Simon Magus." Aquila got up and smiled at his parents. "I think I'll find Marco and see if he wants to go with me over to Uncle Niko's inn. It feels like we haven't seen Titus and Adriana in ages and I bet Longina and her husband would love to meet the new wolves in the pack—I mean, family. Wingshadow and Nighthawk are probably ready to feel the wind in their manes. I've got to find Marco." He took off at a trot.

Adan reached for Dulcibella and she nestled in his arms. "I think Marco and Aquila have given me a most unexpected gift," said Adan after kissing the top of Dulcibella's head.

"Really, what is that?"

"Gray hair."

Dulcibella touched the side of his face. "Ah, yes, I see it. Right here at your temples. Yes, that's new. Makes you look even more handsome, I think."

"I think you are seeing with your heart, Dulcie, rather than your eyes."

Dulcibella smiled and gently wove her fingers through his hair. "Ah, so much the better since the heart can still see even when the eye is blind."

Adan cuddled her closer and looked out over the sea. "This quest of Marco's has taught all of us a lesson, I think. Anything can happen at the most unexpected times."

"Life is precarious to say the least," agreed Dulcibella. "How did our children survive their childhood? It was a miracle."

"No, it was a miracle that *we* survived their childhood," said Adan with a grin.

"Would you have it any other way?" Dulcibella cooed in his ear.

Adan leaned down and gently kissed her. "Not in a million years."

"So, what's next, my love?"

"What do you mean?"

Dulcibella smiled knowingly. "I know you. I can see wheels of mischief turning in those eyes of yours. You're planning something."

Adan huffed a short laugh. "You know me so well. I do have a plan. After we escort Aurelius to meet his sister, I think Niko and I will need to do some investigating."

"Investigating?" Dulcibella looked at him suspiciously. "For what?"

"I think we need to find a certain wooden box that belonged to his father."

"Ah, sounds like a mystery. What's in it?"

"The greatest mystery of all. I think it holds the future." Adan smiled at the laughter in her eyes.

www.ingramcontent.com/pod-product-compliance
Lightning Source LLC
Chambersburg PA
CBHW080725020726
47503CB00010B/2795